THE PERJURED CROWN

A
Historical Novel
by

Berwick Coates

Published by Berwick Coates

Publishing partner: Paragon Publishing, Rothersthorpe

ISBN 978-1-78792-031-6

Cover design Stephen Goodwin
sgssdesign.co.uk

Book design, layout and production management by Into Print

www.intoprint.net

+44 (0)1604 832149

Contents

Dedication

To my son Stephen
A rock and an inspiration

Introduction

PERHAPS THE BEST-KNOWN single fact about English medieval history is the Battle of Hastings, when Duke William of Normandy successfully challenged and defeated Harold of Wessex, the last Saxon King of England. It is surely not entirely coincidence that probably the best-known piece of non-written evidence from our medieval history also concerns Harold and William – the Bayeux Tapestry.

But the Tapestry depicted not only the conquest itself in 1066; it also covered the events of 1064, when Harold was shipwrecked in Normandy and met William. According to the Tapestry, Harold, before returning to England, swore an oath the gist of which was that he would not stand in William's way for the crown of England.

Historians are not agreed – naturally – on the details, particularly as to Harold's motives for appearing in Normandy in the first place, shipwreck or no shipwreck. But they are agreed that the Tapestry's version of events, from Harold's visit to Normandy in 1064 to the end of the Battle of Hastings in October, 1066, is a sustained piece of shameless Norman propaganda.

So – what really happened in 1064 when the two rivals met? This novel attempts to suggest another version of events, before they came to be doctored by the Norman apologists.

It follows then that many of the characters are real people. The fictitious ones naturally have invented names, but the people they identify were real enough. The lives of humble priests, waiting-girls, monks, cooks, dog-handlers, common soldiers, and so on offer a counterpoint to the 'events' involving the great and the powerful.

Curiously, the ladies who stitched the Tapestry were aware of this truth, and many a menial pops up in margins – working, fighting, lusting – to show that history is by no means merely the actions of famous people.

List of Characters

Earl Harold of Wessex, 1052-1066
Duke William of Normandy, 1035-1087
Wulfnoth, brother of Harold
Matilda, wife of William
Lanfranc, Abbot of St. Stephen's, Caen
Sir William Fitzosbern, chief adviser to Duke William
Sir Roger of Montgomery, senior vassal to the Duke
Sir Walter Giffard, another senior vassal
Maurilius, Archbishop of Rouen, appointed 1054
Yves of Bellême, Bishop of Sées, appointed 1035
William, Bishop of Evreux, appointed 1046
Odo, Bishop of Bayeux and brother to Duke William, appointed 1049
Geoffrey de Montbrai, Bishop of Coutances, appointed 1049
Hugh, Bishop of Lisieux, kinsman to Duke William, appointed 1049
John, Bishop of Avranches, appointed 1061
Robert of Beaumont, a young Norman nobleman
Guy, Count of Ponthieu
Arnulf, chaplain to Duke William
Adele, Arnulf's daughter
Arlette, waiting-woman to Matilda
Ralph of Gisors and Bruno of Aix, scouts for Duke William
Gilbert of Avranches and Nigel Fitzhenry, young soldiers in the Rouen garrison
Gerard of Ghent, chief cook at the Duke's castle in Rouen
Thierry, courier to Bishop Geoffrey
Goscelin, cathedral-builder to Bishop Geoffrey of Coutances
Hubert, a monk of le Tréport
Aldred, captain of Earl Harold's ship
Edwin, a dog-handler in Earl Harold's retinue
Robert, Cecily, William, Richard, Matilda, Constance, Agatha, children to the Duke

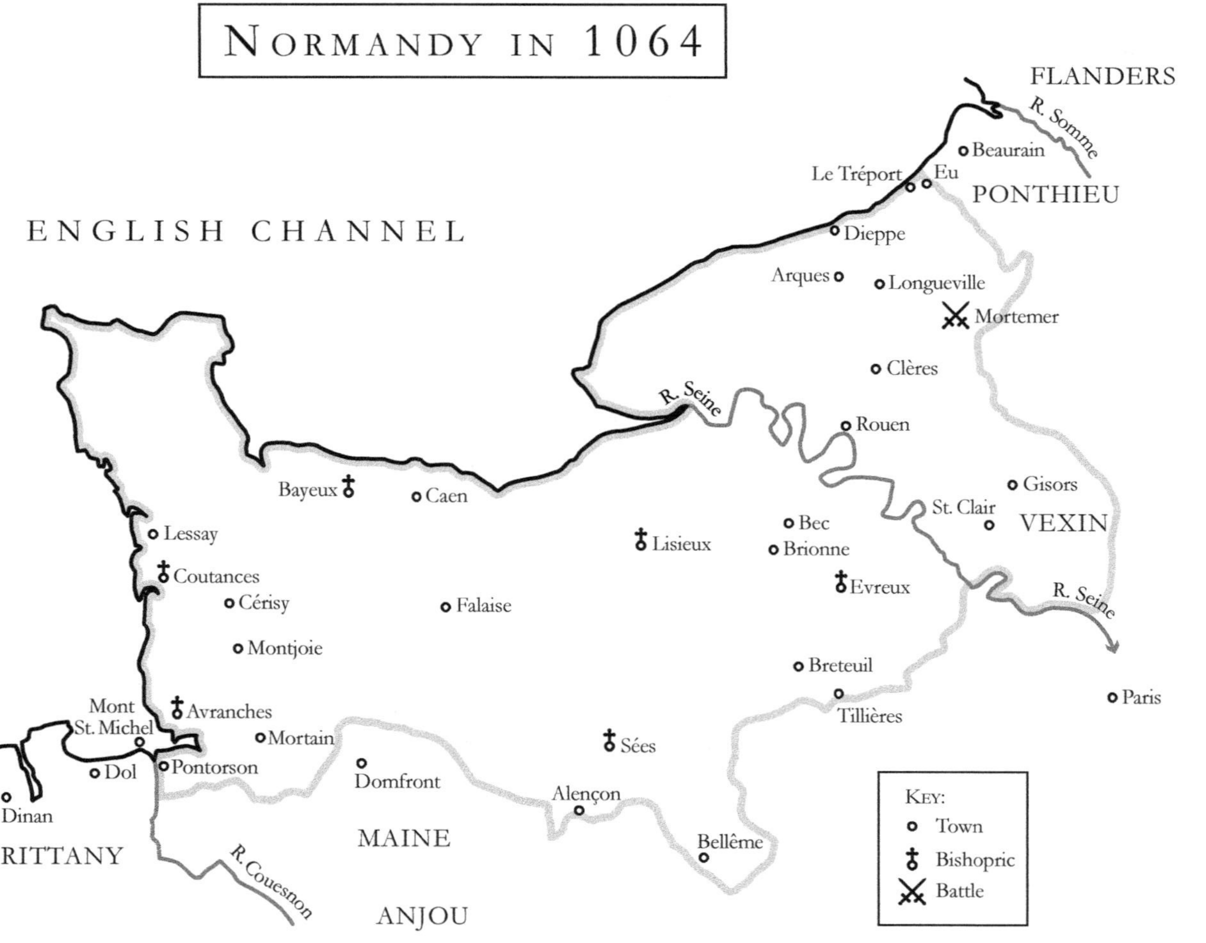
NORMANDY IN 1064
FLANDERS
R. Somme
Beaurain
Le Tréport
Eu
PONTHIEU
ENGLISH CHANNEL
Dieppe
Arques
Longueville
Mortemer
Clères
R. Seine
Rouen
Gisors
St. Clair
VEXIN
Bayeux
Caen
Bec
Brionne
Lisieux
Lessay
Coutances
Evreux
Cérisy
Falaise
R. Seine
Montjoie
Breteuil
Paris
Tillières
Mont St. Michel
Avranches
Mortain
Sées
Dol
Pontorson
Domfront
Alençon
Dinan
MAINE
BRITTANY
Bellême
R. Couesnon
ANJOU
KEY:
Town
Bishopric
Battle

Chapter One

The Coming

'Bring it up, son. You can only lose it once.'

They ambled off, laughing, bare-footed, sure as cats.

Edwin had felt odd long before the first raindrops splashed wetly on to the back of his hands. He had felt uncomfortable before the first breeze had ruffled his fair hair. The dogs, restless and worried, strained to be somewhere else, in the manner of all dogs. Their pulling straightened Edwin's arms, and he was too uninterested to drag them back; it was easier to sit there, with his arms waving straight and puppet-like. If they hauled him into the sea, he did not much care; it would be a happy release.

He had felt sick before they cleared the harbour at Bosham. He was the only one – then. The crew clapped him noisily on the shoulder as they passed about their mysterious business with the oarports and the forests of rope and the huge square sail that flapped overhead like a god's line of laundry.

'Bring it up, son. You can only lose it once.'

Everyone else was enjoying himself. Valets and falconers alike roared with delight as each large movement of the swell lifted and dropped the boat.

It was a novelty for them.

'Why did those quill-cutters make such a fuss? This is good fun ... '

My lord's clerks and bodyguard had not thought it was good fun.

'You wait till you have to do it every month. In all weathers. Devil take the Normans.'

'What have they done? I thought you would be pleased that the King threw them out.'

'We are. But look what happened. Harold snapped up a lot of their manors, and we have to run them for him. And look at the roads in Sussex. So Harold gets this bright idea of travelling between them by sea instead.'

'Saves time.'

'Not our stomachs.'

'What about Harold?'

A soldier spat.

'That man is not human. Nothing upsets him.'

'Well, we are looking forward to it.'

The soldier laughed.

'You will see ... '

They soon did. The roars of delight subsided and the jokes became fewer.

Within an hour not a man was speaking. Faces wore an absent look, as if their owners were concentrating mightily on something. The first shivers made their way under tunics. Cloaks were drawn more tightly.

Edwin glanced about him. The crew seemed busier. Not one dog-handler or falconer was now so much as looking at anybody else, never mind speaking to him.

Edwin gazed miserably at the mist-shrouded coast of Sussex. All those Norman estates that Earl Harold had recently obtained now seemed very attractive. If only, if only ... He looked inboard again. At least nobody was teasing him any more.

The dogs tugged without mercy. Edwin's arms, held by the leather thongs round his wrists, shook helplessly. Frankly, if they dragged him over the side, he would not complain.

He winced as he felt a slap on the shoulder.

He looked up at the mane of fair hair, the broad moustache.

'Some adventure, eh, lad?'

For the first time since he had entered the Earl's service, Edwin disliked him. He remembered the bodyguard's remark: 'Nothing upsets that man.'

Harold snuffed the air and beamed with well-being.

'I said "some adventure".'

Edwin sniffed.

'Yes, my lord.'

* * * * * *

'From His Holiness Pope Alexander II, Vicar of Christ, Bishop of Rome, servant of the servants of God, to my lord Lanfranc, Abbot of the newly-consecrated house of St. Stephen's, at Caen, greeting ... '

The wind rattled the closed shutters, and blew through the cracks with enough strength to flutter the letter in Lanfranc's hand. Lanfranc squinted in the bad light, and leaned across his desk to hold it nearer the flickering flame of the hooded candle.

It was an official letter of congratulation on his appointment as Abbot the previous year. Lanfranc's eyes skimmed quickly across the orotund phrases of Vatican verbosity ... 'God in His Infinite Wisdom had seen fit so to guide the judgment of His Grace Duke William II of Normandy' ... 'having taken full and honest consultation with learned fathers and bishops of the Holy Church of the said Duchy' ... 'your fame throughout Christendom as scholar, teacher, theologian, disputant, champion of the Holy Faith against the recent abhorrent heresies of the Devil-inspired Berengar of Tours' ... 'indubitably welcomed by the faithful brothers and novices and officers of the said Abbey of St. Stephen's'

… 'every confidence that you will pursue with consummate energy and urgency the comprehensive reforms which have been initiated by His Holiness and his illustrious immediate predecessors' … 'the mighty burden which has fallen upon the unworthy shoulders of His Holiness in Almighty God's Design for the extirpation and utter removal from our Holy Mother Church of corrupt and evil practices, and for restoration of the Body of the Holy Catholic Church to its former health, to the greater comfort of the Faithful … '

Three long pages of it. Lanfranc's experienced legal eye rapidly distilled the value. A flicker of irony disturbed the corners of his mouth.

He was proof against the fulsome praise. Ever since his days as a young lawyer in his home town of Pavia. He had once allowed such compliments to tempt him into local politics; it was a short but bitter lesson. Never again. Thereafter he had cursed himself for the sin of pride, but only because of what he thought of himself, not because of what others thought of him. Others did not understand the struggle he had had to find his true path in life.

He thought he had found it as Prior of Bec, in the quiet little house founded by the old soldier Herluin near Brionne. And then, just when he was beginning to look forward to a lifetime with his books and his pupils, had come the call from the Duke to take over as Abbot at his new house at Caen. 'Having taken full and honest consultation with learned fathers and bishops'? Rubbish! William, for some reason known only to himself, and after five minutes' talk with Fitzosbern, had summoned him from his retreat at Bec.

Perhaps it was a quirk of William's robust sense of humour. Lanfranc had once opposed the Duke's marriage on the grounds of blood ties that were too close. There had been long and tedious dispute throughout Normandy, even as far as Rome itself, which had nearly resulted in Lanfranc's banishment. When William and Matilda went ahead anyway and got married, they each promised to found a house by way of lifting the weight of sin off their immortal souls – both at Caen. William's house was for men, Matilda's for women. William's was completed first – St. Stephen's. William probably saw some neat soldier's justice in inviting to lead it the very man whose opposition to the marriage had necessitated the Duke's breaking of the law and his subsequent attempt to make amends.

As for the obedient brothers of the new house giving him an 'indubitable welcome', the best he could hope for was wary acquiescence. A mere novice took only six months to learn the hard lesson that abbots had to be lived with like one's feet; sometimes they bore you up and sometimes they were a pain, and there was no chance of changing them. The brothers at Bec may have wept when he left (and Lanfranc's stern conscience for once allowed him to be moved by that), but the new brothers at Caen did not know him from Adam. He may have a wide reputation as a teacher, but a born teacher was not a born abbot. He had to prove himself all over again.

The 'comprehensive reforms' which the Holy Father was undertaking – trying to stop laymen from making clerical appointments, putting an end to the open sale of benefices, reinforcing the old decree about clerical celibacy, proper canonical election to sees – one would have thought was more a matter for the nobility and the Duke himself, and the pastoral clergy. There was not a lot the average abbot could do about that, except perhaps to clear a few furtive concubines out of the dormitories and warming-rooms. It was more a responsibility of men who were out in the world. He smiled again. He understood the vassals of Normandy well enough to know that pious pronouncements from episcopal thrones, or papal thrones for that matter, rarely cut much ice. To move the average Norman knight, it would take something more imaginative than gentle pastoral requests.

He noticed that there was an extra page after the official signature and seal. He smiled with genuine pleasure this time. It was in the Pope's own hand; he recognised the slightly sloping style of his old pupil.

'I greet you in the name of God, and trust you are in good health. The Duke has chosen wisely; I can think of no man better qualified to fill your new post. His Grace will be well served, and so will Mother Church.

'I fancy the Duke's vassals might take a little notice of our latest decree: I propose to make it an offence to attend Mass said by an incontinent priest. Perhaps we shall make more headway if we make them worry about imperilling their own souls than if we simply ask them to try and avoid imperilling the souls of their married clergy. I hope it will put the cat among the pigeons rather nicely.

'Perhaps you can whisper something of the wisdom of this course when the Duke comes to consult you, as I am sure he does very often. We all did.

'And now farewell for a while. I shall try to write when time permits. Meantime, my fond respects. Believe me, I still sit at your feet.

'Your friend in God,

'Anselm. (Only the Lord Himself knows whether I can live up to the name of Alexander. I can not conquer myself, never mind the world.)

'Postscript: You will see that my handwriting still leans and droops most slothfully. Not even you could change that!'

There was a polite knock at the door. Lanfranc put the letter away in a chest.

'Come in.'

A servant came in and bowed.

'Father Abbot, my lady Matilda waits on you.'

Trust Matilda never to give warning. She rarely visited people; she descended on them, usually with her ever-growing brood of children in tow.

Lanfranc nodded.

'Give me a moment, then show her in. When you have done that, bring some refreshment. Does she have any children with her?'

The servant winced.

'Several, my lord.'

'Then bring some sweetmeat or other.'

'Yes, my lord.'

'Why are you limping?'

'One of them kicked me, my lord.'

'Which one?'

The servant turned wearily at the door and winced again.

'Does it matter, my lord?'

Lanfranc waved him away, and turned to open the shutters to let in some light. Matilda hated shadows and gloom. She seemed impervious to draughts and chills. Raised in Flanders, where it was always raining, or so they said. Lanfranc shivered. He would never learn to like the northern climate. Here was a wind, in the middle of May, fit to freeze a Christmas feast.

He went to a cupboard and took out two glasses in the finest Italian style. A precious legacy from his doting father. He should not really have them. Surely the Father Abbot, of all people, should set the example about the forsaking of personal property. But they had not long since arrived, borne with great love, care, and patience, all the way from Lombardy. What could he do? Destroy them? It would have been unbearably thoughtless to the carrier, and a sacrilege to the memory of a beloved parent.

Matilda swept in like a tiny gale. Behind her, a forest of feet scuffed up the straw on the new flagstones of the chapter house. Lanfranc kept a corner of it for clerical business.

Robert, the eldest, and Cecily, the next, both pouting on the verge of adulthood, already topped their mother. Even Richard, at nine, was nearly the same height. Two more girls and another boy jostled at the end of the line.

Matilda snapped her fingers.

'Say hallo to Father Lanfranc. Properly now.'

'Good morning, Father Lanfranc.' Their treble voices soared in well-practised sing-song. Robert bowed stiffly. Cecily managed a self-conscious curtsey. Matilda stabbed a finger into the air.

'Stay there. And still, mind!'

Without waiting to see if her commands were obeyed, she came forward smiling with pleasure and well-being.

'How are you, Father Lan?'

Lanfranc bowed slightly. Matilda knelt and kissed the ring.

'All the better for receiving you, my lady.'

It was a change not to see her with an infant slung from her hip. Lanfranc cast his eye along the line by the door.

'Where is – er – ?'

For the life of him he could not keep track of their names.

'With the nurse. She is getting her ready.'

Lanfranc raised his eyebrows.

'That is why I am here,' said Matilda, answering the question on his face. 'To say goodbye.'

She walked to the open window, and breathed deeply.

'A fine, clear day, Father. Ideal for a journey.'

Behind her, Lanfranc smiled in spite of the cold he felt. It was hard not to be affected by Matilda's admittedly robust charm.

'Where to this time?'

He did not need to ask why; she travelled only in order to be with William.

'Rouen,' said Matilda, turning back from the window. 'He lies at Rouen. He has – '

There was a knock at the door.

'Come in.'

They waited while the servant set out plates, some food, and wine. As the door shut behind him, Lanfranc waved her familiarly to the table.

As Matilda sat down, the children jostled suggestively.

'Would they like to sit down?' said Lanfranc. 'I have something for them.'

They pleaded with their eyes. Matilda kept them dangling while she pretended to consider.

'Well ... as it is quite a long journey.'

A small avalanche of humanity clambered on to the benches.

'I have two more glasses,' said Lanfranc. 'Since they are now so big.' He nodded in the direction of Robert and Cecily, who were whispering heatedly to each other.

'Behave yourselves,' snapped Matilda, 'or I shall tell Gerard when we get to Rouen. And that goes for all of you.'

Lanfranc passed round the plate of sweetmeats.

'One each – no more!' said Matilda.

Podgy hands nursed the fragments with miserly care.

Lanfranc set out the glasses, and poured the wine. Matilda made no comment about the beautiful workmanship. Aesthetics completely passed her by.

'To a safe journey,' said Lanfranc. 'And may God go with you.'

'Amen.'

Cecily hissed in Robert's ear.

'You should pass me my glass. Ladies should have their glass passed to them.'

Robert sneered.

'Ladies – maybe. Not you. Get your own.'

Cecily glared at him, and stretched across him to reach her glass. As she did so, Robert pinched her upper arm.

She cried in pain and jerked her hand against the glass, which toppled and smashed on the pale, unmarked wood of the new table-top.

'There! Now look what you have done.'

'Not me,' said Robert smugly. 'You.'

'Tit for tat! There!'

Cecily swept Robert's glass away to the floor, where it too smashed, staining the rushes red.

'Enough!'

Matilda stood up.

'Come here.'

They both rose and came before, a good head above her.

Without warning or hesitation, she slapped each of them roundly across the cheek.

'Outside.'

'Do I have to?' whined Cecily.

Matilda pointed remorselessly. Both stumped out.

Lanfranc fondly gathered the pieces that were scattered on the table.

'I shall pay for the glass, of course,' said Matilda. 'And so will they.'

'No,' said Lanfranc. 'It is no matter ... No matter.'

At least it had helped to solve his problem.

Lanfranc stooped and piled all the broken glass together on the floor in a corner. A silent blessing slipped between his lips as gentle as a mother's kiss. Then he stood up.

'Now – Rouen.'

'Yes,' said Matilda. 'William has sent for me. And the children. Cecily does not want to go, naturally.' She mimicked her whine. ' "Do I have to?" '

They smiled.

'Robert will enjoy the castle and the soldiering. They always make a fuss of him there. And the chicks will like seeing Gerard again. Eh?'

'Yes, mother,' they chorused.

Matilda was imperious, wilful, and outspoken. She was also a devoted parent. But William came first. Whenever he summoned her, she packed up the entire household – children, furniture, servants, and all – and went wherever he happened to be. Sodden camp or chilly castle, it was all one to her. She was prey to none of the whims and vapours that constantly beset ladies who drooped bonelessly over their tapestry work in effete courts like Paris or Cologne.

'William can not mount his campaign against Brittany yet,' she explained. 'Damned vassals haggling again. Old wives' laments about dates and omens. Pox-ridden excuses. God's Blood! – I should like to tell them a thing or two.'

My lady Matilda's rich resources of broad language were renowned, and secretly admired, among the Duke's soldiery.

Lanfranc had not lived in Normandy for nearly twenty years without gaining an understanding of the military and political problems that constantly faced the Duke. An understanding, it seemed, fully shared by Matilda.

'An invasion of Brittany?' said Lanfranc innocently. 'To what purpose?'

Matilda made a face.

'Turds of Hell, Father Lan. Do not play the saint with me. You know as well as I do, we have Maine. Anjou is riven by civil war, and will be no rival. My father is guardian to the infant King of France; Paris is no threat.'

Lanfranc smiled.

'I know, I know. And Montgomery and Fitzosbern have made the southern frontier safe at Alençon, Bellême, and Tillières. And the Vexin?'

'Quiet.'

'And in the north?'

'Ponthieu?' Matilda almost spat. 'Pah! Count Guy is a worm.'

'And a sworn vassal.'

'And a sworn vassal. But it is not his oath that keeps him virtuous, Father Lan. It is fear. After what William did to his brother.'

Lanfranc felt a shudder of revulsion. They had needed a coffin and a half to collect all the pieces by the time William's mercenaries had finished with him.

'But why Brittany? If everything is safe?'

Matilda wagged a finger.

'There you go again, Father Lan. Count Conan needs to have his claws cut – as you well know.'

Lanfranc smiled wryly.

'And if the Duke's vassals will not follow him across the Couesnon against Conan?'

Matilda was unmoved.

'If they really are as womanish as that, then William will not sit idle. He is not one to cry over what can not be done.'

Lanfranc nodded. William would fume and fret, and fling himself into the saddle, bawling for beaters. But sooner or later, he would tire of the chase, even tire of Matilda. For all her devotion, she was not always the easiest of company over a long period. But God alone knew in what direction William's demonic energy would take him.

However, Matilda's next remark told him that she shared this intelligence with the Almighty.

'He says it will be a good chance to give some time to the Church.'

She laughed at Lanfranc's surprise.

'And you surely can not object to that, Father Lan. He has summoned the bishops – all except Coutances, who asked for leave.'

They looked at each other for a moment, then both laughed.

'Geoffrey and his cathedral.'

Matilda confirmed it.

'Geoffrey and his precious cathedral.'

'They have been away campaigning for two full years. Geoffrey must be curious to see how it grows; it is only natural.'

Matilda nodded, still smiling.

'True, true. But I really think Geoffrey is afraid it will fall down if he is not there.'

Bishop Geoffrey de Montbrai, Bishop of Coutances, was a valuable member of the Duke's military council, but he was also a conscientious bishop, and devoted to the reconstruction of his western diocese after so many plunderings by the Northmen.

Matilda looked up straight into Lanfranc's face.

'He wants you too.'

'Why me?'

Matilda snorted.

'Father Lan, I may not be able to read your books, but I am not one of your stupid court women. I deserve better of you than that. You know very well why William wants you.'

Lanfranc conceded with good grace.

'So be it. I am corrected.' He smiled. 'But why is it that your Duke always desires me to be somewhere else? I was settled at Bec; then he wanted me to be Archbishop. I talked him out of that. Now he has persuaded me to come here, to St. Stephen's. And just when I begin to set his new house on its feet, he summons me to Rouen.'

'Do not forget the time you opposed our marriage,' said Matilda. 'He wanted you out of Normandy altogether.'

'That was a long time ago.'

Lanfranc offered some more wine. Matilda declined. Like her husband, she was not self-indulgent at the table.

Lanfranc sipped thoughtfully, his inward eye on an angry young duke ...

'Splendour of God, where do you think you are going?'

'Out of Normandy, my lord. You banished me, remember?'

'What, on that donkey?'

'Give me a good horse, and I shall leave Normandy that much faster.'

William glared, then roared with laughter.

'Get off that animal. You look ridiculous ... '

Matilda looked at him with her head on one side.

'Do you still?'

Lanfranc looked surprised.

'Still what?'

'Oppose it. Do you still disapprove of our marriage?'

Lanfranc allowed a flicker of humour to ruffle the corners of his mouth. He indicated the young faces on either side of the table.

'The saying about shutting the stable door after the horse has bolted is not an especially apt one, but it covers the situation, I fancy. And God has clearly shown His Divine Blessing to you.'

'Amen to that,' said Matilda with fervour, pattng Richard's wrist. 'Every single one. We are truly favoured.'

Lanfranc knew very few families, noble or peasant, who could boast that every cub in the litter had survived. Matilda's gratitude was genuine. It was a soft side that she rarely showed. It did not last long.

She rose.

'And now we must be on our way. Shall I tell William you will come?'

Lanfranc sighed.

'Yes, you may tell him that. When these winds have dropped.'

They clattered out, Matilda's voice rising and falling as she heaped abuse on the impenitent heads of Robert and Cecily.

Lanfranc went to the chest, and fished out the letter he had been reading ... 'an offence for anyone to attend Mass said by an incontinent priest ... '

The Duke's chaplain had a daughter.

Lanfranc rolled up the letter again.

If the Duke wanted his advice on Church reform, he would be in no position to grumble if his new Abbot of St. Stephen's at Caen regaled him with the very latest decree from His Holiness.

* * * * * *

Edwin was now more than sick; he was cold. God in His inscrutable Wisdom had now seen fit to turn the wind from west to north-west. And to make it stronger.

Two or three falconers, grey-faced, sat hunched close to the oarports, obsessed by the mutiny building in their stomachs. It was as well to be in position.

At least the crew were not teasing him any more; they were too busy. The captain was shouting orders more frequently.

Only Earl Harold seemed the same. Unmoved alike by the swelling seas around him, and the growing human distress before him, he stood by the mast, gazing expectantly forward, his long blond hair and beard whisking about his head and face.

Edwin had not been in his service very long, but already he had become acquainted with his master's gift for being able to take unforeseen events in his stride. Difficulties became jokes against himself; dangers were turned instantly into adventures to be savoured. His self-confidence seemed boundless.

Edwin had not met the Earl's brothers, but if Gyrth and Tostig and Leofwine were anything like their elder brother, it was small wonder that King Edward had felt hemmed in by them. When their father, Earl Godwin, was alive, it must have been unendurable. Edwin had often listened round the fire while his father discussed the matter with friends. They passed the pot and put the world to rights ...

'It was all Edward's fault, bringing the Normans here in the first place.'

'He was half-Norman himself – raised in Normandy too. What else would he have done but bring his cronies with him?'

'Bring his friends for drinking and hunting, yes. But not give them so much land and power. God's Teeth – he made one of them Archbishop of Canterbury. What was Godwin supposed to do? Lie down and accept it?'

'Godwin pride – that was the reason. Godwin wanted no rivals.'

'Well, he got his way in the end. Got them all out. And got their land back.'

'Good riddance, I say. All foreigners are parasites. They did nothing but feed on the body of England.'

'Well, Godwin's brood are getting fat on it now – Harold in Wessex, and the other three in Northumbria, Kent, and East Anglia. The King can barely move for Godwins.'

'He is no friend of them, mark my words. Why else did he invite the Bastard to come and see him? Why else did he promise the crown to the Bastard?'

'You believe that story?'

'The Bastard keeps on about it.'

'He would.'

'It makes sense. We know the King has banished the Queen from his bed.'

'His way of getting at the Godwins – through their sister.'

'Maybe so. But we all know there will be no heir of his body. There must be an heir. The Bastard and he are cousins. The King likes Normans. As I said, it makes sense.'

'The Godwins will never wear it.'

'Neither will the rest of England.'

'It will not stop the Bastard trying.'

'Pah! A bastard ruler, in a seedy little duchy, with half his vassals traitors? Reaching out his hand for the greatest kingdom in northern Christendom? He must be mad as well as misbegotten.'

'If the Bastard really means what he says, let him come and get it ... '

And so the talk had gone to and fro. As the Bastard's visit faded into the mistier corners of memory, so did the potential threat it embodied. It became a stupid dream of grandeur, such as would appeal to a bastard with no breeding and no true standing. The son of a tanner's daughter, for God's sake! A preposterous joke to enliven an evening's drinking. Besides, every piece of news which came out of Normandy seemed to be about civil war or a frontier campaign somewhere or other – Maine, Anjou, the Vexin, Touraine, the Bessin, Brittany. It was difficult to keep track.

It would be only a matter of time before the Bastard was picked off by a stray arrow at a petty siege or hacked to pieces in a squalid ambush. His uncle had probably been poisoned. His father had died in mysterious circumstances in the East, leaving him an orphan at eight. All his guardians had been murdered. Treachery flourished there like nettles on a ruin. The menace was laughable.

The King sighed gently and kept silent. He folded his pale, veined hands in his lap, and listened patiently to the endless petitions from his faithful subjects, and turned them down so graciously that they all went away convinced that he had done them a favour.

But the Godwins grew in strength and popularity; each of the four earls was amassing a fortune in his earldom. Harold, in Wessex, was the second man in the kingdom, and the King had no children. How long would it be before he moved to become the first? Edwin's father and his friends talked round the fires. They did not venture to predict the future openly, but the signs were there for anyone with eyes to see. Even a dog-handler.

Edwin's stomach lurched. The hounds skidded and scratched and whined. Edwin's arms ached so much that he felt tempted to slip their leashes and let them fend for themselves.

Harold turned, saw his plight, and came aft towards him.

'Courage, lad. What is a little sickness? Think what a clean stomach you will have afterwards.' He gestured overboard. 'And with this breeze we shall arrive all the faster.'

Breeze!

'Yes, my lord.'

* * * * * *

Geoffrey de Montbrai shivered, as much with the cold as with nerves. The spiky shroud of scaffolding round the new tower, with its wooden platforms and splintery poles, creaked and rattled in the rising wind. He hoped that Goscelin, his engineer, knew what he was doing.

Taking great care to hang on with both hands, he turned himself about and looked at the other two towers that rose above the west facade. The shiver was one of pride too. Three towers! Bishop Odo at Bayeux had only two.

Geoffrey looked further, out over the great fields of his vassals' manors; towards the forests where the wood had been cut for the very poles that now supported him; towards the quarries of Montjoie, whence had come the granite blocks of the towers and the nave; northwards towards the heaths and moors of Lessay; west towards the sea, the Great Western Sea, the end of all the world.

'The end of all the world!'

He remembered his bitter complaint to his brother Mauger when he had first been saddled with the lands and mitre of Coutances. There had been nothing here – no cathedral, no town worth the name, no episcopal palace, no mills, no bridges, no garrison, no market – nothing.

And Mauger, who had bought the bishopric for him from an impoverished Duke, had dismissed him without a care: 'Then the end of all the world is what you have, brother, and it is all you have. I suggest you make the most of it.'

Geoffrey sighed. Fifteen years ... fifteen years of unremitting toil, travel, and worry. But he had a town now. Indeed, he owned half of it himself – bought it as a ruin from the Duke, as his brother had bought the bishopric. Built it up. He had not neglected the countryside either. The rivers had been cleaned out and their banks repaired, walls rebuilt, mills set up, a market established. Sprawling cattle tracks had been turned into passable roads with rubble from the masons' yards round the cathedral. He was especially proud of the stone bridge that Goscelin had built for him over the River Vire at St. Lô. It had taken all his tact and guile to inveigle Goscelin into doing it, to take him away from his 'great work' at Coutances for a few weeks.

'A bridge, my lord bishop? Did you say a bridge?'

The furrows in Goscelin's cliff of a forehead had twisted themselves into pyramids of agony at the thought of an artist such as himself being so demeaned as to be forced into the mere contemplation of throwing a few boulders together over a marshy stream.

It was Thierry who had come up with the right idea. Feed Thierry, and he usually responded.

'Flattery, my lord – remember?'

So said Thierry, between mouthfuls. Thierry was Goscelin's friend, and ought to know.

So Geoffrey had laid it on with, appropriately, a trowel, and he got his bridge.

Of course, it turned out to be a splendid bridge. The fact that Bishop Odo of Bayeux made so many sarcastic remarks about it only showed how good it was.

Around the town of Coutances, the manors of Geoffrey's new vassals fattened and prospered. New stalls were added to the market every month, or so it seemed, as more and more peasants came in, if only to sell a few eggs or surplus chickens. With each passing year of his rule, men felt safer. The new episcopal palace was both cause and symptom of his growing strength, wealth, and reputation.

But it was the cathedral that consumed him. This passion had grown, from the tiniest grain of reluctant interest, from the moment they had laid the first course of granite blocks in the nave. It was an emotion which had come to him unexpected and unbidden. As the cathedral of Our Lady of Coutances rose heavenward, yard by yard and year by year, the intensity of the excitement often surprised him.

Now he grasped the scaffold beam beside him, looked about, and felt a surge in his heart that he could never have foreseen when he had first been faced with this town that was no town at the end of all the world. It was like a shiver too, though not of cold, nor of fear, nor yet of pride.

He would never have admitted to it, of course. Kept it to himself. Had he but known, it was the most open secret in all Normandy. Bishops and vassals alike joked among themselves about it.

'It takes a miracle or a crisis to dig Geoffrey out of Coutances.'

He did not like admitting it even to himself. To have owned to anything like satisfaction in being a bishop would, in his own eyes, have somehow implied saying goodbye for ever to the prospect of attaining satisfaction in being a knight and a vassal.

His friend Lanfranc, who had seen the great potential in him when he was a young man, had argued many times with him ...

'Why struggle against what is clearly God's Will?'

'I only have your word for it that it is. I do not see it. Why does God tell everyone but me?'

'Because you do not listen. Look – if you had not become a bishop, what would you be? A second son of an undistinguished Cotentin vassal. No land, very little money, and no prospects.'

'I had my wits.'

'You still have them; Coutances has not taken them away. Now look at you – you have a mitre, a town, a cathedral, a palace; you are a trusted adviser of the Duke; you have lands, a fortune, a reputation. And you can still use all your military skills and experience to help build up the best-run duchy in France.'

'But I did not seek it. It was forced upon me. I have no calling for it.'

Lanfranc smiled. 'Geoffrey, anyone who has achieved what you have achieved has the calling for that particular type of work. It is not only being a bishop, or only being a knight. *It is being both – successfully.* Very few men have that gift, and the Duke knows it.'

Geoffrey growled.

'You did not want to be pulled out of Bec. Or sent to St. Stephen's at Caen.'

'No. But I went. Perhaps the Duke saw that I was the man for the job. Who of us knows what the next step in life is going to be? We must simply go along with the Will of God ... '

Well, that was as may be. There had been times – many of them – when he had wished his mitre to the Devil. It was because of that cursed mitre that he had lost Sybil. Damn the cloth, and damn the tonsure, and damn everything which had taken him away from her – or her away from him, into the convent of St. Amand.

And yet, and yet ... why was it that he could never wait to get back to Coutances after every campaign? Why was it that he resented every call to the Duke's Council, be it at Caen, Bayeux, Rouen, or wherever? Why was it that he never grudged any time he spent with the gloomy Goscelin, poring over scrawled diagrams on slates, clambering over piles of masonry, squinting up at lofty windows and columns, arguing over the siting of statues?

Why was he so glad that the latest campaign in Maine was over? No more imminent rebellions. No more frontier raids from Anjou. No more threats from Paris. No more tiresome training weeks with the Duke's knights and mercenaries. No more camp councils with Fitzosbern and Giffard and Montgomery.

He began to climb down, slowly, hanging on very tightly. The wind, out of the north-west, out of that end-of-the-world sea, whipped his cloak about his ears.

He did not get angry. He was looking forward to several weeks of peace and quiet with Our Lady of Coutances. But first, a good meal. He had fasted since before he had said early Mass. And up there for so long in the wind and the cold. Jesus and Mary! He felt as hungry as Thierry.

* * * * * *

Edwin had tried to hold it back at first. A forlorn attempt to keep his dignity. He had seen the ugly postures of the other dog-handlers and falconers as they curled and convulsed and heaved. None of that for him!

The smell of vomit came to him through the spray. The wind carried the ghastly noises of distended throats. Sadly he knew that he was going to lose the battle. He had as good as surrendered before his stomach at last claimed the victory.

In his weakness and preoccupation, he lost his control over the dogs. A sudden tug on the leashes pulled him over. He found himself on his hands and knees as a second spasm hit him. He watched helpless as the matter slid across the timbers, slipped between cracks and dribbled down into the bilges.

One of the crew, his face set and hard, slipped in it. He stumbled and cursed as he passed on an urgent errand. Through the slapping of the sail and the hiss of the spray came the raised voice of the captain. No anxiety. But demanding instant compliance.

No sailor stopped now to slap his back with a hearty jest.

As Edwin continued to kneel, he began to feel the rain seeping through the clothes on his back. The deck heaved under his hands like a live animal. If he were not cold enough with the wind and the nausea and the rain, fear now laid its chill hand on him as well.

'Bear up, son. Not far now.'

The Earl was squatting beside him, his blue eyes a mixture of amusement and sympathy.

Edwin struggled to a sitting position, and hauled on the leashes.

'Just as you say, my lord.'

* * * * * *

Arnulf paused at the porch of the garrison chapel and looked up at the weather. Gusts of wind snatched at the long, greying wisps of hair that clung round his tonsure like cobwebs to a cruck. Clouds were building. He would have just enough time to reach his chambers before the rain.

He clutched the large leather satchel of vestments to his ample stomach and began to cross the main courtyard, his frightened eyes shooting to right and left in case of he knew not what. He was always in a hurry, and he was nervous in case anything should happen. He knew this, but, no matter how hard he tried to arrange his day, he ended by feeling late; and while he was rushing to complete something, something else usually managed to take him by surprise.

In the chapel behind him, he had upset a candlestick in his haste and broken a new candle – one of the new tall ones he had put aside for High Mass whenever my lady Matilda should arrive. He knew it was any day now, and he was determined not to be caught unawares. He heard the altar boys sniggering to each other, aimed a blow at one of them, and missed. He overbalanced, fell down an altar step, dropped another candle, and broke that too. They ran out, laughing openly, leaving him to fold the vestments himself.

When he reached the porch, he heard them scampering away towards the guardroom, still laughing. Within minutes he knew that this latest trivial skirmish would be elaborated into a great adventure, in which he would play the major part of the fool. His walk would be mimicked, his puffing exaggerated; the soldiers on duty would chortle, and would be persuaded in their good humour to give the boys some free beer.

In a corner of the courtyard, a detachment of men-at-arms were practising with spears at a wooden target on a wall. They paused to watch his half-scamper, half-waddle progress.

' 'Morning, Father.'

'Late again, Father.'

'Mind how you go, Father.'

Sly grins were exchanged. As soon as he had passed, one of them stuck out his stomach in crude parody and mimicked a desperate stagger.

Arnulf sweated with effort and embarrassment. The flush on his cheeks was almost permanent.

When he reached his quarters, he bumped into another soldier coming out. The man smirked, then turned away from Arnulf to shout over his shoulder at someone inside.

'Here comes your father, Adele. Make sure you are nice to him too.'

He laughed at his own joke, and was gone before Arnulf could think of a crushing reply.

Adele was bent over a table when he came in, apparently absorbed with some kitchen task. Arnulf felt another surge of heat. His daughter seemed to have grown hips almost overnight.

He put his vestments into a chest.

'What did he want?'

'Who?' said Adele without turning round.

'That boy.'

'You mean Nigel?'

'I mean that boy who just went out.'

'He is not a boy.'

'He is to me, girl.'

He came forward to see what she was preparing. She kept her head down, but he could see that she too was flushed.

'He is older than I am,' said Adele.

'He should still know better.'

Adele looked up and challenged him openly.

'What is he supposed to have done?'

Her mother's dress was too small, and she knew it. They both knew it. Her figure was already fuller than her mother's had ever been. She was trying to hide the fact that she was breathing deeply. There were times when she was willing to flaunt the tightness of the bodice. Without mercy.

He wrenched his eyes away from her chest.

'That is for you to tell me.'

She pouted.

'Now Father, who would dare to lust after me, the innocent daughter of a priest? The Duke's own chaplain.'

She looked him full in the face.

After a moment, he broke away from the stare.

'What do we have to eat?'

He wiped the sweat off his cheeks, and went to pour something to drink. Adele heard the cup clattering against the tap, and smiled devilishly.

Arnulf want back to the door he had left open, and held his face to the wind.

Let Father Lanfranc come soon and hear his confession. Let him also pray for this torture to be ended. God had taken his wife; was that not punishment enough?

* * * * * *

'Splendour of God, Fitz! It is not to be endured!'

The Duke flung his knife on to the table, and began pacing up and down the hall.

Sir William Fitzosbern continued imperturbably with his breakfast. A lifetime of campaigning had taught him to avail himself of every meal that presented itself – when it presented itself. He had also just come through a long and late Mass, with another rambling sermon from that pot-bellied garrison chaplain. What the Devil was his name? Curious how the stomach grumbled more on the knees than it did in the saddle.

The Duke spat a piece of rind on to the rushes.

'We have the best chance we have had in years. Maine is quiet. Anjou is in confusion. Matilda's father has the King in his care. We could tame Brittany in a month – two months. And all they do is make excuses about days of bad omen and shortage of horses.'

Fitzosbern took another mouthful.

'They are right about the horses. There are no trees full of destriers.'

William stopped in front of the table.

'Look at the new lands I could give them. With Conan as sworn vassal the possibilities are enormous. Then, Fitz – then! – we should be secure all round.'

'Except for Ponthieu.'

William waved a hand.

'Bah! A fly to be swatted, and only then if necessary. Think, Fitz. All round – Brittany, Maine, Anjou, the King, the Vexin, Ponthieu. All quiet. We should be ready. Ready.'

William never spelt it out, but every man near him knew how, with each passing year, the great project increasingly dominated his thinking.

Fitzosbern still declined to be moved.

'You will not be ready if you forget your goal, if you stop to buy pretty goods on the way to market. No, hear me, my lord.' William had opened his mouth to object. 'You could mount a campaign in Brittany, yes. You could bully de Montfort and de Warenne and Beaumont and all the rest into putting their full force in the field. You could perhaps defeat Conan – even depose him. And what resources would you have left? How would you make up the further losses in destriers? How would you afford the cost of more mercenary infantry? Flemings are not cheap. Baldwin says our supply columns were stretched to the limit in Maine last year. He must have time to rebuild.'

The Duke sat down.

Fitz was right – of course – damn him! His quartermaster, Baldwin de Clair, had been saying much the same thing ever since they had returned from Maine. Baldwin was a shocking old woman, but he was a boyhood friend, he was loyal, and he too was right.

There was no point in having Brittany under the heel if he had no breath left to move when the great moment should come. Come it would – he was sure of it. He had to be ready.

And yet. And yet! Timing was everything. Conan had a full-scale rebellion on his hands, and half the rebels were looking towards Normandy. William's every instinct cried out to him to hit Brittany now. If Conan put his rebels down, the moment would pass – possibly for years. And Edward would not live for ever. Fitz must know that. As for his stupid vassals ...

'Can they not see, Fitz?'

Fitzosbern passed his tongue across his teeth, and reached out for the pot.

'They are not the Duke of Normandy, my lord.'

They were ordinary vassals, like vassals everywhere, go where you will in France or Germany. They had estates and boundaries that needed maintenance just like a duke's. They had to recoup losses, collect further supplies, find the funds to purchase weapons and trained destriers. Their greed was limitless, but now and again their prudence put a rein on it.

William plonked his elbows on the table.

'So we do nothing?'

Fitzosbern sighed gently. They had had this conversation four or five times already.

'No, my lord. We compromise. We pay the leash out a little. Let them rest on their estates, count their loot from Maine, enjoy their wives, go hunting. In short, let them do what you are planning to do.'

William ignored the thrust.

'All summer?'

'No,' said Fitzosbern patiently. 'For a while. Then, when their larders are full and their wives begin to nag, talk about a short, punitive expedition.'

'You said we do not have the resources.'

'Just so. Not for a full campaign. But for a show of strength, yes. We do. Some marching, controlled looting, lift a siege or two. And withdraw. We rap Conan over the knuckles, and we give encouragement to the rebels.'

'Bluff, you mean?'

'Yes. We often make the mistake of assuming that others know what we know. They do not. You should play chess more often, my lord.'

William shrugged.

'No patience for it.'

Fitzosbern sighed again. William had very little patience for anything, except his family. Please God Matilda and the children arrived soon. His own patience would not put up for ever with this restlessness.

'Remember too, my lord, there is work to be done elsewhere. You have sent for the bishops. And Lanfranc. Ask him. He will say the same as I do.'

'Lanfranc is not my military adviser; you are.'

Fitzosbern finished his drink and stood up.

'I have given you my advice, my lord – several times. And now I must ask you to grant me the same favours that you should grant everyone else – and are about to grant to yourself. I have not been to Breteuil or Tillières since Christmas. And my mother is here, in Rouen, in the convent of St. Amand – not half a mile from where we sit, and I have not yet seen her.'

It was a rebuke. William accepted it. He would have tolerated it from no other man. He fought the tiniest of rearguard actions before he withdrew.

'So we just make a noise outside Conan's door?'

Fitzosbern paused at the end of the hall, and looked back.

'We can not take Brittany. Better to leave it divided, perhaps, than to leave it alone. My regards to the lady Matilda, my lord.'

* * * * * *

'We must run before it, sir.'

'If you say so.'

Harold and the captain bellowed at each other through a wall of rain.

'If we can make the mouth of the Seine … '

'Do what you think best. We are in your hands.'

In God's Hands, thought the captain, as he turned to give the orders. Though now was not the time for fine points of navigation and theology. The Seine had a broad estuary; God would at least have a lot of space at His disposal. They were not asking Him for a miracle.

Even as he bawled orders to his crew, the captain spared a thought for the conversation which had got him into this. If he had had the time, he would have allowed himself a wry smile …

'I need a ship.'

'I have a ship, my lord.'

'You do not know my charge yet.'

'Make me an offer, my lord.'

Harold grinned.

'Very well. I need to travel a lot. I have gained all these manors in Sussex.'

'From the Normans.'

'From the Normans. I am fed up with the bogs and bumps of Sussex lanes. It will be quicker – and easier – to travel from one part of the county to another by sea. You agree?'

'I agree, my lord. But then I am a sailor.'

'Precisely. And I am not. Will you take me?'

'Yes, my lord. For a fee, of course.'

Harold named one.

'Agreed.'

'Whenever I wish?'

The captain revealed some double-door gaps in his teeth when he grinned.

'For what you are paying, my lord, any time you like.'

He spat half-way across the waist of his ship.

Several journeys later, Harold came to him again.

'Could you take dogs and falcons instead of soldiers and clerks?'

'I see no reason why not, sir. So long as your people keep them well tethered.' He chuckled. 'If we are shipwrecked, they will fare better than we shall; the dogs will swim and the birds will fly.'

Harold chuckled too.

'True. But do not tell my dog-boys and my falconers. I have told them it will be a great adventure.'

'So be it, my lord.'

'Are you content?'

'It beats crossing the Channel any day, sir ... '

And here they were, crossing the Channel. With the mother and father of all winds in pursuit. Ah, well – that was the sea for you.

Harold grasped a rope and gazed into the streaming curtain before him.

The Seine ... if they could reach the mouth, they could manage a few more miles to Rouen. William's capital. What an interesting possibility! It was going to be worth it if only to catch the look of stupefaction on the Bastard's face. To say nothing of the look of bafflement on the faces of his vassals, as they tied themselves in knots to try and work out what he was doing there. That was the trouble with Normans; they gave themselves headaches trying to work everything out before the truth hit them between the eyes. So much so that they often missed the truth when it did. It probably came from playing all that chess.

Would Wulfnoth be there? He hoped so.

He was so absorbed that he failed to notice the heap of humanity beside his knees.

Edwin had given up trying to stay dry. Three or four falconers had found a large piece of spare sailcloth, which they wrapped over and round themselves. Pressed together, they retched and spewed over each other and their charges. In the confined space, with the smell and the noise, two or three of the birds went berserk, lashing out with beak and claw. Two men clambered out, and fell prone on the streaming timbers of the deck, blood from their scratches running pink in watery vomit. Anything was preferable to what they had just escaped.

Edwin had heard what the captain said. Normandy! If the man had said Constantinople he would not have cared. He had long since lost sight of the coast of Sussex. What did it matter where they went so long as this – this – he could think of no word to describe it – so long as this would be ended.

The fear had left him, to be replaced by longing.

* * * * * *

'Bring them out!'

Sir Walter Giffard shouted through the open door of his stables. He turned back to his friend, and grinned in triumph.

'Now, Roger! Be prepared to go green with envy.'

Sir Roger of Montgomery hitched his thumbs in his belt. Walter had been like a child with a new toy since dawn ...

'Come and see me before you go back. You must.'

'I am tempted, Walter. I am tempted.'

Longueville was only twenty-five miles or so from Rouen. After months of campaigning, and further tedious weeks during a hard winter spent in numberless council meetings with the Bastard, it would be a pleasant interlude to be a mere guest – and with his old friend. Before he faced all the problems piled up for him at home.

Walter's hall was a shambles, outside and in. Neither he nor his wife seemed to notice it, but their welcome was genuine and warm. Ermengarde, her grey hair a mess as usual, soup stains down the front of her dress and a hole in one elbow, remembered the names of all Roger's children.

Walter was so pleased with himself that he could talk of nothing but Spain and horses. Roger listened and nodded in all the right places. He watched Ermengarde, who had no doubt heard it several times already. She gave quiet orders to the servants while she sewed. Roger compared Longueville with Bellême; Mabel would never be content to sit in the background like that. Ah, well ...

The wind blew wisps of straw around their leggings.

'Come on, boy, come on! Lively. Walk them round. Easy now! At their own pace.'

Sir Walter Giffard, never a patient man at the best of times, was now quite impossible. Nothing was right. Everyone at Longueville, from the lady Ermengarde to the lowliest swineherd, understood. This really was a special circumstance. Sir Walter's pride knew no bounds, and he was able to transmit it. His mighty purchase was a triumph for the whole fief of Longueville.

After one glance Roger understood too. They were the two most magnificent creatures he had ever seen.

Walter patted a rump. He could not stop grinning.

'What do you think?'

Roger of Montgomery spread his hands.

'I am lost for words, Walter.'

He really was.

'Half broken already. And shod. Look.'

That made sense. It was a long way from Spain. How on earth had Walter managed to get such spirited creatures over the passes in winter?

'Took the pilgrim route,' said Walter, answering one of the questions on his face. 'Bad enough, even then. Lost a mule or two. One man deserted.'

Roger was still amazed. He had spoken to pilgrims back from Compostela. They swore, one and all, that, no matter how meritorious the journey to the shrine of St. James, it would take a mortal sin of Hellfire certainty weighing them down to induce them to make it again. (Though some of them still did, years later.)

'I shall answer the other question on your face,' said Walter. He grinned. 'Mind your own business.'

Roger spread his hands again.

'But two, Walter – two! How did you manage it?'

Walter's grin of satisfaction threatened to split his face.

'That is the clever part. I plan to sell one of them to the Bastard. Quickly. Before he spends all the loot of Maine.'

'How do you know he will meet your price?'

'When I tell him how many kings and emperors spend ransoms to own one of these – ' he patted an arched white neck ' – he will pay.'

Anything which put a bastard duke on a level with the King of France would be too big a temptation, enough to overcome any amount of budgetary prudence.

There was a military reason too.

'You know what the Bastard has been on about too. More mobility. Our destriers are too stodgy.'

Roger nodded.

'Geoffrey has been saying the same. The last eighty paces of the charge take too long. It gives too much time for the formations to break up. Geoffrey says – '

'Exactly. We must not sacrifice weight, but we must have more speed.'

'Well, Geoffrey is the one in charge of training. And William listens to him.'

'That was my chance. In half an hour I had sold him an Arab stallion.'

'And all you had to do was go and get one.'

'Two. Precisely. God's Face – he even gave me permission to miss the whole Maine campaign.'

Roger smiled.

'I had wondered how you managed it. The whole autumn and winter in Spain. But how did you raise the money? Steal the Emperor's crown?'

'That would have been easier.'

What Walter had in fact done was little short of moving Heaven and earth. He put out some of his best outlying estates on short lease to the monks of the new house at le Tréport; he screwed up mill dues as high as he dared; he doubled the fines for illegal fishing in the Scie; he raised stud fees for the stallions he already owned, and ignored the grumbles of his neighbours; he sent a trusted negotiator to extract a loan from the Jews of Cologne. He 'borrowed' the dowry of a niece of Ermengarde's who was in his care.

Walter made a face.

'Ermi would not speak to me for a week.'

He had to hire extra men-at-arms to guard the money throughout the journey to Spain, and the haggling with the Moorish dealers nearly broke him.

But now, after a terrible return journey, he was back, and triumphant.

'If the Bastard becomes convinced, and orders the new cross, I shall have been vindicated. What the Bastard wants today, every vassal will want tomorrow.'

'If they can afford it.'

'Pah! They will afford it – for that. So will the Bastard.'

They watched while the stable boy returned them to their stall. Walter swept on.

'With the money the Bastard pays me, I shall buy some more mares from Flanders. I have seen Count Baldwin. There are thirty already on their way. We can start putting them together as soon as they are settled. It will be just in time for foaling next spring.'

Roger smiled. Walter had made thorough preparations. If the Duke wanted this cross, the lady Matilda would put pressure on her father, Count Baldwin, and the Count would give Walter a favourable price. Another reason, no doubt, why the Bastard had invited my lady to come to Rouen. Before long, an invitation would go out to my lord the Count of Flanders.

No wonder Walter was so pleased with himself. It was a very long-term investment, but in four or five years he could be the master of a fortune.

Walter read his thoughts again.

'I shall invite down payments on the foals. That, plus fees for breaking and war training, then the rest of the purchase price ... Think, Roger. Just think.'

Roger did not have the heart to suggest to his friend that the cross might not be successful. Walter's enthusiasm was unstoppable.

It began to rain. They walked back towards the hall, hunched against the heavy spots borne on the wind.

Walter looked up at the grey sky.

'I have had enough of the elements for a while. Just give me my hall, my stable, and my lovely white babies – and the rest of the world can go to the Devil this summer.'

'You know the Bastard wants Brittany, I suppose,' said Roger.

Walter snorted.

'Madness. After last year. I saw Baldwin a few days ago.'

'What – Count Baldwin?'

'No. Baldwin de Clair. Our Baldwin. He says we are already overstretched. And a quartermaster ought to know.'

'Walter, *everyone* says we are overstretched. Guess who is the only one to disagree. I left Fitz to talk some sense into him. He will not listen to anybody else. He goes on about the frontier – total security.'

'You know why,' said Walter.

'We all know why.'

'But it helps me,' said Walter. 'If he is thinking that far ahead, he is thinking about destriers – more and more of them – fitter and faster. I tell you, Roger, his dream may or may not get him a crown, but it stands a good chance of getting me a tasty little nest egg.'

* * * * * *

Edwin looked at his hands as if they did not belong to him. He was fascinated by the colouration. At first they had gone pale with the cold. Then red. Then a blue tinge became noticeable. Now he noticed flecks of yellow as well. Did they turn black before the end came? He had heard tales of limbs going black with disease or poison. Was it just the tall stories of old soldiers? He had once thought so. Now he was not so sure.

Some of the dogs had broken free. Two falconers had hurled their birds overboard, and sat hunched, their arms tight about them, nursing their pains and their gashes.

The captain tugged at Earl Harold's cloak. Harold lowered his ear towards the captain's open mouth.

'We have missed the Seine, my lord. Wind has gone round a touch to the west.'

Harold nodded.

'Dieppe, then?'

The captain spat the spray off his beard.

'I doubt that, sir. More like the Somme, I should say.'

Harold nodded again.

'So be it.'

The captain turned away to give orders. Harold caught him by the sleeve.

'Captain Aldred?'

'Sir?'

'I am sorry.'

The captain blinked.

'Sir?'

'Sorry you are caught up in this. This was not in your contract, was it?'

Aldred grinned.

'They told me that working for you would not be dull, sir. They were quite right.'

Harold laughed.

'I am finding that the sea is not a dull place either. I had always thought it was.'

'The sea is a wayward mistress, sir. But I do not think she is ready to take us to her bosom just yet. Not just yet.'

Harold looked about him. Perhaps Aldred should try telling that to the huddled figures on every side.

Harold watched Aldred bellow his orders, though his voice barely carried above the wind. It was worth a storm, though, to see that gleam in a man's eye, and to know that he had put it there.

* * * * * *

'By the Nails, boy! You call these knives sharp?'

The booming voice echoed round the great kitchen.

Young men-at-arms lounging over scraps grinned at each other across the trestle table. Two scullions paused at work on a spit to look over their shoulders.

A third boy stood limp and silent. The cook stumped towards him, still brandishing a knife. The foot of his crutch caught at the rushes on the floor.

'I said do you call these sharp?'

'No, Gerard.'

A point was waved under his nose for his inspection. A great black beard bristled.

'You could not cut butter with this for a midsummer feast.'

'No, Gerard.'

A gleaming eye raked the boy from head to foot.

'Well, what are you going to do about it?'

'Do them again, Gerard.'

Another piercing gleam.

'Be about it, then, be about it.'

A wallop across the rump from the crutch sent him on his way.

The two boys on the spit giggled.

Gerard whirled on them and glared. They fell to their work at once.

The young soldiers chuckled.

'Make sure they baste it well, Gerard. We are looking forward to a fine chop when we come off guard.'

Gerard jammed the crutch under his arm and made surprisingly good time across the kitchen floor. One soldier, still smiling at the joke, felt a huge hand grab him by the collar. He was lifted bodily off the bench.

'God be merciful to your wagging tongue, Nigel Fitzhenry.'

Nigel could feel Gerard's breath on the back of his neck.

'Your appetite comes not from gazing out over castle walls, my lad. You get it from staring at tight dresses in priests' houses.'

Nigel, still hanging like a cloak on a hook, was not put out.

'No harm in looking, Gerard. Like looking at nuns – all right so long as you never get into the habit.'

He winked at his companions, who roared with delight. Gerard noticed that one of them still blushed through his laughter.

Gerard dropped Nigel back on to his seat.

'Begone, the lot of you. And stay gone. This meat is not for the likes of you.'

He brandished his crutch.

They clattered off, throwing rude remarks over their shoulders, from a safe distance. Gerard flung a rolling pin, and hit Nigel, which pleased him.

He subsided on to the bench, well content. They were coarse, and callow, and not very bright, but they were young, and their eyes and ears were sharp. They missed nothing. And their tongues were easily loosened by a full stomach. A scrap of food for a scrap of gossip – it seemed a fair exchange.

Gerard eased his bad leg into a better position. He rarely went outside his kitchen, very rarely beyond the castle, but there was not much that he was unaware of.

For example, he already knew all about the little spat in the chapel that morning, when Arnulf had broken the candles. Poor devil! He could not even discipline a couple of altar boys, much less handle his own daughter. Although, come to think of it, perhaps that was just what he had done. Some people were born unlucky; God seemed at times to take a perverse delight in placing certain people constantly in situations that He knew they could not deal with. Poor Arnulf. He had not particularly wanted to be a priest. He was certainly not the scholar for it. Gerard suspected that half the so-called Latin he muttered during the Mass was gibberish. He had married his wife only because his wretched conscience would not allow him to keep a concubine. When Adele was born Arnulf was taken unawares once again; had not the faintest idea what to do with a daughter. And now that she had grown up, and especially since his wife had died, he knew only too well what one did, or at least what other people did, and that left him totally at a loss too. He could not cope with a hungry young wolf-cub like Nigel, and he could not cope with his own feelings.

Nigel was not the only one. Gerard was prepared to wager that every young buck round his table just now had nibbled the forbidden fruit in Arnulf's kitchen. All except one. Gilbert had blushed. And Gilbert probably was the only one who longed for her. The others merely lusted.

God, who loved all men, surely had a lot to answer for. That explained why men desired to be kings and emperors and Popes, but they never longed to be God. Ah, well ...

'Keep at it, boy, keep at it.'

The spit turned.

If my lady Matilda came on the morrow, or even today, he would be ready. My lord duke had been to the chase twice already since Sunday, and the larder was beginning to fill. It needed to be fuller still if all those bishops and their trains were to be properly fed. Then there was Count Baldwin. The invitation had gone out. It would be good to see his Count again. Flanders gossip was the best gossip of all.

It was going to be a busy time. But not too busy to see the children. Robert would be thirteen now – beginning to grow some muscle. Ready to try a man's bow? Somehow he would make time to take the boy into the courtyard. Devil take his leg – if only he could move properly!

Would Cecily still be a misery?

* * * * * *

'I tell you, she is coming. With all the children.'

Gilbert cut another piece of pork off the cold joint he had stolen from the kitchen, and tossed the remainder to one of his companions on the next bunk.

Ralph of Gisors caught it, and sliced off the rest of the meat on to two wooden platters. He shared out a small dark loaf.

'Why so sure?'

'Got it from Gerard. And he should know.'

'Never trust a Fleming,' said Bruno from the third bed.

'My lady is Flemish,' said Gilbert. 'What do you say to that?'

Bruno of Aix took the plate Ralph offered him with a nod.

'My lady is different.'

For once Gilbert did not argue. The lady Matilda was well liked in the man's world that surrounded the Duke night and day. Totally unabashed by her lack of inches, she went briskly about her business of being mother, consort, and regent in the Duke's absence, and expected everyone else to mind theirs. She was tough, resourceful, and totally oblivious of the most appalling weather conditions. She could laugh – unusual in a Fleming, so they said – she could drink with the best of them, if she had to, and she could outswear most inmates of the guard-room. She was a devoted mother and wife, but she regularly beat her children regardless of size, and her rows with the Duke had staff by the dozen bent double at cracks in wooden walls. She shouted things to his face the mere thought of which caused sweat to run down the cheeks of strong men.

'Well, anyway, she is coming,' said Gilbert. He waved airily with his knife. 'As a scout, I weighed the information, and my judgment is that it is reliable.'

Ralph looked at Bruno, who raised his eyes to the rafters.

They munched for a while in silence.

'Could do with some beer,' said Bruno. 'Damned altar boys stole the last jug.'

Gilbert did not take the hint.

'Afraid of him then?' said Bruno.

Gilbert flushed.

'Who?'

'That nice man with the crutch.'

'Damn you!'

Gilbert got up and stamped out of the guardroom.

Bruno grunted.

'Works every time.'

'How long do you think he will go on taking it?'

'Till you tell him flatly no.'

Ralph struggled for a reply.

'It takes time.'

Bruno wiped the blade of his knife.

'I can tell him now if you like.'

Ralph put out a hand.

'Just – just leave it, eh? I am not afraid to tell him, but I want to be fair.'

'You do not want to lose him.'

Ralph ignored the remark.

'It means a quiet time then. No move to Brittany.'

'Nothing in force. Fitz is trying to drive some sense into him. Perhaps getting my lady here is Fitz's idea; I would not put it past him. Devious devil.'

Bruno got up and shut the door left open by the irate Gilbert. The wind was driving the rain inside. His great height brought his head on a level with the lintel.

'You have no excuse this time.'

Ralph fidgeted.

Damn Bruno. Why was he always right? Ralph lay back and shut his eyes ... How many times had he been home in the last fourteen years? 'As often as I can – I promise.' He squirmed at the memory of his own words. He had meant them too.

But brother Aubrey now had full control of the knight's fee in Gisors; their father waved his stump of an arm and shouted defiance to the world, but he was getting weaker, and the winters got into his bones. His mother, her mind broken by the raid, talked mostly to herself in corners. It was seeing them like that. Last time he had nearly cried over his mother's hands. He remembered them as soft, round, able to stroke away a world of troubles; now they were the white claws of a witch, twitching at a smoke-stained coverlet. Aubrey did not really want him, and his sisters were married with families – worries enough of their own.

And Michael. Visiting the grave would be worse than holding his mother's hands.

Gilbert was here. Alive. Not eaten like Michael. The likeness was magical.

'He may have your brother's face; he does not have your brother's soul.'

Bruno again – damn him!

What if the mud of the plough still clung to Gilbert's boots? All men came from the soil in the last resort. He had travelled Normandy as keeper of hounds to Bishop Geoffrey de Montbrai; he must have picked up some knowledge of the world. He had begged the bishop to let him join the garrison at Rouen. He was big, strong, dying to learn the profession of soldiering. His eagerness and innocence were touching. He wore his feelings on his sleeve like a badge.

It was obvious, for example, that he was smitten with Adele – made cow's eyes at her all the time. And he was probably the only one who had not made a pass at her.

Now he wanted to be a scout. Ralph was flattered by the boy's admiration. If they took him on, he would have Gilbert with him all the time. It was like re-creating his family; his father would have two good arms, his mother would smile once more and soothe his brow, and Michael would be born again free of fever.

'You are chasing a ghost,' said Bruno. 'The boy is a clod, not a dead saint.'

'Go to Hell!' ...

Ralph opened his eyes, and watched Bruno sit down and start some mundane task of cleaning. Bruno's hands were always moving, rhythmically, steadily; they were reassuring, like a pulse.

'You never talk about your family.'

Bruno did not lift his head.

'Nothing much to talk about.'

'Will you go home? To Aix?'

'Depends.'

Ralph gave up.

The door banged open. It was Gilbert with three mugs of beer. He remembered to kick the door shut again.

'Great Jesus – this wind!'

* * * * * *

The sickness seemed to have finished with him. Having shaken every scrap of food and moisture out of his contorted body, it had dumped him down like a pile of beggar's rags. He was past pain, past fear, past longing. It was the quiet before death. Edwin had seen it on his father's face, just before the end ...

For three days they fought the flesh rot. Edwin and his mother suffered with him. It had not been such a great wound either – only a dagger thrust, and not in a vital spot. But the poultices and the bleedings were of no avail. When he ceased to struggle, everyone breathed a sigh of relief. He spoke clearly and serenely.

'It is just a little earlier than I had expected.'

His mother held his father's hand.

That evening, Earl Harold himself had come to see him. Up till then, he had been a popular lord, and Edwin regarded had regarded him with almost the same respect that he had had for his father. Now, in his anger, he was barely civil.

'Your father died a brave death.'

'He still died,' said Edwin.

Harold looked down at him, and gave him his full attention.

'Yes, he did. And he died protecting my property.'

'So?'

'What should I have done? Let those Normans disobey the law and keep the estates that I had been granted? I sent in my bailiffs. In the same position, your father would have done the same. Even at your tender age, you know that.'

Edwin's mother nudged him in the back, as if to silence him. In any case, he could think of nothing to say.

Harold fixed him with a sharp eye.

'Nevertheless, you are right in a sense. Your father was my man, and I am responsible for his family now that – now that – '

'Now that he is dead,' repeated Edwin, finding his tongue again.

His mother began to splutter excuses, but Harold waved them aside.

'I need another dog-handler. Will you come?'

Edwin gaped.

His mother pushed him in the back again ...

Now the dogs were all gone. He did not know how, nor did he care. The marks of the leashes on his hands had almost faded. There were no falcons either. So much for the captain's joke about the animals surviving longest.

All around him bodies were curled up as if they were trying to return to the womb.

Only Earl Harold seemed untouched. He still stood by the groaning mainmast, the sides of his hood lashing his cheeks, his long moustacbe blown wide, his jaw jutting into whatever lay before them.

How long was it since he had seen Wulfnoth? Nine – ten – Great God! – was it twelve years? He would be a full-grown man now. He tossed his head. Whose jaw would drop further – his brother's or William's?

Aldred came alongside, clutching the stays.

'We shall look a sorry sight when we arrive, my lord. Sorry about that.'

Harold clapped him on the shoulder.

'Not the end of the world.'

Edwin wished it was; it would be preferable.

* * * * * *

'Will you stay for a game?'

'No time.'

Gerard offered another drink.

'Not even a quick one?'

Wulfnoth put up a hand.

'You can not play chess quickly.'

Gerard laughed.

'I can. Much more fun.'

'I have too many things to think about.'

This boy always had; that was his trouble. Whether in play or in work, it was the same. He pondered every move on the chessboard as if the Last Judgment depended on it. The bishops and abbots would not be arriving for at least two or three weeks, and he was behaving as if he had to arrange a Papal election by the evening.

The Duke had made a good choice when he appointed this young Saxon nobleman as his junior chamberlain. The boy was dutiful, conscientious, and thorough. But oh, what a worrier! A great pity. He was tall, healthy, good-looking in a lean, suffering sort of way. No wonder the girls were drawn like flies to honey. Arlette could hardly believe her good luck when he looked at her. But it was she who had had to make all the running …

'What should I do, Gerard? She is a Norman.'

'Very pretty one too.'

'But I am Saxon.'

'So?'

'I shall return to England one day.'

'So you either desert her or take her with you.'

Wulfnoth spread his hands.

'What does that make me?'

'Anything you wish to make of yourself.'

' How do I do that? Saxon till I was twelve. In Normandy as a hostage for twelve years. Now what am I?'

'Anything you care to be.'

'Gerard, I can not "be" anything. If I follow my Saxon star, I must pine for Harold to come and take me back. And the Duke will never let me go. If I follow my Norman destiny, I shall be haunted by dreams of my mother and brothers for the rest of my life. What am I to do?'

Gerard refilled his mug.

'You admire them both, eh?'

'You know I do.'

'Then do what they do. Seize life!' Gerard made a snatching movement with his free hand. 'Look at our Duke. When Mother Church and Father Lanfranc forbade his marriage, did he sit down and mope? Did my lady Matilda?'

Wulfnoth shrugged.

'No,' said Gerard. 'They went ahead and got married. A trifle unofficially, I grant you. But the world came round to them in the end.'

Wulfnoth sighed.

'I wish I could seize life.'

'All you have to do is put out your hand, boy. Just put out your hand.'

* * * * * *

The boat was wallowing. Water lapped everywhere. Edwin was up to his knees. The wind had ceased to roar, but not before it had eaten the mast. The splintered stump stood alone, with torn canvas and frayed ropes clinging to it like frightened children to a bereaved mother.

Aldred clamped Harold's hands on the steering oar.

'Just keep her pointed, sir!'

Harold nodded.

The coast of Normandy was not far away now. The crew were sweating on the oars like Greek galley slaves.

'Pull, lads. If you want a gentle bed of shingle tonight, pull!'

Aldred turned to the wretched passengers.

'Your turn, my beauties.'

Edwin stared in disbelief.

'Look at us. We have no strength. Look at us.'

'You have enough for the work I want. Bail.'

'Why? We are going to die anyway. Our dogs have.'

'And our birds,' said someone else.

'Damn your dogs and damn your birds. Damn you too.'

Edwin rose in fury.

'How dare you? What do we bail with, you idiot – our hands?'

Aldred whirled on him.

'If you are too stupid to think of anything else – yes.'

'I shall see you in Hell first,' roared Edwin. 'Let us at least die with dignity. Scooping out water by the spoonful!'

Aldred nearly felled him with a great slap to the side of the face.

'I have no wish to stand before the Gates of Heaven or of Hell beside the likes of you. Damn you, bail! Or, so help me, you go over after the hounds!'

* * * * * *

Sir Roger of Montgomery allowed his horse to take its own pace. Now that he was away from the Duke's presence, and all the pressure that that entailed; now that he was actually on his way to Bellême, the attractions of home were not entirely unmixed.

The brief stay with his old friend Walter Giffard had been a relaxing interlude. He would soon have to bring his mind to bear, in detail, on the many problems awaiting him ...

How much money had Mabel spent this time in his absence? Whenever she showed him her latest purchase, he found it difficult to enthuse because he was always doing sums in his head and arriving at frightening answers. He could dismiss the extra kitchen staff she had taken on, or call a halt to ambitious building projects; but he could not bring himself to burn the latest piece of oak furniture, or tell her to take off the new dress she had bought from the seamstresses at the royal court in Paris.

Whatever he did there would be high words.

'Do you want me to live in the sort of squalor that Ermengarde has to tolerate?'

The cat coming out. A careful swipe at both his friends at the same time.

'You should see what Fitz has had done at Breteuil and Tillières. Are we to become everybody's poor relations?'

Then try telling her she was a snob.

'How can we ever entertain Matilda here? In this – this midden.'

Mabel in fact was a very efficient manager, and God help any of the household who did not agree with her when she reminded them of it – as she did nearly every day. The living at Bellême was infinitely more comfortable than it was at Longueville. You could almost eat your meals off the floor. There were no holes in Mabel's elbows. But Roger always enjoyed his stays with the Giffards, in the same way that, as a boy, he had enjoyed his time with the stable lads and their families, who did not mind if he forgot his knightly manners now and then.

The children would be pleased to see him. And he them ...

A pity he would not see the lady Matilda. He liked her. And she would take the Bastard's mind off politics for a while. Give everybody some peace.

Probably not for long, but a few weeks was better than nothing. Saints and angels! The work he had to do at Bellême. Long before midsummer he would be receiving messengers from the Bastard, to ask how the new fortifications were coming along. When would they be ready? How did they compare with those at Alençon and Tillières and Breteuil? Did he know that his brother Robert had done wonders at Mortain?

Montgomery sighed. Of course he knew what the Bastard's brother Robert was doing at Mortain. He wished he had a handful of silver for every time he had visited some border fortress or other in order to compare notes and exchange ideas. At every council the Bastard went on about the same theme ...

'Secure. We must be secure. All round. From Brittany to Ponthieu. In case.'

In case. In case. Always the dream.

The restless eyes darted continuously to left and right. Part of the Bastard never sat still. Rumour had it that he never stayed in the same position in sleep for more than a few minutes at a time.

The frontier, the eternal frontier.

'We have Maine under the thumb.'

The Bastard's rasping voice was unmistakable.

'What about Anjou, sir?' said one brave soul, from the back.

'Bah! Of no account.'

'Can we make their civil war last for ever, my lord?'

'We can if we place our bribes wisely, and tell our tales to the right people.'

The Bastard was probably right.

'The south is safe – now.'

He was right there too. A compliment, if only a back-handed one. Between them, Fitzosbern at Breteuil and Tillières, Montgomery at Bellême and Alençon, and the Bastard's brother at Mortain had seen to that.

And everyone knew that the young King in Paris was in the guardianship of Count Baldwin, the lady Matilda's father.

That left two ends – Brittany in the west and Ponthieu in far north-east. Nobody wanted to mention Brittany, in case the Bastard brought up the question of invading it again. As a feeble diversion, somebody let fall the word 'Ponthieu'.

'Could be a problem, sir.' Fitzobern dealt with that.

'Guy is a bandit, little more. He saw what happened to his brother. Took him three days to count the pieces. Besides, he has sworn homage. We scared the life out of him.'

The Bastard allowed himself one of his rare laughs.

Roger of Montgomery was not so sanguine. Guy of Ponthieu was not only a rogue; he was a fool. He would not have learnt the lessons that had been dealt out so finally to his brother Enguerrand.

It may be true that Count Baldwin in Flanders was breathing down Guy's neck, but that would not stop a fool if he thought he could steal a march. Ha! Try saying that to the Bastard in his present mood.

Still, there was always Fitz, with his endless patience, to tell him some home truths, and the lady Matilda to tell him some more. And the children. Perhaps they might get a peaceful spring and early summer after all ...

Roger of Montgomery patted his horse's neck, and looked back at his column of men-at-arms.

'Right behind you, Sir Roger,' said his sergeant. 'We want to get home too.'

Home.

Home. Bed. Mabel was quite good at that too. So long as you told her so immediately afterwards.

* * * * * *

'Let go!'

The ship rode gently on the anchor cable.

Harold swore to himself.

'You would never think there had been a storm.'

Aldred grunted.

'That is if you look at the sea, sir. Look at the ship.'

It was a pitiful sight. Deck and thwarts awash with blood, water, vomit, and worse. A splintered mast barely a yard high. Torn awnings, flapping stays, broken oars. Shreds of canvas trailing in the water. Flotsam in the wake. Bowed shoulders, drooping jaws, grey faces. Even the crew were wan with exhaustion.

Harold turned and looked at the shore. A small group of horsemen waited at the back of a rough jostle of peasantry.

'Quite a crowd.'

'Must have been watching us for hours,' said Aldred.

As Harold and Aldred left the ship at the head of their men, some of the crowd rushed into the sea in front of them. Harold thought at first that they were coming to help. Instead they waded right past him.

Aldred spat.

He had seen that look on men's faces before, when he was once wrecked off the coast of Devon.

Pieces of litter and wreckage were pulled from the water, examined with tight jaw, and hurled back again with an oath.

Harold, his cloak bundled round his waist to keep it from the sea, struggled out of the water, and shouldered his way through the remaining spectators. They recognised a nobleman and instinctively made way for him. He marched right up to the group of horsemen, singled out the corporal in front, and flung an arm at the looters.

His anger lent him fluency in a language he did not use much now that the King's Norman friends had left his country.

'Is this what you call charity?'

The soldier twitched his reins slightly to bring his horse's head round.

'No.'

'Are you going to stop it?'

'No.'

His voice had the usual disembodied tone that resulted from its issuing from a head almost covered by mail coif, iron helmet, and the ugly, projecting nasal between the eyes.

Harold drew himself up.

'Have you no authority?'

'It is the custom.'

'Whose custom?'

'Our custom. All wrecks are lawful prize.'

Harold jerked a thumb over his shoulder.

'Their prize?'

The soldier shook his head.

'Only the droppings. They will not touch the ship itself.'

Harold took the man's bridle and looked him in the eye.

'When I have talked with your superiors, they will be sorry they touched anything.'

The soldier shrugged. He made a sign to his companions, and they all dismounted.

By this time, many of the crew had caught up with Harold. Captain Aldred stood closest.

'Do you recognise this part of the coast?' muttered Harold.

Aldred nodded towards the wide sand flats.

'River estuary, obviously.'

'The Somme, as you said.'

'Probably.'

This was strictly outside Normandy, but the Bastard's influence would be felt. His father-in-law held sway in Flanders to the north; they could squeeze the vassals in between into homage, or at least into sulky obedience.

The soldiers drew their swords, and one unlooped a coil of rope from his saddle horn.

Ah, so that was it – ransom. Not only were the ships lawful prize; their passengers were too.

Harold looked at the expressionless soldiers, who were clearly following orders, then at his soaked and shivering men. They were in no condition for a fight against armed opponents. If they lost, their deaths would be upon his head; if they won, they were still in a foreign country, and whoever had sent these soldiers could no doubt send more.

Better to try a surprise.

Conscious that he was the centre of attention, Harold advanced on his own, towards the man with the rope, and held out his wrists to focus the soldiers' eyes. As they gathered round him to complete the arrest, Harold suddenly shouted, 'Run for it, lads!'

Nobody moved.

Harold felt a movement behind, turned, and saw all his men at his shoulder. Aldred made a face of mock sternness.

'Now, sir, you should know us better than that. We can not have you wandering about Ponthieu all by yourself, can we? Whatever should we say to the King if we lost you?'

'He would probably make you Earl of Wessex in my place,' said Harold, and they both laughed.

Harold, flushed with the joke and with pride, turned back to the baffled soldier in charge.

'Do you still wish to bind us like common criminals?'

The corporal inclined his head by way of salute, and waved away the man with the rope. He made a sign that they were to follow. The horsemen remounted. The corporal ordered two to remain to watch the ship; they steered their horses among the jostling peasants still on the beach, shouting and swearing. The rest fell in on either side of the untidy column. Nobody noticed the prostrate body of a young Saxon, masked by clumps of seablite which grew almost to the water's edge.

They moved inland, picking their way over the soft surface between shallow pools and wide patches of the blue-green seablite. After half a mile or so, as the ground began to rise slightly, another rider approached from the landward side. The procession halted as he cantered up to them and made a great show of reining in his horse. Its mane was clipped and bound – not in the Norman style. Garish trappings in vulgar colours hung from the saddle.

The new arrival wore no mail. His head was bare; he wore his hair longer than the severe Norman fashion allowed. His short cloak, held at the neck by an ornate brooch, was flung in casual manner back from his chest.

He rode right round the column, deliberately going so close that several men were nudged to one side by the flanks of his destrier. He returned to the head, and approached Harold as the obvious leader.

He halted, surveyed the group once again, then placed his gloved hands on the pommel of his saddle.

'I am Guy, Count of Ponthieu. Who are you?'

* * * * * *

Chapter Two

The Telling

'All wrecks are lawful prize.'

Edwin's ears had told him that. After his years in the service of Robert of Eu in Sussex, he knew enough French to follow, sometimes say, simple sentences. When a Norman reeve gave orders, you quickly learned to obey. The corporal had a difficult accent, curiously flat and thin. Flemish influence probably. Edwin had heard Aldred say they were in Ponthieu, and Ponthieu was close to Flanders.

Edwin's eyes told him the rest. He saw the horses, the weapons, the rope, the column moving off. There seemed little doubt; the Earl was a prisoner.

There was nothing he could do. The slightest movement on his part would have led to his own arrest. It needed fine timing to stay quite still while the soldiers were within sight, and then to choose the exact moment to move carefully away before the looters came back out of the water. It occupied him so completely that he forgot his wet clothes, his tortured stomach, his earlier despair. Nothing mattered now but to avoid being caught.

He gave no thought to any plan. His reactions were completely instinctive, those of a rat in a cat-infested kitchen. For an hour he crawled through the thick carpet of sea-blite. After a rest, he crawled again till he reached rising ground, from where he looked down at the wreck on the beach. The scavengers had nearly all gone, up the river valley.

He gazed about him. Cropped grass and well-groomed woodland as far as he could see. Sheep slopes. Half-grown lambs still skipped and tumbled near their mothers.

Shelter! He had to find shelter. There would be shepherd's hides, but he needed to be careful. Three times he came across traces of recent fires outside them, and moved on. By the time he reached the fourth, broken and lopsided, he was nearly weeping with fatigue.

Luckily the wind had now dropped completely, and there was a glorious sunset. His clothes had dried on him during his wanderings. He crawled inside, made what bed he could of stale sheepskins, and was instantly asleep.

It was the wind, now alive again, that woke him, not the sun. It whined outside like a lonely dog; it chilled him with daggers of draughts that stabbed through the gaps in the hide's derelict walls.

Outside, the countryside was empty except for animals. Each sheep was tethered to a stake, and grazed in a perfect circle round it. He could still make out the wreck, still riding secure on its anchor. All the looters had gone. No sign of soldiers.

The sight of the ship struck his mind so forcibly that he almost reeled with the recollection – the storm, the misery, the landing, the arrest. Earl Harold a prisoner. And he the only one still free! Where was he to go? What was he to do? He had never been out of Sussex in his life, never mind out of England.

He had no idea where he was, except that it was Ponthieu and outside Normandy. He had overheard captain Aldred; the storm had blown them beyond Normandy. The only person he had heard of in Normandy, except for his old master, Robert of Eu, was the Duke himself. He remembered the captain saying something about the River Seine. The Duke lived at Rouen, and Rouen was on the Seine – he knew that much. All he had to do then was to follow the coast back to the mouth of the Seine, and trace the river back up its course until he reached Rouen.

The Duke had to be told about the arrest. He was not the ideal person to be given this news, but Edwin had no other choice. If he did not tell somebody, it might look as if Earl Harold had vanished off the face of the earth. Count Guy might ransom him when he had won the highest terms, but that could take months. If he found no suitable bidder, he might choose the obvious means of ridding himself of an awkward burden.

Having made up his mind, Edwin was now assailed by the demands of his stomach. If he did not get some food and drink soon, he would not be going anywhere. He decided he could expect little charity where he was. The news of the wreck would already be common knowledge in the valley behind him. His dress and hair style would proclaim him as English at one glance. Far from feeding him, or even turning him away, they might arrest him and take him off after the others, in an attempt to secure the favour of Count Guy.

He must turn his back on the valley, make for the coast again below the wreck, and begin his journey south. He had no idea how far it was going to be, but reasoned that if he followed the coastline far enough, he had to come to the mouth of the River Seine sooner or later. He could look for food on the way. It looked a fat, green countryside; the pickings should be quite good. He had spent a whole boyhood avoiding the eagle eyes of reeves, bailiffs, haywards, and manor cooks, both by day and by night. He still had his knife, and some twine and leather straps on his belt; there were always rabbits.

He walked towards the coast, and reached it where the estuary of the river met the white cliffs that faced the sea. Turning to his left, he began his journey towards the Seine. Surely the Earl Harold would be most grateful when he, Edwin son of Edward, brought none other than the Duke of Normandy to his rescue.

* * * * * *

'She likes you. Told me herself.'

Gilbert blushed.

Nigel Fitzhenry winked again at his companions.

'She slapped my face. Sent me packing. Said there is only one she is interested in.'

Gilbert bent down and pretended to tie a loose lace. At least it would be an excuse for a red face.

'Why me?' he mumbled.

'Because you do not chase everything in skirts.'

Gilbert rose to the bait.

'Oh? Who said?'

Nigel put on a serious face.

'I told her. I said you only had eyes for her.'

Gilbert flushed more deeply.

'You did what?'

'It is true, my dear boy. We can all see that. And we say, good for you. A fine thing – fidelity. And she is a fine girl. Any of us would be proud to have her – to have her for his own.'

Two of the soldiers spluttered into their beer.

Nigel slapped Gilbert on the back.

'Why do you delay? I have prepared the ground for you. She is too shy to make the first move – priest's daughter and all. Eh, lads?'

The faces round the table were in agonies of enforced composure.

Gilbert stood up.

Nigel gave him a push in the rump.

'Go on. No time like the present. Strike while she is – while the iron is hot.'

When Gilbert had left the kitchen, everyone burst into silent hysterics.

'Nigel, you are a bastard!'

Nigel drained his beer, stood up, and beckoned them after him.

'That was just the digging of the trap. Wait till he falls into it.'

As they stumped out, Gerard swung his cleaver again. The thud made the scullions jump.

'Get on with it, you worms. Or the onions will not be the only things to make you cry.'

They wrenched their eyes away from the open door.

Gerard arranged the chops in a pan. They would taste better cooked separately in herbs and butter. The lady Matilda had a good appetite, and young Robert had begun to eat like a horse.

If there was to be no campaign this year, the Duke should either go out more often to the chase, or he should pack these young bucks home on leave for a while. There would soon be no end to their mischief. Town brawls, irate fathers, or worse.

Finding a virgin in a garrison town in peacetime was like looking for a jewel in a midden. Only lovelorn ploughboys like young Gilbert still hoped to find them.

Gerard whistled under his breath as he hobbled about his kitchen.

They did things better in his Flanders. Packed off most of the unemployed young men as mercenary soldiers. Let them cause trouble in the Empire or Italy or France. Somebody else's headache. Count Baldwin had a long head on his shoulders. Made the very most of his assets – surplus manpower, heavy horses, looms, and family connections. Commission on mercenary contracts, breeding fees for his mares, cloth sales in every market and fair in Christendom, and status as the Regent for young King Philip. To say nothing of father-in-law to the most successful prince in France.

No wonder the world made bad jokes about Flemings. Jealousy. Pure jealousy. Let them say one word against my lady Matilda though. Just one word – in his hearing.

* * * * * *

'Best thing you could have done, son – falling in with me.'

Edwin was not yet so sure. He already had an uncomfortable feeling that this garrulous monk was more pleased to see him that he was the monk.

'Spotted you for English straight away. Hubert, I said to myself, that boy is English. What is more, that boy is in trouble.'

Hubert may have had a useless arm, but there was nothing wrong with his eyes. He had noticed Edwin's hiding place beside the track when he stopped for a necessary moment. There was nothing wrong with his fieldcraft either, because he came up on Edwin totally without warning. Before Edwin could move a hand to his knife, a sword point was waving under his nose.

'Soldier, you see. Teaches you to take notice. Things you never forget either. Me – I did everything – scouting to scavenging. Catching you was child's play.'

Edwin pointed to the habit.

'Why the sword now?'

'Got to take care of yourself. The roads these days. Never know who you might meet. It takes people by surprise; they do not expect a man of the cloth to carry a sword. Useful.'

Edwin was offered a meal, a drink, and a ride on a cart. The only price he had to pay, it seemed, was Hubert's voice.

'I am with St. Michael's – Robert's new house at le Tréport. Robert of Eu.'

Edwin jumped at the familiar name.

'Robert of Eu? He was my lord in England – before the Normans were expelled. He lost all his land there. My father was killed during – '

'Yes,' said Hubert. 'Robert of Eu. Good thing you did not seek shelter at Eu. Just up the road. You must have passed quite close. Folk round here do not take kindly to visitors, much less vagabonds like you.'

'I am not a vagabond,' said Edwin, nettled. 'I am on a most urgent mission.'

'You see, this is on a direct line between Flanders and Normandy. All sorts of travellers pass through these parts. Not all with the best manners. We had a detachment of Flemish mercenaries through here not long ago. Stripped the place bare, they said. On their way to Brittany. The Duke is planning a new campaign, so the gossip has it. Easy pickings, I expect. Nasty lot, Flemings. Gloomy, godless. Must be all that rain. You would have received poor charity, I can tell you.

'Oh, yes – poor charity. You see, I know. I was like you once – a piece of wreckage.'

Edwin opened his mouth to object, but he was not quick enough.

'Piece of wreckage, I was. Cast up from the wars. Look at this.' He shook his useless arm. 'Been everywhere too – France, Germany, Italy, Provence, Spain. All I wanted was to come home to my family and our land. Do what my dear old father had done. And what did I find when I came home?' He turned to Edwin. 'I say, what did I find?'

Edwin looked blank.

Hubert answered his own question.

'Nothing. Nothing is what I found. My father dead, my family gone, my land stolen. No lord, no court, no redress. I tell you, I was angry, angry. Enough to try a saint, and I was no saint.

'Oh, no – no saint.'

Hubert broke off to encourage the donkey.

'Hup, hup, Rollo. Carrots, carrots!' He turned towards Edwin. 'He understands, you know.'

'Ah,' said Edwin.

'See Rollo?' said Hubert, pointing. 'See that animal? Well, my young friend, I was like that. Like the animals. I sank that low. Crime, dirt, lust, madness – the drink, you know.'

'Ah,' said Edwin again.

'But I was lucky,' continued Hubert. 'I am no saint, as I said, but I was lucky. I *met* a saint. I tell a lie – God forgive me.' He swiftly crossed himself. 'I met two. I was pulled out of a ditch near Brionne. You are acquainted with Brionne?' He turned again and raised a pair of tufty eyebrows. 'No, probably not, being an English refugee.'

'I am not a refugee – '

'It is on the other side of the Seine from here.'

Edwin pounced on the word 'Seine'.

'That is where I want to – '

'In the fief of Sir Baldwin de Clair. To be more precise, in the land of the great house of Bec, which is in the fief of Sir Baldwin. In a ditch, as I say. Just like an animal. Like Rollo here. And Herluin found me. Herluin was his name, He is the first of the two saints I told you about. Soldier, he was – once. Just like me. When he finished with the wars – or when the wars had finished with him – he was a lost soul. Loose end, and all that. Bit of a guilty conscience too, if the truth be told. So he collected a few men like himself who wanted to put something back into the world, and they set up their house of prayer at Bec. Got some land from Sir Baldwin's father. Herluin's own mother came in to do the washing. And that is how they started. Prospered too. God's work, you see. Simple, quiet, holy – genuine, you might say. St. Benedict's rule, to the letter. More men came. And God rewarded them by sending them the second saint.'

He looked at Edwin once more.

'Not boring you, am I?'

Edwin shook his head. Suddenly offered the chance to interrupt Hubert, he could think of nothing to say.

'Well, my young friend, it was Herluin who raised me from being an animal. It was the second saint who turned me into a man of God. Lanfranc. Ever hear of him? No, of course. I was forgetting. English. All that fog.'

Edwin wiped a hand across his brow. Hubert ploughed on.

'Greatest teacher in Christendom. I tell you, if a man can teach me, he can teach anybody. Lanfranc did. They come from all over, you know, just to be taught by him. Burgundy, Italy, Germany. He became Prior in the end. Got me through my vows. I was not sure at first – loss of liberty, you see. Soldier's life. Herluin seemed happy enough. But I had wanted land, pride in growing things of my own, independence. Building a manor. Creating something.'

Rollo slowed slightly. Hubert prodded him with a long stick.

'Home tonight, Rollo. Home tonight. You see.'

He made clicking noises with his mouth.

'Then Sir Robert of Eu set up his new house at le Tréport – St. Michael's. They wanted brothers to get it going. Not easy. I knew from what Herluin said. And Lanfranc said to me, "Hubert," he said, "you can do that. Just what you need. Fine work." "No, Father," I said. "I am not strong enough in my vows. I am not a saint like you." "Nonsense," he said. "We want workers, soldiers of Christ, not milksop saints with books in their hands." He smiled, did Lanfranc. Smiled.

I am not good with letters, you see. And Lanfranc understood. So – to cut a long story short – off I went. St. Michael's of le Tréport.' He chuckled. 'Everything was so new we were getting splinters off the table tops.

'But Lanfranc was right. It was the work for me. Setting up a new fief, making things grow. It was just what I had wanted. And you see, Lanfranc knew that. And then, last year, our house leased some manors from Sir Walter Giffard, near Longueville, where we are going. And two of us have to go there – we take turns – to see to them. It is just like being on detachment in the army. Better. I had wanted independence. Now I have it.

'My abbot at St. Michael's said the brothers were happy for me to go – I can not think why. But then I keep myself to myself. So here I am. Every so often I set off to relieve Brother Stephen at Longueville, and spend a month or two there. I am doing exactly the work I wanted to do – in my own way, in my own time. I travel, which I like. My habit is my pass on the road. And I can keep my sword, which I could never do in the house. I am truly a lucky man. God has been very kind. And now I fall in with you – lucky again. You are good company. I like your style. Yes, your style ... '

It was well over an hour before Hubert asked Edwin what his errand was.

* * * * * *

'That was a feast fit for a king.'

Matilda leaned back and stifled a burp.

Gerard took the plate and limped away towards a wooden sink.

'Fit at any rate for a duchess, your Grace.'

Matilda threw an empty cup at him.

'God's Blood, Gerard. I did not come down here to stand on ceremony. I get enough of that in the hall.'

Gerard came back with a small barrel tucked under his free arm. He carried it as easily as if it were a bunch of kindling.

'I see that life in the hall has not improved your manners, lady Matti. Or perhaps too much life in camp. Not a good thing, if you ask me.'

Matilda wiped her fingers on the kerchief that Gerard pointedly provided.

'Nobody is asking you. Mind your own business.'

'What sort of example is that to the children? Do you want them to grow up like you?'

'If they are bad, it is because you spoil them. You certainly did not spoil me. And let me remind you, if I had not followed William to every camp, there would be no children for you to spoil. Think about that.'

The kitchen was empty for once. Gerard usually cleared it of company whenever Matilda came in for a gossip.

In the early days they had talked together in Flemish, so that nobody could overhear. But as her marriage relationship with William deepened, Matilda increasingly used French even when she was out of his company, and Gerard wisely did not press her.

He knew exactly how far Matilda could be pushed. He had had enough practice. By the time she was five, it was clear that no female in the household could exercise a scrap of control over her. In desperation, the Count made Gerard responsible for her safety. Since then, scarcely a day had gone by without some kind of outburst – of rebellion from her, of impatience from him.

She cried, kicked, whined, pleaded, plotted, scoffed and sulked. He nagged, cuffed, hectored, threatened, and blackmailed. Over the years they built a relationship in which each practically knew what the other was thinking. She felt unsettled until she had seen him in the morning, and he was not at ease until he had seen her into the hands of her nurse at night. Each naturally professed total indifference to the other.

The other inmates of the guardroom teased him at first, but the taunts of 'nursemaid' very soon dried up amid the bruised ribs and bloody noses. Swords had come out once under pressure of drink. Gerard pinned a soldier against the wall and waved a point under his terrified nose.

'Anything is man's work if there is a man's reason for doing it.'

To outsiders it looked a most unusual partnership, but to everyone in the Count's household it became as normal as the sunrise. Such was the respect, and awe, in which Gerard was held by his fellow-soldiers, and such was the affection that they felt for Matilda, that everyone became almost proud of the bond between them.

When, in defiance yet again of her father's strictest orders, Matilda went climbing up some scaffolding around a new tower and became stranded by some falling poles, Gerard was instantly sent for. He climbed up and reached her, and people on the ground could hear him berating her as he fixed the ropes round her body for the lowering to begin. She was swearing back at him. But on the descent it was he who fell. He spent days in pain, and Matilda was inconsolable.

The pain went in the end, and he was able to get up. However, the bone had not set properly, and it was clear that he was a cripple. Matilda was beside herself with grief and remorse.

Gerard built himself a crutch, and learned to make very good speed with it, as many a jeering stable-boy found to his cost. His shoulders and wrists grew yet thicker and stronger. To save time, he grew a beard, which made him look more threatening.

Everyone knew, however, that his soldiering days were over. After a memorable week's drunkenness, which cost the Count a small fortune in guardroom damage, and which only Matilda could get him out of, he accepted it himself.

He became the Count's cook; it was the only way he could think of to remain close to Matilda.

They teased him again about aprons and stewpots. After he had thrashed them with his crutch, he would bend over them, thrust his black beard into their faces, and repeat, 'Anything is man's work if there is a man's reason for doing it.'

Such was the power of his personality that, after being the focus of the guardroom for years, he became the focus of the Count's personal household. Constable and chamberlain alike went in awe of him. Only Matilda, it seemed, could say what she thought to him. The Count himself treated him with a mixture of humour and deference.

Whatever the fresh problem or the new talking point, Gerard heard about it, and sooner or later Gerard was consulted about it.

He approved of the young Duke as a husband when the stormy courting began.

'Son of a tanner's daughter,' said Matilda, sniffing, when the first approaches were received.

After the first meeting, she complained of his lack of grace.

'Muck from the midden!' said Gerard. 'He is the only man you have met who has seen through you.'

Matilda replied with yet more vulgar expletives, but within two days she and William had become inseparable.

When the Church forbade the marriage on the grounds of a family relationship that was considered too close, Gerard craftily suggested compliance.

'Go against Mother Church, lady Matti? Is that wise?'

Matilda tossed her head.

'Trust you to give me some old woman's advice. I shall do exactly what I want. It is time you married too. I shall find a wife for you.'

'I am getting rid of you,' said Gerard. 'God save me from another shrew.'

He did marry, though – a long-faced, rangy seamstress from the Countess's women.

It did not stop him from appearing in Matilda's train when it set out for Normandy.

Matilda put her hands on her hips. 'And where are you going?'

'You can not live on the fruits of love for ever,' said Gerard. 'You have to eat like anybody else.'

'I suppose you think William has no cook?'

'Not from what they tell us. He has lived round camp fires most of his life.'

Matilda pointed imperiously.

'Get off that cart!'

Gerard jumped down with surprising agility, and fixed his crutch under his arm.

'Want me to walk, do you? Very well. I may be a day or two late. So long as you have no objection to cold food. You are right; the exercise will do me good.'

So Gerard installed himself at Rouen. He went back to his wife whenever Matilda visited her father, but was always pleased to leave as well.

His wife never conceived, so when Matilda's numerous children began to come along, he spoilt them outrageously.

He devoted much time to Robert, the eldest, and spent hours teaching him horsemanship and the handling of weapons. When other members of the garrison gave him lessons as well, he scoffed at their poor technique.

'They will get him into all the wrong habits. No real grounding, you see.'

Matilda gulped some beer.

'And I suppose you have. You will be finding me a husband for Cecily next.'

Gerard looked genuinely surprised.

'Is she not too young?'

'Twelve. Too young to marry, I agree. But we could think about some betrothal or other. It might put a smile on her face. She would be the centre of attention for a while. She is jealous of Robert.'

'You have a Fleming in mind, of course,' said Gerard innocently.

Matilda put down the cup.

'William wants a Norman.'

Gerard for once did not argue. He knew the depth of Matilda's attachment to the Duke. Here was an area where she could be pushed by only one person.

He changed the subject.

'When is Father Lanfranc arriving?'

Matilda screwed up her eyes.

'How did you know that?'

Gerard laughed a great boom of a laugh.

'By the Nails, lady Matti. I am not blind and I am not deaf. The walls store secrets here just like anywhere else.'

Matilda stood up.

'Well, careful not to poison him with the cooking. William needs him.'

* * * * * *

'And what makes you think the Duke will receive you?'

Edwin had already learnt not to answer at once, because he knew that Hubert would answer his own question.

'Have you any idea – I say have you any idea – what sort of life the Bastard has had? He was eight when his father died – eight. And a bastard, as I say. He spent all his childhood escaping from fond members of his family who were trying to seize his inheritance. All his three guardians were murdered, one of them in the same room as he was, and this before he was fully grown. He has put down three full-scale rebellions, repelled countless invasions – Anjou, Maine, Brittany, the King himself. Oh, yes, the King too. And he has survived by being watchful, ever watchful. They say his eyes never stay still. Do you think he will receive any stray Saxon who comes to him with a tall story?'

'I mean him no harm,' said Edwin. 'I want his help.'

'How does he know that? You are English. How does he know that you are not some spy from Harold? Does Harold love him? Will Harold sit by when your King dies and let the Bastard take the throne?'

Edwin spat.

'Let the Bastard come and get it. Our crown will go to the man named by our King and by our Witan.'

Hubert poked Rollo thoughtfully.

'Try telling that to the Bastard. How does he know that you are not sent by Harold to do his work for him? To save him a campaign. A quick spring, hands round the throat, or a hidden knife. A small matter for a desperate man.'

Edwin sighed.

'Let them take me to him stark naked. Just so long as I can give him my news.'

Hubert had not asked him what that news was, and Edwin had not told him. Five minutes in Hubert's company had made him realise that anything told to this portly prattler would be all over Normandy in a couple of days.

Hubert had chuckled.

'Secret, eh? Ah, well, keep it then. Just as well. They used to call me Hubert the Tongue in camp.' He took a pull from the leather flask at his side. 'Still, we can enjoy the journey. It is company I treasure, not secrets. I hoard company; I spend secrets. It was a good thing you fell in with me, I tell you. Have you any idea how long it would have taken you going by your road?'

Edwin had at first shown impatience at Hubert's slow progress. The monk shook his head.

'Rollo must not be rushed. He goes at his own speed. Just like his namesake. You have heard of Rollo, I take it? Rolf they used to call him in the old days. First Duke of Normandy. So big and fat, they said, that he used to go everywhere on foot; no horse would carry him. Rolf the Ganger. Yes. Rolf the Ganger. There is a good story about Rollo. It seems – '

Edwin interrupted.

'Devil take Rolf the Ganger. I need to reach Rouen quickly.'

Hubert paused in mid-flow, his mouth open. His tufted eyebrows lifted a fraction.

'Allow me to say, young fellow, that you are going the wrong way about it. Oh, very much the wrong way. Definitely the wrong way.'

He launched into a detailed explanation of the geography of Normandy, none of which Edwin understood. He tried again.

'If you follow the coast it will take you a week to reach the mouth of the Seine, assuming you do not get beaten up, locked up, or cut up on the way. Then you must double back on yourself, and the Seine winds like a spilt ball of thread – a spilt ball of thread. It will take you thrice the time. And how will you eat? Very badly. Raw rabbits, and pig slops when nobody is looking.'

Edwin could think of nothing to say. Hubert offered him a piece of cheese.

'Come with me – company, comfort in a cart, food and drink, and I know all the best stopping places. When we reach Longueville, I can put you on the right road to Rouen. An idiot can follow it. Use your wit, boy.'

Edwin sighed.

Hubert slapped him on the back.

'Glad to see one Englishman has some sense. More than the soldiers I served with when I was there. Now – we are coming soon to Envermeu, where we will stay for the night. There is a reeve I know. He puts us up, and we pay him with a little something.'

Edwin turned in alarm.

'A little something? I have no money.'

'Tut, boy. Who said anything about money? Put your hand behind you, under the canvas. Those small casks? Feel them? One of the skills we have already developed at le Tréport. Keeps a man warm in winter. Better than any money. Come on, Rollo, home soon. Yes ... good place, Envermeu. Now, there hangs a tale too. Did you know that the Bastard's grandfather, Duke Richard the Second, married a girl from Envermeu? Yes. Second wife. Popa they called her. Popa of Envermeu. Had two sons by her. Bad lots, both of them. One of them became Archbishop of Rouen – yes!' He chuckled. 'The other, William, became Count of Arques. We shall pass that way tomorrow. You will see the castle, or what is left of it. Would you like to hear the story of William's rebellion?'

* * * * * *

'Ha! You think to surprise me?'

William gestured to a clerk.

'Show him.'

The clerk blinked, clutching a sheaf of parchments to his chest.

‘My lord?’

William waved his hand impatiently.

‘Splendour of God, man! The one we have been talking about all this week.’

The clerk swallowed, and began fumbling.

‘Ah – you mean the letter of my lord Maurilius?’

‘What else, you idiot. Show him. You were quick enough to show me when it arrived.’

He pointed at Lanfranc, who was sitting on the other side of the table.

The clerk shuffled frantically, while William, unable to stand the delay, stood up and began pacing.

At last the clerk fished out the document William wanted. The Duke pointed again.

‘Well, show him, show him!’

The clerk nearly dropped the rest in his haste to lay the letter before Lanfranc the right way round.

Lanfranc skimmed through it. William stopped his pacing.

‘Well?’

Lanfranc smiled.

‘Maurilius has indeed said no less than I. He is well informed.’

‘Well, of course,’ said William. ‘You are not the only person the Pope writes to, you know. He does write to my archbishop as well.’

Lanfranc refused to be overawed.

‘The fact that you have received such news from not one, but two authoritative sources, my lord, should serve to convince you all the more that the Holy Father is in earnest.’

William sat down again.

‘I suppose you expect me to run round like a scalded cat to do their bidding for fear of Hell Fire?’

Lanfranc pushed away the letter.

‘No, my lord. I expect you, as a man of honour, to do what you have often said you will do, both as a matter of personal interest, and as a matter of declared partnership in the desires of Mother Church.’

‘You want me to clean up the Norman clergy.’

Lanfranc remained impassive.

‘I should not have ventured to express such a complex policy with the vigour and over-simplicity of your own camp-fire vernacular, my lord, but that, indeed, is what it amounts to.’

‘Then why did you refuse the archbishop’s throne at Rouen when I offered it to you?’

This was an old gambit, and Lanfranc dealt with it with tired ease.

'Maurilius is a fine son of Fécamp, and he has performed the duties of Archbishop for ten years with just as much success as I could have done – probably more.'

William conceded the point.

'So be it, so be it. I suppose I should be grateful that you condescend to become the Abbot of St. Stephen's.'

Lanfranc said nothing. William was contentious at the best of times, especially when forced to be inactive. He was still chafing at the advice Fitzosbern had given him to stay his hand in Brittany. It was clear that he had made up his mind to turn his attention to Church matters in the meantime, but his manner showed that he was going to be a difficult partner in the process of 'cleaning up the Norman clergy'.

'I have not been idle,' said William. 'The bishops are on their way here. Maurilius sits and sucks his quill in his palace round the corner, and awaits my summons. I have given leave of absence only to Coutances.'

And let Geoffrey get on with his cathedral. William was rough, harsh, and impervious to paper learning, but he had breadth of vision. He was not one of those obsessive reformers of limited mind who could concentrate on only one thing at a time. He understood the importance of building and resources and furnishings; he was beginning to appreciate the value of administration and writs and letters, for all that he could not read a single word; he was prepared to listen to good advice about recruitment, as Lanfranc himself could testify. The very appointment of Maurilius was a break with tradition; for over sixty years the throne of Rouen had gone to a member of the ducal family. But in 1054, after the villainous Uncle Mauger had disgraced himself in a rebellion, William had taken advice and appointed a monk from Fécamp. Maurilius had impressive qualifications of scholarship and wide experience in France and Italy; he had already held church councils which had attracted attention as far afield as the Holy See. Lanfranc admired William. The only problem was restraining his energy; he treated everything as if it were a military campaign.

If not held back, or at least steered carefully, William would summon his bishops – from Sées, Bayeux, Lisieux, Evreux, and Avranches – issue his orders, and expect them to jump to it. But it was all very well to dismiss all non-celibate priests, so long as there were enough celibate ones of sufficient scholarship and qualifications to take their place. It would need delicate handling. There was also the awkward question of non-celibate bishops. The Duke's own half-brother, Bishop Odo of Bayeux, had at least one bastard. Rumour had it that Bishop Geoffrey of Coutances had had one too, though his old paramour had at least had the grace to retire to a convent.

The trick was to find a way of making the Duke see the value of discretion and balance, while at the same time not letting him think that difficulties were being strewn in the way by hair-splitting bookworms. It called for the finesse of the chess-player.

Lanfranc raised his eyebrows innocently.

'I take it that the bishops know the reason for the summons?'

'They do. And if they know what is good for them, they will come armed with lists of new men. I have told Maurilius to have a list of possible candidates from the new houses.'

'You can not strip the monasteries,' said Lanfranc. 'It will undo all the good work there. Especially the new ones. They are just getting on their feet.'

'Like St. Stephen's,' said William. 'Exactly. That is why I appoint good men to be abbots. Why do you think I wanted you in Caen?'

First trick to William. Lanfranc decided to take the attack on to his home ground.

'I still maintain, my lord, that each case must be judged on its merits. You must allow your bishops the range of power and discretion that befits their rank. After all, apart from Yves of Bellême at Sées, you appointed them all.'

William tapped the letter in between them.

'Do you want this reform or not?'

Lanfranc was ready for him.

'I presume then, my lord, that you will start with your own household by way of of setting an example. Your chaplain, Arnulf, I understand, is still with you. His daughter is well, I trust?'

William hesitated for a fraction.

'Arnulf married us. When nobody else would,' he added pointedly.

Lanfranc nodded.

'I do indeed recall, my lord. And you were so confident that the ceremony was valid that you arranged for Maurilius to repeat the service at Rouen cathedral as soon as he was appointed.'

'Matilda and I built the two houses at Caen. That was the agreement. We have fulfilled it.'

'That, my lord, was by way of doing penance for the marriage within the prescribed bounds. This – ' he too tapped the letter ' – is a ban not on consanguinity but on non-celibate priests. Do you wish to endanger your own soul by continuing to hear Mass from them? Or that of my lady Matilda? Or of your own garrison?'

William glared.

'The matter will be gone into carefully.'

'Exactly my point, my lord. Carefully, fairly, on the merits of the individual case. Taking in the implications for the full picture. And while you are about it, no doubt you will give attention to the small matter of your brother, my lord Odo of Bayeux. How is his son these days? John, I believe his name is, if my memory serves me correctly.'

* * * * * *

'I remember as if it were yesterday,' said Hubert.

Edwin glanced up at the ruins of the castle of Arques. It commanded the junction of the Rivers Béthune and Varenne. Here was the only bridge for miles which could take carts. Hubert, on leaving Envermeu, had been forced to swing slightly westward.

'In those days I was running with Fulk the Angevin. You may have heard of him. No? Just as well. A son of Satan if ever there was one. Mercenary captain – one of the best. But a swine.' Hubert crossed himself. 'God forgive me that I should speak evil of a man. Unless he already were evil ... ' He shook himself. 'Where was I? Oh, yes. Well, we were trying to get into the castle. Fulk's men – us – had just left the walls unguarded for a while, and the enemy got some supplies into them. The Duke was furious; put the siege back months, he said. Yes, months. The Duke laid into Fulk in front of us; we could hear him in the tent.

'Well, Fulk came out of that tent looking like thunder. "Bring the prisoner," he said. We had captured one of the rebel leaders – Count Enguerrand of Ponthieu.'

Edwin started. Ponthieu again!

'Yes, Count Enguerrand. Very big fish indeed. The Bastard wanted him kept alive; his sister was married to the man. Fulk had other ideas. He knew that Enguerrand also had a sister – inside the castle. He shouted for her to be put up on to the walls. And do you know what he did? I say do you know what he did?'

Edwin had long since learned not to interrupt.

'He brought a wooden block, and he laid Enguerrand on it, and he proceeded to cut off parts of him and show them to his sister. Nose – ears – hands – feet.'

Hubert crossed himself.

'I shall hear his screams on my bed of death. What his sister went through up there ...

'By the time the Bastard arrived it was too late. Fulk went right up to him and flung Enguerrand's privates on the ground before him. "Behold!" he said. "The keys to the castle of Arques." '

Edwin shuddered.

'Yes,' said Hubert. 'Terrible. It worked of course. The gates were open. But the

Duke was furious, as I say. Furious. His sister a widow. And one of his nearest neighbours a sworn enemy. For the new Count of Ponthieu was Enguerrand's brother, Guy. He and his sister swore homage, but with gritted teeth. And Count Guy, as he is now, has been no friend ever since. Hardly surprising. I say hardly surprising.'

Hubert prodded Rollo thoughtfully.

'If Count Guy ever finds a chance to get his own back ... '

* * * * * *

'Did you miss me?'

'What? Oh – yes, I suppose so.'

Wulfnoth finished counting out blankets, and placed a pile of them in the arms of a servant. He followed the man to the door of the store.

'If that is not enough, come and tell me at once.'

Arlette trailed after him.

'I missed you.'

Wulfnoth barely turned round.

'Mmmm?'

Arlette stamped her foot.

'Wulf, you are impossible.'

He looked genuinely surprised.

'What *is* the matter?'

Arlette made as if to go.

'Well, if you have no idea, I am sorry for you.'

Wulfnoth ran a hand through his blond hair.

'Arlette, please! I have so much to do. If there is really something wrong, then tell me and I will do my best to – '

'Do your best! Is that all you can manage? Do your best?'

Wulfnoth sighed. He would never understand her. How could he do better than his best?

'Arlette, try to understand. I shall soon have five bishops under this roof. Five. And all their staff.'

Arlette made a sarcastic bow.

'Oh, I was forgetting. My lord high master overlord chamberlain. He must be about his sacred work. His Grace the lord Duke has ordered.'

Wulf turned on her.

'I notice you do not stand still either when my lady Matilda summons you.'

Arlette rose to the insult.

'I am here. At least I prefer you to that string of brats. Or rather I did. You do not seem to prefer me to your bishops and their blankets.'

Outside the door of the storehouse, the servant paused, leaning slightly backwards with the weight of his load, his head cocked. There was usually some ripe gossip to be had when these two young people were together. On his way to the dormitory being prepared for the visiting clerics, he would stop off at the kitchen. Gerard would have a hot drink on offer, and the usual trade would be done – hospitality for information.

Within an hour, each remark and insult, suitably garnished with irony and wry comment, would be served up to every hungry ear in the castle. Every stage of this couple's courtship had been bargained across Gerard's great kitchen table, and relayed to cellar and scullery, buttery and bailey, sentry post and stable yard, chapel vestry and chancellery office.

Opinion was divided, usually upon lines of sex. The men on the whole preferred Wulfnoth, for all that he was a Saxon. It was agreed that he was a likely young man. Considering his hostage status at the Bastard's court, he had shown willing, and had made positive strides towards becoming a Norman knight, which by common consent was the only thing really worth becoming. He rode and hunted well; he handled the knightly weapons with acceptable skill – none of those outlandish axes that the English were supposed to favour. He accepted Norman fashion, dress, and hair-style, and looked well in them. His French was fluent, and nearly free from the shocking accent that tormented it in the mouths of most visiting Englishmen. He had even become a competent chess player – most un-English.

It was clear that he had found favour with the Bastard. William had supervised his training and his upbringing. How old was he when he first came? Ten? Eleven?

'The Bastard likes him. Why else would he have made him an under-chamberlain? Shows he trusts him.'

'Keeps him under his eye. He is only half a warrior too. He *likes* it in the castle. No true knight enjoys being indoors.'

That was the feminine element. The women resented his good looks, and his ability to break hearts, while at the same time saying that he was 'lovely'.

The men shook their heads. How like a woman!

The general feeling at the laundry stones down by the Seine was that Arlette was a touch too good for him, for all that he was the brother of four earls, and she only the daughter of a knight. He did not deserve her.

'He should make more fuss of her.'

'Why should he bother?' said the men. 'She already follows him with doe eyes. Why run after a quarry that is already caught?'

Wulfnoth's slightly long-suffering good looks had already captivated Arlette, and she had sufficient common sense left in her head to realise that an earl – even an English one – was a good catch.

'Besides,' said the men, 'the Bastard has arranged it. It will get her off his hands very nicely.'

'Serve his own purpose too, if he can bind the boy to his own cause. I heard him say once to her, "Make a Norman of him, girl." Six months beside those eyes in bed, and she will, I say.'

Arlette's father had been killed fighting for the Duke in his last civil war – at Mortemer in 1053. She was under age then, and so by feudal law became the Duke's ward. It was conceded, however, that William more than acknowledged the debt he owed to her father; it was not mere feudal obligation that made him take her into the household.

'It was more than that. If you ask me, her name was her fortune. He has never forgotten his mother. Remember Arlette?'

Grins all round.

'The tanner's daughter from Falaise.'

'Ssssh! Never out loud. The Bastard was devoted to his mother. Never looked at a woman till she died and he met Matilda.'

'He has a soft spot for this girl, I tell you. She plays on it too.'

'Matilda sees through her though. And *she* does not like *Matilda*.'

'Would you, having to look after all those brats whenever my lady descends on the castle?'

Arlette liked nothing about children – their noise, their spitefulness, their appetites, their quarrels and talebearing, their impudence, their disobedience. In the case of Matilda's brood, it was their sheer numbers which overwhelmed her. They ran rings round her. They defied her. They threatened to betray her to Matilda, or, worse, to Gerard. Like everyone else, she valued Gerard's esteem, and, with the instinct of the hunter for the weak spot, they knew it. They looked forward to being placed in her care with cruel glee.

However, Arlette's dislike of children ran deeper than that. She felt repelled by the very thought of parenthood. She could not bring herself to contemplate the idea of another body inside hers. The actual process of giving birth both terrified and revolted her. At Matilda's regular and frequent confinements, she backed against the wall in a vain attempt to seclude herself from the horror before her eyes, while her ears burned at my lady's lurid language. Two or three times she had been packed from the solar as worse than useless – once by Matilda herself.

'Get that gaping bitch out of here!'

Yet she refused to face the implications of her pursuit of Wulfnoth. He was what she wanted, and that was enough.

At the moment, of course, she needed to hurt him, because he was not taking enough notice of her.

'Why I come here I can not imagine. You are no joy to anyone. You are as miserable as – as – as Cecily! "Take me for a walk, Wulf." "Do I have to?" '

* * * * * *

'Did you ever see horseflesh like that? Did you ever?'

Edwin shook his head.

'No, I never did. Whose are they?'

'Belong to Sir Walter Giffard. That is his hall you can see by the river. He has another on the higher ground behind us, commanding the valley.'

'Ah,' said Edwin, remembering. 'The man who leased the manors to your house.'

Hubert patted him on the shoulder.

'Well done, lad. Yes. We shall be there in another mile or two.'

'Do you have to pay your respects to him?' said Edwin.

'Not if I can avoid it. Sir Walter is not the best-tempered of men. And he can think of nothing but his precious horses these days.'

Edwin gazed down at them again.

'I can see why.'

'Breeding stock,' said Hubert. 'Oh, yes, fine stock. Arab.'

'Why?'

'More destriers, of course. The Bastard has plans. Huge expense. Huge investment. Sir Walter will make a fortune. A fortune.'

'Why?'

Hubert cleared his throat.

'Well, it is not for me to say to an Englishman.'

Edwin understood.

'He is planning that far ahead?'

'You do not know the Bastard. It has been on the bottom shelf of his mind for years.'

Edwin spat.

'Well, let him try – let him just try.'

Hubert looked at his set jaw.

'Are you *sure* you are not planning to murder him?'

Edwin saw the raised eyebrows, the innocent eyes, the faintest gleam of mischief, and grinned.

'An idea, eh?'

They laughed together. Hubert's tongue had been a stiff price for the last few days of food and protection, but it was a price that Edwin, on balance, had been content to pay. It was impossible to get really cross with him. Edwin enjoyed the man's easy ability to convey wisdom without preaching. He savoured the good sense buried among the constant chatter like plums in a pudding. He had grown fond of the patient Rollo, and had been pleased when Hubert let him take the reins.

Hubert slid him another, even more innocent glance.

'I suppose you will still keep secret the nature of your errand?'

'You suppose correctly,' said Edwin. 'I do not wish to arrive behind the news of it. If I tell you, it will take wings ahead of me.'

Hubert took the joke against himself with good grace.

'Ah, well, it was a good try. I thought I might catch you while you were in a good mood.'

He pulled the cart to a halt, and Edwin jumped down.

'Now – you follow the valley of the Scie – this valley – as far as the house at Auffay. I know some of the brothers there. Just say my name and they will give you a roof and a meal. Then you go due south again from there, through Vassonville, St. Maclou, and Grugny, to Clères. From there – '

He paused, looking at Edwin's blank face.

'Is there any hope of you remembering that?'

Edwin grimaced helplessly.

'I have forgotten already.'

Hubert sighed.

'Get up on the cart.'

Edwin hesitated. Hubert gestured with his bad arm.

'Get up here. I thought it would come to this all the time.'

Edwin sat up beside him again, and mumbled his thanks.

Hubert jabbed Rollo into action.

'You see what I mean by me being a lucky man. My own master, you see. Brother Stephen will not mind me being a little late. There is no reeve to chase me. I am my own reeve. Besides, lad, I like your style.'

'You mean you like my company,' said Edwin, now familiar through confidence.

Hubert leaned back and looked at him as from a distance. The eyebrows went up yet again.

'But of course. What better way is there of passing this vale of tears that we call life other than in the company of our fellows?'

Edwin grinned.

'Hubert, you are impossible.'

The monk laughed.

'One of Nature's minor miracles. Very well – I shall go with you to all those places I mentioned, and on past them to the River Cailly. Then I really must return. Stephen will think I am lost on the road.'

Edwin looked disappointed.

'Do not worry,' said Hubert. 'You follow the river till it joins the Seine at Rouen itself. I take it even an Englishman can follow a river?'

Edwin laughed.

'I think I might manage that.'

'Good. If you keep on laughing like that, your secret might tumble out of you before we get there.'

But Edwin was ready with the parry.

'I have a better idea. Tell me a story. What was it you were saying the other day about Rollo?'

Hubert took the bait completely.

'Ah, yes. Rollo. It is funny that you should be going to Rouen, because that was Rollo's first title, you know. Count of Rouen. Yes. Count of Rouen. It happened this way ... '

* * * * * *

'You can stop that.'

Nigel sat back in surprise. Then he leered, and returned to the assault.

'You think you can fool me? You want it as much as I do.'

Adele stood up and adjusted her bodice. Nigel came and stood behind her, his hands over hers. He squeezed.

Adele squirmed.

'You can stop that, I said. Or I shall tell my father.'

Nigel laughed loudly.

'Why? Do you want to make him jealous?'

Adele burst from his hold, turned, and slapped him as hard as she could.

Nigel put his fingers to the red marks on his cheek. He frowned.

'You have been in a funny mood since I got here. And it is not my fault.'

'That makes a change.'

Nigel took a chance shot.

'Is it because of Gilbert?'

Nigel had been surprised that Adele had made no reference to the gaping, tongue-tied yokel that he had sent blindly into her arms. After Gilbert had been sent away, baffled and burning with shame and fury, Nigel went to share the fun with her. She had not laughed with him, and she had not sworn at him. Nigel felt put out; his joke had not gone as well as he had planned.

She had not flirted with him either. She had not played the usual game of hunter and quarry, either with words or actions. It was not like her at all. Nigel had at first wondered whether he was losing his touch, and once or twice had looked round guiltily to see if any of his drinking companions were on hand to laugh at his lack of success.

'I said, "Is it because of Gilbert?" '

Adele arched her neck and looked down her nose.

'I have no idea what you are talking about.'

Adele was not really listening. She was so used to flirting, or to keeping young men at arm's length – whichever suited her at the time – that she could go through the various moves almost with an absent mind. And Nigel was such a buffoon – only one idea in his head most of the time. Though he was good company, and he did know how to give a girl a good time. But not now. Not now ...

Since dawn – or since he had returned from Mass, which had been said by the formidable Father Lanfranc – her father had unable to carry on a sane conversation.

'What are we to do? What is to become of us?'

He paced up and down, he wrung his hands, he sweated mightily. Adele had to shake him before she could get anything coherent from him. It came out in fragments, like pieces of a broken pot scattered on a floor. She had to work hard to make a shape out of them.

'A letter from the Holy Father himself ... impure priests ... God knows, I have struggled with the flesh, no man harder ... Archbishop Maurilius is preparing an announcement ... was it my fault that God took your mother? ... was it my punishment after all? ... the Duke has called all the bishops here ... I married the Duke and the lady Matilda, when nobody else would ... is this all the thanks I get ... ? Father Lanfranc claps his hands and even the Bastard jumps ... it is not fair; all those years of loyal service ... when have I asked for any greater reward than to be his chaplain? ... have I really imperilled his soul? ... all those who laughed and mocked behind my back, they were happy to come and receive the Host at my hands, to save their precious souls ... have I suddenly lost the power to consecrate, just because a Pope sends a letter? ... everyone will turn against us, you see ... it is not fair. What are we to do? Dear God, what are we to do?'

'Father, sit down and talk sense. How can I help when you are in this panic?'

It was useless; her father was beyond all reason, at any rate for the time being.

Adele needed time – time to find out if the ghastly possibilities that her father was hinting at had any chance of becoming reality.

Nigel could not have come at a worse moment. How could she get rid of him? She looked coyly up at him.

'If you must know – yes, it *is* because of Gilbert.'

'Ah!'

Nigel felt a small surge of returning confidence. Adele simpered.

'Well, partly.'

'Partly?'

'Well, at least he had some decent motives.'

Nigel smirked.

'Likely.'

'He talked marriage – which is more than you ever do.'

'Marriage?'

Nigel looked at her as if she had suddenly sprouted wings and danced on the head of a pin.

Adele pressed home her advantage.

'Yes. Marriage. Do you ever think of marriage, Nigel Fitzhenry?'

Nigel began backing to the door.

'God, no, Look – beg pardon for what has happened. No offence. Some other time, eh? I – I must go. Guardroom duty – should have gone before. Just remembered.'

He forgot to shut the door.

Adele tossed her head in disgust.

She began to follow him at first out of the house, but changed her mind and sat down. Perhaps she needed to think first, before she did anything rash.

* * * * * *

Edwin had never seen such a huge river in his life. There was no need to ask anybody – not that he dared; this had to be the Seine. Nor had he seen such a castle, such a town, such a bridge. There was no question about this either; it had to be Rouen.

He sat down at the edge of a wood near the mouth of the River Cailly above the town, taking care to keep within cover. He heaved a big sigh. He would have liked to turn and tell Hubert that even a stupid Englishman was able to follow a river.

Just as well, though, that Hubert was not there, because nothing else had gone right, as Hubert would have delighted in telling him. 'Everything wrong, boy – oh, yes, everything wrong. You should use your wit, you see – your wit.' Since leaving the Tongue, his cart, and his donkey, Edwin had stumbled from one mistake to the next. At every bad turn of luck, Edwin cursed him and missed him at the same time.

Twice he had nearly been caught stealing food from swineherds' huts on the edge of the village waste. A crowd of children crept up on him while he slept, and drove him away with their screams. Worse, they followed him, pelting him with horse manure. An irate forester came upon him looting from game traps, and chased him a mile. This put him off coming too near habitations, and when houses came down to the edge of the River Cailly, he was forced to make detours. So he got lost more than once, and wasted valuable time getting back to the watercourse. Deciding next that it would be better to stick to the river come what may, he had to wade through marshes and drainage ditches. Once, running from an inquisitive ploughman, he slipped and fell in completely. It was a good thing the weather had turned warm.

He sighed at the memory. Well, at least all that was over; he had arrived.

He sighed again as a fresh problem presented itself. How was he to get into the castle? 'First things first, boy,' he heard Hubert saying. 'If you see the next step, do not worry about the next step but one.'

The next step was clear. He could see the road right up to the castle. Where it approached the gatehouse, it was thronged with people. He would not be noticed in that crowd.

Half an hour later he was gazing up at the huge rounded arch of the main gate, totally at a loss. He had had no idea from a distance that it was so vast; its sheer scale robbed him of initiative.

As he stood and gazed, a hubbub behind him caused him to look round. A column of horsemen was pushing its way through. As it drew closer, Edwin saw the forbidding aspect of a military escort – the conical helmets, the chain mail, the iron nasal guards that rendered the wearers faceless and unearthly. Swords banged against thighs; spears were carried formally upright as on a parade; kite-shaped shields swung on thongs between shoulder-blades. The great destriers, the largest animals a man ever saw, swept aside anything in their path like a great wave released from a dam; their hooves hammered on the spread anvil of the cobbles.

Behind came the man who was clearly the centre of the column. A nobleman, dressed for the road, with no marks of rank other than the quality of his clothes and the habit of authority etched on his face. Behind again came a bobbing bundle of clerics, grimacing with the unaccustomed effort of trying to look dignified on horseback before peering yokels and stallholders. Two covered waggons rattled and bounced behind them, and a final trio of men-at-arms brought up the rear.

'Who comes?'

The sentry, who was perfectly able to see how important the new arrivals were, nevertheless went through the correct procedure.

The soldiers paused and broke ranks, allowing the nobleman to make his way to the front. He lifted his staff, and Edwin now noticed that it was no lance but a crozier.

'Yves of Bellême, lord Bishop of Sées, on business at the command of my lord Duke.'

'Robert of Beaumont,' said a young man at his side. 'On the Duke's staff.'

The wicket gate was shut, and the great gate itself was swung open, with much heaving, swearing and creaking. The column clattered inside.

Edwin, on an impulse, pushed his way to the front of the craning crowd. He was just tensing himself when a voice made itself heard from the back, some distance down the road.

'Make way! Make way! Keep the gate open.'

Two riders only this time. No formality. Their horses, light scouting ponies, had been ridden hard. Equipment and clothing alike were spattered with the dirt and discolouration of travel.

The fatigue party, glad of the respite from heaving on the gate, paused, and watched the new arrivals.

The sentry came forward.

'Who comes?'

The scouts reined in their horses with much snorting, stamping, and slapping of leather.

'From my lord Guy, Count of Ponthieu. Urgent messages for his Grace, Duke William of Normandy.'

The sentry nodded.

'Leave your weapons at the guardroom. Follow him.'

He gestured to another sentry lounging by a water trough in the outer bailey.

Count of Ponthieu! Edwin did not know whether to gape, swear, or cry. But the surprise jerked him into action.

Hardly aware of what he was doing, he stepped forward.

The sentry relaxed and sneered. He slipped off his helmet and mail coif.

'What do you want, Saxon?' said Nigel Fitzhenry.

Edwin drew himself up.

'I have business with my lord the Duke of Normandy.'

Nigel raised his eyebrows, looked quickly to left and right to make sure that he had a good audience, and set about enjoying himself.

'That almost sounds like French. Fancy. An educated Englishman!'

The fatigue party grinned. Nigel offered a deep bow.

'Perhaps my lord would care to identify himself.'

Off-duty soldiers, sharing a drink outside the guardroom, threw glances of amusement at each other.

'I must see my lord the Duke. It is most urgent.'

Nigel bowed again, even lower.

'And may I ask your loftiness on whose authority you come?'

Edwin was too excited to become incensed at the sentry's attitude.

'I come on the business of Earl Harold of Wessex, the second man in the Kingdom of England.'

Nigel stood up again, dusted his hands, and decided that the joke had gone far enough.

'Yes, and I am the Pope's uncle. Now, if you know what is good for you, boy … '

He did not bother to finish the sentence, but turned away. To his amazement, he felt his sleeve caught. Turning, he saw the mad Saxon vagrant at his elbow.

'You do not understand. It is a matter of life and death. It concerns the Earl Harold and Count Guy of Ponthieu.' He looked desperately at the soldiers. 'Will nobody believe me? How could I possibly have made this up?'

A man detached himself from the group of soldiers. He handed to one of them the pot of beer from which he had been pouring, and began to come nearer. Edwin noticed that he limped so badly that he needed a crutch.

A tall, dark, man, with a brow like a cliff of granite. There was something about his manner that silenced the sniggers and the jibes in the crowd. No word passed between him and the sentry, but by the time he had stumped across the flagstones of the entrance, mysteriously, the sentry had surrendered the initiative to him.

His great black beard loomed over Edwin.

'I am Gerard of Ghent, master of the Duke's kitchen. Who are you?'

* * * * * *

Chapter Three

The Gathering

'Out of my way, you great lumps!'

The rear bailey boiled with people and animals. Horses drank thirstily from a wooden trough. Dogs flopped in corners with lolling tongues. Tired beaters grunted with relief as they sagged back on to benches. Kitchen staff struggled with bleeding carcases towards the storerooms. Gerard had set up a small barrel in a corner beside a water pipe. Men queued to soak their faces and necks and wrists – the sudden hot spell, coming so hard on the heels of a week of cold and wind, was that much harder to bear, and the Bastard had driven them hard for hours. Two scullions poured and handed out mugs of drink as fast as their thin white hands could move. Soldiers stood about and swore in their usual meaningless way as they slurped beer over their chins. Matilda kicked a mailed rump.

'God's Blood, move, you oafs!'

They took one look at the familiar tiny, compact figure, and shuffled to make a path for her without a grumble. One or two smiled indulgently.

'Sorry, my lady.'

'I should think so. Hell's teeth, sergeant, with all that fat round you, how you persuade your wife to open her legs for you I shall never know. Crush the life out of her.'

The sergeant grinned.

'Puts even more into her, my lady.'

Matilda looked up at him.

'Sergeant, you are a vulgar swine.'

The sergeant grinned again, and saluted.

'Yes, my lady. Let me come with you and clear the way.'

Matilda swept into the hall. At the end, below the solar, William was pacing restlessly. She went right up to him and waited. He stopped, but looked annoyed at the interruption.

'What is it?'

His eyes went past her, as if he expected more people to follow her.

Matilda stood her ground.

'I expect you to tell me that.'

William frowned.

'Make yourself clear, woman. I have business.'

Matilda folded her arms.

'Very well. Do you believe him?'

William frowned again.

'Who?'

'Guy's courier.'

William stopped glancing to left and right, and focused on her.

'How do you know that?'

'Do you believe him?' persisted Matilda.

'This is politics.'

'There is no Fitz to talk to. You will have to make do with me.'

William bridled, but thought better of it. He motioned her to a table, and sat down opposite. He spoke half to himself, as if he found it hard to take it in.

'Harold. In Ponthieu.'

'Do we know why?'

'Guy says something about a coastal raid that he has scotched. Long story. Most of it lies, I expect. He has been looking for a way of making trouble for years. Ever since the Arques rebellion.'

'You tried to save his brother,' said Matilda.

'Guy does not see it like that. Enguerrand died, and Guy blames me. He will make the most out of this that he can.'

You mean he thought all this up?'

William shook his head.

'Not the brains. No. His story is a lie. But I believe he holds Harold. He could never have made up a lie as big as that. Nobody would swallow it.'

'I too believe he holds Harold.'

William looked hard at her.

'Why? What else do you know?'

Matilda met him head on.

'I know what a Saxon boy has told me, in the kitchen just now. Gerard pulled him in from the front gate. He has run all the way from the Somme. Escaped the arrest.'

Matilda told Edwin's story.

When she had finished, William stood up and began pacing.

'Splendour of God! Why? Why?'

Matilda watched him for a while.

'Well?'

William stopped beside her at the table. Matilda stood up too. Totally unabashed by the difference in height between them, she folded her hands in her sleeves and flashed a challenge with her eyes.

'What are you going to do about it?'

* * * * * *

Edwin almost staggered into the bailey. He put his hand to his forehead, and it was not to keep off the sun.

'Where? When? How many with him? How many casualties? Did you see the Count of Ponthieu? Did you hear anything?'

The hard, rasping voice; the speed of thought; the urgency.

'Why? How? How long ago? Why? Why? Why?'

Above all, the eyes – focused like needles at the end of a question, never still while he pondered the answer. Edwin told the truth, and all the truth as he saw it. He could have done no other, and it was not through fear. Respect was there, certainly – even awe. William completely filled all the space around him; Edwin simply did not see anybody else. He could have told no more truth had he been speaking to the Pope himself.

He retained enough wits to suspect that William did not entirely believe his story, but he clung to it like a castaway to a piece of driftwood.

'Hounds? Did you say "hounds"?'

'Yes, my lord.'

'And falcons?'

'Yes, my lord.'

'Where are they now?'

'At the bottom of the sea, my lord.'

William took him through the whole story once more. By the end of it Edwin was sweating. He became conscious that my lady's eyes were on him too. He had barely noticed her before.

At the end there was a pause. William and my lady exchanged glances. My lady shrugged.

Edwin felt afraid for the first time. What were they going to do with him?

'Out. Get out. Get food and drink. See my kitchen-master. Go where you will, but do not leave the castle. I have given my sentries orders.'

'My lord.'

When he came into the light, Edwin was conscious of a raging thirst. He saw the boys and the barrel, and made his way towards it. He felt a hand on his shoulder.

'Who says you can drink?'

It was the sarcastic sentry. Probably little more than his own age. After the Bastard, a puny threat.

'The Duke himself,' said Edwin. 'He said I can have what I like. And it is up to you to stop me escaping.'

Nigel looked taken aback, but recovered.

'Make sure you give me no excuse to chase you and whip you. And make sure you say “please” for everything. Eh, my dear?’

He looked at a young woman who was passing on an errand.

The young woman tossed her head.

‘Much do I care.’

Nigel went after her.

‘Now is that the right way to treat an old friend? Surely we are still friends?’

Edwin watched them go. He noticed the sentry’s hand, which had been resting on her shoulder, sliding down towards her hips.

He turned away to the panting dogs. Dogs were something he understood. He crouched in front of one and held out his hand. After a sniff or two, the dog allowed his head to be touched.

Edwin smiled ... They were pretty ample hips, too.

* * * * * *

‘You will tell the Count that he must postpone his visit. He will render me far more service by bringing pressure to bear from Flanders. Force is the only agency Ponthieu will respect.’

‘You will give my father my love and tell him that I shall miss him. But I agree with his Grace.’

‘Pressure, remember. Pressure.’

‘And the chicks send their love too.’

The courier looked intently from one to the other, anxious not to miss anything.

‘Yes, my lord. Yes, my lady.’

Lanfranc stood a little way down the hall and watched patiently. Neither William nor Matilda had seen him.

‘Keep good company through Ponthieu; we want no more hostages in Guy’s lap. Tell the sergeant to give you four good men. Draw rations for a week. Waste no time.’

‘My lord.’

The courier hurried out.

‘Why, Father Lan,’ said Matilda, noticing him, and coming forward. ‘A good day to you.’

She kissed the ring.

‘My lord abbot.’

William acknowledged him stiffly, but offered no formal kiss.

‘It is past the time we arranged for the first session, my lord,’ said Lanfranc. ‘I came to ascertain the cause of the delay.’

He raised his eyebrows in innocent inquiry.

William was taking off his spurs and his belt.

'I have the sweat of the chase on me, as you see, my lord abbot.'

'Rather the glow of politics,' murmured Lanfranc.

William paused and glared.

'What was that?'

'Nothing, my lord. A pleasantry, no more.'

'No games, Father Lan,' said Matilda. 'Guy's messengers are down in Gerard's kitchen; so is the Saxon boy. Their story is all over the castle by now. The gossip is ripe enough to tempt the ear even of an abbot.'

'I did not come here from Caen on matters of gossip or of politics, my lady,' said Lanfranc. 'My time is valuable.'

'So is mine,' said William. 'And you came here on my business, not on yours. If that business should change, it is still my business, and you will hold yourself at my disposal. I made you abbot, and you are my vassal.'

'Some of your bishops may lead troops at your orders, my lord, but not your abbots.'

The door of the hall opened, and a young kitchen boy announced in his piping treble, 'His Grace the lord Odo, Bishop of Bayeux.'

Talk of the Devil, thought Lanfranc.

Odo stuffed his gloves into the arms of the boy, and came forward, unlacing a light jerkin.

'What is all this about Ponthieu?' he said, ignoring Lanfranc. On his small round face the red pimples shone.

'Have you brought your mitre, my lord bishop?' asked Lanfranc with heavy irony.

Odo looked blank.

'Because if you have,' continued Lanfranc, 'it was a waste of time. You will need your mail coif and your helmet.' He turned and bowed formally to William and Matilda. 'I await the pleasure of your Grace. Or should I say the pleasure of my lord the Count of Ponthieu.'

'Get out!' bawled William.

* * * * * *

'So – there is to be no council after all.'

Yves of Bellême, Bishop of Sées, leaned his elbows on the parapet of the keep, and gazed downwards. Heights troubled him, but this was preferable to the smell and confusion in the bailey below.

Odo, Bishop of Bayeux, lounged beside him.

'Not yet. Give my brother time; there will be.'

Robert of Beaumont picked up a stick and tossed it mischievously to the ground. He watched it fall beside a fair-haired boy with a dog, and laughed as they both jumped.

'When I and the Flemings have put the fear of God into Guy of Ponthieu, you will have your council soon enough, my lords.'

Odo and Yves glanced at each other and smiled.

Young Beaumont was a typical senior vassal's son – loud, arrogant, and convinced of his own immortality. Not without ability, but as yet it was more promise than proof. His father, Roger of Beaumont, thought he was the greatest gift to warfare since Roland and Oliver, and was anxious to push the boy's career. The Bastard, who owed Roger one or two services, offered to let the boy become attached to his staff. As a sop to his vanity, he was designated 'liaison officer' to the incoming Flemish mercenaries. Their commander, a gritty captain from Brabant, would take his orders direct from the Bastard, but Beaumont would serve to take messages between them, and he would certainly learn about the rough side of campaigning around the Flemish camp. It was a commonplace that it took six months to learn the good habits of soldiering with the Bastard, and it took a week to learn the bad ones with the Flemings.

Odo knew, from his recent conversation, that his brother planned to halt the Flemings on their march towards Brittany; the campaign would have to wait. They would be held in reserve in case Guy of Ponthieu did not see reason at once. William had no intention of paying the enormous ransom demanded by Guy, and by a timely parade of his Flemish force, he would probably induce Guy to see reason. Guy, pleased with own cunning, had gambled on the fact that the Bastard had recently dismissed most of his vassals' forces after the expenses and losses of the previous year. He had not known about the Flemings. They were not enough to mount a full invasion of Ponthieu, but they would be sufficient, together with the Bastard's household contingent and a regiment of sappers, to burn Guy out of his castle at Beaurain. The surprise alone would wrong-foot him. And just to keep him on the hop, the Bastard's father-in-law, Count Baldwin of Flanders, would make some well-timed patrols in strength from behind Guy's rear. One of the things that Odo, and many enemies, were forced to admire about the Bastard was the swiftness of his responses.

So Beaumont would receive his marching orders any moment now. He was to halt the Flemings, and put them into temporary camp near Longueville – Sir Walter Giffard would go purple in the face about that – ready to lead them back to the north-east in the event of Count Guy proving impervious to reason.

Bishop Yves scratched an ear.

'I suppose there is no chance that Guy might kill him.'

'Chance in a million,' said Odo. 'Harold is the best piece he has on the board.'

The English earl was of use only if he were alive. Guy could not bargain if

Harold were dead. Such a death would bring down on Guy's head not only the punishment of his feudal overlord, the Bastard, but also the full might of a King. The Confessor might be no lover of Harold, but national pride would dictate that he could not allow an earl of the kingdom to be cut down like a pedlar in an ambush by a frontier adventurer. Count Guy of Ponthieu might be a brigand and a fool, but he was not a lunatic.

Yves nodded.

'Yes, I agree. By the way, do you fancy a game?' He gestured over the parapet. 'We are too late for the boar.'

'Should we not pay our respects to Maurilius?'

The archbishop still waited in his palace in the town, unwilling to share the privations of castle life until it was absolutely necessary.

'Plenty of time for that,' said Yves. 'Besides, he will probably want to talk theology.' He shuddered.

They were just moving off when they heard agitated footsteps coming up the steps. They just caught an urgent whisper: 'Look your best. And pull your shawl tighter.'

Arnulf came out on to the top catwalk of the keep, dragging Adele by the wrist. Both bishops recognised him at once. Yves had always wondered why the Bastard kept such a seedy sack as a chaplain; could he not do much better? Odo sneered; the man was just as fat and sweaty as ever. Beaumont's eyes fastened at once on a well-turned ankle.

Arnulf came forward, and made a great show of kissing both rings.

'My lord. My lord.'

He addressed himself to Bishop Yves.

'Forgive me, my lord, for intruding on your deliberations, but I saw you come up here, and it is so – well – so private that I knew the moment presented the perfect occasion for me to broach a matter of some delicacy.'

He paused and licked his lips, and looked to Adele for inspiration. Adele had noted Beaumont's interest, and pulled her shawl even more primly round her body. But her eyelashes were anything but prim.

'You may not be aware, my lord,' went on Arnulf, 'that I may find it necessary to terminate my service with my lord the Duke. A long story – I shall not bore you with it, my lord. Time passes – one must – er – one must move on – ' he conjured up a sickening half-smile – 'fresh fields, to coin a phrase. And it is not as if I were without skills and experience in many directions. I have – um – responsibilities, as you see – the love of a father for his only daughter.'

He tugged Adele's wrist as if it were some kind of curtain cord and he were about to reveal a pageant.

Adele stood stock still, and met Beaumont's gaze now full on. The arm her father was pulling on scarcely belonged to her.

Yves spread his hands.

'No use coming to me. I have nothing.'

Sweat was now pouring down Arnulf's face. Adele could feel the moisture from his palm through the material of her sleeve.

Yves gestured towards Odo. 'Perhaps my lord of Bayeux ... '

Arnulf turned towards Odo, and swallowed in anticipation.

'Oh, my lord, if only you could see your way. My daughter is good in the kitchen too.'

Beaumont laughed.

'Is she good somewhere else then as well?'

Adele blushed in fury, and tore her arm away from her father's loathsome grip. The movement shook the shawl loose from her shoulders. She gathered it round her again, but not so hurriedly that Beaumont did not get a good look.

Odo dusted his hands. There was no more enjoyment to be wrung from this pathetic charade.

'Come my lord – the board. As for you, priest!' He poured a bushel of heavy irony on to the word. 'Look to your own soul before you try to save those of others.'

As he and Yves began to go down the steps, he flung a last dart over his shoulder.

'Your loving daughter will bring you – comfort – as she has no doubt done in the past.'

* * * * * *

'I should have known better.'

Wulfnoth flopped on to a bench and helped himself to some of Gerard's beer.

'We should all have that carved on our graves,' said Gerard. He looked at Wulfnoth from over his mug.

Wulfnoth grunted.

'Priest's daughter! I should have realised when she offered.'

'Offered?'

'Yes. To serve in place of Emma.'

Emma, one of the usual serving girls, had taken to her bed amid tears, wailings, and excuses about women's complaints.

'All eyelashes and eagerness to help.'

'Ah,' said Gerard. The boy was building up for one of his bouts of breast-beating.

'All she did was make eyes at Beaumont. Practically offered herself on the plate instead of the food.'

'Has she never made eyes at you?'

Wulfnoth pretended to consider briefly.

'She may have done. I have not noticed. She is already doing his laundry, you know.'

'Ah. How is Arlette, by the way?'

Wulfnoth hid his face in his cup.

'She is well. Well.'

'Ah.'

It was a question of waiting. The boy would get around to it sooner or later.

Wulfnoth put down his cup, and heaved a huge sigh.

'When will it be paid? I should guess that Earls of Wessex should come quite expensive.'

'Who said anything about a ransom?'

'Guy did.'

'All right – who said anything about the Bastard paying it?'

Wulfnoth gaped.

'You mean the King? Oh, have some sense, Gerard. Edward is – wary of my brother. Why should he pay to have his greatest embarrassment brought back to England?'

'No, you have some sense, boy. Guy will have to hand him over. He has few brains, but he does have just enough to know that.'

Wulfnoth poured some more beer.

'Very well, suppose Guy hands him over. What then?'

Gerard turned to the new crutch he was fashioning.

'No danger of William cutting his throat, if that is what is on your mind. If he wanted Harold dead, he would have let Guy do it, and keep the blood off his own hands.'

Wulfnoth moved restlessly, but did not stand up.

Gerard spoke, but kept his head down over his work.

'You are not worried about the ransom, or about Harold's life. Why not try speaking the truth?'

'What do you mean?'

Gerard looked up.

'Either admit it, or leave me in peace. You have a face longer than a mile of refugees. By the Nails, boy, you should be overjoyed.'

Wulfnoth drank once or twice, twiddled the stem of the cup, and finally set it down.

'Twelve years, Gerard. It has been twelve years.'

Gerard brushed some slivers of wood off the table.

Twelve years was indeed a long time to a lonely lad of ten. Left in a foreign country as pledge for his father's good faith. Earl Godwin had promised not to oppose the succession of Duke William to the throne when the holy Edward would be finally called to the company of his fellow-saints. Wulfnoth was living proof of his promise.

Now Godwin was dead. So was his eldest son, Sweyn. But the others were alive and well – all four of them. Harold ruled in Wessex; Tostig in Northumbria; Gyrth held East Anglia; Leofwine was lord of Kent. Between them they practically owned England. Would they stand by the promise made by their father, a promise no doubt extracted through gritted teeth?

In all those twelve years, Wulfnoth had never left Normandy. Nobody from the family had ever visited him. He had had to adapt. To do him credit, he had made a good job of it. But the fact remained that he was a dreadful agoniser, and a shocking worrier. To show sympathy for him now would be to do him a disservice.

'What are you afraid of? That Harold's charm will no longer work? Or that it will?'

Wulfnoth looked thoroughly wretched.

'What do I do, Gerard?'

'Stop whining like a girl, that is what you do. Harold is your brother. He loves you – you used to tell me that often enough.'

'I am not a child any longer.'

'That will not stop Harold loving you. A brother is always a brother. You are a man now. Greet him as a man, as an equal.'

Wulfnoth smote the table with his fist.

'Harold is at this moment in Guy of Ponthieu's prison. The Duke's messengers are on their way there now, and it is surely not in order to put him on a boat for England. Harold will not be coming here as an equal of anybody. How will it turn out, Gerard? You know everything.'

Gerard let out his great booming laugh.

'Not before it happens, lad. And by that time it is too late. There is little we can ever do about anything. So why worry? The sooner you realise that, Wulf, the better.'

* * * * * *

'Believe me, Sir Walter, I take no pleasure either in the journey or in the message I bear.'

It was a kind of honesty.

When they had received the Bastard's orders to proceed to Beaurain by way of Longueville, Ralph did not know whether to be pleased or sorry. He had still not decided about going home to Gisors, to his crippled father and his mad mother.

'Saves you the trouble of making up your mind,' observed Bruno, striking the very nerve of the truth as usual.

They both knew that Sir Walter would be furious at the interruption. Everyone had heard about his fabulous new stallions.

'He stays so close to them he is practically mating with them himself.' Or so ran the castle joke.

'The Duke stressed the urgency of the matter, Sir Walter,' said Ralph.

'God's Face, you need not spell it out. I shall go, damn you.'

The lady Ermengarde fed them, and they resumed their journey.

Ralph said very little. Bruno glanced at him, and said less.

The man they were going to see, Count Guy of Ponthieu, was the brother of the late Count Enguerrand, the man who had carried out the raid on Ralph's home, the raid that had left his father with one hand and his mother with half a mind. Ralph did not believe in the enjoyment value of revenge, but he took satisfaction from the fact that they had it in their power, thanks to the Duke's commission that they carried, to make Guy squirm.

The Duke was taking a chance with an embassy of only two, but he had already taken other precautions, of which Guy would be fully informed.

The message was brief and to the point. The Earl Harold was to be released at once, and brought with full honours and with all possible speed to the frontier at Eu, where the Duke would meet him in person. There was to be no bargaining, there were no terms, there was no mention of any ransom.

The rest of their party, about half a dozen of them, were to turn off at the Somme, locate the wreck of Harold's ship, and arrange for local sailors to bring it to the small harbour at le Tréport. Once there, the Duke's men were to requisition wrights and labourers to carry out full repairs.

Gilbert had begged to be allowed to go on with Ralph to Beaurain. Ralph had hesitated, but only briefly. Bruno's remarks still smarted.

'The boy is a castle joke. Besides, he is not a loner; you are. I should know.'

So Gilbert was to go to the Somme with the main party. All the way he had to endure the nettle of Nigel Fitzhenry's tongue.

'I hear you once herded hounds for the Bishop of Coutances. Have more luck handling the bitches, did you? Lot easier than women ... '

On a hillside near Longueville, above the road, Hubert the Tongue rubbed his chin as he stood beside his donkey's head and looked down.

'Now there is a funny thing, Rollo. My Saxon friend comes from the north-east, and goes on to Rouen. Suddenly, a whole patrol of the Duke's men comes up from Rouen, calls on Sir Walter, and disappears towards the north-east. And look – Sir Walter is stabling his prize horses, and it is a long way from dusk. Where do you suppose he is going?'

He climbed up on his little cart.

'Hup, hup, Rollo! There is some news lying about somewhere near. Time we went to look for it.'

* * * * * *

'For shame, girl!'

Arnulf, for once feeling himself in a strong position, puffed out his chest with righteous indignation. He addressed himself to Adele's heaving shoulders.

'The Lord God has given us our position in society. It is not for the likes of you to try and question the Divine Will.'

Adele's sobs punctuated his sermon.

'We of the people have our dignity too, you know. You have shamed your class and shamed your sex.'

Adele rose in sudden wrath from her bed of misery, her face blotched and wet.

'Did I shame my sex with you in the dark after the midsummer feast?'

Arnulf went dumb with shock and surprise. He tried to mouth a reply, but nothing came out. Adele, sniffing and wiping her nose, pursued him.

'You grovelled to confess to my lord Lanfranc. And you crawled for a position with my lord the Bishop of Sées. And then my lord of Bayeux. And only yesterday my lord Maurilius.'

Arnulf retreated to a bench, fell on to it, and wiped his face.

'Providing for our future, you ungrateful brat. Do you not realise the danger we are in?'

Adele came and stood over him, her hands on her hips, her bosom heaving.

'What else was I doing but provide for the future? I at least was seeking a sacrament, not the breaking of one. If I had gained the object of my desire, I should not have had to go on my knees to the first priest I met.'

Arnulf, beginning to relish a good family row, began to lose his embarrassment.

'With a nobleman? What did you have to offer a stallion like Beaumont but your body?' He sneered. 'Your fortune? Your inheritance? Your dowry? Your rank?'

Adele faltered.

'What is wrong with me? Am I not pretty?'

'Of course. And there a dozen like you within half a mile of here. Beaumont can have any of them he likes, without having to go up the aisle to get them. When you told him your price, I should think his desire drowned in a sea of laughter.'

Adele flushed.

'Yours never did. You never found me funny.'

Arnulf stood up and slapped her.

Adele turned back to the bed, and fell on to it again.

'What is to become of us? What is to become of us?'

Arnulf collected some shreds of dignity.

'I am your father. I shall think of something.'

He patted a bare calf.

* * * * * *

'His Grace did stress the urgency of the matter, sir.'

Sir William Fitzosbern rubbed the back of his neck.

In the awkward silence the courier fidgeted. Sir William's legendary self-control could be as unnerving as other lords' outbursts of temper.

Fitzosbern glanced up.

'Are you quite sure he said "Harold"?'

The courier nodded eagerly.

'Yes, sir.'

'Of Wessex?'

'Yes, sir.'

Fitzosbern grunted.

'God's Teeth! What a man!'

The courier, already filthy from miles of dusty riding in the sun, began to sweat afresh ...

'I know what he will say,' the Duke had said to him. 'He will go on about Brittany and about his precious castles, and about his mother and his wife. But stand your ground. Make my meaning clear. Do you understand ... ?'

The lady Alice came and stood behind her husband. Fitzosbern looked up at her.

'Brittany. The Brittany bee is buzzing again – already. This other business – Harold and – um – '

'Guy of Ponthieu, sir,' prompted the courier.

'Just so. Guy of Ponthieu. There must be some confusion. Such a story – ' he gestured towards the courier ' – preposterous.'

He fixed the hapless courier with his eye.

'Do you realise what you are saying? I have just been released after fourteen months – fourteen months – of continuous presence at the Duke's side. I have only just arrived from St. Amand, after my first visit to my mother in a year and a half. I have barely exchanged greetings with my wife.' He patted one of the hands on his shoulders. 'I have to attend to the maintenance of two castles – two ... '

'Stand your ground,' the Duke had said.

'Yes, sir ... '

The courier – tired, hot, hungry, thirsty – thought of his partner, Philip, who had craftily offered to attend to the stabling of the horses.

'Breteuil and Tillières are two of the most important fortresses on the southern border, and they demand immediate attention. The Duke himself has said so ... How am I to be expected to ... '

At the end of the next forty-mile ride, Philip could go in at Bellême and break the news – and see how he got on with my lord Sir Roger of Montgomery. And when Sir Roger had finished with him, the lady Mabel would be there to chew up the pieces. Serve Philip right!'

* * * * * *

Wulfnoth made his cast with great care. He did not know it, but anyone who knew him could have told him that, when he was concentrating, he stuck out the corner of his tongue.

The line dropped exactly where he wanted it. Holding his rod with gingerly finesse, he eased himself down on to his haunches, and then to a full sitting position. He fixed his eyes on the spot where the line entered the water, screwing up his face against the bright reflection of the sun off the surface of the river.

It was Harold who had taught him to fish.

'The man who has no time to fish, Wulf, has no peace in him.'

The noises of the town and castle reached him as a faint babble. At intervals on the opposite bank, just visible among the reeds, or vague in the shadows of trees, were the hunched figures of more men and boys, still and silent as statues over a grave ...

The Bastard never fished.

Wulfnoth lifted his whole body in a huge sigh.

'Wulf! Where are you?'

Wulf cursed to himself and flung down the rod. Might as well wade the river with an army.

'I am over here.'

There was a rustle of long grass. Arlette kissed him on the top of the head.

'Gerard said he thought you would be here.'

'Then Gerard was right – as usual.'

Arlette did not catch his mood.

'Move over. Share the dry grass.'

Wulfnoth did so – just. Arlette plumped herself down close beside him.

'What bliss! To get away from those wretched children for a while ... Well, what do you think of it?'

'What?'

'My new dress.'

'Oh. Yes. Very nice.'

He barely looked up. Arlette made a face at him.

'Gerard said you would be in a mood.'

Wulfnoth flared.

'I am not in a mood!'

'You see?'

'I repeat – I am not in a mood.'

Arlette laid a hand on his shoulder.

'You must learn to tell me things, dearest. I know there is something wrong. Husbands and wives must tell each other things.'

'We are not married yet.'

'We soon will be, when the Duke names the day.'

Wulfnoth grunted. Arlette frowned.

'What does that mean?'

'He will be too busy to, for quite a long time, I should think – now.'

Arlette crept closer.

'Believe me, Wulf, I do understand.'

Wulf picked up the rod and fiddled with it.

'Is that what Gerard sent you to do – to "understand" me?'

Arlette sat back.

'Really, Wulf, you are impossible. What is there to worry about? You are going to see your brother.'

Wulf threw down the rod again.

'Yes, but under what circumstances?'

'Does it matter? You love him; he loves you.'

'Arlette, you know nothing of politics.'

'What have politics got to do with it?'

'Everything. What is William going to do?'

'Gerard said you were worried about what *you* were going to do.'

'You see – I was right. Gerard sent you here to understand me.'

A thought suddenly crossed Arlette's mind.

'You are not afraid, are you?'

'Afraid?' Wulfnoth looked genuinely surprised. 'For myself, no. William would not harm me. If he were going to do that, he would have done it by now. Even if Harold took the crown, William would gain nothing by killing me.'

'You trust him,' said Arlette.

'Yes,' said Wulfnoth. 'As regards myself. But what will he do with Harold?'

‘Entertain him. The whole town knows he has arranged for Harold to be brought from Beaurain. Hardly to kill him. He could have let Guy of Ponthieu do that.’

‘You still do not understand. What will William do?’

‘You speak as if Harold will be clay in his hands. Have you no faith in your own brother?’

‘I know my brother. Harold is a charmer.’

‘Are you afraid his charm may not work with you again?’

‘I am afraid because I know it will not work with William. William is a schemer. He will arrange for something to happen.’

Arlette frowned.

‘Like what?’

‘If I knew that, I could warn him.’

Arlette smoothed out imaginary creases in her dress.

‘I still say you are making problems where none exist.’

Wulfnoth turned and grasped both her arms.

‘The crown. The crown of England. Does that not exist?’

‘Wulf! You are hurting.’

Wulfnoth almost flung her away.

‘The crown, Arlette! They both want it. And each knows the other wants it. Each is locked into this prison of ambition, and now, thanks to Guy of Ponthieu, William has had all the keys dropped into his lap. And you say there is nothing be worried about?’

Arlette rubbed one of her arms.

‘Gerard said you always look too far ahead when you play chess. You are doing it now. You speak as if King Edward were dead.’

‘He can not live for ever.’

‘He can yet father children.’

Wulf spat into the river.

‘He has not touched our sister Edith in years. The “Confessor”, remember?’

‘Whether Edward lives or dies tomorrow, the question still exists: who will be the next King.’

Wulfnoth frowned at her change of tack.

‘What do you mean?’

‘I mean,’ said Arlette, ‘that the question would still exist whether Harold came to Normandy or not.’

‘So?’

‘So – you are worried about more than you say. You are not frightened of Harold meeting William; you are worried about Harold meeting you.’

'Ridiculous!'

'Yes,' said Arlette. 'It is ridiculous. Harold loves you.'

'He is my brother.'

'Your big brother.'

Wulf blazed.

'Yes! If you like – my big brother!'

'Well then.'

Wulfnoth tossed his head in frustration.

'Arlette, when he last saw me I was a ten-year-old.'

'Well?'

'A Saxon ten-year-old.'

Arlette frowned. Wulf persisted.

'Look at me. What do you see?'

'The man I want to marry.'

'A man. The first thing. Not a boy. What else do you see?'

'A handsome man,' said Arlettte dreamily.

'Arlette, do be sensible.'

'I am being sensible. I do think you are handsome.'

'I mean look at me as an outsider.'

'No. I am biased. I love you.'

'Look at the other side for a moment.'

'I have no wish to; I like this side.'

'Arlette, please!'

Arlette put up her hands.

'Very well, I know what you are trying to make me say. So to please you, I shall say it: you look like a Norman now. After twelve years, Harold would hardly expect otherwise.'

Wulfnoth gestured helplessly.

'But look at my clothes. Listen to the language I am speaking.'

'Well, it would be no good speaking English to me, would it?' She giggled. 'Apart from those rude Saxon words you taught me. Do you want me to talk those now?'

'Arlette!'

'I will if you like.'

Wulfnoth stood up and turned away.

'You are laughing.'

'Because it is not serious.'

Wulfnoth turned back, his face twitching in his effort to hold back tears.

'Arlette, what will Harold think? Dress, hair, habits, language, manners

– everything about me is Norman. He will think I have betrayed him.'

Arlette shook her head, but Wulfnoth rushed on.

'But what else could I have done? Alone in Normandy, ten years old. Mourn myself to death? Bite the hand that fed me? Be ungrateful to the man who has become like a second father to me? I can not betray William either.'

'There is no need to "betray" either of them.'

'He has even supplied me with a wife.'

'Do you regret that?' said Arlette, pouncing.

Wulfnoth tossed his head wearily.

'No ... no.'

Arlette put her arms round him.

'All three of us love you. Gerard loves you. I have seen that priest's bastard girl making eyes at you. You should be on your knees to God. Though, when you are in this mood, I wonder why we all do.'

Wulfnoth struggled, but faintly.

'But what must I do?'

'Do? Nothing, you silly. Come to think of it, you could make love to me.'

Wulfnoth tore himself away.

'Do you take me for a coward? Someone who can not face his problems?'

'My love, you make problems where none exist. If William gets his precious crown in England, you will go with him, and you and Harold together will serve him. If Harold gets the crown, you will go to England to join him; William will not kill you just from spite; he loves you. Either way, you will get what you want.'

Wulfnoth sat down and picked up the rod again.

'So I sit and do nothing.'

'Yes,' said Arlette firmly. 'When there is nothing to be done, you must be content to do nothing.'

Wulfnoth undid a tangle in the line, and spoke with irony.

'Is that a priest's holy wisdom?'

'No. It is woman's common sense. If you were a woman for just five minutes in this world, you would know that. We are weaker than men; we owe our shelter, our protection, our welfare to men; me must marry according to the wishes of men. And what can we do about it? Nothing. And where should we be if we fretted ourselves about such a state of affairs? Mad with fantasies and fevers we could not control. No use to our fathers, our brothers, our husbands, our children, or ourselves.'

'Nobody is forcing you to marry me,' said Wulfnoth by way of rearguard action.

'I am one of the lucky ones,' said Arlette. 'But you are a Saxon; I can do nothing about that. You are the brother of an earl; you are a hostage. I can do nothing about that either. You are proud, and you are silly, and you are – you are wonderful – and I do not wish to do anything about that.'

Wulfnoth moved impulsively to interrupt, but Arlette held up her hand.

'And one day you will go with your brother Harold back to England, and as your wife – God willing – I shall go with you. I shall leave Normandy – the land where I was born, the land I love. Its broad fields, its forests, its orchards, its lambs tumbling on the downs above the sea. I shall leave all that, not because I shall betray Normandy, but because I love you.'

Wulfnoth moved again, and this time she did not stop him.

'Wulf! You are squeezing ... Really, for a man who finds it hard to make up his mind ... Wulf! ... My dress ... Just a minute ... there ... Only if you promise to enjoy me ... I warn you, I shall make you laugh too ... And I remember the Saxon word for ... What about the fish? ... I thought you did that to me, not the fish ... '

* * * * * *

'Pass the cheese, Goz.'

Thierry cut himself a liberal chunk, sliced it up, and began laying the pieces on large lumps of bread. When he had finished, he laid down his knife, and contemplated the prospect ahead of him on the table with satisfaction.

'Fidget and curse, fidget and curse. We shall be on the road by noon. This will be my last square meal for three days.'

'Ah.'

Goscelin also enjoyed his food. He too had suffered the rough side of my lord Geoffrey's tongue.

'Between you and me, Thierry, I shall not be sorry to see him go. He only gets in the way. He will never leave a plan alone – always adding things. He lives on afterthoughts.'

'I know, I know,' mumbled Thierry through the crumbs. 'I see him up there – all weathers too.'

'And he is hopeless with heights. Barely talk for fear of it. Now, if he were a true artist – '

'And when he is on the ground, he is always prowling round the masons' yard like a hungry wolf in February.'

For a while they munched and solemnly sympathised with each other. Goscelin leaned across and poured some more wine for his friend.

'Mind you, I fancy you will have the worst of it for a while.'

'Too true.'

'You know what they say: "Takes a miracle or a crisis to dig lord Geoffrey out of Coutances". This Harold must be quite a man.'

Thierry stuffed in some more bread and cheese.

'You know what I think? I think it is nothing to do with Harold at all. When the courier first told him, you know what he said? He said, "I care not if Harold and all his brothers are lined up in parade on the shore." And he said, "Do you know how far I have travelled this last two years in the service of the Bastard?" I tell you, I felt sorry for that courier. But he kept his head. He said, "The Bastard has also called my lord Odo of Bayeux to his side. My lord Odo has his ear at the moment we speak." '

Thierry took a long swig of the wine.

'That did the trick. He is always terrified that if Odo gets too close to the Bastard for too long, some mischief will be afoot.'

'Or else Odo will conjure some fresh privilege for his own cathedral. Lord Geoffrey would tear his hair.'

'I tell you something else too, my friend,' said Thierry. 'He will be sending me back here every other week to see what you are getting up to. So mind the roof stays up.'

Goscelin allowed another half-dozen lines of anguish to etch themselves across his cliff of a forehead.

'If only we could be allowed to get on with it. God preserve us from fussy Philistines. Can you do nothing? You have known him longer than I.'

Thierry wiped his blade and inserted the knife in its scabbard.

'The lady Sybil is still at St. Amand. If things get too bad, I shall suggest that he pay her a visit.'

* * * * * *

'No wonder you held your news tight, boy. Though you might as well have thrown it to the wind; it is all over Normandy now.'

Edwin had never thought to see Hubert again. Even if he had, he had never expected to be glad to see him.

But it was a joy to meet someone who was willing to talk – just talk. In whatever language. Wherever he had wandered in the castle, he had found, at best, turned shoulders; at worst, insults, jibes, and threats.

The Duke had once pulled him into the hall – almost literally – to ask some more questions. That was one conversation he would willingly have done without. The sarcastic young sentry had been sent off on some patrol or other, but he had been left under the eye of a fat sergeant, who barely uttered a word to him. A large portion of the castle garrison had been sent off on various missions to all parts of Normandy. There was a great deal of bustle and fuss. Edwin kept coming upon urgent, whispered meetings in corners of courtyards which suddenly fell silent when one of the participants caught sight of him.

Only in the great kitchen did he feel, if not welcome, at any rate not unwelcome. The big cook frankly frightened him – those huge wrists – the obvious menacing strength coupled with the lopsided limp. But Gerard never grudged him a meal, and was willing to exchange a word.

It was there that Hubert found him.

'Guardroom or kitchen, my boy. One or the other, if you want news. In your case, more likely the kitchen.'

'Nobody tells me anything. I know that this is because of the word I brought – '

'Or Count Guy's messengers,' interjected Hubert, who was already surprisingly well-informed.

'Yes, if you like. But they know I am telling the truth. Yet nobody will tell me what is happening now.'

Hubert patted his arm.

'Leave that to me.'

Edwin's disbelief showed on his face, for Hubert answered it.

'Think I talk too much? Maybe. But there is talk which makes eyes close, and there is talk which makes mouths open, and I do know the difference.' He held out his good arm. 'See that?'

Edwin frowned.

'Your arm?'

'No, foolish boy. The sleeve. Look at me.' He stood up, twirled himself round in front of Edwin, and sat down again. 'Men tell far more to a habit than they do to a jerkin or a hauberk. Or a skirt, for that matter,' he added thoughtfully. 'Something I have noticed since taking the cloth. It makes them think of the confessional. They fancy that pouring it into my ears is like pouring it down the drain.'

'But what about your work?' said Edwin. 'Your manors at Longueville.'

Hubert, already at home, poured himself a drink.

'They will never run away. Did you ever meet a villein who worked when he could gossip? The manors were still there when he had finished.' He stood up. 'Give me a day, and I will have the whole picture. But I can tell you this now, my friend: you have certainly started something.'

* * * * * *

Chapter Four

The Guessing

'You are to bring the lord Harold to the frontier at Eu. My lord the Duke will be there to receive him. There are to be full military honours and proper compliments to be exchanged.'

Guy of Ponthieu sucked a large, vulgar ring on his index finger. Ralph of Gisors, one of the Duke's couriers, stood before him, his attitude a nice mixture of formality and swagger. Behind him towered his partner, Bruno of Aix, silent and cold as one of the great stone monuments that were said to stand in crowds in Brittany.

'Nothing else?' said Guy.

Ralph bowed low enough to transmit irony.

'Nothing, my lord.'

Guy flushed.

He had expected anger, bluster, bargaining ... something! Instead it was he who felt the anger. It was he who fell back on bluster.

'And if I do not?'

Ralph bowed again, even lower.

'His Grace did not favour me with an account of his future policy, my lord. But he did instruct me to acquaint you with certain details of current events, which I was to pass on to you as a possible means of assisting you to make up your mind.'

Guy glared. Ralph continued.

'First, his Grace's father-in-law, my lord the Count of Flanders, is at this moment mounting patrols in strength. On your northern frontier, my lord. Routine security, you understand. You will also recall, no doubt, that my lord the Count's sister, the lady Judith, is married to my lord Harold's brother, the Earl Tostig. Understandably, my lord the Count has the usual worries of a kinsman that my lord Harold is receiving the hospitality that is due to the second man in England. Finally, my lord the Duke has detached a contingent of Flemish infantry to temporary garrison duty at the frontier near Eu, where they can act as guard of honour when my lord Harold arrives. Another routine precaution, as you might say. As your lordship knows well, a full awareness of the current situation is helpful towards a correct decision about future actions.'

'And the Duke sends you his salutations,' said Bruno.

* * * * * *

'So there you are; now you know.'

Hubert fastened his flask.

Edwin stared.

'How did you find out all that? And so quickly?'

Hubert scratched an innocent cheek.

'I must confess I cheated; I talked to Gerard.'

'That bear? Why would he tell you anything? You have never met before. Have you?'

'No.'

Hubert tossed the flask on to his cart from his seated position beside Edwin on the side of a horse trough. Edwin frowned.

'Well?'

Hubert grinned.

'Old soldiers, my boy. Old soldiers. If they come from opposite sides of the world, old soldiers always have much to discuss. Besides, I can now do Gerard a favour.'

'Oh?'

Edwin did not sound very interested.

'A favour,' said Hubert. 'You see, Count Baldwin will not be coming now, I should guess.'

'Count Baldwin?' asked Edwin, in spite of himself.

'The Duke's father-in-law, Count of Flanders. He will remain at home to watch our Count Guy from the rear. Make sure he gets up to no mischief, no cheating. Make sure he hands over your Earl Harold in one piece.'

'He had better,' said Edwin.

'I agree,' said Hubert, 'but you can never make too sure with creatures like Guy of Ponthieu. I should know; he is a neighbour of ours at le Tréport.'

A thought struck Edwin.

'What is Count Baldwin to Gerard?'

Hubert raised the tufts of ginger hair that served as his brows.

'Oh, come now. The accent. Gerard is a Fleming. He and my lady Matilda are very close. He used to be her nursemaid.'

Edwin sneered.

'Nursemaid. That cripple? And you believe everything you are told?'

'By a man like Gerard of Ghent – yes.'

Hubert had no need to take offence. Edwin was lonely, worried, frightened, a long way from home. Small wonder the boy's moods were liable to rapid change, his words like the paws of a startled cat.

Hubert clapped his hands on his thighs and stood up.

'I must be on my way. Count Baldwin will not come to Rouen and talk to

Gerard, so I must go to Flanders, collect the gossip, and bring it back to Gerard. That is my payment for what he told to me. I think it a fair bargain.'

'And what about your precious farms at Longueville? Do they grow weeds waiting for your tongue to fall idle?'

Hubert again refused to get cross.

'I am an overseer, not a ploughboy – or a dog-boy,' he added as an afterthought.

Edwin glared.

'Do not tell me my business, son,' Hubert went on. 'I do not tell you yours. And I can do a favour to you as well. Le Trèport is on my way to Flanders; I can look in and bring you news of how the ship repair is going. I take it you do wish to return home?'

Edwin dropped his eyes and sighed heavily.

Hubert patted him on the shoulder.

'There, there. Believe me, old sergeant Hubert understands. And how about this too? I shall travel through the border at Eu, and it is there that the Duke will receive the Earl Harold. Who knows what I might not see and hear?'

'How will you return here before them?'

Hubert smiled.

'Rollo can keep a steady pace when I tell him. We have an understanding. The Duke and the Earl will be in no hurry.'

'Why not?'

'Because they will wish to get to know each other. If you were either, would you not relish the opportunity – under the circumstances?'

Hubert shook out the folds in his habit.

'And – *and* – I shall still have time to pause at Longueville and stop the weeds growing. Until the next meeting, son. Keep your eyes open; there will be plenty to observe before the Duke arrives with your Earl. You see.'

He paused at the gate and looked back.

'Cheer up. Drive away all those worries that besiege you.'

Edwin sighed again.

'How can I? They are not soldiers; they are in my head.'

'Then put something else in your head. Have you seen that priest's daughter?'

'What about her?'

Hubert laughed.

'Come, boy – you are depressed, but you are not innocent. Her last paramour has been sent to le Tréport with the fatigue party. The coast is clear.'

Edwin snorted, half in disgust, half in amusement.

'Go to – Flanders!'

'On my way, boy, on my way.'

* * * * * *

'Knight to king's bishop three.'

Bishop William of Evreux stood and sipped from a wooden cup as he offered his advice from behind.

'Ah!'

Bishop Yves of Sées grunted with agreement and moved the piece. He looked behind himself at Bishop William, grinned at the cleverness of the idea, and looked back again at his opponent, who now bent, frowning, over the board.

Bishop John of Avranches, a busy writer and scholar, was not a regular player, and it showed. Frankly, Bishop Yves was not much better; his choice of recreation lay rather with the the chase or the field of campaign. He welcomed the help.

For the next few minutes he kept up a stream of comment and gossip with William behind him, until his opponent looked up and said, 'My lord, if we are to do justice to this game, let us at least accord to it the attention it deserves.'

Yves looked again at William behind him, and made a face, but he kept quiet. John made mistakes, and Yves had enough wit to take advantage of them. When he lost his queen, John of Avranches sat back with a sigh.

'There seems little point in continuing.'

'Just what I was thinking about the council,' said William of Evreux, as he refilled his cup. 'With this bee from Wessex buzzing round the Bastard's brain, what chance do we have of getting him to listen?'

Yves got up and went to the fire.

'I agree. Not even Lanfranc can make him see reason. William bawled him out.'

'Has Maurilius tried?' asked Evreux, who had arrived only the day before.

'Maurilius has scarcely left his palace. If he did, can you see him succeeding where Lanfranc has failed?'

Maurilius, Archbishop of Rouen, was a saintly scholar and a good administrator, but he did not have the towering personality of the Abbot of St. Stephen's of Caen.

'We could always try pressure,' suggested John of Avranches.

Yves of Sées turned on him.

'Oh?'

'Pressure,' repeated Avranches. 'Excommunicate that squalid little chaplain of his. His daughter too; I gather she is a garrison whore. Offer to lift the ban when he calls the first session.'

'You mean blackmail?'

The Bishop of Avranches deplored clerical marriage we well as clerical concubinage, and did not care who knew it.

Yves leaned across the table.

'Have you ever known blackmail to work on the Bastard?' He stood up, scoffing. 'Not even the Pope could do it. Look at Matilda. Did it stop him marrying her?'

The Bishop of Avranches was not impressed.

'Are we not all summoned here to discuss the very matter of clerical marriage?'

'Yes,' said Evreux, 'but only among other things.'

'Of equal importance,' added Sées. 'We do not all have an obsession with priestly incontinence.'

'If we all stuck a little more to our principles – ' began Avranches.

' – We would get nowhere,' said Sées. 'Church councils are as much about politics as about virtue. And politics are about means and ends, not about principles. If you try to drive the Bastard into a corner before we start, you will never get your precious council, Harold or no Harold.'

'Is it not precious to you?' said Avranches. 'As a prince of the Church?'

Yves of Sées laughed.

'You should keep your traps for the chessboard, my lord. You will not catch me that way. And see in your turn that you are not trapped by the very lusty fat cleric whom you would cast out into darkness. The poor devil is importuning every bishop and vassal he can find; he can see his own livelihood vanishing into thin air, without you excommunicating him.'

'He has already approached me,' said Evreux, 'and I have barely arrived.' He shuddered. 'It was sickening.'

'He has not seen me,' said Avranches.

'Not desperate enough yet,' said Sées. 'He knows your views on the likes of himself. He has been to me, to Odo, to William here. He will try Geoffrey when he comes too, and Hugh.'

Avranches looked surprised.

'I thought Coutances had leave of absence from this council.'

'He did. It is not for the council that he is coming. The Bastard wants his advice on our guest from Wessex. Geoffrey will be joining a military gathering, not a clerical one.'

Avranches made a sound of disgust in his throat. Geoffrey de Montbrai was a sound bishop, but he was born a knight. John of Avranches deplored this dual function of bishops that the Duke seemed to consider so important. Hugh, Bishop of Lisieux, soon to arrive, was another one – kinsman to the Duke moreover. No question where his first priorities would lie.

John of Avranches twiddled a rook on the board.

'Could we not start the council without him?'

Sées looked thunderstruck.

'Without the Bastard?'

'Yes. There is me – Avranches. You – Sées. William here – Evreux. Bayeux is somewhere in the castle.'

'He is ill – the flux.'

'He will get up from his sick bed when Coutances arrives – anything to stop him stealing a march.'

'And who do you propose should preside?' said Sées.

'You,' said Avranches. 'You are the senior bishop by several years.'

'Near that chair?' said Yves of Sées. 'No fear.'

'What about Maurilius?' said William of Evreux. 'He is the Archbishop of Rouen, after all.'

'He is as unwilling as I am.'

'Lanfranc then.'

'Never. Maurilius sees the need, but has not the courage. Lanfranc has the courage, but does not feel strongly enough about the need. No, my lords, there is no alternative; you will have to wait, and hope that the Bastard deals quickly with this Harold of Wessex, however that may be.'

Yves grinned slyly at Evreux.

'There is always the chase.'

John of Avranches raised his eyebrows in lofty disdain.

'The board then?' said Yves, still teasing.

'For certain we can not keep on saying Mass all the time,' said Evreux. 'There will soon be more bishops here than there are congregation.'

John of Avranches looked gloomily at the chessboard. William of Evreux leaned across to him.

'The trouble is, you handle your bishops badly.'

Avranches raised his eyes, and allowed himself a rare, if wry pleasantry.

'Perhaps we should tell that to his Grace the Duke.'

* * * * * *

'Hoc est corpus meum ... '

Arlette had forgotten which bishop it was who was saying Mass. She had never seen so many together in the castle at any one time. Not that she cared. Nor that she was paying that much attention. She had found a convenient excuse for getting away from my lady's dreadful children. Nobody could blame her for neglect of duty if she was on her knees in the castle chapel. The droning Latin offered a soothing background while she thought ...

If that scheming little cat thought she could make eyes at Wulfnoth and get away with it, she had another think coming. Holy St. Catherine – she had to be desperate. Surely everyone knew that she, Arlette, and Wulfnoth were spoken for each other. It served only to show what a whore the girl was.

And look at her father ... Arlette glanced up towards the altar, where Arnulf held the book of scripture that he could barely read, much less understand, while his Grace the Bishop of wherever-it-was intoned the words of consecration. Even at this distance she could see the sweat on his forehead in the candlelight. Pitiful – the Duke's chaplain, reduced to fetcher and carrier at his own altar – grovelling to every bishop he could find. Oh, yes – Arlette had heard the gossip. And his bawd of a daughter was offering herself to any takers ... Why did whores always hope to get married? Could they not see ... ?

A rustle of material beside her jerked her out of her reverie. Holy saints! It was the whore herself.

Adele was equally startled. Coming from behind, she had not recognised the hooded figure in the shadow. Now on her knees, it was too late. The bishop had almost reached the moment of consecration. Neither dared move.

They remained thus, rigid with shock and revulsion. Some members of the congregation went up to receive the Host. Still neither moved.

It was Arlette who found her tongue first – a needle driven in by the zephyr of a whisper.

'Late to Mass – late to virtue, sister.'

Adele said nothing. Arlette dug again.

'Are you not receiving then? You – the daughter of a priest?'

'No.'

Adele could not think of a suitable excuse. Arlette pressed her advantage.

'Are we not then in a state of grace? Are there sins that still weigh upon our conscience?'

Adele found her voice, also a sibilant whisper.

'Are there sins that weigh upon yours? You do not move either.'

Arlette turned to Adele and smiled.

'I heard Mass this morning as well. It is my custom. I received too. Perhaps you were otherwise engaged – in male company perhaps?'

Adele lowered her head behind her clasped hands.

'Perhaps he preferred my company to yours.'

Arlette almost recoiled under the impact.

'Stay away from him!' she hissed with all the venom she could muster.

It was Adele's turn to smile.

'Forgive me. I thought you were nursemaid only to my lady's charming children. I did not know you had been promoted to watch over my lord's ward as well.'

'Stay away from Wulfnoth!' said Arlette, coming out into the open.

Adele arched her eyebrows in mock surprise.

'Unless – forgive me – you have become recently betrothed. My apologies – I had no idea.'

'There has been an understanding between us.'

'But not a betrothal. Had there been a public announcement, I would of course have been more – reticent. We can hardly be blamed if nobody tells us.'

'It is an understanding of very long duration.'

Adele fixed her eyes on the altar.

'Such silent fidelity is most touching.'

Arlette was equal to the contest. She too gazed forward in apparent rapt piety.

'Better to be faithful to one than faithful to the whole garrison.'

Adele flushed.

'At least I do not have to mount sentry duty on any of them; they come of their own accord. Tell me – how do you tether him – with a halter or with a ring through his nose?'

The last of the communicants filed away from the altar rail.

They stood as the bishop and his retinue walked down the aisle. Last of all, puffing and sweating, came Arnulf.

Arlette turned again to Adele and smiled sweetly.

'Tell me – when you do go to confession, sister, do you confess to your father, or does he have to confess to you?'

* * * * * *

'You have the chance; why not take it?'

Ralph pretended not to have heard, and busied himself with unsaddling his horse.

Any normal man would. Gisors was only two or three days' ride away. They had fulfilled the Duke's instructions. There was nothing to do but wait for Guy to bring Harold to Eu. When he did, and when the Duke arrived to welcome him, there would be nothing to do but witness the formalities. Two scouts more or less made no difference; William would bring plenty of men-at-arms with him as escort.

In the event of trouble, there was also the company of Flemish mercenaries who had been cooling their heels for a fortnight and who would welcome the action.

Any normal man would go home to see his family.

Ralph sighed. Any normal man would have a normal family – not a cripple for a father and a weeping, mind-wandering old crone for a mother. Not an elder brother who would only pretend to be pleased to see him, and who would pray for his departure to be early and peaceful. He was bound to fall out with Aubrey sooner or later; he always had, ever since infancy. After Michael died, it had got worse.

His sisters had families and worries enough of their own. It was very unlikely that he would manage to see them at all.

If he went home, he would be drawn to Michael's grave like a starving bear to honey. It would be a deeper pain than seeing the stump of his father's arm or holding his mother's pale claws of hands and listening to her ramblings. What good could he do them?

All that damage had been done in a brief half-hour of a brigand's raid – an irruption of bloody force as sudden and random as a bolt of lightning. And the victims were as helpless as they would have been before the lightning.

It was the swiftness and completeness of it, the blindness of it, the implacable permanence of it, that made Ralph angry – not its perpetrator. The fact that it had been Enguerrand of Ponthieu, Count Guy's brother, was purely coincidental.

He had felt no grim joy when the wretched Enguerrand, bound on display before the castle of Arques, had suffered the sword strokes which deprived him first of ears and nose, then hands, feet, eyes, privates. Would it bring back his father's hand, his mother's mind? If for one moment he had thought it might, he himself would have ripped open the remains of the screaming torso, and with his bare hands have dragged out the entrails.

True, they had watched Enguerrand's brother, Count Guy, as he squirmed and blustered, but that was little more than the satisfaction of seeing a bully cut down to size. Ralph had never met Guy before, and Guy did not know him from Adam. There was nothing to be gained from reminding Guy of the manner of his brother's death; the chances were he rarely forgot it anyway.

Ralph knew that their mission was a delicate one: Guy was to be brought to heel with the minimum of naked force. Any unnecessary provocation could recoil on Harold, and then there would be the Duke's wrath to face.

'I said you have the chance; why not take it?'

Bruno rarely repeated himself. Ralph would have to answer.

'The horses need resting. Here is as good a place as any.'

Bruno lifted his saddle from the horse's back.

'And Eu is only a stone's throw from le Tréport. You can go and see how he is getting on.'

Ralph kept his head down.

'I may do, I may do. I have not made up my mind.'

'Oh yes you have. You can not face Michael at Gisors, so you will console yourself with a reflection at le Tréport.'

Ralph swore.

'God's Breath! Why do you disapprove of everything I do?'

Bruno was ready as ever.

'Why do you disapprove of everything I say?'

'Go to Hell!'

Bruno ducked his head under the lintel of the stable door as he left.

'Just let me know when you plan to leave for the shipbuilder's yard.'

'Go to Hell!'

'To pick up the ploughboy.'

* * * * * *

'Heave, my lads, heave.'

'Our oars, or our stomachs?'

Nigel laughed.

'Both, if necessary. If you want to reach harbour by nightfall.'

'All right for you.'

A dozen men-at-arms, their hauberks stowed in canvas to protect them from the salt and the water, grimaced and swore as they stretched unwilling muscles to unfamiliar work.

There was no sail, and no mast, after the storm, and there were a dozen leaks.

'Then we row,' said Aldred, Harold's captain.

When this was translated, soldiers threatened to down tools.

'What choice do we have, boys?' said Nigel. 'I for one should be happy to tell this Saxon water-rat to go to the Devil, but who among us is to tell the Bastard that we refused to carry out his orders?'

So, grumbling and blaspheming, the soldiers stripped off helmet and sword belt – and hauberk when the sweat ran – and fumbled for a grip on the huge oars. Before an hour had passed, it seemed as if their hands had been cast in iron around those oars, and would never unfold again. They looked forward to the end of their turn, when they could exchange the back-breaking slavery for the lowly grovelling and bailing.

Nigel Fitzhenry, as usual, had found himself the most congenial task, at the huge steering oar in the stern, where he lent his weight to assist Aldred. Infuriatingly, too, he was one of the few who did not feel sick.

A handful of sailors were skipping here and there with vital running repairs, though the main reconstruction would have to wait until they reached le Tréport.

Nigel kept up a flow of jibe and repartee.

'See this captain of ours? Speaks no French – not a word. And I can tell you, lads, that he is the smelliest, crudest, most vulgar creature ... I should know; I am right beside him ... Think what is in store for you when we reach harbour.

All those girls waiting on the dockside, eager for ... Do not waste all your energy on the oars; keep some for the whores ... more for the whores than the oars, eh?'

'Nigel, you are a bastard!'

'I bet you save the best one for yourself.'

Nigel looked injured.

'If I go ashore first and do the scouting, surely I deserve the first choice? You know me, boys; I shall find the best places to go.'

'As good as the priest's house in Rouen?'

Nigel glanced towards Gilbert, who was crouched in the bilges, white-faced and staring. Each move with the bailing bucket was a teeth-gritting effort.

Nigel winked at those nearest, and raised his voice slightly.

'Now there is a girl for you. Give you a better ride than you are getting now, my lads. God, what thighs! Softer than any saddle. I say, better than any saddle, eh, Gilbert?'

Gilbert, pale and shivering, kept his head down and pretended not to hear.

Great Jesus! He would find a way to shut this braggart's mouth. Somehow, somehow ...

* * * * * *

'Why not stay and welcome him here at Rouen?'

'No.'

' More dangerous at Eu.'

'No.'

'Guy could still make trouble.'

'No.'

Matilda made a face at William's back as he busied himself with dressing for the road. A valet hovered.

'Well, then take me with you,' said Matilda. 'And the chicks.'

'No.'

'Just me then.'

'No.'

'Why not. You brought me all the way here from Caen.'

'That was for the council.'

'There will be no council if you go chasing off to the frontier to wait on Harold.'

'You want to come just because you are curious to see him.'

'And you want to go just because you want to get away from Lanfranc and the bishops. It is the next best thing to going on campaign in Brittany.'

'Attend to your own business, woman.'

'You were willing enough to tell me yours when Fitz was away.'

'Well, now he will soon be here.'

'And what am I to do? Stuck in an empty castle knee deep in bishops?'

The valet began to concentrate more. This conversation had the makings.

'Entertain those bishops. Talk to Lanfranc. You like that; you told me. Keep them here until I return.'

'How do I do that?'

William tightened the buckle on his sword belt.

'I expect you to think of something.'

'And what about the children? We were going to discuss them too – remember? Cecily is becoming impossible; she is driving Arlette mad. And that reminds me: what are you going to do about Arlette? Will you let her announce her betrothal to Wulfnoth?'

'Not yet. Not yet. When I am ready.'

William put out his hand for his travelling cloak. The valet was almost as absent-minded now as his master; he was listening as hard to Matilda's words as William was neglecting them.

'And what about Arnulf? What am I to tell Lanfranc? Will you really banish him? He did marry us, you know.'

'Yes, yes ... '

'You have an eldest son too, may I remind you. Robert is dying to come with you.'

William, his patience thinning, nevertheless turned to give a scrap of attention at the sound of Robert's name.

'There will be no campaigning at Eu. Only ceremonies. Robert will simply get bored.'

'He will be even more bored here. Do you want him to learn bad habits from that fat sergeant?'

William fastened the buckle. If he could get away now ...

Matilda did not give up easily.

'Robert needs discipline. He will get nothing but spoiling here. Gerard says – '

William's patience snapped.

'Gerard says! Splendour of God – to the midden with Gerard! Am I to be ruled by a stumping cripple from Flanders with a ladle in his hand?'

'How dare you abuse Gerard! He has given more attention to that boy than you have these last two years, and I tell you ... '

The valet could not make up his mind: should he stay and enjoy it by himself, or would it last long enough for him to run to the kitchen and scoop up a few more to make an appreciative audience behind the door?

* * * * * *

'We thank you for your service to our house and to our daughter in God.'

Robert of Beaumont bowed low.

'Believe me, Reverend Mother, the pleasure was all mine.'

He meant it.

What had begun as a demeaning imposition had ended by becoming a joy that had ended all too early.

It had started with the Flemings. Moved from pillar to post by the Duke's orders, and deprived of action and pay, they had become restive and insubordinate. Worse, they refused to take Beaumont seriously.

'Liaison officer? Ha! Bastard's messenger.'

When, flushed and furious, he turned to their captain for support, he was met with little better.

'I take my orders from the Duke, not from beardless boys. You merely transmit; you do not command.'

The captain turned a blind eye when his men carried out a little discreet looting around Eu; they craftily did just enough to avoid a major incident. In vain Beaumont blustered about telling the Duke and about dire punishment. They spat into the fire and turned back to their gambling boards.

Beside himself with rage and injured pride, Beaumont rode back to Rouen to tell the Duke. He stopped the night at Longueville, at Sir Walter Giffard's hall.

Sir Walter's stallions took the edge off his feelings. He had never seen such magnificent beasts.

'My husband's pride and joy,' said the lady Ermengarde.

'I can understand why.'

Ermengarde was a good hostess. She was a good listener too. Robert of Beaumont felt a lot better by the end of the evening.

'You should never trouble yourself about Flemings,' said my lady. 'Especially unemployed Flemings. Only the Bastard himself can keep them on a leash for more than a week or two. It is well known. Besides, from what you tell me, you were only trying to do your duty.'

'Well, exactly.'

Ermengarde let him talk on. She liked this young man. Had seen him grow up. She knew his father well, Sir Roger of Beaumont. Yes, he was spoilt, arrogant, quick to anger at imagined insults; then so were most his age. Especially with a doting father like Roger.

But he had virtues too: he was a cut above the usual horse-prancer with nothing in his head but battles and boar-spears. True, he was ambitious and he was impatient, but he possessed a natural kindness, when he thought nobody was looking. There was an engaging innocence about him, though he would have been most offended if it had been suggested or implied. And there could be no denying that he was extremely good-looking. He was the sort of son that Ermengarde would have liked to have herself. Perhaps that was why she enjoyed talking to him. Perhaps that was why she asked him the favour she did.

There was this girl, she said. A ward of Sir Walter's. They were going to put her in the convent of St. Amand at Rouen; there was little for the child at Longueville, and she would be well cared for by the sisters. Give her a little education too in the arts of the household; the girl would have to marry sometime.

Robert wondered what was coming.

The problem was the journey, continued Ermengarde. Sir Walter was going to take her himself, but had been called away suddenly by the Duke – the Harold business. She hesitated to send Judith (that was her name, by the way – Judith) in the company of her bailiff, especially with all those awful Flemings in the neighbourhood. Anything might happen.

Robert felt the trap begin to close.

Now, said Ermengarde, Robert was a brave knight, with a strong entourage, and it just so happened that he was journeying to Rouen. If he could see his way to escorting Judith to the mother abbess at St. Amand ...

'Those Flemings – for all their rudeness, Robert, I am sure they would never dare flout a man of your standing. Or your bravery.'

Robert had no defence. What could he do? My lady Ermengarde had given him shelter, food, and sympathy. Nor did he wish to offer gratituous offence to her husband, Sir Walter, a man not noted for patience or slowness to anger. A great friend of his father's too.

Ermengarde retired to sleep that night well satisfied. Walter may have stolen her niece's dowry to raise the money for his wretched horses, but he would not be able to steal their ward's dowry to pay off the moneylenders of Cologne. That was going to St. Amand with Judith, where it belonged.

Robert of Beaumont had a surprise when Judith appeared, promptly at dawn, quite ready for the journey. He had expected a squalling infant in a litter. He saw a slender girl of about thirteen on horseback.

He received his second surprise when the ride began; she came up beside him and began talking. She was actually interesting. Her eyes fairly shone when she laughed – which she did, often. Her small, gloved hands swung and dipped like swifts to accompany her voice. Once, when she released the reins the better to give point to a story, she nearly fell off – and laughed again.

They stopped for the night at Clères, at the hall of a cousin of Ermengarde's. Robert's valet came to him in the stable.

'Where do we put the child for dinner, sir?'

Robert whirled on him.

'Child! She is a young woman. She is the daughter of a knight. She sits beside me.'

Throughout the second day, Robert allowed the pace of progress to become slower and slower as they neared Rouen. His retinue, anxious to stable their horses and be off to the delights of the town, grumbled among themselves, but nobody dared pass a remark to his face.

When they at last passed the front gate of the convent of St. Amand, Robert found his curiosity fighting a battle with his delight in Judith's company. He had not been in a nunnery before, and was intrigued to see what actually went on. Moreover, the mother abbess in this house was none other than the lady Emma, the mother of Sir William Fitzosbern.

'We thank you for your service to our house ... '

The dignity, the stillness of visage, the measured tones of the voice, the imperturbability – they had come about from character rather than from the contemplative life of seclusion. Robert could see where Fitz got it all from.

Standing at my lady's elbow was Sister Sybil, now under-abbess, whom the lady Emma introduced.

Robert turned to look. So this was the lady Sybil, sister of the twelve sons of Tancred of Hauteville, so many of whom were carving empires for themselves in Italy. What a brood! He gazed at her. Was there in her features a trace of the mighty Robert Guiscard, the most magical of the twelve?

The lady Sybil had another claim to fame; she was, or had been, the paramour of my lord Geoffrey de Montbrai, Bishop of Coutances. Many years ago now; he remembered his father and uncles talking about her. The broad forehead, the clear, open face, determined jaw, the high colour – not a great beauty, but he could see, even at this distance of time, that a man could easily have lost his heart to her when she was young.

It was not a question of ... God's eyes, what was it a question of? All he knew was that it was ridiculous, but he did not want to say goodbye to Judith, and he would very soon have to.

* * * * * *

'You should have been Archbishop, not me.'

Lanfranc sighed.

That was the best Maurilius could manage. Nothing positive. Maurilius was a good scholar, and a sound administrator, but lacked the personality to stand up to William. Nor did he have the subtlety of the chess player.

Neither did Bishop John of Avranches. His suggested method was too stark – a sentence of excommunication on the Duke's chaplain. A lot of ice that would cut with his Grace. It would put them back, not forward. The wretched man's so-called wife was long dead anyway.

The warriors among the bishops – Yves of Sées and Geoffrey of Coutances – would be no use. Yves was waiting to get back to his castle and his hunting, and Geoffrey would fret about his cathedral. The Duke's kinsmen – Hugh of Lisieux and Odo of Bayeux – would follow whatever family policy the Duke laid down. That left Evreux and Avranches. William of Evreux would follow the majority; there were sound virtues in Evreux, but none of the saint or the prophet. If the odds became too long, he would back down. The main interest of John of Avranches was his books, apart from his obsession with clerical celibacy, which would offend William long before they could get any assurances out of him about more general reform.

Lanfranc sat on the edge of a horse trough in an outer bailey, and idly stirred the water with his finger.

'A sou for your thoughts, my lord abbot.'

Lanfranc looked up. He had not heard Gerard coming, for all that the 'tok tok' of his crutch on the cobbles was one of the best-known sounds in the castle.

The beard bristled. The broad mouth broke into an even broader grin.

'I saw you from the buttery. It struck me that you could do with some stimulation.'

He held up a pot and two wooden cups.

Lanfranc smiled and moved along. Gerard flopped down familiarly beside him. He stood his crutch carefully within reach, then poured out the wine and balanced the cups on the edge of the trough.

For a while they sipped in silence. At last Gerard spoke, gazing into space.

'Maybe the problem needs more than wine, Father Lan.' He had slipped into Matilda's habit.

Lanfranc hesitated.

'Maybe.'

'Difficult to keep bishops together.'

Gerard was as usual better informed that Lanfranc had given him credit for. He had struck the first of the nails smack on the head. How to hold the bishops in Rouen for what seemed like an indefinite period, with no prospect of council business. Half of them had not wanted to come anyway.

'And to bend his Grace to your will.'

That was the second – smack on the head again.

Lanfranc laughed.

'Is there anything we can keep from you, Gerard?'

'Not in a castle, Father Lan. Come and have a game. It will sharpen your wits and – who knows – it may produce an idea ... '

Gerard laid out the pieces.

'I have no great expertise at handling dukes, Father, but I have a lifetime's experience at handling lady Matti. And she is the Duke's other half.'

Lanfranc settled his skirts on the other side of the board and began the game. 'Well? I am listening.'

After only a few moves, Gerard did something that at once drew Lanfranc into a space.

'If I may make so bold, do not try to push him. Pull him. With all the resources you have here – six bishops and an archbishop – there must be something you can do that will make him listen.'

'All he can hear is the name "Harold".'

'What is he hoping to do with Harold?'

'Outwit him, I should imagine.'

'Then offer him something towards that end.'

'What?'

Gerard moved another piece that put Lanfranc under threat.

'You are the clever one, my lord abbot. I expect you to think of something.'

* * * * * *

Think, man, think!

Arnulf paced up and down, shaking his fists in a frustration that took him to the edge of tears. He was sure the whole garrison was laughing at him, with the cruelty that men, and women, showed when they crowded to look at the cornered stag or the condemned criminal on the scaffold. It was their way of tasting a death which they all knew was not far from themselves, tasting it with impunity – for a while. With him too they sensed an end, a sort of death, and he had never been liked. He fancied he could see his blood on their lips.

Hearing a noise, he whirled round, but nobody was in the doorway.

He forced himself to sit down. This was hopeless. He had to regain control. It was a mercy that Adele was not in the house to sneer and pout, to flaunt her body and toss her head.

He knew that if they spoke they would end by shouting. Shameless trollop! After Beaumont it was now the Saxon hostage. Stupid too. And if she failed to see how blind she was to aim so high – brother of an earl – she would fall that much harder.

He reached for the pot. It was empty. He rummaged in a cupboard and found another, with some dregs in the bottom. It tasted awful, but it was wet and it was strong.

With the end of a broad sleeve he wiped his jowls.

Think! What was it Gerard had said? 'Facts, man. What has actually happened?'

'But the council, the decree from the Pope. Bishop John of Avranches is a scourge of married priests – '

Gerard had to shake him.

'The truth, man. Not fears – they can unman us all. What has actually happened? Has the Bastard actually called you in and formally dismissed you?'

'Well – no. But – '

'No but's. You are still his chaplain. And you married him, remember that too. William does not forget a favour. You are a tonsured priest, with the power to loose or bind a man's soul. Stop counting your fears and count your advantages. Fight, man, fight. Nobody respects a loser ... '

The Duke had gone to Eu. Not back for a week at least. That gave him time. And what had he been doing? Going round behaving as if he were already cast out. No wonder the bishops wanted nothing to do with him.

For a moment he almost stood up and began pacing again, furious at his own stupidity.

He wiped his mouth. So – no more crawling. He would not demean himself before the Bishop of Avranches, or Lisieux when he arrived, or Bishop Geoffrey of Coutances.

All right, so far so good. A new chill came over him. But what then? If there was nobody to go to, what should he do? Stand still and wait for the inevitable?

Gerard had had the answer to that too ...

'Count your advantages.'

'You have done that.'

'And count your allies.'

Arnulf spread his podgy hands.

'I have none. Everybody despises me.'

'By the Nails, man. You – a priest – you *must* know. Praying is your trade. You have the greatest ally of all, and you have His ear. We have to make do with our knees; you have your altar. You have the Host, the body of God, which all men want. All these blessings. Use them ... '

Yes, of course, Gerard was right. Gerard was always right. He would go and pray. God would find a way. There was always a way. Foolish to despair so readily.

He looked around. But just one more drink first. It might be a long vigil.

* * * * * *

Sir Walter Giffard, wet and uncomfortable from riding in the rain, trudged across the main bailey towards the door of the hall. In the porch, he paused to take off his riding cloak, glancing at the sky from force of habit. The leaden, unremitting grey promised more rain.

He cursed silently, put his hand against the door, and pushed. Feeling resistance, he pushed again, harder. The obstacle was still there. With another oath, he shoved savagely, and nearly knocked over a boy who was coming the other way.

A pot smashed on the floor.

'Have a care, boy.'

'Sorry, sir.'

One of Gerard's scullions, Peter, stood helpless for a moment, not knowing whether to stand to attention or stoop and gather the pieces. Giffard frowned.

'Well, pick it up, pick it up.'

'Yes, sir.'

As he grovelled in the muddy rushes around the entrance, Giffard pushed past.

'Get me something to eat and drink.'

'Sir.'

Peter tried to clutch the pieces and rise to do his bidding at the same time. Blood appeared on a finger.

Giffard pulled back the curtain that hung behind the door, and moved into the main body of the hall. Two figures were seated on a bench before the fire.

He recognised Sir William Fitzosbern and his old friend, Sir Roger of Montgomery.

'Hallo, Roger. Fitz.'

He sat down and put out his hands to the blaze.

'God's Teeth, what weather! And almost June too.'

'Have you eaten?'

'On its way. As soon as I have, I change these clothes.'

In the kitchen, Peter sucked his finger and struggled with the cheese knife in one hand.

Giffard puffed as he took off his spurs.

'Well, do you know any more than I do?'

'I doubt it,' said Fitzosbern. 'Harold of Wessex was shipwrecked in the mouth of the Somme, and Guy of Ponthieu has him.'

'Was nobody with him? I presume he did not cross the Channel by himself.'

Fitzosbern made allowances for Walter's hunger and bad temper.

'There was no military force, if that is what you mean. A few retainers, and the crew of the ship obviously. Oh – and some dogs and falcons. At least, that is what the boy says.'

'What boy?'

'The boy who brought us the news. Apparently he escaped when Guy's men captured Harold. Came straight to Rouen.'

'Why should we believe a frightened Saxon refugee?'

'Because Guy's couriers arrived at the same time with the same message, and Guy's demands.'

'Ransom?'

'Yes. Which William has ignored. He has told Guy to deliver Harold to the frontier at Eu. He has gone to meet him.'

'Why has Harold come? And why Ponthieu?'

'That is one of the things we are summoned to discuss.'

Giffard shook his head in amazement.

'The nerve of the man! Do you suppose – '

The door creaked open, and Giffard stopped abruptly. They all turned and peered into the shadows at the end of the hall.

'Your food, sir,' said Peter.

Fitzosbern pointed to a table. The boy deposited his plates and poured some beer into a cup, overfilling it. A drop of blood from his cut finger fell in. He glanced up quickly to see if Sir Walter had noticed.

'There is bread, sir, cheese, and a piece of cold pork. We have some onion stew if you wish, but Gerard says – '

Giffard waved a hand.

'Just leave us. Pull the curtain and shut the door,' he shouted after him.

Giffard began filling his mouth.

'Starving. Hardly a bite since dawn.'

He listened while Fitzosbern and Montgomery talked.

'Do you suppose that Guy is cooking something up with Harold?' said Montgomery.

'Or that Harold is cooking something up with Guy – more like it. Guy would not have the brains.'

'And Harold brought the dogs and falcons as presents? Feasible, I suppose.'

'But unlikely,' said Fitzosbern. 'What could Harold possibly gain from an intrigue with a border bandit like Ponthieu? He knows William could swat Guy just like a tiresome insect.'

'Well, it is clearly not a military expedition,' said Montgomery. 'I take it that there have been no landings anywhere else on the coast?'

'None that I am aware of.'

'No warships sighted standing off the shore?'

'No. Edward would have no motive for attacking Normandy; he has promised the crown to William. As for Harold, what possible reason could he have for attacking Normandy before he secures the crown of England? It would be lunacy.'

There was silence for a while, broken at last by Giffard, still with his mouth full.

'He is hardly here on a pleasure trip. You say there is no plot and no raid. So – why?'

'To see William, presumably.'

Giffard waved a chunk of cheese in the air.

'Then why go to Ponthieu? Why not come straight here?'

'There was a storm, Walter, remember? Harold was simply blown off course.'

Montgomery frowned as he pursued a line of his own.

'Why would Harold come?'

'To see William – I just said.'

'No, no. Listen. Harold wants the crown – we agree? He must do. No man in his position, with the King childless, and his family owning over half England, could wish otherwise. We also know that the Confessor promised it to our own Duke. At least, that is what the Bastard has always told us.'

'Get to the point, Roger.'

'My point is this: why would the Saxon claimant to the throne come here and put himself completely at the mercy of the Norman one?'

'Perhaps the King sent him,' said Giffard.

'Why?'

Giffard shrugged.

'Well – um – perhaps he feels his age and wants the two claimants to be at peace before he dies. You know – rule a peaceful kingdom and leave a peaceful kingdom.'

Fitzosbern shook his head.

'Unlikely. Edward is not an old man, and was in good health the last I heard. Do not be fooled by all this gossip about his holiness. I happen to know that he puts as many hours into the chase as any of us.'

Giffard was reluctant to give up.

'Suppose Edward sent Harold to make a formal offer of the crown? What better man could there be? One claimant offering it to the other. It would end all the argument.'

It was Montgomery's turn to disagree.

'No. The King does not have the authority; Harold and his brothers are too powerful. He would never dare to order him.'

'Perhaps he came willingly.'

'If you were Harold, would you go on an errand like that?'

Giffard drained his cup and stood it noisily on the table.

'So here we are – going round in circles, when we really have no idea of what the man is up to. I am going to change these clothes.'

'No – just a minute, Walter.'

Fitzosbern put up a hand. Giffard sighed, but sat down again.

'You agree,' said Fitzosbern, leaning forward, 'that there seems no reason in politics that would induce Harold to come?'

'No good reason, no.'

Fitzosbern sat back to give emphasis to his suggestion.

'Suppose the reason did not lie with politics at all.'

Giffard looked blank.

'Where then?'

'With the family.'

'The what?'

'The family. Harold's family.'

Giffard stared in bafflement. Montgomery slapped his knee.

'Of course! The Saxon hostage. Wulfnoth!'

Giffard now stared at his friend as well.

'Ridiculous! That boy was sent here twelve years ago as a pledge of Saxon good faith. It is a proof of the promise to the Bastard. A guarantee of Godwin's word.'

'Godwin is dead.'

'Harold's word then.'

'Harold wants the crown.'

'All the more reason to hang on to Wulfnoth. It would be madness to let him go.'

'I do not say William would let him go,' said Fitzosbern. 'I said only that Harold might be coming to ask for him.'

'No. Not in all logic.'

'Families are not logical things, Walter. Look at Godwin's brood. Sweyn, I agree, was a bad lot. He is dead. Tostig is not much better; I hear that he is a poor Earl of Northumbria. But the other two – Gyrth and Leofwine – are devoted to Harold. They are all three very close. Their mother is still alive too. For all we know, Wulfnoth may share this bond. Baby of the family and all.

'Another thing you must remember – these Saxons are not like us. They are dreamers, romantics; they act on impulse.'

'But even if you are right, Fitz, Harold must know that the Duke will never let him go. So why come?'

Fitzosbern nodded as if he had expected it.

'Just so. I will tell you why. You forget that Harold has a reputation for charm. That is one of his great strengths, but it is also a source of weakness. One thing that never crosses the mind of a charming man is that his charm might not work. We know William is proof against it, but Harold naturally relies on it.'

'So you are saying,' said Giffard, 'that Harold has risked his neck, and his chance of the crown, simply in order to collect his baby brother?'

Fitzosbern shrugged.

'Possible.'

Giffard stood up.

'Well, now I have heard everything. I leave you to your fortune-telling, because that is about all it is.'

He collected his spurs and made for the door. He paused by the curtain.

'Oh – how about this for a good reason? Harold was going hunting, and decided to take his animals for a sea voyage instead just for fun, and all of a sudden a storm came up and blew him all the way across the Channel – dogs, birds, and all.'

Chuckling in harsh irony at his own joke, he pulled open the door and flung one last shaft.

'Let me know when Geoffrey gets here from Coutances. I can not wait to hear the latest divinations from a prince of the Church.'

* * * * * *

'Wulf, you must stop this.'

Wulfnoth flung a piece of rotten stick into the water.

'Is it my fault Harold is coming?'

'I am the one who should be miserable,' said Arlette.

Wulfnoth turned in genuine surprise.

'Why?'

'Because Harold may be taking you home.'

Wulfnoth laughed bitterly.

'William will never let me go – not until he gets the crown. And Harold will never charm him.'

'But at least you are going to see him – your brother. You love him.'

Wulfnoth tossed his head in anguish.

'But what am I to do? I have become half Norman. Harold will think I have betrayed my family and my country. If I try to throw off everything I have learnt here, the Duke will think me ungrateful.'

'You admire him.'

Wulfnoth nodded, if unwillingly.

'Yes. He is fearless, and he gets things done. And he has no favourites. I like that. But what is the use?'

Arlette smiled.

'I think he likes you.'

'Hah!'

'Not in the way Harold does, maybe. But his Grace is not Harold. He has not taught you to swim or taken you fishing. But he has had you with him everywhere – expeditions, battles, sieges. You know the men close to him. You sit at his council table.'

'I am not allowed to say anything.'

'You are allowed to listen. He has given you every chance to learn. I tell you, he has watched over you like any father. You could not have asked for better care. I said – he likes you.'

'He likes you, you mean.'

Arlette smiled coyly.

'That is silly.'

'I can see.'

'You mean you are jealous?'

'No, no.'

'Oh,' said Arlette, disappointed.

'Your name, I expect. The same as his mother's.'

'Wulf!'

'Now what have I said?'

Arlette sighed.

'Never mind.'

'You should be flattered,' said Wulfnoth, not seeing the signs. 'Arlette of Falaise. She was pretty, she had character, and she was courted by a duke.'

'And she had a bastard child!'

'What of it? Harold has a whole family of bastards, and he loves their mother.'

Arlette began to get up.

'Wulfnoth of Wessex, you are impossible. It is the women who bear the bastards, and it is the men who say that there is nothing to make a fuss about.'

'It has not stopped the Duke.'

Arlette stayed long enough to get the last word.

'You will simply not be helped. You love Harold, and will not admit it. You love William, and will not admit it. They both love you, and you will not admit that. Why will men never admit to loving or being loved? And as for women, they are good for bearing bastards, and that is nothing to make a fuss about. Stay with your beastly fish!'

'Arlette!'

Wulfnoth called after her again, but she did not come back.

He sighed, sat down, and cast his line again. His tongue poked out ...

He felt more like a fish than a fisherman – flashing towards whatever bait shimmered before him. The Duke held out a new life, a new career, and he ran to be his shadow. Arlette shone her eyes at him, and he was after her like a young stag. Now Harold came out of the past, radiating memories like a midsummer dawn even before he had arrived – fishing, swimming, brothers' arms round shoulders, a mother's hand on his head – turning in an instant the busy years of exile into a desert. He wanted all three, and he was denied all three.

He twitched the line. Come to think of it, the fish was better off than he was. At least the fish got caught, or it escaped. Either way, it knew its fate. His destiny was to chase, always to chase, and never to know if he would attain his goal, or even whether he was chasing in the right direction.

What was it Gerard said about 'seizing life'? Fat chance!

* * * * * *

'Greetings, my lord bishop. I am overjoyed to see that you have been able to leave your sick bed.'

Geoffrey de Montbrai, Bishop of Coutances, bowed low, a trifle too low.

Bishop Odo of Bayeux, looking like death, had not the strength to return the sarcasm. Even his spots were pale.

After a perfunctory nod, he sat down with relief, near the head of the table. Though half-brother of the Duke, he automatically left the top place to Sir William Fitzosbern, the Duke's right hand.

Geoffrey smiled quietly to himself as he sat opposite. He knew that it was not the arrival of Harold that had dragged Odo from his sick bed and his privy bucket. It was his own presence. Odo had been looking forward to a church council without his rival of Coutances; now that his brother had summoned a full meeting of his chief military advisers, it was imperative that he came to see what Geoffrey might be getting up to.

The curtain was drawn back, and the scullion Peter in his high treble announced, 'Sir William Fitzosbern.'

The table servants paused and gaped.

Fitzosbern came forward.

'Good morning, Odo. Oh – good morning, Geoffrey. I heard you arrived late last night. Good journey?'

Geoffrey nodded.

'Standing on ceremony, Fitz? Announcements and all?'

'Formality is a good thing, in the right place and at the right time.'

'I agree,' said Geoffrey. 'Kiss the ring.'

Fitzosbern bent and did so. Odo, flushing slightly, thrust out his hand.

'And mine!'

Fitzosbern barely touched it. Odo flushed again.

Sir Roger of Montgomery and Sir Walter Giffard smirked at each other.

'To business,' said Fitzosbern, taking the chair.

He watched in silence while the servants completed the furnishing of the table, then dismissed them. The dogs were roused from their warm straw beside the fire and driven out. A sentry was stationed outside.

'No clerks?' said Montgomery, gesturing to an empty side table.

Fitzosbern shook his head.

'This is highly sensitive, and unofficial. Not to be recorded.'

'You mean we can speak our minds?' said Giffard.

'Yes.'

'Good,' said Giffard. 'When are you going to dismiss those Flemings? If they come back from Eu, I shall have them looting round Longueville again. I tell you, Fitz – '

Fitzosbern raised a placatory hand.

'All in good time, Walter. Let us remember the occasion of this meeting. We are summoned to offer advice to his Grace. It must be ready by the time he returns from Eu. The Flemings will have to wait. This latest news has driven Flemings, Brittany, the council, his family, everything out of his head.'

Giffard snorted.

'How can we do that? We have no idea why Harold is here. How can we formulate plans to deal with an enemy until we know what his intentions are?'

'We know what his intentions are in general terms,' said Montgomery.

'Yes,' said Giffard. 'The crown. The world knows. The Bastard has not called us here to repeat it, surely. When the time comes, we fight, and that is that.'

'My lords,' said Fitzosbern, 'let us examine the dimensions of this problem before we get trapped into glib solutions.'

He poured himself a drink while he collected his thoughts. Such was his reputation for cool and clear thinking that not a word was uttered.

He wiped his lips, picked up a knife, and began to trace idle patterns on the wood of the trestle boards.

'The situation, as I see it, is this: there is a competition going on, and the prize for the winner is the crown of England. There are at present four competitors.'

'Four?' said Giffard, impulsive as ever. 'How do you make that?'

Fitzosbern looked patiently at him.

'Our own Duke – one. Earl Harold of Wessex, our unexpected guest – two. King Harald of Norway – three. Edgar the Atheling – four.'

'What are you trying to do – make difficulties?'

'Be patient, Walter,' said Montgomery. 'Let Fitz finish.'

Fitzosbern continued in his measured way.

'It is a wise precaution to know the number and strength of one's rivals. I am merely summarising the forces against us. We should look foolish indeed if we were to fail through simple underestimation of the competition. Now – each of these four has his own peculiar advantages.'

He numbered them off on his fingers with the point of the knife as he spoke.

'Our own Duke. William has Normandy, the best-governed province in France. He has his own military prowess and reputation. He has us; and we can put into the field some of the finest heavy cavalry in Christendom.'

He left their own ambitions eloquently unspoken.

'Best of all,' he continued, 'he has Edward's promise. He is the officially designated heir.'

He tapped his second finger with the knife.

'Now Harold. Harold is also a proven soldier and a fine leader. He and his brothers already hold most of England between them. Tostig in Northumbria, Leofwine in Kent, Gyrth in East Anglia, Harold himself in Wessex.'

'I should not count on Tostig's loyalty,' remarked Odo.

Fitzosbern dealt easily with the objection.

'I am concerned with the present, not the possible future. Tostig, I repeat, holds Northumbria. The family has its grip everywhere. Their sister is married to the King himself. Edward is a Saxon; England is Saxon; Harold is a Saxon. He keeps near-regal state already. He is ambitious, he looks the part, and he is popular. If ever there is a natural king of England, it is Harold.'

'And we have him!'

'Be silent, Walter!'

Fitzosbern tapped his third finger.

'Competitor number three – Harald of Norway, King Harald Hardrada, the Stern Ruler. Another warrior, with a legendary reputation, which our own Duke would not grudge him. A giant by all accounts, with a string of military exploits to his credit that would be the envy of any Viking alive or dead. His dream is to re-create the empire of Canute. Frankly, I should not put it beyond him.'

'Norway is a long way from England,' observed Montgomery.

'The sea has never deterred a Viking yet. They are the best boat-builders in the world. They know far more about seaborne invasions than we do, may I point out. Crossing the North Sea would be like jumping a ditch to them. Remember too there are Viking settlements all round Britain from Ireland to the Danelaw. Danish kings ruled for nearly thirty years. Scandinavian roots go deep there. How deep do Norman roots go? Ten years, till Godwin kicked us out.'

Nobody saw fit to argue, though they growled at the memory of the disgrace.

'Your fourth,' prompted Geoffrey.

'Edgar the Atheling. A mere boy. His family spent a generation in exile. But because the King is childless – and, from what we hear, likely to remain so – this little sprig on a distant branch of the family tree is brought from the cold of exile into the unfamiliar warmth of the court. His father died in mysterious circumstances, but the boy lives. Suppose he survives – what is his strength?' He pointed with the knife. Legitimacy! He is the closest male relative. By all custom, habit, and tradition, he is the rightful heir. The blood of Cerdic runs in his veins.'

He laid the knife carefully on the boards in front of him, and sat back.

'Four competitors – one who will claim by virtue of nomination, one by popular acclaim, one by conquest, and one by blood.'

'That Edgar is a boy,' said Giffard. 'He counts for nothing.'

To his surprise, Fitzosbern agreed with him.

'Just so. And that brings me to the disadvantages. The boy, as Walter says, has youth against him.'

'My brother became Duke at the age of seven, and survived,' said Odo.

'The Duke was well served, and he was extremely lucky. We do not know whether Edgar has either of these benefits. Nor do we know whether he will show the Duke's military qualities as he grows up. All we know is that his father's death has never been fully explained, which indicates that he may have had more enemies than friends.'

Geoffrey smiled. Fitzosbern had slipped through the net of a possible argument against Odo with his usual skill.

'What about Norway?' said Montgomery.

'I fancy that Hardrada's skills may lie with conquest rather than with government. He can take England, but can he hold it? Vikings find the arts of administration too humdrum for their taste.'

'Canute did not,' said someone.

'Canute was the exception that proves the rule,' countered Fitzosbern. 'Look at his two sons – awful.'

'And the other Harold?'

'Harold of Wessex,' said Fitzosbern, 'is not a blood relative, and the King is most unwillingly married to his sister. He has not been designated. Will the Saxons tolerate the crown going outside the royal family, outside the line of Cerdic? Harold has nothing to promote him except obviousness. He is the obvious next king.'

'Not my brother?' said Odo, prickly again.

'Think, my lord,' said Geoffrey. 'If you were a Saxon, and Edward died tomorrow, whom would you have as king?'

Odo sniffed. Fitzosbern interposed smoothly.

'Which brings me to our Duke. He has the skill to mount an invasion, and possibly the resources, and between us we have the will and the experience to run another country besides this one. But how will the English take to a Norman king? We shall not conquer with a single battle. It could be a long and bitter campaign. Have we the resources for that? And can we guard our back here against Anjou, Brittany, the King? And now maybe Ponthieu as well.'

Everyone looked at everyone else. Then Montgomery laughed.

'Well, Fitz, in your usual careful, thorough way, you have covered all sides of the matter. I am impressed as I always am. You have balanced the problem beautifully. The trouble is, what do we do?'

'All Fitz has done is to outline the situation,' said Geoffrey. 'Now – suddenly – one of those competitors, thanks to God's inscrutable Wisdom, is in our hands. A most extraordinary piece of luck. God will, I am sure, help those who help themselves.'

Geoffrey poured himself another drink. Fitzosbern looked round the table. There was a long, long pause.

It was Giffard who broke it.

'Somebody has to say it. We are all thinking it. Kill him. If there are four people after the throne and you remove one, it becomes easier for the other three.'

'Are you suggesting we commit public murder?' said Geoffrey.

'Well – no. But I am saying that Harold's death must make the Duke's future career easier. Sheer numbers tell me that. As for the actual manner of his – er – demise, I am sure something could be arranged.'

'Oh?'

'People have had hunting accidents before. People fall ill and die before their time. Edgar's father did. And the Duke's father. Who is to say whether it is poison or rotten meat? There is no need to make a public sacrifice of him.'

Geoffrey's face set into stone.

'My lord of Bayeux and I are prelates of the Holy Church, and in this instance I am sure my lord of Bayeux is in agreement with me. To impute murder, or any association with possible murder, to us is blasphemy, and I will not have it.'

Odo nodded.

'You will retract,' he said.

'He is better to us dead than alive,' said Gifffard. 'I only said what we all were thinking.'

'You will retract,' repeated Geoffrey.

Giffard looked round the table. Fitzosbern and Montgomery kept their heads down.

'Oh, come on now.'

'Do as Geoffrey says, Walter,' said Montgomery, without lifting his eyes.

After another moment of hesitation, Giffard gave in.

'Very well – if you insist – I retract.'

Fitzosbern took a deep breath.

'Good. Let us continue.'

'Suppose we say he drowned. Nobody in England knows yet that he has been rescued.'

'Walter!'

'All right, all right. Just an idea.'

'What about ransom?' suggested Montgomery.

'No good,' said Odo. 'The English will pay.'

'Yes, but we could charge enough to cover our own invasion when it comes. How about that? A full-scale invasion with all expenses paid.'

'And Harold alive and well in England, ready to deal with it,' said Giffard.

'What does that leave us with?' said Montgomery. 'Prison? Let him rot for a few years and hope it saps his strength?'

Fitzosbern shook his head.

'I think we are approaching this problem from entirely the wrong standpoint. You have all assumed that the one thing we must prevent at any cost is Harold's return to England. I put it to you that Harold's return, on the contrary, could serve our purpose very well.'

Giffard's voice was loudest in the chorus of objection and disbelief.

Fitzosbern, who had expected it, waited with his arguments ready.

'Consider – there are four claimants. You agree?'

'Go on.'

'Not one of these claimants will stand aside for any other. Yes?'

'Go on, go on!' said Giffard.

'If we – er – were to eliminate Harold now, it will make all England hate the Normans far more bitterly than before. It will pull the whole country behind young Edgar in defence of justice and legitimacy, all Saxons against the foreign conqueror. Our task will become doubly difficult. And we shall hardly get our breath back – assuming we succeed – before we have to face Harald Hardrada from Norway. And if you were English, which would you choose – the Vikings you have absorbed before, or the Normans you loathe as murderers and foreigners? Foreigners whom you have already expelled in the last fifteen years.

'How could we hold all England – after our losses in the invasion – an England half of whose people are descended from Vikings – against a Viking army led by a man like Hardrada. Think of our numbers. Think of our lines of communication and supply.'

'What are you saying, Fitz?'

'I am saying, let Harold do our work for us. If he is in England when Edward dies, he will take the throne. That is as near a certainty as we can have. If he does not, we shall have no problem. So – he takes the throne. There may be a small legitimist group who hold out for Edgar, but that too will help us. It will split England's loyalty. Harold will not – we hope – have the undivided support of his people.'

'And then we wait to strike – is that it?' said Giffard.

'No. We wait for Norway to strike. Harold will have to march north to meet the threat. There will be a battle. While they are at each other's throats, we cross the Channel and land unopposed. Whoever wins that battle in the north will have to march south to meet us on ground of our own choosing. They will be tired and depleted after such a fight. If it is Harold of England, he will be doubly tired after the double march there and back. If it is Hardrada, he will have less knowledge of the country. Our battle, the one that really matters, will be fought on our own terms, in our own time.'

He looked round the table.

'If we keep Harold here, we shall probably have to eliminate all three claimants ourselves, and we may not have the resources to do it. If we let Harold return, he may well eliminate the others for us, or they will him. Either way we shall have only one left to deal with.'

He picked up the knife and began doodling again.

Montgomery blew.

'I should never have thought of all that in a thousand years.'

'Too clever by half,' said Giffard. 'We have him. Let us do something with him.'

Montgomery turned to the Bishop of Coutances, who had the reputation, after Lanfranc and Fitzosbern, for deepest thought.

'What do you think, Geoffrey?'

'I tend to agree with Fitz, though for different reasons. His are political; mine are moral.'

'If this Geoffrey the vassal speaking, or Geoffrey the bishop?' said Giffard.

'Walter!'

'All the suggestions we had before,' said Geoffrey, glancing at Giffard, 'were outrageous – murder, imprisonment, a contrived accident, poison – not so much because they are offensive to the Church – though they are, of course, deeply offensive – as because they put us all at fault. However you dressed it up, we should be, in the eyes of the world, and God, committing a crime against a visitor in distress. Harold really was shipwrecked, remember.'

'Who cares what the world thinks?' said Giffard.

'The Duke does, for one. And I care what God thinks, for another. I am sure I speak for my lord of Bayeux. And Lanfranc. The whole Norman church, whose princes, may I remind you, are presently assembling in this very castle for a council of reform. The Duke is a good son of the Church, and however ambitious he is, he will not listen to a plan which will put him out of favour with the Church. Look at the trouble he took to induce the Pope to recognise his own marriage.'

Giffard began to fidget. Geoffrey was more long-winded than Fitz. Must be the sermon habit.

'When the Duke invades England,' continued Geoffrey, 'he is pledged to depose Stigand from the see of Canterbury because his election was uncanonical. The Holy Father will support this worthy motive. It is a reform dear to his heart. He will not back the invasion of England by a brigand who murders foreign princes at will – foreign princes whom he has offered to entertain as guests.'

'What are you saying, then, Geoffrey?' asked Montgomery, anxious to head off another interruption from his friend.

'I am saying what Fitz says: let him go. But force him into error – moral error – before you do. An enemy's place is in the wrong.'

'What do you suggest?'

'Between us we should be able to think of something.'

Giffard's patience gave out again.

'This is ridiculous. All this talk, and we are going to hand him back. The biggest fish we are ever likely to catch, and we are going to throw him back into the water.'

'I said nothing about letting him go straight away,' said Geoffrey.

'What is the difference?'

'Time, Walter. That is the difference. Watch and wait. However long we hold him, the initiative is ours.'

'I agree,' said Fitzosbern. 'One can not create opportunities; one must simply be quick to use them.'

Giffard threw up his hands in despair.

Odo leaned forward.

'So the advice we give my brother is – no advice.'

'No,' said Fitzosbern. 'The advice we give his Grace is very hard, well-considered advice – to do nothing at the present.'

Giffard swore under his breath. He had left his prized Arab stallions to come all this way in the rain – for what? To tell the Bastard to do nothing. That fat monk pottering about on his donkey could have done it just as easily.

* * * * * *

'Gerard, men are rotten!'

Adele stirred the huge pot that hung eternally over one of the fires in the great castle kitchen.

Gerard glanced at the ample hips, the glowing flesh on neck and arms, the flash of soft calf as she stretched over the embers. Small wonder that men were liable to decay when so much ripe fruit fell against them. What a good thing he was married. Still, even his watchful seamstress of a wife could not stop him thinking.

'Men are not made of stone, girl.'

'Then they should not nibble at the fruit if they are not prepared to carry it away and nurture it.'

'When such delights are placed at the front of the stall, it usually means that there is something on offer.'

'Yes,' said Adele. 'For a price.'

'Your price is too high.'

Especially when the price was considerably lower not so long ago.

'I am fussy about my clients.'

'You aim too high as well – an ambitious Norman knight and the brother of an English earl. If you play for high stakes, you must be prepared for big losses. In pride, if in nothing else.'

Adele took out the ladle, and scooped some soup from the inside of it with a finger.

'Somebody has to do something. Look at my father.'

She nearly spat out the soup in her contempt, but it tasted too nice.

'On his knees to every bishop who shows his face, and now on his knees in the chapel by the hour.'

'A person can only use what the Almighty has given them. Your father uses knees for praying on; you lie back and offer to raise them. I blame neither of you.'

Adele hung the ladle from a great iron hook beside the trivet.

'Gerard – you are a typical man.'

Gerard loosed his great booming laugh.

'Be practical, girl.'

Adele glared, but sat down.

'Well?'

'You are in too much of a hurry. You have condemned your father to limbo when the Duke has not yet dismissed him.'

'But the council?'

Gerard waved a ham of a hand.

'That council will never sit until the Duke has dealt with Harold. Your father has time. Time. And so have you.'

'Time for what?'

'For thought. You are rushing into the church square without studying the market first. Select your customer. Find someone who is more likely to buy. Someone with a gap in his cupboard. Make him come after you.' He grinned. 'It should not be difficult.'

'I might get somebody awful.'

'I did not say scrape the barrel. But you are after something very definite. If you wish to succeed, you must leave aside all dreams and girlish fancies. Ask yourself honestly – do you want passion and aching thighs and an empty hearth from a greedy lover, or boredom and warm straw and a meal on the table from a faithful husband?'

Adele put her hands on her knees and stood up.

'I might have guessed I should get no sympathy or comfort from you.'

'No. But you get the truth – much more valuable.'

Adele paused at the door.

'I could always try the lady Matilda. That little priss Arlette is hopeless with the children. You could put in a word for me. She listens to you.'

Gerard laughed again.

'Over Arlette's dead body. Think what you have just done to her.'

Adele was forced to smile.

'Yes – I forgot that. Milk and water ninny.'

Gerard punched the air.

'Much better. You are yourself again. Now stop thinking about the future. You have no control over it. And think about the present. You *can* do something about that. Go away and – and – ooohh – do somebody a favour. Anything. Anybody.'

'Such as?'

Gerard waved his crutch.

'I have no idea. That young Saxon – he is lonely and frightened. Missing his hounds. Be nice to *him*.'

Adele laughed.

'That dog-boy? He is quaint. Besides, he is English.'

'So was Wulfnoth.'

* * * * * *

Chapter Five

The Waiting

'What is your word?'

William glanced round the table in his usual urgent way, as if he had a mere minute to spare. He had come straight from the stables, without taking off his gloves.

Sir William Fitzosbern alone was impassive. The others showed signs of having been wrenched from table, bed, chessboard, or pew.

Sir Walter Giffard was already suffering from wind, after bolting his meal. God's Face – it was always a feast or a famine with this man. One minute you were breaking your leave and rushing from your home to give urgent advice; the next you were left cooling your heels for days while he went to welcome the Saxon earl. Now, here he was again, out of the blue, ahead of time as usual, demanding instant action.

Sir Roger of Montgomery sighed. It was typical of the Bastard to catch them on one foot. Everyone had expected him to arrive in company with Harold, and here he was alone, leaving the Saxon to dawdle on the road with his escort of garrison troops and unwilling Flemings.

'He is quite happy,' said the Duke. 'Says he is content to see what he can of Normandy. Well, let him.'

Montgomery shrugged. If that was true, Harold was showing remarkable coolness for someone who had been shipwrecked, arrested, and handed over as virtual prisoner. What was more surprising, William was showing unusual patience too; he was, apparently, happy for the man to wander round the duchy and feed his eyes. Either negligent, or supremely confident. Knowing what he did of the Bastard, Montgomery inclined to the latter view. But what was he up to?

Montgomery shrugged again. Problems like this were best left to experts in human behaviour like Geoffrey de Montbrai, or deep thinkers like Fitzosbern.

Geoffrey still wore his episcopal robes. He had been dragged from a mass, told to leave the rest of the service to the duke's chaplain – that fat, sweaty creature who seemed in a permanent state of nerves.

Fitzosbern glanced at the young man by the Duke's elbow. Now why had he brought the Saxon hostage with him? To reassure him that no harm was intended to his brother? Because he often included him in council meetings, and to exclude him now would be to raise his suspicions? Was it William's way of saying that the game must not be allowed to break cover just yet? Fitzosbern was not sure.

He toyed with his knife again, making patterns on the table top. If the Duke wanted careful phrasing, he could provide it. Before he could open his mouth, Sir Walter Giffard jumped in.

'May I ask, my lord, if this is diplomatic?'

'What?' said William, deliberately letting him fumble.

Giffard tried again. He half nodded in Wulfnoth's direction.

'Well, my lord, under the present circumstances … '

William let him stew, while he fidgeted himself into a more comfortable position.

'It will not hurt him to listen to your advice. He has heard it before. He has no means of knowing whether I shall take it. Neither have you.'

'My lord.'

Giffard flushed, and edged to one side to make room for Wulfnoth, without looking at him.

Geoffrey and Montgomery both looked at Fitzosbern, who took the cue. He placed the knife carefully in front of himself, and stood up. He gazed directly at the Duke, speaking as if William were totally alone.

'I speak for us all, my lord. We have deliberated long and carefully, as you instructed. The Earl Harold is a guest, a foreign prince, who has fallen in among us by – by – mischance. It is incumbent upon every prince and vassal to offer such a distinguished visitor, by whatever means he should come, courtesy as befits his rank and hospitality as dictated by christian duty. This duty we should perform as long as – as – long as seems fitting. No doubt he, being a true knight, will afford us some sign of his – um – gratitude before he – before we make the necessary arrangements for his return.'

He sat down.

'Is that all?' said the Duke.

Fitzosbern half rose again.

'That is all, my lord.'

The Duke's eyes flashed to every face round the table. Not a flicker of emotion met him. He stood up.

'Very well. You will hold yourselves available to meet the Earl Harold when he arrives. The formalities will be the responsibility of my under-chamberlain. See to it, Wulf.'

Wulfnoth had barely time to gasp in surprise before William had turned and left. After a glance of bafflement at the members of the council, Wulfnoth hurried after him.

Giffard stood up and began pacing.

'Now where does that get us? Are we simply to play host and guest? Is that why we are all here?'

'It is the game the Bastard wants to play,' said Geoffrey, 'so we have little choice.'

'It is the game that Harold seems to be enjoying,' said Montgomery. 'Dawdling on the road like that. He must know what sort of stir he is causing.'

Fitzosbern smiled.

'Let him think so. Let him think he has the initiative.'

Giffard snorted.

'As far as I can see, the man *has* the initiative. Shipwreck, prison, handed over like a prize pig in a market, and he has not turned a hair. And all we have done is rush about like headless chickens.'

'Well, now we sit still,' said Geoffrey.

Giffard turned towards him.

'Yes, for what? I tell you again, we are being too clever by half. What are we going to do with the man?'

* * * * * *

'I tell you, Gerard, there is no pleasing him. I almost live on the roads between Coutances and Rouen, and whatever news I bring puts him in a bad mood. He paces and pouts, and tears his hair.'

Thierry reached for another pasty. Gerard refilled the cups. Thierry had earned it.

Half an hour in the kitchen on an empty stomach, and lord Geoffrey's courier had spilled enough news to satisfy a dozen gossips. Gerard had wisely deduced that the best way to get information out of this portly ex-peasant from the Cotentin was to keep his food back. Once he had a tight belt, his talk became more and more diffuse, rambling, and irrelevant.

The real bite in Thierry's news had come in the first few minutes, as he pulled off his gloves and gazed hopefully at the great pot over the fire.

'Brittany. Count Conan is in the field again.'

'Where?' prompted Gerard.

'Dol this time. He has decided to move against the rebels there.'

'Why do it now? Everyone knows that Norman men and money have been trickling in there for months.'

'Show of strength. He thinks the Bastard has gone to ground; no more funds for a campaign.'

'Listening to Viking merchants again?'

'Yes. You know those salt-crusted villains. Swindle a widow of a shoe. Think little and talk much.'

'So Conan wants to clear out the nest of rebels at Dol?'

'Something like that. Show the world that the Normans are behind it. Tweak the Bastard's nose. He is talking loud about crossing the Couesnon.'

Gerard raised his eyebrows in mild surprise.

'Big ideas.'

Thierry glanced towards Peter turning the spit.

'It will not amount to much. Some looting and burning. He will run when anyone comes.'

Gerard stumped across to the fire, gave Peter a clip round the ear just for the Hell of it, and cut off some slices of meat. If Thierry had already seen lord Geoffrey, his news was now known among the members of the Duke's council. What would the Bastard make of that? It would be no surprise, that was sure. Conan in the west, like Guy of Ponthieu in the north-east, rarely missed a chance to cause trouble if he thought William was at the other end of his duchy. And to be fair to him, the presence of rebels in Norman pay, in one of his own towns, must be a constant annoyance.

A few weeks ago, it would have goaded the Bastard into frantic action; he would have hectored and bullied his unwilling vassals into yet another campaign: 'Splendour of God, what did I tell you? Conan must be crushed once and for all, whatever the cost.'

Now, of course, he had another bee buzzing round his nose, from Wessex. And this bee was much more full of honey – not a pocket-breaking invasion of a wet duchy at the end of the world beside the Great Sea, but the prospect of a step nearer the greatest prize of all – the crown of England. Would a dozen Conans divert him from that course?

Thierry almost wept with pleasure and relief as he contemplated the plateful placed before him.

'By the Rood, Gerard, if you knew how long it has been.'

The rest of the talk came between mouthfuls, but Gerard was content that the real fat of the news was now out and in the pan.

'That bishop of mine ... restless like a bug ... dying to go home to Coutances ... furious when the news comes about Harold ... now he is furious because nothing is happening.'

'They are all waiting for Harold to arrive.'

'Yes. He is furious because he is bored. I thought he might be pleased with some real events. But no! Do you know what he said? "That is all we need." Just what he said. "That is all we need." I thought they would rejoice to have something to take the Bastard's mind off Harold for one minute.'

'No pleasing some people,' said Gerard.

Thierry almost choked in his eagerness to agree.

'Just what I say. Mind you, I know what he will do.'

Gerard frowned. Perhaps there was one more titbit of real news to come after all.

'Oh?'

'Oh, yes,' said Thierry, burping. 'He will go and see the lady Sybil. Always does when things get too much. And he is here, in Rouen. A stone's throw from St. Amand. Every man is human ... even lord Geoffrey.'

'Ah,' said Gerard.

Thierry wiped his mouth.

'Would there be another pasty, do you think? They are so good.'

* * * * * *

Adele punched the dough.

God alive! Was there nothing of interest in this midden of a castle? If she heard one more word about the great Earl Harold, she would go mad. Men and women alike could talk of only one thing. Soldiers told stories about his campaigns in Wales – wherever that was. Hard enough to say the word, never mind get interested in details of ambushes and chases through mountain gullies.

'A great captain, they say. His men adore him. Go through fire for him.'

The women gossiped about ... what they always gossiped about.

'A face and a body to make you go weak at the knees. Look at his baby brother. And he is only a cub.'

'He keeps near-royal state in Chichester. Edward is jealous.'

'Have you heard of his mistress – Edith of the Swan Neck? Now there is a grand passion for you. Five children, and they still rush to get into bed.'

Adele lifted the dough and slammed it on to the board again.

Nobody wanted to talk about anything – well, interesting. Even Gerard had no conversation.

'Your trouble, girl, is that every able-bodied man in the castle is away.'

Gerard was right, as usual – damn him. A third of the garrison was at Eu, waiting to escort Harold. Harold again! Another third was at home. The Bastard, having despaired of another immediate campaign against Brittany, had sent them on leave while things were quiet. It was their.due. When the news about Harold's shipwreck had arrived, William had sent the remaining third as couriers to summon every senior vassal to Rouen.

Nigel was away at le Tréport, repairing a ship – Harold's ship! Nigel was a tease and a nuisance, but he was company. At times he was fun. Rough, perhaps, and, like all men, thought he was a great lover. He was teachable, though. And – she had to admit – she usually felt better afterwards.

What was there left? A hall full of bishops and their pinch-faced clerks.

Adele left the board and walked round the room. For the life of her, she could not bring herself to finish the baking. She picked up half a dozen things that needed her attention in a busy kitchen, and immediately put them down again. She went to the door and gazed up at the weather. It was overcast – no excuse to go out in search of she did not know what.

Her father was usually home by this time. Sharp words from him would at least have relieved the silence. Given her something to think about. The stupid fool was probably still on his knees. A lot of good that would do him. God helped those who helped themselves. That was what Gerard said. 'Do something.'

In God's Name, what? She sat down, and pressed her hands into her lap. In God's name, what?

'Be nice to the Saxon boy.'

All very well for Gerard to offer advice. Well, she had tried that. And she was right – he was quaint.

He had made her laugh though. His accent was funny. When he saw her laughing, he had laughed too. She found herself laughing with him, no longer at him. He looked as if he had not laughed for a long time. Grateful – that was it.

Without thinking, she had flirted with him.

'Your hair is a lovely colour. So fine.'

He blushed at first, then returned the compliment.

'You are ... very pretty. Very pretty.'

Adele was so adept at flirting that she could almost blush to order. She did so.

When Edwin, becoming bolder, had moved to put an arm round her waist, she had slapped his face.

But before they parted company, they had laughed again, at a trifle.

Adele returned to the table, and picked up the dough. She turned it over and began kneading. Edwin was quaint, but he was different. Whenever Nigel left her, she had no wish to see him again for a while.

She threw down the dough once more. What was she to do? Was all this – this unease because the future hung over her like one of those storm clouds outside? God knows, she had tried, she really had.

What about the lady Matilda? Had that bitch Arlette really made it impossible to approach?

Adele's eyes narrowed as she sank her fingers once more.

There ought to be a way of getting back at her.

* * * * * *

'Now there is a man for you, Rollo.'

For the tenth time on the trip, Hubert shared his thoughts about the Saxon earl.

'You would have thought *he* was in charge of the party, not Count Guy. Did you see his clothes? God knows, the Duke was dressed to kill, but he did not eclipse Harold.

'Did you see his horse? The finest in the whole assembly, Duke and all. Spurs! Hawks! He must have had Guy eating out of his hand. I tell you, Rollo, nothing can outface that man.

'You would have thought he was an ambassador from the Emperor himself. And charm! Before they had gone a hundred paces together, he had the Duke talking like an eager squire. I would not have believed it had I not seen it with my own eyes. I am sure you liked it too, Rollo. It was a great sight – one to remember.'

Hubert chuckled.

'You should have seen Father Abbot's long face.'

Hubert had leave to travel between le Tréport and Longueville, but he knew that he had been stretching his abbot's patience with his travels to Rouen and Eu and Flanders ...

'Do not take advantage of your privileges, brother Hubert. Our house is new and undermanned, and the liberties you have been granted can be easily revoked if you abuse them.'

Hubert bowed in penitence, and lowered his eyes to hide the mischief.

'I value the trust you place in me, Father Abbot. I shall be diligent in attending to my duties.'

'And only your duties,' warned Father Abbot. 'Take care. I am in the process of writing a letter to my lord Lanfranc of Caen.'

'I could carry it for you to Rouen, Father Abbot. My lord Lanfranc is there for the council. It is scarcely out of my way.'

Father Abbot gave in.

'Hubert,' he said familiarly, 'you are incorrigible.'

Hubert bowed again, lower.

'Oh, I do hope not, Father Abbot. Surely God can work a small miracle.'

'I am sure he can, my son. I suppose we had better give Him the time to do so while you are on the road to the Duke's castle ... "

Hubert smiled. A good father to his flock, my lord Abbot. Understood men. Men of the world too. An old dog needed a longer lead than a puppy if it was to see the virtue of training.

Brother Stephen did not mind; the longer Hubert was absent, the more he, Stephen, could delay his return to the parent house at le Tréport. Someone had to look after the Longueville manors. Stephen was human too.

So Hubert had been to Flanders, gathering gossip for Gerard, and, while he was about it, for himself. He had supped in Count Baldwin's kitchen, and was full of titbits which might be of interest even to his Grace's daughter, the lady Matilda. He had passed through Ponthieu, and learned of Earl Harold's stay at Beaurain, Count Guy's seat.

'I tell you, Rollo, the man was knee deep in tailors, shoemakers, jewellers, embroiderers. Paying on credit too. Six days out of house arrest, and they were offering him credit. Falconers were lining up to show him their birds. Count Guy is helpless, a mouthing sideshow.'

From Ponthieu, Hubert had jogged with Rollo to le Tréport, where, after wriggling out of trouble with Father Abbot, he had sneaked down to the boatyard. He had promised Edwin that he would find out how the work was proceeding. Earl Harold's captain, Aldred, and the crew were working steadily on the repairs, despite language difficulties with the local shipwrights. Hubert shared a supper with Nigel Fitzhenry, Gilbert, and the rest of the Duke's fatigue party. They were tired and bored. Nigel had been dealing with boredom in his usual way ...

'You should see the girls here, Brother.' He glanced at Hubert's habit. 'Though, come to think of it, perhaps you should not.'

Hubert twitched the tufts of eyebrow on his forehead as he looked innocent.

'As an old soldier, I understand. As a monk, I am not tempted. Continue.'

Nigel leaned closer.

'Like mating with bags of close-stacked corn. I think they must be half Fleming. They say Flemish girls are dull and damp, like the weather up there.'

'I see.'

Nigel glanced at Gilbert, who was cleaning mud from his boots. Nigel grinned and raised his voice.

'Now, if it were Adele from the castle, it would have been much more fun. Eh, lads?'

Hubert saw Gilbert go red ...

'It seems, Rollo, that our little Saxon boy may have a warm welcome if he – er – presses his suit. Poor Gilbert. Is it not so often the way, Rollo? The one who is truly smitten is the last to find out the truth?'

But it was to the Earl Harold that Hubert returned most often in his musings.

'I am sure Father Abbot would not grudge me my stay at the frontier – to see the Earl arrive. It was worth the wait. I would wager, Rollo, that Harold kept us waiting on purpose. I noticed the Bastard was impatient. But within minutes of sighting the Earl, the Bastard was shaking hands, and meaning it.' Hubert shook his head. 'And it has been the same ever since. All the way from Eu. It is not the summons of a rescued prisoner; it is a triumphal procession. What a man! Have you seen, Rollo? They turn out at the roadside, they fill every village square, they swarm over every bridge. No wonder the Bastard left him to get on with it, and went on to Rouen. Fed up with it, I should think.'

Rollo paused to nibble some grass. Hubert leaned back into the cart and tugged out a leather flask from under the canvas. He took a long swig, wiped his mouth, and looked about him.

'I fancy we shall be in Rouen tonight, Rollo – God willing. And the Earl with his train not far behind.'

He stowed the flask again, picked up the reins, and chirruped.

'And do you know what I think, Rollo? I think they will have not the faintest idea what to do with him. All their plans and schemes and plots will go for nothing. Earl Harold will be like the tide coming in.'

* * * * * *

In the event, Ralph did not enjoy going to see Gilbert at le Tréport any more than he would have enjoyed going to see his family at Gisors. Bruno did not say 'I told you so', but the expression on his face was just as eloquent. Ralph almost swore at him for something he had not said.

Gilbert was no company. Ralph found him the worse for drink ...

'That bastard Nigel ... one day I shall take a knife and spoil those pretty features ... foul-mouthed lecher.'

Ralph tried at first to bring him round with argument.

'Has Adele promised herself to you?'

Gilbert flushed, and buried his face in his cup.

'There you are then,' said Ralph. 'A hunter like Nigel only chases game that runs. Stop running.'

Gilbert swung the empty cup in the air.

'All very well for you. You are not stuck here, miles from anywhere. There is nothing here – no soldiering. Do you know what I am? I say, do you know what I am?'

Ralph glanced at Bruno, who raised his eyes Heavenwards. Gilbert stabbed the air with a finger.

'Carpenter's mate – worse than that. A hammer and nail carrier.'

'So is Nigel, I presume.'

Gilbert leaned back and made an expansive gesture.

'Great Jesus, no! Nothing like that for my lord Nigel Fitzhenry. He has made friends with the Saxon captain. They go off to the best places.'

'Jealous?' said Bruno.

Ralph saw the trap, and tried to change tack.

'Part of soldiering,' went on Bruno. 'You wanted to do it, and you must accept whatever it brings.'

Gilbert spat.

'This is not soldiering. Any serf could do what I have been doing. Any serf's brat.'

Ralph tensed himself, waiting for Bruno to say it. He did not. But he thought it – Ralph knew. 'It should come easy then.' Bruno might as well have said it. It hurt just as much.

It was unfair, of course. Gilbert was not a serf; he was the son of a respectable villein in the Cotentin, some miles from Avranches. But the ties with the village were unarguable. The very fact that Gilbert liked to style himself 'Gilbert of Avranches' – naming a distant town that he had probably visited only once or twice in his life – showed his eagerness to separate himself from his lowly beginnings.

This was Bruno's constant theme: 'No background – no staying power.' The number of times Ralph had nearly struck him.

Instead he struck Gilbert, knocking him off the stool. Gilbert stretched out a hand to retrieve his empty cup, but Ralph kicked it away.

'God's Breath! You disgust me.'

Gilbert grasped two handfuls of dirty rushes.

'I disgust myself. But what do I have left? I am no soldier; Bruno is right. I am the butt of jokes. Adele laughs at me behind my back. This – ' he waved the rushes in the air ' – this is all I am fit for. I shall go home. Or I shall go back to my dogs, back to lord Geoffrey.'

Ralph kicked him and sent him sprawling. As he turned, Bruno was ready to offer him a full bucket of water. Ralph flung it full in Gilbert's face.

Gilbert spluttered and swore. Ralph shook him by his jerkin, recoiling at the smell of stale sweat and beer.

'Think yourself lucky that is all I am doing. Now clean yourself, and find some fresh clothes; you smell like a Turkish midden. While you do that, reflect. You are as strong as Nigel. If you wish to be rid of a pest, think of a way of doing it. You are as presentable as Nigel, or you could be. If you wish to pay court to Adele, in the name of all that is holy, go back to Rouen and do so. If she says no, then forget her.'

Ralph pulled him to his feet and dumped him back on the stool. He dusted his hands.

'And reflect too on what is happening. Think who is coming to Normandy. Think of the meeting of two remarkable men. Each of them can make history. And you are here, in the middle of it. You should be on your knees to your God in thanks, not grovelling in the dirt and licking out an empty cup.'

Ralph left the tavern, glaring at Bruno as if challenging him to say anything.

Bruno said nothing until the morrow, when they were on the road again, and then only when Ralph asked a question.

'Well, did I do the right thing this time?'

'You tried.'

'Is that all? Tried?'

'You are up against a powerful force.'

'What?'

'The weight of the mud on his boots – the mud of the furrow.'

'Go to Hell.'

'I do agree with one thing you said, though.'

'Oh?'

'About Harold. He seems to be a man who can make things happen.'

* * * * * *

'Just look at that.'

Sir Walter Giffard and Sir Roger of Montgomery stood on the edge of the main outer bailey of Rouen castle, under a dripping stable doorway. They gazed at the puddles, lashed and dancing in the heavy rain.

Giffard sighed and tossed his over-gloves to a servant.

'No getting out in this.'

'The beaters are exhausted anyway,' said Montgomery. 'The Bastard has run them off their legs.'

Giffard fidgeted.

'I could be with my horses.'

Montgomery looked sidelong at him. His old friend was not the most patient of men at the best of times. He could not stand inactivity. He could not go home. He had no orders other than to sit and wait. Now he was denied even the pleasures of the chase. As far as Montgomery was concerned, a day or two of peace and quiet was not entirely unwelcome. The alternative was being back at Bellême – with Mabel. Besides, something was bound to happen sooner or later. Harold was on the road, and would soon arrive. Then we should see.

Giffard hawked and spat.

Montgomery tried to take his mind off the boredom.

'What do you think of this news then?'

'What?'

'This word that Geoffrey's man has brought from Brittany.'

'You mean Conan?'

'Yes.'

Giffard shrugged.

'May be true. What of it? It will not divert the Bastard from our Wessex earl. Even if we mounted a punishment column, Conan would be gone before we arrived. In my opinion, if the King himself invaded in force, I doubt if the Bastard would take much notice right now. He sits and waits like a cat at a hole, and we have to wait with him. God's Face!'

He spat again, and kicked a stone.

'Suppose we do something ourselves.'

'What?'

'Go and get him.'

Montgomery looked at him.

'What do you mean?'

Giffard looked steadily ahead.

'Our Wessex earl is enjoying a progress through Normandy – yes?'

'Yes.'

'Without the Bastard as guardian.'

'So?'

Giffard kicked another stone.

'Dangerous place, the open road. Anything might happen.'

Montgomery stared.

'Are you sugg – '

'People get ambushed all the time. The very devil to find the culprits. We could blame it on Guy of Ponthieu. Getting his own back.'

'Walter!'

'No, no, hear me out. Blame it on Guy of Ponthieu. The Bastard could invade Ponthieu, punish Guy, secure his northern frontier for good and all. He would be one step nearer the English throne, and we could all go home for the summer. And we should have done everyone a favour.'

Montgomery raised his eyebrows.

'Have you forgotten the small matter of Harold's escort? And maybe the Flemings as well?'

Giffard lifted his chin in disdain.

'Bribes open scabbards and close mouths.'

Montgomery shook his head.

'Walter, have some sense. The smell would rise to Heaven itself. How could the Bastard ever remove himself from it? He could swear on a hundred relics, and nobody would believe him.'

'Would he mind?'

'I should give not a fig for our chances if he found out who had done it.

Always remember: he must have a path of virtue to the throne, or it is not worth treading. How else could he attain it? Or hold it?'

Giffard looked unconvinced, so Montgomery pressed him.

'Look at the Confessor's brother. Godwin was accused of murdering him. Half England believed it. Half Normandy believed it, by the time they had finished flinging the mud. The Confessor himself believed it. Godwin swore himself blue in the face that he was innocent. Remember? At the feast? "If I am guilty of the prince Alfred's death, may this piece of bread choke me." And it choked him.'

Giffard retreated to his last ditch.

'Who would fling the mud?'

'Who would not? God knows, the Bastard has enemies enough. And with gossips like your little fat monk at Longueville bouncing round Normandy on his donkey, the Bastard would sink beneath an avalanche of mud.'

Giffard sighed again.

'Ah, well ... '

Montgomery smiled to himself. Poor Walter! How he missed his Arabs.

* * * * * *

'In this weather, sir?'

'God's Blood, man, do as you are told!'

'Very good, Sir Robert.'

The groom set about fitting saddle and bridle, smiling to himself. Young Beaumont had arrived in a bad mood, which had not improved since. Probably some imagined insult. Touchy, these spoilt sons of noblemen. Fancied themselves too. Copied their betters. Even the oath – he must have heard my lady Matilda use it, which she did often enough ...

Later, in the warmth of the hay loft, over a pot of ale, the groom gossiped with some beaters enjoying a day off.

'My guess is the Flemings told him to lose himself.'

'He has come here to tell tales to the Bastard, and the Bastard has told him to vanish too.'

'I expect he will run home to fond father. Pass the pot, Serlo ... '

Robert of Beaumont was baffled as well as annoyed.

Why was the Bastard doing nothing? Why did he not care what the Flemings were getting up to? He had hired them, after all. He would not dismiss them, and he would not pay them. That was something else with which the Flemings teased him.

'You know what you can do with your "special commission" – sir! Better still, take it back to the Bastard and ask him where our money is.'

Beaumont flushed at the mere thought.

And why was the Bastard not shepherding the Saxon earl like a broody mother hen? Having Harold at large in Normandy was like having a rogue boar running loose on a common. The man would be capable of anything.

Most baffling of all, why did the Bastard not react to the news about Conan? A few weeks ago, he could think of nothing else but Brittany. Now it all seemed to go in one ear and out the other. He just carried on with that infuriating tuneless humming of his.

There would be no campaign. There would be no orders for him to carry to the captain of the Flemings. How he would have enjoyed getting them off their backsides and away from their gaming boards.

The weather was abominable.

So – there would be no action. Nothing ...

He steered his horse at the walk through the castle gateway and acknowledged the sentry's salute. Glancing up at the leaden sky, he pulled the hood of his heavy travelling cloak over his head, and turned towards the town.

The convent of St. Amand was on the far side, beyond the archbishop's hall. Somewhere inside its walls, a young girl skipped and laughed, and waved quick hands in excited talk.

* * * * * *

'I very nearly took him on principle.'

Geoffrey of Montbrai, Bishop of Coutances, laughed at the recall of the conversation.

The lady Sybil smiled. She had smiled at meeting him again. It was always a deep, deep pleasure. Now she smiled too at his amusement, the more so for its wryness. She smiled at the memory of all the many happy thoughts and pleasantries they had shared. Above all, she smiled at the thought that, no matter what had come between them, they had always retained their capacity to take amusement at the same things.

Geoffrey had said to her once, 'I wonder if Jesus made his disciples laugh?'

Sybil had been ready with an answer: 'If they loved each other half as much as we once did, he must have done.'

Geoffrey had been bringing her up to date on castle gossip.

'This wretched man, I gather, has been badgering every bishop to take him into service. Most of them wriggled. Odo turned him down flat, of course. Said something nasty as well. Typical of Odo.'

He grunted.

'So, as I said, I nearly took the man on principle, without being asked.'

'I think you might have regretted it,' said Sybil, who was better informed on castle affairs than an under-abbess should be.

Geoffrey nodded.

'Yes. I found out just in time. I had a word with Fitz. You can always trust Fitz to put the full picture.'

'How is he?'

'Fitz? Oh, fine, fine. He is with his mother right now. Came with me.'

'Reverend Mother told me she was expecting him.'

'Is she well?'

'As well as can be expected, considering her age.'

Everyone always asked after the lady Emma's health. It was partly out of the universal respect in which her son was held, from the Duke downwards. Partly, too, because she represented a link with the bad old days of the Duke's childhood, when William, a bastard infant of eight or nine years, went in constant fear of his life from ambitious and dangerous relatives who considered they had a better claim to the ducal throne. Her husband, Osbern the Steward – Fitz's father – had been one of the Duke's guardians. When Osbern was murdered, William and Osbern's son, also christened William, had escaped by a whisker. As a security measure, the boys were split up and taken into hiding, and Osbern's widow, the lady Emma, was spirited into the convent of St. Amand at Rouen.

There she stayed, while her son William Fitzosbern – known far and wide as 'Fitz' if only to distinguish him from the Duke – helped Duke William to bring his unruly inheritance to order. By the time it was safe for her to come out, she no longer had the taste for the outside world. As a widow, there was nothing for her to do. Her son ran the family castles at Tillières and Breteuil, and had a wife and family of his own.

She rose in the convent hierarchy, and became in the end the abbess – a status for which she was well fitted by rank, by ability, by experience, and by temperament. It was a position which contented her. Her son visited her as regularly as his duties permitted; there was a strong bond between them, as between any parent and child who have been through stern adversity. Since the Duke's mother, the much-respected Arlette of Falaise, was now dead, the lady Emma became a sort of mother to the whole duchy. Everyone relished the reassurance that she was in sound health.

'Well,' said Sybil, 'are you looking forward to meeting him?'

Geoffrey shrugged.

'I suppose so. Curiosity, if nothing else.'

Sybil laughed.

'Geoffrey, if you are not curious, you must be the only such person in the whole of Rouen.'

Geoffrey looked surprised. Sybil put a hand on his arm.

'People talk of nothing else.'

'How do you know?'

Sybil laughed again.

'Because the sisters talk of nothing else. I tell you, Geoffrey, vows count for very little when such a man is involved. They are human under the habit.'

Geoffrey suddenly looked intent.

'Are you?'

Sybil hesitated.

'Me?'

'Yes. Human. I did not come here to talk about Harold. I came here to talk about us. I came here to get away from – from all that.'

He waved a hand vaguely towards the window.

Sybil shook her head.

'My dear, you may not want to talk about Harold, but you think about him. Just as you do about your cathedral.'

'That is not fair,' said Geoffrey. 'I have not mentioned my cathedral once.'

'No need to. I can see it on your face all the time. Now be honest. Look at me, and tell me you do not think about it.'

'I think about you too.'

'Maybe. But I was right: the cathedral turned out to be bigger than me, bigger than us.'

Geoffrey's dark eyes glowed with tenderness. After all the years, she looked just the same. The honest, open face, the broad brow, the high colour, the hearty laugh, the gentleness in the eyes.

'There is hardly a day when you are absent from my thoughts. And with you comes – '

Sybil put up a hand as if to ward off a blow.

'No,' said Geoffrey, 'I will say it. Of Raoul.'

'Raoul is dead. Raoul – '

For a moment neither could speak. Then Geoffrey leaned forward and took Sybil's hand.

'Son or no son, *we* are not dead. Do you think I enjoy the endless travel, living in a saddle, the campaigns, the sieges, the councils? And when I return to Coutances, the building, the courts, the markets, the endless demands on the time of a lord. When that is over, can I rest? As a priest and as a bishop, never. How often do I lie awake, too tired for sleep, and think of the early days – when I was a young knight, and we were spoken for.'

'Not by my mother,' said Sybil.

'You know what I mean,' said Geoffrey. 'We knew – we knew.'

Tears appeared in Sybil's eyes, but she withdrew her hand.

'Oh, my dearest Geoffrey, I hear you, and I know you mean what you say. Now. But you are tired. I can see it in your face. When you are tired, you yearn for rest. And I represent rest, because I represent harmony for you.'

Geoffrey moved to interrupt, but she forestalled him.

'No, no, hear me. I know you love me; there is no need to say or cite examples. I know you speak honestly when you tell me. Now tell me this honestly. If Harold had arrived yesterday, would you be here today?'

Geoffrey lowered his head.

'And supposing something happens to Harold.'

Geoffrey looked up sharply.

'Impossible. We are pledged to – '

'All right, all right. So Harold is safe. But supposing he has come to offer the crown to William. And supposing King Edward dies, and William goes to claim his inheritance, will you then turn your back on the new kingdom and return to me at St. Amand?'

'Harold will make no such offer.'

Sybil was ready for him again.

'Very well. Suppose Edward dies and Harold seizes the throne. William will invade England. Will you then refuse to join him because you must return to an under-abbess at Rouen?'

Geoffrey lifted his shoulders in a colossal sigh.

'I can think of nothing to say by way of answer.'

'That,' said Sybil, 'is my very answer. It always has been. When they placed the mitre on your head, our paths were destined to separate. There was nothing either of us could do about it. Our paths cross from time to time, and that is good, but they will never run alongside again, and that – that is a shame – because – '

Her face puckered in pain.

'God's Will is truly hard to understand at times.'

'You can say that again,' said Geoffrey.

They looked at each other, and both smiled through tears.

'You see?' said Sybil. 'God can still make us smile. So perhaps Jesus really did make the apostles laugh.'

* * * * * *

'Are you ready for your soup now, Father?'

Arnulf looked up in surprise. Adele usually placed it in front of him without a word. With a pout and raised eyebrows as often as not.

Better still, she had charmed a choice joint out of Gerard, which she had garnished with some well-cooked early vegetables. Arnulf could not remember when he had last eaten so well.

Even more mysterious, she kept up a flow of chatter throughout the meal. About everything and about nothing ... the lady Matilda was nagging the Duke about their son Robert; the boy had to be found proper military employment – getting out of hand ... so was Cecily. Answering back to Arlette.

'A proper little miss. I found her myself inside the guardroom, watching the gambling. I took her back to my lady. And do you know what my lady did? She had Arlette beaten for neglect. Very right and proper too, if you ask me. Letting a girl run wild like that. Who knows what might happen ... ? '

Arnulf felt the suspicion rise like mist in an autumn evening, but said nothing. At least his daughter was no longer throwing herself at young noblemen, either Saxon or Norman, and making a fool of herself and her father.

It was no use coming straight out and asking her; she could always flutter out of reach. Ah, well ... He wiped his mouth on his sleeve and stood up.

'Off to the chapel, Father?'

The voice was like poisoned honey, but he went without a word. .

When he had gone, Adele cleared the table. As she washed the platters in a bowl beside a horse trough, she had a contented smile on her face.

Cecily had been shown a few of the facts of life. Arlette was in hot water with my lady. Edwin was showing definite interest, and was being led a merry chase – and Father had no idea what was going on. If that arrogant buck Nigel Fitzhenry should come back, he would be shown that he was not the only pebble on the beach.

One way and another, it had been a most gratifying day.

She could not resist going down to the castle kitchen and showing Gerard how pleased she was.

'A welcome change, I must say,' said Gerard, taking in her mood at a glance. 'Is he still quaint?'

Adele flushed.

'I am sure I have no idea what you mean.'

Gerard let go one of his great booming laughs.

'By the Nails, girl! It was my idea, remember?'

Adele shrugged.

'Well. Father has thrown himself at every bishop in sight. So ... '

* * * * * *

Abbot Lanfranc of St. Stephen's, Caen, closed the Testament that he had been reading for over an hour. He stood up and went over to the open window. For a few moments he gazed down into the teeming cathedral square of Rouen.

Everyone seemed so purposeful, from the pompous Arras cloth merchant counting out his money at the change table to the urchins teasing a sow with a stick.

Lanfranc turned away and looked round the room. Archbishop Maurilius had provided this chamber for his sole use, and had placed at his disposal a young novice, who would take dictation, bring refreshment, and generally fetch and carry. The resources of the cathedral library were open to him.

Maurilius was doing his best. Lanfranc sighed.

He had read his correspondence from Caen several times, and the boy had written his answers; the letters had gone off days ago. There was nothing else to do but wait for replies from his prior. He had looked at nearly every book in the library, and was frankly not very impressed. His old library at Bec dwarfed this one. But then – he smiled wryly at the irony – who was he to criticise? He had not given them his full attention.

He glanced back at the Testament he had just closed. What had he been studying? Half the words had danced round before his eyes. All he could recall was something about the parable of the talents. Not much for an hour's work.

He thrust his hands in the pockets of his robe and looked out of the window again. It was not like him to be unable to concentrate. One of his earliest memories was of his beloved father saying to family friends, 'Look at him. Nose in a book. You can rattle a fire iron and he will not hear.' But there was pride in his father's voice. Both he and Lanfranc knew that he would become a scholar.

That was all he now wanted to be. After a false start in Pavia as a lawyer, then another as a hermit – a shameful episode that filled him even now with discomfort at the mere thought – he had found himself as a teacher and man of letters. He had been happiest at the monastic house of Herluin at Bec, and would have stayed there, had not the Duke commanded him to take over the new house of St. Stephen at Caen. He had rejected the archbishop's mitre here at Rouen. He wished poor Maurilius joy of it; it was not for him.

And just when he was beginning to settle at St. Stephen's – finding the challenge more to his taste than he had expected – had come this summons to the Church council. It was a compliment in a way, a sign of the esteem in which William held him. But frankly he now had better things to do. Council business was best left to bishops; they had the authority to implement the decisions that were taken.

However, he was reluctant to leave, for all that the work was not to his taste. It meant quitting unfinished business, and the lawyer in him liked to tie up loose ends. Yet the council could not be further from the Duke's mind.

He rested his elbows on the window sill and looked at the boys with the stick.

They had now turned their attention to a bear on a chain. Dangerous.

What was the chance of inducing one of the bishops to take the initiative? John of Avranches would follow his principles; Yves of Sées would follow the chase; Hugh of Lisieux would follow his kinsman, the Duke; William of Evreux would follow the crowd. Geoffrey of Coutances – ah! now there was an independent spirit for you. But Geoffrey had wanted to attend least of all; in fact had managed to negotiate leave of absence, until this Wessex earl had upset everybody's plans. That left ... Odo, Bishop of Bayeux, who followed his own self-interest.

Lanfranc recalled his game with Gerard.

'I expect you to think of something, my lord abbot.'

Lanfranc glanced back at the Testament ... the parable of the talents ... he had been accused in his young days of having a canny legal brain. 'Cunning,' his enemies had said. And Odo was a born intriguer ...

Lanfranc almost knocked over his young secretary as he swept out. Crossing the cathedral square, he did not notice the bear lunge towards the boys and make them scamper away in fright.

Bishop Odo looked blank.

'Draw him on? How?'

'You are his brother; I thought you might have an idea.'

Odo scratched a pimple.

'Hardly, my lord abbot. To be honest, I must confess that I too am more interested in Harold than I am in the council. I do not see what I can do.'

Lanfranc was one of the few people to whom Odo was always civil. It was a measure of the huge respect in which the abbot of St. Stephen's was held by one and all. Some said that Odo was slightly afraid of him.

Lanfranc raised an innocent eyebrow.

'You are looking forward, no doubt, to the unexpected pleasure of the company of my lord of Coutances?'

Odo scowled.

'I wish he had stayed away. Let him get on with his darling cathedral.'

'Ah.'

Having planted one seed of intrigue, Lanfranc proceeded to sow another.

'I presume all the bishops will be presented to my lord the earl?'

'I imagine my brother will arrange it. It could be quite an occasion.'

Lanfranc tossed in the third.

'What are you going to do with this Harold?'

Odo offered a sly, unpleasant smile.

'Catch him out.'

Lanfranc nodded.

'I see. Well, I wish you good day, my lord.' He paused at the door of Odo's chamber. 'If you should get any good ideas ... '

'You will hear, my lord abbot.'

Lanfranc recrossed the square.

Perhaps he too would come to the castle to meet this Harold. At least he would be paying more attention to him than he had to the Scriptures.

The two urchins were dancing up and down in cruel parody of the bear's half-upright stance – but this time at a safe distance.

* * * * * *

Arnulf placed the second candlestick back on the altar and stood back to look at the pair of them. Would the Duke be satisfied? As God was his witness, he had tried. Left on his own. Those devilish little imps of altar boys had barely put their heads in the door since the Duke's son Robert had arrived. Always out. Some mischief or other. If they got caught, Robert would charm himself, and them, out of trouble. Spoilt, thoroughly spoilt. The younger generation these days.

Useless to complain. People laughed behind their hand. Oh, yes, he had seen them. But who would get into trouble if the chapel was not decked with finery and the altar silver polished like a sunbeam when the Earl Harold arrived? And with half a dozen bishops to find fault as well.

Arnulf looked at his blackened hands. Why was God so unfair?

And why did He not listen to his prayers? To the prayers of one of His ministers. Did He really mean to stay aloof while His faithful servant was cast out like an unwanted old dog who had lost his teeth? His daughter too?

Arnulf sighed as he wiped his fingers on a piece of rag torn from an old skirt of Adele's. He looked at the bright colour. Trust Adele to wear the most lurid dye she could afford.

Shameless creature!

He might have known she had been up to something. Getting the Duke's daughter into bad habits was one thing; that did not surprise him. Anything to get back at that haughty little miss, Arlette. Frankly, Arnulf did not like her much himself. But throwing herself at the Saxon boy – how low could she stoop ... ?

'Really, you amaze me. I can understand Beaumont and the hostage – that was simply stupidity, and you are a stupid girl.'

Adele flared. Arnulf spread his podgy hands.

'But a Wessex serf!'

'He is the son of a reeve. A good family. He told me.'

'A dog-boy. A fugitive. Have you no pride or shame?'

'I reach where I wish.'

'Up to the moon, I can understand. But not down into the drain.'

Adele flashed her eyes.

'You reached into the family hearth ... '

Arnulf felt his face red at the recall of it.

She was probably in the oaf's arms at this very minute.

Arnulf knelt down, but his knees were too sore, and he stood up again. As he rubbed them, his eyes fell on the boxes at the back of the chapel.

The Duke's travelling altar. He would be expected to have that clean too. There was no military campaign being planned, but suppose the Duke went on a progress with Earl Harold? Only one person would get into trouble if everything were not ready.

Arnulf sighed and set to work. As he lugged one of the boxes towards the light, he heard a sliding and rattling.

The relics. Time and again he had promised himself that he would have them properly fixed in a suitable setting. But the carpenters and seamstresses always made excuses. Nobody fell over himself to do Arnulf the Sweater a favour. But there was more to it than that; nobody liked having anything to do with holy relics. Praying at arm's length away was the limit of their chosen involvement.

'Work for priests, not for sinners.'

The Duke set great store by them. Took them everywhere. Even wore one or two of the smaller ones in battle, or so they said.

Arnulf stood up, stretched his back, and looked down at the battered box. If they did favours for dukes, perhaps they would do favours for chaplains. It was worth a try.

* * * * * *

'What will Earl Harold say?' said Adele, nuzzling a cheek.

Edwin pulled back.

'How will he know?'

'In a castle? With no campaign going on? Everybody knows everything. Nothing else to do.'

Edwin shrugged.

'The Earl's young brother has a Norman lover.'

'That is different. They are betrothed – well, in a way.'

'In a way?'

Adele sniffed.

'She would like to be. He is hanging back. Bit of a misery, if you ask me.'

'Do you want to be?'

'What?'

'Betrothed.'

Adele laughed out loud. Edwin flushed.

'What is so funny?'

Adele kissed him on the end of his nose.

'I must be the first girl you have ever chased.'

'Nothing of the sort. And I have caught a few too.'

Adele sat up and smoothed her dress.

'My, my. Quite the talker!'

Edwin put his arm round her again.

'Earl Harold has a mistress.'

'Yes – in England. Out of sight.'

'Who cares about us? Not you, for one. And I wager your father knows.'

Adele tossed her head. What if he did? So much the better. She turned back to Edwin with renewed interest.

She knew she was bored. If she had understood this young Saxon with his fractured French, she would guess he was bored too. When Harold arrived at last, this boy would rush off and leave her like a dog running to his master's whistle. To be fair, if Nigel came back, she could think offhand of no particular reason why she should prefer a foreigner – for all that he made her laugh.

It was better than listening to her father's wailings. It was better than the recent humiliations at the hands of arrogant young knights and gloomy hostages.

Besides, she was good at this. It was medicine for her sick self-confidence.

Gerard had noticed it – of course. Only an hour since, when they had gone together to gossip and scrounge in the kitchen, he had boomed at them, 'A relief to see a smile on your faces – both of you.'

* * * * * *

'Tell us a story, Gerard.'

The great brows came down like the bar on a castle gate. The black beard bristled.

'A story?'

'Yes!'

He put up his hands and pretended to recoil at the loud chorus of treble voices.

Then he frowned again.

'I am very busy.'

'Please, Gerard.'

It was a charade they always played.

Gerard pretended to go into deep thought. Several pairs of young eyes glittered in suspense. Gerard cleared his throat.

'Very well.'

He held up a hand to still the clamour.

'But no interruptions, mind. There – before me.'

Cross-legged on a rush mat before the main spit, they fidgeted with excitement.

'And be still.'

Gerard fixed each one in turn with his eye. Each child met his glare with mouth open but head unbowed.

'Now – '

Gerard suddenly turned and swiped the scullion Peter across the rump with a ladle.

'Get on with it, you!'

Peter, who had been staring like the Duke's children, jumped, and began turning the spit handle again. The bandage on his finger was grimed with dirt.

Gerard settled himself on a stool, leaned his crutch between his knees, and rested his hands on the arm-pad.

'I am going to tell you the story of the very first Duke of the Normans – '

'Rollo!' The audience erupted into delighted chorus.

'Silence!' thundered Gerard.

'Sorry, Gerard.'

Hands were folded piously into laps. Cecily forgot her growing years and looked forward to the treat from force of habit.

'Once upon a time,' said Gerard, with a final warning stare all round, 'there was a chief of the Northmen called Rollo. He was a great warrior and a great voyager and a great leader.'

Robert, the Duke's eldest son, felt a tingle of excitement. Fights, adventures, leadership – this was what stories should be about!

'He travelled far and wide,' said Gerard, 'across the seas of the north, and fought many great battles.'

'And he was very big,' said Richard. 'You left that out.'

Robert could have hit him.

'I was coming to that,' said Gerard. 'Yes, he was indeed very big. Very tall.'

'Was he taller than Bruno?' said William through his freckles.

Gerard nodded vigorously.

'So tall and so fat that there was no horse that could carry him. When he came off his ship and travelled on dry land, he had to go on foot. He was known to one and all as – '

'Rolf the Ganger!'

The younger girls clapped in delight.

Gerard pretended to be cross again.

'What did I say?'

Heads bowed.

'Sorry, Gerard.'

'Now, where was I?'

'Rollo's battles,' said Robert, seizing his chance.

'Ah, yes. Well, this Rollo – Rolf the Ganger – came in the end to France. The King of France was a weak man, and was no protector of his people. King Charles the Simple they called him.'

Robert sneered.

'And Rollo,' said Gerard, 'was a mighty hunter who provided well for his men. He came right up the river Seine and fell like a wolf upon the lands of King Charles. He laid siege to the city of Chartres.'

Cecily sat up straighter. She always liked this bit.

'The people of Chartres ran into their church and prayed to the Holy Virgin to save them. The Holy Mary told them to take out from under the altar their most holy relic – the shift of the Virgin Mary herself. Her very own. It would protect them, she said.

'So they tied it to a staff and flew it from the ramparts of the city as a holy banner. When the Northmen laughed at it, the citizens rushed out of the gate and attacked them and put them to flight.'

Cecily looked sidelong at Robert and tilted her head in triumph.

'But Rollo came back again, and again. He raided in Evreux, here in Rouen, and right up to the gates of Paris itself, and the King was powerless to stop him.'

Robert made a face at Cecily.

'In the end,' said Gerard, 'the King had to give way. He said to Rollo, "If you will stop fighting, I shall give you some of my lands." Rollo, who was a man of honour, did not see the cunning behind the King's words. For the King was planning to make Rollo his vassal, to make him swear homage, to make him accept the King as his overlord.'

Robert spat.

'So the King met with Rollo at the town of St. Clair on the River Epte, not very far from here, and he gave to Rollo all the lands around Rouen and Evreux and Lisieux. And he became the Count of Normandy. And the King said that Rollo must kneel and place his hands between the hands of the King, according to the custom.

'Rollo said that he had never done that obeisance for any man, nor his father, nor his grandfather. But there was a silver-voiced man among the King's court who spoke well the tongue of the Northmen, and he said that if Rollo was a man of honour he should respect the ancient customs of his new country.

'Count Rollo looked at the King and looked at the wide lands around them on the banks of the river. To seal such a gift with a clasp of the hands – it seemed a small sum to take out of the purse of pride as the price of such a realm.

'So he knelt and the King placed his hands round those of Count Rollo – so.'

Gerard leaned forward and did so with William's extended hands. He sat back again. William smiled with pride at the others.

Gerard paused deliberately, and took a swig of beer.

'Tell us about the kiss,' said the young girls.

'Yes, tell us about the kiss,' said Richard.

Gerard wiped his mouth.

'Ah, yes – the kiss. Well, the chamberlain of the King said to Rollo, "There is one more thing. One more custom. You must kiss the King's foot in token of your obeisance."

'Rollo was very cross at this trick. "No, by God I will not!" he said.

' "But it is the custom," said the King's chamberlain. And do you know what Rollo did?'

Six pairs of eyes gleamed.

'He said to one of his men, "You kiss the King's foot." And Rollo's man stepped forward, and do you know what he did?'

A taut bowstring of a silence. Peter had stopped turning the spit.

'He stood before the King, took the King's foot and lifted it to his lips, and tipped the King over backwards, throne and all.'

A gale of laughter filled the great castle kitchen.

Richard deliberately propelled himself backwards on to his shoulders, heels in the air. Robert and Cecily found themselves clapping together with delight – still.

Gerard waited for them to subside.

'And Rollo took for his wife the daughter of a Norman nobleman – the lady Popa of Senlis. And he had a son called William.'

'William Longsword,' said Robert.

'True. And William had a son.'

'Richard the Fearless.'

'And this Richard had a son.'

'Richard the Good.'

'And Richard's son was – '

'Duke Robert,' said Robert, his face flushed with pride. 'Duke Robert the Magnificent. My father's father.'

Duke Robert had died on a pilgrimage to the Holy Land. A truly brave and Christian knight. One day, Robert promised himself – one day – he too would go to the Holy Land and do great deeds.

* * * * * *

'Is Harold really a great warrior?'

'So they say.'

'Where has he fought?'

'Here and there.'

'Has he won victories?'

'Now and then.'

Arlette made a face at the hunched shoulders. She would never understand what men saw in fishing.

'Wulf.'

'Ssshhh!'

'Very well then.' Arlette whispered through a set jaw. 'Wulf!'

'What?'

'Is he like you?'

'Who?'

Arlette struck him on the back and stood up to go back to the castle. As she turned to fling the last word, she heard a single horse approaching. It came right down to the bank. Arlette gasped.

'Wulf!'

'What?'

'Wulf! Get up.'

Wulf half turned at the urgency in her voice, and he too gasped. He scrambled to his feet.

'Your Grace.'

William glanced to left and right, as if he expected the fish to leap out in ambush.

'Are you alone, boy?'

Wulf gestured to Arlette. William tossed his head in impatience.

'I can see that. Well, I have some news for you.'

Wulf stood to attention.

'Sir.'

William looked at Arlette.

'What have you done to him, girl? Nailed his tongue to his teeth?'

'He is anxious, my lord.'

'Arlette!' Wulfnoth pleaded and glared at the same time.

'There is no need,' said the Duke. 'I have had word that your brother will be with us on the evening of the second day, maybe before.'

'Sir.'

William stared.

'React, boy. You are my under-chamberlain. There are preparations to be made. Half my senior vassals are already here, and the rest I expect hourly. There is much to be done.'

'I shall see to it, my lord.'

'I should think so.'

William turned his horse and began to move away. He paused at a gap in the bank brambles.

'I thought you liked him.'

He went off, humming tunelessly to himself.

Wulfnoth began to gather in his line. Arlette put her hands on her hips.

'There you are. You see?'

'See what?'

'The Duke will make a great fuss of your brother. Every senior vassal in Normandy will be here. What greater compliment can you imagine?'

Wulfnoth tied his pouch of bait, flung it into his satchel, and looked straight at her.

'Arlette, Harold is a prisoner.'

'You mean he was.'

'I mean he is. Only he is now the Duke's prisoner instead of Guy's.'

'William means to entertain him. He said so.'

Wulfnoth flung out an arm towards the castle.

'Fitzosbern, Montgomery, Giffard, Beaumont, de Montbrai, de Tosny, de Montfort, de Warenne. I could name a dozen more. Are they all coming here to shake my brother by the hand?'

Arlette shrugged.

'How should I know?'

'And why is the Duke so pleased with himself? Humming like that?'

'It could be that he likes you. Pleased to see you. Did you ever think of that?'

'Why is he telling me this?'

'He could have sent anybody. But he came himself. Surely that tells you something?'

'No. And that is what worries me.'

Arlette shook her head.

'Honestly, Wulf, I think you enjoy being worried. You are going to see Harold, the man you love most. And he is going to be entertained by the Duke, the man you admire most. One loves you as a brother, and the other cares for you like any father.'

Wulfnoth began to stump up the hill towards the gate of the rear bailey.

'William has children of his own. Why should he care for me?'

Arlette sighed.

'I sometimes wonder.'

Wulfnoth did not wait for her. One could never expect women to understand politics. A great trap was beginning to open at Harold's feet – a great formless void – and there was nothing he or his brother could do about it. There were no precautions possible, because the danger had not declared itself. There was no going through it, no going round it. And there was no stepping back. No escape.

* * * * * *

'Did you miss me?'

Adele put her hands behind her head.

'Where is it you stayed?'

Nigel frowned.

'Le Tréport. Awful place. Why?'

Adele raised her eyebrows.

'I missed you as much as you miss the last girl you had in le Tréport.'

Nigel flopped on his back beside her.

'That is not fair. I came all this way just to see you.'

'You deserted.'

'How dare you! The idea!'

'This is me – Adele. Remember?'

Nigel sighed.

'All right. Yes. Nobody will care. If you could see le Tréport. The smells! Nothing but Saxon sailors' feet and Flemish whores' armpits. Besides, the work is going well. All up to the carpenters now. No need for me.'

'So you deserted.'

'Yes! I deserted! Satisfied?'

'To come and see Harold.'

'Harold?'

'Everyone else is.'

Nigel looked at her keenly.

'It seems to me you know a lot all of a sudden.'

'Not difficult with you.'

Nigel fell back on his charm again.

'I thought you would be pleased to see me.'

'Overjoyed.'

'I am touched.'

'Are you complaining?'

'Somebody else, is there?'

Adele laughed.

'Here? With the whole garrison on leave or on courier duty or rushing about Normandy as bodyguard for the Saxon earl? You are the only able-bodied man for miles.'

'I see. Making do, are we? Perhaps I should have brought Gilbert back with me.'

'Gilbert?'

'You know – the one who made cow eyes at you all the time. He still is. Oaf!'

Adele fell back on flirting from force of habit.

'And you do not make cow eyes, I suppose.'

Nigel smirked.

'I play the bull, not the cow. Did you notice?'

Adele had noticed. Very much so. She felt slightly ashamed of herself. And she did not know why.

* * * * * *

Chapter Six

The Watching

Oh, the blessed silence!

Wulfnoth propped his rod along a groove in a rock, put his arms round his knees, and gazed at nothing.

For an hour at least, no more shouting, no more rush, no more stupid servants constantly at his elbow whining for fresh instructions. At first, it had been quite heady. The Duke had made it clear that his under-chamberlain's orders were to be obeyed without question. For a brief, dizzy spell he had been, after his Grace, the most powerful man in the entire castle.

Grooms, valets, launderers, and kitchen serfs tripped over each other. Extra stabling and fodder, fresh carcases, dry clothing, spare footwear, clean bedding, new sconces and candles ... Gerard's voice boomed everywhere. Bundles of fuel, baskets of eggs and early vegetables, barrels of beer ... guardrooms and barracks stripped of trestles and benches to provide extra seating in the hall; there was the escort to cater for as well, and Flemings, it was well known, drank as much beer as Saxons ... Peter and the other scullions, smarting from Gerard's crutch across their rumps, took up sticks and did the same to the host of stray dogs that seemed to be able to smell extra food from across the river.

Arlette had been made to lay out clean clothes for all the children, to air the best embroidered linen for napkins and pillows. The precious 'chicks', for once, were too excited to be rude to her. And she was too busy to seek out Wulfnoth.

He sighed. That was something.

The sun shone. The line dipped sleepily.

A voice called out.

'Ho! You there.'

Wulfnoth gasped. He would know that voice anywhere, even after twelve years.

Harold did not recognise him, even when he stood up.

'Yes, you.'

Wulfnoth gave no sign of understanding. Harold edged his horse closer, and spoke as all visitors do in a foreign country – slowly, loudly, simply.

'Never been here before. Looking for a young man. A young man. They said he would be here. Down by the ... '

'Hallo, Harold.'

Harold swallowed.

'Wulf.'

He dismounted hurriedly.

'Wulf!'

'Yes.'

Harold embraced him fiercely.

'They said you would be down here.' The words did not come out easily. 'Always fishing, they said.' He stood back. 'But look at you. That chest. Those shoulders.'

'Yes.'

'My brother. My baby brother. Ha!'

'Yes.'

Harold forced a laugh.

'Can you say nothing but "Yes"?'

Wulfnoth gestured helplessly.

Harold put out a heavy hand and rubbed Wulfnoth's head.

'With that Norman haircut, you look like old Sawin the hayward. Remember? How he used to rub his bald pate like this? Remember?'

'Yes.'

'There you go again.'

'Sorry.'

Harold laughed.

'If our brothers could see us now.'

'Gyrth, Leofwine – how are they?'

'Fine, fine.'

'And mother?'

'Well, very well. Misses you, of course. Misses her baby.'

'Yes.'

Harold cleared his throat.

'Still fishing, I see.'

'Yes.'

'Not forgotten all I taught you, then? Remember when we took you out on the Severn?'

'Yes – the big thunderstorm.'

'The lightning too, remember?'

'And I was so frightened.'

'And you rushed to Gyrth so suddenly that you tipped him out of the boat.'

'I was only eight.'

'And Gyrth came up spouting like a fountain. I can still see the look on his face.'

They laughed together. They stopped laughing at the same time. Harold tried first to fill the silence.

'Do they treat you well?'

'Yes. Well enough.'

'You are not ... I mean, you can move around as you please?'

'Oh, yes ... yes.'

'Good. Good.'

Wulfnoth made his effort.

'The Duke takes me round with him.'

'Ah. Good.'

Harold found an absorbing catch in the reins.

'Let me see ... You are twenty-two now, eh? Been here – '

'Twelve years.'

'Yes, yes. Twelve years. Long time.'

Harold's interest shifted to the bridle.

'I hear you have yourself a woman.'

'Yes.'

'Betrothed?'

'There is a sort of understanding.'

'Nice girl, is she?'

'Why?'

'What?'

'Why, Harold, why?'

Harold continued to examine his horse's harness.

'Does it matter? I am here.'

'Just like that.'

Harold frowned.

Just like what?'

'Twelve years. After twelve years, you expect to snap your fingers and your baby brother will come running. Come fishing, Wulf. Come riding, Wulf. Show you father's sword, Wulf.'

Harold gazed intently as the words tumbled out.

'And now – after twelve years – it is the same again. Like to see England, Wulf? See your brothers, Wulf? See your mother? Fishing in the Severn? Wag your tail, Wulf. Harold is ready to play again.'

Harold became serious.

'Who said anything about going back to England?'

'Ah! So you realise that much.'

'What is that supposed to mean?'

'Obvious, I should have thought. You are the Duke's prisoner.'

'No. I was Guy of Ponthieu's prisoner, for a very brief time. I am William's guest.'

Wulf almost spat.

Harold held out his hands.

'Look at my wrists. Do you see any irons? Look around you. Do you see any soldiers? I was allowed – nay, encouraged – to ride down here alone to find you.'

'I suppose you rode all the way from Ponthieu alone.'

'No. I had soldiers.'

Wulfnoth sneered.

'How many?'

'About four or five score, actually. An entire Flemish detachment.'

'There you are.'

'An escort, my boy. Befitting a Saxon earl. William wanted to give me barely thirty. I asked him to treble it. What does he think I am – a bare-top bishop or a border count? I am Earl of Wessex, in all England second to none save the King himself.'

'I am sure his Grace is aware of that.'

'Well, he knows it even better now. By the way, talking of bishops, what are all those bishops doing here? The main gateway was full of them. I must be in line for the Papacy as well as the crown.'

Wulfnoth ignored the question.

'And how long do you think this will go on?'

'What?'

'Oh, Harold, open your eyes. How long will you be treated like this?'

Harold tied the horse to a willow.

'As long as it suits me to stay. William is a correct host. And I hope I know how to behave as a correct guest.'

Wulfnoth's line suddenly jerked. He turned to wind it in, and held up the silver, shaking body.

'See that? That is what you are. Trapped and helpless. Worse, you are not aware of it.'

Harold shook his head.

'I am neither trapped nor helpless. I was caught in a savage storm. I was shipwrecked. I was Guy of Ponthieu's prisoner for a short time. Each of these troubles I have survived. I have since demanded, and been granted, the full honours due to my rank. Now tell me – am I like your fish?'

'Maybe not then. But you are now.'

'Wrong again. That fish came to your bait. I did not come to William's bait; he came to mine. When he heard I was in Ponthieu, he could not get to Eu fast enough.'

'Exactly. To rescue you. To put you in his debt.'

'No. To find out. And that gives me the advantage.'

Wulfnoth stared.

'The advantage!'

'Yes. I know what is in William's mind, but he has no idea what is in mine.'

'All right – clever. What is he thinking?'

'One thing: "What is Harold up to?" '

Wulfnoth opened his mouth, but no answer came out.

'You see?' said Harold.

He strolled down to the river bank, and began tossing twigs into the water. Wulfnoth walked after him.

'All right. Answer me this. When do you plan to return?'

'I have no plans at the moment.'

'Ha!'

'Something has come up.'

'What?'

'Have you not heard the news from Brittany?'

Wulfnoth frowned.

'What has Conan to do with it?'

Harold skimmed a pebble and watched it bounce across the water.

'Only three times. Must be losing my touch.' He stood up. 'My guess is that William will go to Brittany to rap him over the knuckles. Lift the siege of Dol.'

'Well?'

'I shall go with him.'

'How?'

'Get William to invite me.'

'Why would he do that?'

'I told you – curiosity. He is dying to find out what I am up to.'

'What are you up to?'

Harold laughed loudly, then put a finger alongside his nose and winked.

'Secret.'

Wulfnoth glared.

'It is bad enough that you patronise me. Please do not laugh at me as well.'

Harold put an arm round his shoulder.

'I am sorry. How about this, then? Suppose I wish to take the chance to find out how he wages war. Would that knowledge not be useful?'

'Suppose you get killed?'

Harold shrugged.

'I take that risk wherever I go campaigning. I ran that risk when I put to sea two or three weeks ago.'

Wulfnoth tossed his head in impatience.

'Harold! Do you not see? Suppose – ' he looked furtively over his shoulder, as if he expected to see spies lurking in the brambles ' – suppose he arranges to have you killed. Leave you in an exposed position, and let the Bretons do his work for him.'

Harold skimmed another stone.

'No. If he had wanted me dead, he would have let Guy of Ponthieu do it, and let him take all the blame.'

'I know the Duke; you do not. He – '

'Maybe. But I know what he is thinking. I told you. And I tell you now that William will not harm me, not because my death would be murder, but because my death would be a mistake. A crime to stink through Christendom.'

Wulfnoth began to flounder.

'But he wants the crown.'

'Of course he does.'

'Why are you not worried?'

'Because he is not going to get it.'

Harold shook him gently by the shoulders.

'Wulf! Use your brains. Look at the size of England; look at the size of Normandy. William has had trouble with his vassals since he was on his mother's knee. He has treacherous neighbours like Guy of Ponthieu and Conan of Brittany. The Duke of Anjou and the King of France are waiting only for him to turn his back before they fall on his duchy. We have the sea as a wall; William has nothing.'

'You should see his castles. You should see him wage war. He is brilliant. He has some of the finest knights in France.'

Harold grinned.

'Here, here! Whose side are you on?'

Wulfnoth tossed his head again.

'I wish I could make you see, Harold. All your clever arguments will not stop him trying.'

'Trying is one thing. Succeeding is quite another. I would expect him to try.'

Wulfnoth sighed. Harold saw his distress, and softened his voice.

'Wulf, William is a gambler. That does not mean he is a fool; it means he counts the odds with great care, and takes calculated risks. He knows that the conquest of England is the greatest gamble of his career, and it behoves him to try and reduce the odds by whatever means he can find.'

Wulfnoth opened his mouth to object, but Harold held up a hand.

'No, no, hear me out. There are men in England who are jealous of me, who would shed no tears over my grave. But if I, a Saxon earl, were to be murdered by a bastard Norman adventurer, while under his roof, it would unite all my friends with all my enemies to defend the precious soil of England.

'Whereas – and this is for your ears only – if he leaves me alone, he knows I shall see off Hardrada should he fall upon Northumbria. And – between you and me – the Witan will almost certainly prefer me to the Atheling. Time of crisis and all that. So, if the Bastard stays his hand against me, he will not be lengthening the odds against himself; he will be shortening them.' He grunted. 'And even then they will still be too long.'

Wulfnoth pondered this before speaking.

'So you think the Duke will be killed?'

'Maybe, maybe not. I simply said he would fail. Anyway, why should you worry? A minute ago you were worried about me getting killed.'

'I want neither of you – '

Wulfnoth stopped himself, but not soon enough. Harold smiled kindly.

'Like him, eh?'

Wulfnoth looked the picture of misery.

'Take me to England, Harold. Take me home.'

Harold put a hand on his shoulder.

'All in good time, lad. All in good time.'

* * * * * *

'Well, I say this for him – he can certainly drink.'

Sir Roger of Montgomery leaned his chin on his hands, and stared down into the main bailey.

Sir Walter Giffard snuffed the air in relief.

'I have had more headaches in a week than in a month of midsummer feasts. What do you say, Fitz?'

Sir William Fitzosbern pretended to massage a tender rump.

'I would complain of the man's stamina in the saddle. He can almost outstay William.'

Alone of the Duke's vassals, Fitzosbern referred to him by his Christian name. Evidence of the bond between them, of the shared dangers when young.

They gazed together for a while. The sentries on the catwalk kept well away from three such important officers.

'Good company too,' said Montgomery to nobody in particular.

'No sign of nerves,' said Giffard. 'You would think he was on his own estates.'

'No fidgeting.'

'No worries.'

'He seems to have no plans at all.'

'Damn and blast him.'

Giffard stood up and dusted his hands.

'What do we do with the man, Fitz?'

Fitzosbern rubbed the back of his neck.

'Early days, maybe.'

Giffard gestured down into the bailey, where Flemish soldiers were standing about in random groups, joking and jostling. A beer mug shattered on the flagstones. A gale of laughter swept up to them.

'Early days! We shall have trouble with that lot before long. They have had young Beaumont in tears twice already. Only a matter of time before they cut loose in the town.'

'Why does the Bastard wait so long to pay them off?'

'What with?'

Montgomery looked at him.

'Bad as that?'

'He is waiting,' said Fitzosbern.

'For what?'

'News.'

'News?'

'From Brittany. Not long now, I would guess.'

Giffard snorted.

'It had better be quick. Another week, and this Saxon earl will have half the garrison eating out of his hand.'

Montgomery shook his head and smiled.

'Alone, in a foreign land. Not a Saxon soldier in sight. You have to hand it to him.'

'God's Face, Roger! What are we going to do with him?'

* * * * * *

'It could be worse, my lord. Only the scaffolding. The wind, you see. The stonework remains in place. Goscelin is more annoyed than anything.'

For once, Thierry was not complaining about his stomach. He looked too exhausted for that. Must have been in the saddle for two days non-stop.

Geoffrey de Montbrai, Bishop of Coutances, poured his courier a drink with his own hand.

'Anybody hurt?'

'Ah! Bless you, my lord. Two masons dead, my lord. From Isigny. Only been with us a week. Four injured. Broken bones mostly. The father Abbot from

Cérisy sent his infirmarian.'

'Hm.'

Geoffrey stood up. Thierry glanced at him over the rim of the cup. It was only a matter of time before his master began pacing. What he was about to say would certainly start him off. He swallowed.

'But we need more money, my lord. Hiring labour for the new poles. New masons. Alms for the father Abbot. Goscelin says the last delivery of stone was below standard – '

'Yes, yes, yes.'

Sure enough, Geoffrey began pacing up and down.

Thierry took another furtive swig. To be fair, the news he and his companion had brought was enough to start any Norman knight pacing.

'I picked him up at Lisieux. We crossed the Risle together at Brionne. Sir Baldwin de Clair gave us fresh horses. Ours were blown. You should have seen that man ride. I tell you, my lord ... '

Small wonder. The news was all over the castle almost before they had dismounted in the main bailey.

Count Conan of Brittany had stolen a march on everyone. Captured the castle at Dol, and most of its rebel garrison. His scouts had been seen close to Pontorson. Rumour put them beyond the River Couesnon, even at the walls of Avranches. Where scouts went, raiding parties could follow. It was only a matter of time before Conan found out that most of William's senior vassals were at the other end of the duchy – to say nothing of the bishops of Avranches and Coutances.

Small wonder too that Sir Baldwin de Clair at Brionne had given them fresh horses. It was vital to get this news to the Bastard as soon as possible.

The courier was hustled into the Duke's hall as soon as his feet touched the ground. Two off-duty soldiers watched the poor wretch being almost carried away.

'I wonder if this will take the Bastard's mind off Harold at last,' said Bruno to Ralph.

* * * * * *

'And drink! You should see him drink.'

Adele carried on with cutting vegetables. Nigel helped himself to a handful of cress.

'Stories too.'

'Yes?'

'Not for your ears, of course. We were rolling on the floor.'

'A handsome sight, I am sure.'

Nigel leaned back and propped his feet on the table.

'My guess is we shall be off to Brittany soon.'

'Oh?'

'You have heard the news, I take it. About Conan?'

Adele sighed.

'I have heard nothing else. It has made a change from Harold. Now it seems you are bewitched with both.'

'We shall get away from this dead-and-alive place.'

'I see.'

Nigel prodded some dough.

'Never seen Breton girls.'

'Red in the face, I hear. All that wind and rain.'

'Who cares? When one pokes the fire, one does not talk to the trivet.'

Adele swept his feet off the table.

'Then the sooner you go the better. I am busy.'

She suddenly found him boring.

Nigel watched her as she moved about the kitchen. She was getting plump. Not the energy she used to have – get her knees and ankles anywhere once upon a time.

'I shall go, then.'

'Shut the door behind you.'

Nigel thrust his thumbs into his belt and trudged across the bailey. Adele was not herself these days. Could be worry, of course. About her father. Ah, well – a few weeks without her darling Nigel, and, when he came back from Brittany, who knew where she could not get her knees and ankles up to next time?

* * * * * *

'You sing the same tune, then?'

'Just so, my lord,' said Fitzosbern. 'We could not afford a campaign then, and we can not afford it now. The more so after what the Wessex earl will cost us by the end of the summer. And I would remind you that the Flemings are still waiting for their pay.'

William turned to the man on his left.

'Brother?'

Robert of Mortain, the Duke's younger half-brother, put down his cup.

'My land is in the path of any advance that Conan may make, so I say, naturally, attack him before he attacks us. Surprise. He thinks we have our hands full with Harold.'

William nodded, and looked further down the table.

'Coutances?'

'I agree with my lord of Mortain. There is only one language that men like Conan understand. Just like Guy of Ponthieu. Force. The sooner it is applied the better.'

Odo, Bishop of Bayeux, the Duke's other half-brother, interjected.

'The fact that my lord of Coutances has had bad news about his – um – highly-valued cathedral has not, of course, influenced his opinion.'

Geoffrey glared.

'If my lord of Bayeux were building his cathedral near the Breton frontier, I venture to suggest that his advice would be yet more biased than usual.'

'Enough,' said William. 'Montgomery – what is your word?'

Sir Roger cleared his throat.

'I incline to agree with Fitz. We are in the process of completing our frontier defences, though I accept that Mortain is in a specially vulnerable position. But the others – Alençon, Tillières, Breteuil, and the rest – would not benefit from having their garrisons stripped for another campaign so soon after the last one. And Dol is after all in Brittany; Conan is only recovering one of his own towns from rebels that we put there. Perhaps we are over-reaching ourselves. Any sign of strain, and there is no knowing what Anjou might do. Or the boy King if he is badly advised.'

'God's Face, Roger. You sound like Fitz.'

'What do you say, then, Giffard?'

'I say, my lord,' said Sir Walter, 'that we go for him. Quickly. Rap him over the knuckles. It worked with Guy of Ponthieu. And I say something else too.'

'Well?'

'Take the Saxon earl with us. It will give the garrison here something to do, and it will stop them gawping at Harold.'

'It might test him,' admitted Fitzosbern.

'He might make a mistake,' said Odo. 'He has made none yet.'

Giffard muttered to Montgomery at his side, 'With any luck he might get himself killed.'

'Walter!'

'Will he go?' asked Mortain.

'If it is dressed up as a challenging invitation, wild horses will not keep him away,' said Odo. 'He is a soldier too, remember.'

Geoffrey smiled. The plan appealed to the intriguer in Odo.

The Duke stood up and paced the length of the hall two or three times. His vassals waited in complete silence.

William came back to the head of the table. He eyes darted to left and right like sparks off an anvil.

'This is what we do.'

* * * * * *

'Siege work!'

Beaumont grinned.

'You heard.'

The Flemish captain of mercenaries flung his beer mug into the hearth.

'What does he think we are – wood-cutters? Gleaners? He can get any serf he likes to do that.'

'Why should he when he has you?'

'Very funny. Has the Bastard any other military duties for us – like digging out new privies, for instance?'

'I shall put the suggestion to him if you wish,' said Beaumont, who was enjoying himself.

The captain swore. Beaumont grinned again.

'There is also the small matter of the final assault, which requires regular troops. I could tell him you are hesitant, of course. But then, I doubt if you would get your full money. I am instructed to tell you that it will be payable inside the walls of Conan's castle at Dol.'

'I shall protest. This is intolerable.'

'All warfare is, captain. Protest to the Emperor if you like. It will not change the Bastard's orders.'

The captain narrowed his eyes.

'What is your part in all this?'

Beaumont spread his hands in wide-eyed innocence.

'I, captain? A humble liaison officer? As you yourself once said, I give no orders; I merely transmit them. I should carry them out, if I were you.'

* * * * * *

'Must be all of eight months since I did this.'

Harold, totally absorbed, made an expert cast. He watched the float settle.

Wulfnoth fidgeted.

'And you are going?'

'Of course,' said Harold, without looking at him.

'Madness.'

'Oh?'

'What do you know about castles and sieges?'

'Not much. That is one of the reasons I am going. Always a good idea to extend one's knowledge.'

Wulfnoth flung up his hands in despair, and turned away. To his amazement there was the Duke himself, with Arlette on his arm, making his way down from the castle.

Harold saw them at the same time.

'Pull yourself together,' he whispered. 'Not a word. And none of this English emotionalism. Where is your Norman discipline?'

'Harold, please!'

Arlette pointed.

'There, my lord. Did I not say? You will always find him here. And where my brother is, there you will find the lord Harold.'

She tried to hide the regret in her voice, but flashed a glance at Wulfnoth.

Harold gave her a searching, amused look as she approached.

'And this must be the young lady herself. We were just talking about you.'

Arlette began to melt at once.

Harold bowed.

'If I may say so, I admire my brother's taste.'

Arlette curtseyed.

'My lord.'

'You grow good girls in Normandy, William. Had I known there were such charmers here, I should have visited earlier.'

Arlette almost simpered.

The Duke grunted.

'She will do.'

'Is that all you can say?' said Harold, pretending to be surprised. 'I am sure my brother can turn a better compliment than that? Eh, Wulf?'

'Hallo, Arlette.'

Harold laughed uproariously.

'I thought you said there was an understanding between you. You sound as if you have just met.'

Wulfnoth tried to shoot warning looks at his brother, but failed.

'Harold!'

The Duke allowed himself half a smile.

'They will do well for each other. Have you told him?'

'Just about to. But he worries about the idea of my going with you. Thinks I might come to some harm.'

Wulfnoth, appalled, blushed to his eyebrows.

The Duke allowed his restless eyes to settle for a moment.

'Come with us, boy. You can watch over us both.'

Wulfnoth was speechless with embarrassment.

Harold came to his rescue.

'Well, William, I presume it was me you were looking for. Let us discuss this – Conan, is that right?'

He turned to Arlette.

'I must apologise for taking him away from you, my dear, since we arrived. But you will understand that twelve years is a very long time for brothers.'

Arlette ducked her head to hide her own blush.

'Not at all, my lord.'

'Let us leave these two lovebirds, William. Talk war, eh? I take it you have studied the character of this Conan?'

He took the Duke's elbow. To Wulfnoth's amazement, William allowed himself to be steered away.

'Get to know your enemy,' said Harold. 'First principle of successful campaigning.'

Their voices faded as they mounted towards the castle.

'Will you make a feint at Rennes, or go direct for Dol? You see, I have studied the ground ... '

Arlette's eyes glowed.

'Wulf.'

'What?'

'You did not tell me he was so gallant.'

Wulfnoth grunted as he picked up his rod.

'Oh, he knows how to turn on the charm. Like a tap.'

Arlette continued gazing up the hill.

'So good-looking too.'

Wulfnoth wound in the line.

'He is trying to charm the Duke, but it will never work.'

'Did you see the Duke being rude to him.'

'No ... Great God, Arlette! What are they doing? They are mortal enemies. All this politeness. They are stalking each other. They are sizing each other up. It all looks so harmless, and yet it is deadly.'

He turned in wretchedness to Arlette.

'What can I do?'

* * * * * *

'Definite. I heard Fitzosbern himself give the orders. We are off to Dol.'

'Dol?'

Adele did not stop work.

'Conan has captured it. We are going to get it back. Put a Norman garrison in there. Kick Conan in the privates.'

Adele raised her eyebrows and sighed. Nigel watched her over the rim of his cup.

'Could be dangerous. Taking a castle by storm.'

'Really? Not much time for poking the fire then.'

Nigel stood up, came across, and put his arms round her from behind, still holding the cup in his hand.

'Something wrong, is there? Wrong time of the month, maybe? You can tell your uncle Nigel.'

Instead of struggling or pouting, Adele picked his hand off her forearm as if it were a slug, and cast it from her.

'All right, all right – I can take a hint.'

Nigel picked up his helmet.

'You will be pleased to see me when I get back.'

Adele did not bother to reply.

When he had gone, she sat down and pushed a lock of hair from her forehead. Nigel was harmless enough. Had he really deserved it? She had not planned it that way. God knows, the castle was going to be empty enough before long.

She frowned. She would have her father, with his sweats and his worries, all to herself.

* * * * * *

Matilda clapped her hands.

'Time now, chicks. Or my lord Harold will get tired of you.'

Arlette coaxed Richard and William and the girls towards the door.

William turned and shouted through his freckles, 'Can we come tomorrow, my lord, and play with your sword?'

Harold laughed.

'You will have to be early. Your father and I will have much business.'

'We shall be there.'

'At cock-crow,' said Richard. 'Good night, my lord.'

They clattered off, for once doing what Arlette told them.

Matilda looked meaningly at Cecily, who whined.

'Do I have to?'

Harold leaned across the table and pushed towards her a pair of earrings.

'Do not forget your present.' He winked confidingly. 'Leave me with your mother, and I may be able to get her permission for you to have your ears pierced.'

Cecily's eyes lit up.

'Oh, would you, my lord. If you could – '

Harold put his fingers to his lips.

'Ssshh! Or she may hear us.'

He looked at Matilda, who could not repress a smile. It was difficult to deny this man anything.

Robert came and stood beside Harold.

'If you could speak to my father, my lord ... '

Harold made no pretence with him.

'That may be a little more difficult, but I promise you I will try.'

Matilda watched them go.

'How do you do it, Harold?'

'No secret,' said Harold. 'I have five children of my own.'

'Bastards,' said Matilda.

Harold returned her steady gaze.

'Yes. Just like your husband.'

There was a moment's silence. The gleam in Harold's eye turned into a twinkle. Matilda gave way.

'Harold, you are impossible. Are you going to charm me too?'

'No need. We already understand each other. You and William – you are a good team. Edith and I – we too. We have in common the great gift of a lasting love and respect between two people.'

'Not unknown,' said Matilda.

'No,' said Harold. 'But rare. And let us not underestimate ourselves. Such a gift is not won by sloth and a long face, however beautiful that face may be.'

Matilda gestured towards the door.

'It is something that may have to be understood by Arlette.'

Harold nodded.

'And by Wulfnoth too – to save you the trouble of saying it.'

'Is he pleased to be going with you to Brittany?'

'Yes. But worried out of his wits. He thinks William is going to have me killed.'

Matilda shook her head.

'God's Blood. Does your confidence have no bounds?'

'Not confidence. Knowledge. William is a man. Not a furtive border bandit like Guy of Ponthieu. I do know the difference. So do you.'

Matilda swore.

'He will not take me with him.'

You protested?'

'We had words. Stubborn like an ox, that man.'

'I am not surprised. I should not have taken Edith. But I am surprised he is not taking Robert.'

Matilda sighed.

'The boy is dying to go.' She was struck with a sudden thought. 'Do you think – '

Harold held up a hand.

'I know, I know. Leave it to me.'

'A pox on Conan,' said Matilda, 'and I do not want my biggest chick to go, but I know he must one day.'

'And now is as good a time as any – a limited campaign with little more than some leisurely siegework and a rush of looting afterwards. Ideal.'

Matilda poured them both a drink.

'William is not easy.'

'No. But he is approachable on the right side, as you well know. I shall remind him that we are taking my brother. Not to take his eldest son – ' he picked up the brimming cup ' – what would people say?'

Matilda took a long swig.

'Not to his face, that is for sure.'

Harold caught her eye and held it.

'Nor to yours, my lady.'

Matilda masked her face with her sleeve as she wiped her lips.

No wonder even the nuns at St. Amand talked about this man.

* * * * * *

'Why not me? You are taking your brother.'

'You are not my brother.'

Edwin came near to a sneer.

'No, my lord. Just your humble dog-boy.'

Harold smiled.

'And a very good dog-boy too. Edwin, if I were taking hounds to Brittany, I would not have to be begged to take you; I should command you to come with us.'

'I found my way to Rouen for you.'

Harold nodded.

'You did indeed. I have nothing but praise for your bravery and your sense of duty. But you were lucky. That monk – what was his name?'

'Hubert.'

'Ah, yes. Hubert. From le Trèport. On detachment to Longueville.'

Edwin stared.

'Who told you that? Not me.'

'No. Gerard did. The cook. The lady Matilda put me on to him. Mine of information. Stout fellow.'

Edwin marvelled at his lord's capacity, not only to get to know everybody, but to charm so much news out of them.

'Anyway,' said Harold. 'That monk must have been sent by God Himself to put you on your way. It is too much to hope for another Hubert to turn up in Brittany.'

Edwin persisted.

'But you have no bodyguard.'

Harold laughed.

'I have a whole regiment of Flemings.'

Edwin tossed his head in annoyance.

'You know what I mean, my lord. Englishmen. There will be nobody but yourself and your brother. Not one other Saxon. All the others are with the boat at le Tréport. You told me.'

'And I intend to keep them there, till the boat is repaired.'

'Well then.'

Harold put a hand on Edwin's shoulder.

'Edwin, it will hurt you when I say this, but you are not a soldier. You would be in surroundings that you are not equipped to deal with. You might – well, something might happen. And that would be my fault. Your mother is a widow, remember. It is a responsibility I am not prepared to take.'

'You have no objection to risking your brother's life.'

'Wulfnoth is trained. He is a prince. War is the business of noblemen. It is not the business of servants. God would not favour me for moving you out of your station in life just to give me Saxon company or to feed your pride.'

'So I stay.'

'Yes, you do.'

Edwin drew back his shoulders.

'Am I dismissed, my lord?'

Harold stood up, came close, and spoke confidentially.

'Try to understand. We came through the storm with no drownings. We survived Guy of Ponthieu with no casualties. I shall go to Brittany, and I shall return in one piece, rest assured. So will Wulfnoth. And in the fullness of time, we shall return to our home. And it is my intent to go ashore in England without having lost a single man – servant, crewman, falconer, ship's captain, or dog-boy. How I go about that intent is my own business.'

If God shines His Face in the right direction, there might even be an extra man.

Edwin remained formal.

'Now am I dismissed, my lord?

'Yes, by God, you are! And lose that dog-chops look.'

As Edwin reached the door, Harold called after him.

'What about that girl Gerard told me about? You need not be lonely.'

Edwin found himself blushing.

'Oh, her! A tease. Nothing but a tease. She laughs at my accent.'

* * * * * *

'I have said it before: you should have been Archbishop of Rouen, not me.'

Lanfranc shook his head.

'You underrate yourself, my lord. You have led the Norman clergy bravely, and you will preside over an effective council. I do not have the political instinct.'

'But you have the legal instinct,' said Maurilius. 'How many of us have your knowledge of law both civil and canon?'

'I buried that knowledge years ago,' said Lanfranc, 'when I embraced the cloistered life. It is to there that I long to return.'

Maurilius beat his chest in his excitement.

'And do you think I do not wish to return there too?' He swung an arm in a wide, inclusive gesture. 'This – this politics, this playing to the gallery of opinion – this is not for me.'

Lanfranc smiled.

'Then perhaps neither of us should be Archbishop of Rouen.'

Maurilius smiled too.

'You do not catch me as easily as that, my lord abbot. I repeat that you should have been, and do you know why? Because you had the courage to refuse it – to the Duke's face – when it was offered.'

He stood up, and walked up and down the hall of his palace.

'Now look at the ridiculous situation we are in. Summoned to a council that has not had one session, and is not likely to, until this Wessex madness is out of his head. As if that is not bad enough, he now takes half his vassals to smoke out the Count of Brittany. And who is going with him? Half the bishops too!'

Lanfranc looked suitably sympathetic.

Maurilius stopped to count them off with his fingers.

'Coutances – leave of absence to see to repairs to his church. Coutances is near to the Breton border; can you see Coutances resisting the temptation to go and have a look? So my lord Odo of Bayeux must needs go as well, if only to make sure that my lord of Coutances does not steal a march on him.'

'He is the Duke's brother,' observed Lanfranc.

'True. And that also explains why Hugh of Lisieux is going. Cousin.'

Lanfranc sighed.

'Yes, I know. And Yves of Sées will go just for the fun. Much better than any boring council.'

'Precisely. So what are we left with? Evreux and Avranches. Three abbots are talking of going home, and another four never even arrived. The archdeacon from Rome is delayed in Champagne; I heard yesterday. Flux.'

'Prospects are poor, I agree.'

'And what does his Grace say to me? "Draw up an agenda." Ha! An agenda.'

He threw up his hands. 'A forlorn document in the middle of a table surrounded by empty benches.'

Lanfranc stood up as if he had come to a decision.

'Even lonelier, my lord. I shall go too.'

Maurilius stared.

'To Brittany?'

'No. To Caen. I have waited long enough for this stillborn council.'

Maurilius continued to gaze with wide eyes.

'And you will tell this, also, to his face?'

Lanfranc shook some crumbs from his habit.

'If necessary – yes. It will not be the first time. He laid upon me the burden of the abbacy of St. Stephen's. He can hardly complain if – in danger of the sins of idleness and sloth – I return to resume it.'

'But the council. He sent for you especially. He told me.'

'How can I give advice to a duke who will not be here? Council or no council.'

'You see what I mean,' said Maurilius. 'You should have been Archbishop, not me.'

* * * * * *

Arlette gazed at the two broad backs.

'But what do I do?'

'Wulfnoth is your man, my girl – not me,' said Gerard, without turning round.

'A waste of time. He thinks of nothing but his brother. I might as well not exist.'

Gerard glanced at his companion.

'Just one more layer of leather here, across the brow, do you think?'

Arlette stamped her foot.

'Gerard, please!'

'A moment, Serlo. An emergency of the heart.'

Serlo the armourer smiled and poured himself a drink. Gerard swung himself round and propped his palms across the top of his crutch.

'Tell me your miseries, girl.'

Arlette plunged into them with eager relief ... the children were being more beastly than usual ... Robert was ungovernable now that he was about to go on a real expedition ... Cecily could talk of nothing but my lord Harold, was useless for all practical purposes ... Wulfnoth was worried out of his wits about the danger he thought Harold was in – an assassin under every bed ... he was going away to Brittany ... she would be alone in this awful castle, with no company but those dreadful 'chicks'.

'And my lady Matilda,' added Gerard, who knew everything as usual.

'Yes,' said Arlette. 'She is in a foul mood too because his Grace will not take her with him. I am already paying for that. I can do nothing right.'

'Then find somebody who can.'

Arlette frowned.

'What do you mean?'

Gerard gestured with his crutch towards the hall, where Wulfnoth was supervising the preparations for a huge dinner.

'Do you expect any attention from that young man at the moment?'

Arlette 's face began to crumble.

'No. All he – '

'Ah, ah! No tears. Do you ever see my lady Matilda putting her hands in her lap and wailing to the rafters?'

Arlette wiped her nose with the back of a finger.

'Now,' said Gerard. 'Practical. You expect no help from Wulfnoth. Do you expect any from my lord the Duke?'

Arlette stared.

'Of course not. He is – '

' – much too busy. I agree. What about my lady Matilda?'

'Nothing but scolding.'

'So. Who does that leave?'

Arlette grimaced in bafflement.

'I still do not see.'

Gerard slapped the table with a ham of hand.

'What is it you want, girl? A betrothal, is it not? A promise to keep you warm while your young man is away being nursemaid to his brother.'

Arlette blushed.

'I am sure I have no idea what you mean.'

Gerard turned back to the table.

'Show me that rim again, Serlo.'

Arlette sniffed.

'Very well. Yes.'

Gerard put down the helmet.

'Ah. About time. Now, tell me. Who is there left who can help you to get what you want, and who at the present moment can do no wrong?'

Arlette widened her eyes.

'You mean – ?'

Gerard spread his hands.

'Who else but our golden earl? He has every man here open-mouthed in admiration. He tells Matilda to her face that her husband is a bastard, and she laughs. He takes away Cecily's pout. He has persuaded the Duke to take Robert with him. I should think getting a promise of a betrothal out of him would be child's play.'

'But how do I persuade him to help me?'

'By the Nails, girl, think of something. Use your charm. It is the one thing that Harold understands above all others.'

He picked up the helmet that he and Serlo had been discussing.

'Serlo and I have been working on this for weeks. I was going to give it to him at the midsummer feast. But now that – well, it seemed a good idea to do it before he goes away.'

'Who?'

Gerard sighed.

'Robert, you stupid girl. Who else?' He rubbed the metal with his sleeve. 'Do you think he will like it?'

* * * * * *

Thierry slowed down as much as he dared, and eased his aching back. Ahead of him, hunched and silent as any grave, my lord Geoffrey de Montbrai pounded the road as if he thought it deserved a whipping. His two men-at-arms turned in the saddle and looked back, but Thierry motioned them to go on. He would catch up when they watered the horses in the Drome.

It had started off so promisingly too. My lord Lanfranc was leaving Rouen at the same time, after a famous altercation with the Bastard – or so they said – and sought out my lord as a travelling companion. They were friends of long standing. As my lord Lanfranc was a scholarly abbot and no soldier, Thierry had looked forward to a leisurely amble lasting several days, with some fine hospitality at various abbeys on the route where Lanfranc would be welcomed and honoured.

The dream lasted as far as Bec, Lanfranc's old house. Every man on the demesne – cleric and villein alike – turned out to make a great fuss of my lord abbot. Sir Baldwin de Clair himself, lord of the lands of Bec, put in an appearance from his nearby castle of Brionne.

Questions tumbled in on Lanfranc from all sides. How was it to be Abbot of St. Stephen's of Caen? What was the new house like? How big was the new town? How many brothers were there? Did my lord Lanfranc think often of the loving brothers he had left behind at Bec? Did he miss them? What was happening at the great council at Rouen?

Food and wine came thick and fast, as the rules of the Blessed Saint Benedict were discreetly bent to accommodate this most welcome of guests. In the great abbey kitchen, Thierry spent a belt-breaking, tongue-aching evening. The centre of attraction, plied from right and left with treats both solid and liquid, he regaled one and all with gossip from both ends of the duchy.

The only one with a long face was my lord Geoffrey. Thierry sighed. He might have known. Lord Geoffrey wanted to 'get on'. He ate little and drank less.

In the morning, he was astride his horse before Prime was rung, short-tempered and dark in the face, his side hair sticking out like a hay bale, as it always did when he was under stress. He had no patience with Thierry's thick head or tender stomach.

'If we wait for you to pass all the food and drink you consumed yesterday, we shall be here a week. Now mount; we have no time to lose.'

My lord Lanfranc did not come with him this time.

'Can I persuade you to wait another hour or two, and travel in a more sedate fashion? The Almighty did put twenty-four hours in the day, you know. We could stay at Lisieux tonight, and then tomorrow I could show you my new house. You have not seen St. Stephen's yet.'

Geoffrey scraped up enough good grace to hold his horse still while he framed an answer.

'Your house is complete, my lord abbot. Mine is falling down.'

Lanfranc took the cold formality as a rebuke, and released his grip on Geoffrey's bridle.

'The Lord go with you, then. You could still stay at St. Stephen's if you wish. I can send a message with you ... '

My lord Lanfranc might as well have saved his breath. They by-passed Lisieux in the early afternoon. It was only a thunderstorm that persuaded my lord Geoffrey to stop for the night at the abbey of St. Martin at Troarn, about twenty-five miles further on. The house had been founded by my lord's old friend, Sir Roger of Montgomery, so they were at least known and welcomed. Thierry soaked his feet in the great monastery kitchen, and exchanged news with some familiar faces.

At dawn, it was the same again. More aching miles. No question of stopping at my lord Lanfranc's new house at St. Stephen's in Caen. Nor of staying on the main road to Bayeux. They turned off along manor tracks and boundary lanes towards Cérisy.

Thierry winced at the prospect. Trust my lord Geoffrey to avoid calling upon hospitality from the cathedral chapter. Anything rather than be indebted to my lord Odo, Bishop of Bayeux.

It was not only the length and haste of the journey that was getting on my lord Geoffrey's nerves, nor the decision to turn away from Bayeux. Nor again the fresh money that he would have to find to meet the new expenses at his own cathedral.

Thierry had kept his eyes and ears open at Rouen, and he knew the bargain that the Bastard had driven with his master.

'Oh, yes, he let the bishop go to nurse his famous cathedral, but he levied a price … when the Brittany business is over, and Conan retires to bathe his back, guess where the Bastard is going to bring everyone for rest and recreation … Right first time – Coutances. He gave the bishop no choice.'

'He did. He said he could arrange the rendezvous at Bayeux if my lord of Coutances could not manage the hospitality. You should have seen my lord Geoffrey's face!'

'Recreation – you know what that means. Beaters and carriers galore.'

'That is not all. The Bastard wants sappers for the siege of Dol. My lord of Coutances again must foot the bill.'

Thierry stood beside his horse at the edge of the River Drome, and watched it drink. My lord Geoffrey paced up and down a few yards away.

'What does he think I am – made of money?'

Thierry put on his most apologetic expression.

'Shall we be staying with the brothers at Cérisy tonight, my lord?'

Geoffrey mounted again, and looked at the darkening sky.

'I suppose so. Not much choice now.'

Thierry looked at the two men-at-arms and made a face.

Perhaps if my lord Geoffrey had found time to see the lady Sybil at St. Amand before he left Rouen, he might have been in a more human mood.

* * * * * *

There was only one tavern at Eu, and it was awful. Bruno stretched his long legs before a pitiful fire, which he nearly extinguished when he tossed the dregs of his beer into it. Knowing exactly what to expect but doing it all the same, he sniffed the empty mug, and recoiled.

Ralph came in noisily, and came straight across to him. Bruno took his helmet off a bench which he had been saving, and dragged it closer to the feeble flame.

Ralph sat down, and put out his palms.

'God's Breath, is this the best they can do?'

'Food is on its way,' said Bruno. 'I heard you in the stable.'

'Stupid boys – must be the air up here.'

The food arrived. Ralph swore when he saw it. Bruno shrugged.

'That or nothing. Lucky to get that. Nobody else has.'

Ralph made the best of it.

'You saw Guy then,' he said after a while.

Bruno nodded.

'Count Baldwin too. Told him the tale. He will play the cat outside Guy's rat-hole in Beaurain. So the Bastard can prise another rat out of his hole in Dol with a carefree mind.'

'Ah!'

Ralph continued to eat in silence, with occasional sidelong glances in Bruno's direction. Bruno grunted in what seemed like wry enjoyment of a private joke.

'Get it out then. You saw him.'

Ralph wiped his mouth.

'Yes.'

'And?'

'He is delighted – naturally. So are all the others. They are sick of boat-building.'

Bruno grunted again.

'He thinks he is going soldiering?'

'Be fair, Bruno. What was I supposed to tell him? That the Bastard wants as many sappers and general duties men as he can scrape up?'

'He will find out soon enough when he arrives at Dol. Did you tell him about the wasting as well?'

'The Flemings can do that – earn their pay.'

'So Gilbert does only the nice soldiering.'

'Oh, shut up!'

Ralph stood up and went to the inner door.

'You in there! Bring some more logs, and be sharp about it.'

Bruno pulled out a whetstone and began honing his knife. Well, at least Ralph had seen the boy. Had got him on to a campaign, such as it was. For all the good it would do.

It might make Ralph better company during their coming rides in and around the Vexin. Gleaning manpower. From the likes of de Clair, de Montfort, de Tosny, the elder Beaumont. Not a popular task, for all that they bore the Duke's warrant. Then along the southern frontier, twisting the arms of castellans behind the backs of their masters – Montgomery and Fitzosbern – squeezing twos and threes from the garrisons at Tillières, Breteuil, Bellême, Alençon, Domfront, and so on.

It was the Bastard's way of getting round having to use the normal feudal levy. A way of forestalling complaint, or, worse, non-compliance. A sliver here, a thin slice there, a few crumbs somewhere else. Scrounging half an army for half a campaign. It was seedy warfare, soldiering on the cheap, with a handful of silver thrown out months later by way of surly thanks – and only if the looting went well.

Ralph came back, his arms full of wood.

'If you want a job done properly, do it yourself.'

He tossed some on the fire, and poked it vigorously.

The reviving flames began to restore his spirits.

'Do you know what Gilbert asked? He said, "Is Nigel Fitzhenry going to be at Dol?" Why did he do that?'

Bruno shrugged.

'Who knows?'

Ralph clearly did not, and it was better not to tell him. He worried enough about the boy's military career. No point in making it worse by raising anxiety about his love life.

And Bruno, because he wanted Ralph in a good mood, did not ask if Ralph intended seeing his family at Gisors, which would be just off their route.

* * * * * *

Drops of sweat fell on the back of his white hands as he bent over the last knot, tugged, and tied. Grunting with relief, Arnulf sat back on his haunches and wiped his soaking brow.

Now that the effort was over, he bent his thoughts to the morrow – to the dawn departure. Suddenly the outlook was frightening. The fear deepened through the depression brought on by fatigue.

He could think of nothing but unpleasant prospects – the long hours in a cruel saddle, the rigours of the weather (in rain he suffered badly from chills; in sun he sweated more than usual), the jokes and jibes from the travelling company. And there would be no castle lodging to run to. What if the campaign went badly? What if Conan had already invaded, and there was a battle? What if he raided the Duke's besieging camp, and did what treacherous raiders always did to camp followers? What if ... ?

He needed a drink.

Adele said nothing when he poured himself a second cup, and a third.

He frowned at her as if it were all her fault ... At least he would be getting away from his embarrassment of a daughter. Away from her moods, her shameless, stupid flirtings. Away from her tight bodices ... If she was lonely, serve her right. There was scarcely an able-bodied man of any rank whatever left in the garrison.

Would she spare a thought for her father on his harsh, dangerous journeyings? Journeyings that he was undertaking solely in quest of a safer future for both of them. Him being a good father and all.

He doubted it.

How he had already abased himself, more than once, with my lords of Sées and Bayeux, with my lord of Lisieux. If he saw a chance on the road to Brittany, he would do it again. Not that they would spare much thought for him, their heads full of coming clashes with Count Conan. My lord of Coutances had already gone. It was no use trying my lords of Evreux and Avranches again. They were sulking at the stillbirth of the council. And my lord Archbishop Maurilius remained aloof in his palace.

He had tried my lord abbot Lanfranc too – offered to go with him to his new house at St. Stephen's at Caen, in any capacity. At least my lord Lanfranc was gracious in his refusal, but it was just as unflinching. His logic was unanswerable:

'What do you think his Grace the Duke would say if he found out that, after forcing him to part with your services as an incontinent priest, I had taken you into my employment, in however humble a position?'

Arnulf wiped his lips, which were already dry, and brooded on the unkindness of life and the unfairness of those around him.

Who had got him into this position? Gerard! That stumping cripple in the kitchen. All right for him; he would not have to go.

All very well for him to fling his hands to the rafters in quivering frustration and say, 'By the Nails! If I had two good knees!' Nobody was going to wave a magic wand and take him at his word.

Oh, yes, full of advice, as usual ...

'Think, man! Think what is your charge. You have told me about the altars.'

'And the relics.'

'Exactly. The Bastard rarely moves without them. If you do not take them, someone else will. Keep him in the habit of you. Matilda will not be there. He needs normality – if only for some of the time. With what you carry in those altars, you will provide it. In the mud and dust of campaign, he will not stop to worry about decrees from the Pope.'

'Well, if you think it is a good idea.'

Gerard pointed with his crutch.

'And do not forget – his vassals will need Mass too. And confession. Think of what will happen – the assault, the killings, the lootings, the wasting afterwards. They will have great need of the sacraments. And you will be there. They will not question you at a time like that. Any port in a storm.'

'My lord of Sées will be there. And Lisieux. And Bayeux. Coutances probably.'

'Bah! They will be campaigning as hard as the rest. They will need the sacraments too.'

* * * * * *

Pepin clattered his newly-shod hooves on the cobbles of the great outer bailey. He sensed a departure.

Sir Roger of Montgomery, already in the saddle, patted his neck.

'Not long now, boy. Just waiting for Walter and Fitz. Must have some company on the road, eh?'

Pepin snorted, but stood still. A rock of steadiness in the swirl of preparations and last-minute rememberings that filled the bailey.

Grooms, constables, marshals, and a small host of lesser officials, self-promoted to positions of great importance by the urgency of the morning, checked equipment, peered under waggon covers, squatted to squint at axles, bawled at underlings – if there were any such creatures left – and shed sweat and temper in even proportion.

The Duke's private train had been ready well in advance of the others, but then his Grace's frugality on campaign was legendary. 'A soft-headed scullion could pack the Bastard's waggon, and still have room left on it for the donkey.' Or so ran the common gossip.

Small detachments of men-at-arms, the private escort of the Duke's senior vassals, waited in professional calm. Near the main gate, the Flemings, in full marching order, milled round their own supply waggon and snatched one for the road.

The castle detachment of sappers and general duties men had left in dour silence an hour earlier; on foot, they would need the head start. Neither they, nor the more seasoned Flemings, would arrive as soon as the horsemen, but the Duke was hoping, as a sort of long shot, that Count Conan might quit the castle of Dol as soon as he saw the cavalry arrive; he might assume that the rest would be close behind.

It was part and parcel of William's habit of swift reaction. The sheer speed and surprise of his arrival before the walls of Dol, no matter how thin his forces, might knock Conan off balance. He had done it before; enemies had withdrawn in the shock of near-disbelief that he could have covered so much ground in the time.

Of course, he hoped to collect more men on the way, though it would take some arm-twisting. William de Warenne, in the Roumois close by, had gruffly promised to come in person with a small troop of knights. So had Gilbert d'Auffay, equally unwillingly. The Duke's brother, Count Robert of Mortain, could round up men like Lacy and Mohun and William de Briouze and offer them the prospect of timely loot after the wasting was over.

By turning the Flemings loose after the recapture of the castle, the Bastard hoped to avoid having to pay them their full agreed fee. They would do far better raking through abandoned baggage trains and demolished manor houses, and the damage would not be on a Norman conscience. Neat.

William was not slowing himself down either with heavy siege equipment. He had ordered his brother to collect the necessary material at Mortain, and to provide the vital axes.

It was improvisation run riot. No feudal levy, so no vassal could formally complain about annual service commitments being abused. No mention of money, so nobody could grumble about tax or mean reward. No gathering of the host; there *was* no 'host'. In short, there was to be no straining of the duchy's resources – which would please Fitz. Montgomery smiled.

And the Duke would still get what he wanted: a swift, punitive campaign which, if successful, would restore a Norman garrison in a castle in Brittany and so keep a thorn in Conan's side. It would strengthen his western border, and so contribute to his unremitting quest for all-round security – in case! Montgomery shook his head in admiration. The Bastard always got what he wanted.

Mind you, it was an ill wind that blew nobody any good. Roger now had a perfect answer for Mabel. She had been making noises about coming to Rouen for a while. God alone knew how Harold's reputation had reached Bellême, but it had. Mabel could never resist the temptation to do a little social climbing. They had had many an argument over her knack for giving offence to those both above and beneath her.

'I am sure I have no idea what you are talking about. Where is your sense of opportunity? A good job I have some. The trouble with you, Roger, is that you are a pudding.'

She really could not see that she was giving offence.

Montgomery made a face. What a combination – a thick skin and a sharp tongue. If that was what you needed to get on, she was right; he had neither.

Well, she would have to turn her tongue on her serving women at Belléme. She was not coming to Rouen, and she would not meet Harold. Mabel would never contemplate the journey to Brittany, not even to meet the Emperor.

Sir Walter Giffard threaded his way through the throng. For once, when surrounded by inferiors, he was not in a bad mood.

'A fine morning, Roger. Good to be on the move, eh?'

Montgomery smiled.

'Walter, you are the first person I have spoken to this morning who is not grumbling about the rush.'

Giffard made a gesture with a gloved hand towards the bustle all round them.

'At least something is happening. Makes a change from day after day at the table or the chase. Although I must say that the man is devilish fine company.'

Montgomery agreed. Harold's gift for good talk and boisterous spirits had softened the sharp edges of everyone's face. Walter had even forgotten about his beloved Arabs for a while. But it was all impermanent. Even the cautious Fitzosbern said so.

He welcomed the action as much as anybody, though he maintained his long face about the wisdom of the Brittany expedition, more to keep up appearances than for any other reason …

'We can watch Harold under pressure. This endless round of feasts and boar-hunts is child's play to him. We need to see him in different surroundings. We might be able to wrong-foot him … '

Giffard laughed as he remembered the conversation.

'Wrong-foot him. Ha!'

'Harold knows nothing about castles and sieges,' said Montgomery. 'The English have next to no castles.'

'Who told you that?' said Giffard.

'He did himself.'

Giffard laughed again.

'And you think you will wrong-foot him? A man like that.'

He leaned from his saddle and lowered his voice.

'God's Face, I like the man and I admire him. But there is only one way to deal with him. I have said it enough times, but nobody will listen.'

* * * * * *

'Make way! Make way!'

Gerard boomed at the close-packed shoulders and buttocks. When that failed, he made liberal use of his crutch to clear a way to the front. Peter the scullion seized the Heaven-sent opportunity to slip through with him.

'Not long now, son.'

Peter felt a surge of friendship and security at the grip of Gerard's great hand on his shoulder . All round them were castle staff from every bailey and building, every rank and calling. The guardroom was empty, and it took a lot to move off-duty sentries away from their beds.

On the other side of the great gateway, with its huge double doors flung wide, Peter could see two bishops and their chaplains. A large splash of black showed that abbots and their travelling staff were not immune from curiosity. Stretching away towards the town, on either side of the road, were milling half the population of Rouen. Tucked inside it, outside a roadside tavern, was a portly monk standing beside a donkey.

'Here they come!'

A trumpeter first, and not a very good one. The crowd, tense with expectation, and lungs bursting ready to cheer, burst instead into loud laughter at the boy's split notes.

They were so taken up with the joke that they did not notice that the Duke and the Earl were coming until they were almost upon them. There was a moment's hesitation, almost an embarrassed silence, as if they felt that they had been caught poking out their tongue.

Harold resolved it instantly. He gestured towards the straining trumpeter, whose cheeks were now glistening. Harold put his fingers in his ears and winced in agony. The crowd roared its approval in hoots and guffaws that rolled down the street in a tidal wave of mirth. The wretched trumpeter was now red and sweating to his eyebrows, and making even more mistakes.

Beside the Earl, Duke William kept his face straight, but his eyes darted from side to side as if he were approaching an ambush. Behind them came the Duke's senior vassals and their escorts.

'What did I tell you?' said Giffard to Montgomery. 'Listen to it. And the campaign not even started. If we take Dol, what will his reception be? At this rate, he could go for the imperial crown, never mind England.'

The Earl's brother, Wulfnoth, jogged past, his face as long as ever. He never saw Arlette's hesitant hand.

The three warrior bishops – Odo of Bayeux, the Duke's brother, Hugh of Lisieux, the Duke's cousin, and Yves of Bellême, Bishop of Sées – wore conspicuous mail under open episcopal robes, and carried maces, leaving their chaplains, who were indifferent horsemen, to manage their croziers along with the reins. And a bad job they made of it.

Nigel winked at Adele as he trotted by. Adele, smitten by a conscience that suggested she had been a little hard on him, gave him a full smile. Nearly blew him a kiss. When he had passed, she noticed that she was standing exactly opposite the Saxon dog-boy on the other side of the road. Their eyes met.

Adele wrenched them away to wave to her father. Arnulf, bouncing and sweating on his tiny cart, had trouble controlling the patient animal in the shafts. His jowls quivered over the cobbles. Adele felt embarrassed that she had waved and thus revealed her relationship with him. She lowered her head and looked sidelong to right and left. He was so – well, so pathetic.

The laughter kept pace with Harold as he rode between the neck-craning lines of townsfolk, still pretending to be in pain from the helpless herald's efforts. The boy's face was now puce, and tears streamed across his cheeks.

Outside the tavern, Hubert drained the last of his beer.

'Exactly as I said, Rollo. Exactly as I said. Just like the tide. The castle fills to the brim to see him arrive. Now it empties itself down to the lees because he is going. And the whole town is here to see him off. There is not a house here that has more than a rat indoors.

'Did you see those vassals? Fitzosbern, Giffard, Montgomery, and the others? They can not wait to go with him. Oh, yes – they complain about another campaign, and the trouble and the expense. All show, Rollo. All show. They are dying to see how he performs. And shall I tell you something else, Rollo? They are also dying to perform in front of him. Yes! So that he will think well of them.

'Clever. The Bastard knew that. That was why he wants Harold on this Brittany move. What a man! I tell you, Rollo, you would go the length and breadth of Christendom to find two more finely-balanced adversaries.'

The last of the carts and waggons clattered past. Housewives collected the dung for their vegetable patches, and small boys strutted in parody of the soldiers.

Hubert said goodbye to the innkeeper.

Rollo turned his head in inquiry. Hubert levered himself on to the front of his cart. His picked up his light wand of a whip and laid it quietly on Rollo's rump. He sighed.

'Alas! Longueville it must be, Rollo. How I envy those small boys. To be off on campaign again, eh? How many years is it now? And I still feel the pangs now and then. Truly the habit has not yet become a habit, Rollo. We must pray hard tonight, my friend. Oh, yes – very hard!

* * * * * *

'You are rather good at this, you know.'

It tripped easily off the tongue, and it sounded genuine, spontaneous. Adele had often found it useful. It also had the welcome effect of slowing down an over-impetuous lover. He, flattered, was eager to repeat whatever he fancied was especially clever – Adele was careful never to specify. But it gave her a curious sense of superiority. She never ceased to be surprised at what men were prepared to believe in bed; tell them the right things, and you could do anything with them.

They were wary sometimes of what you said before, and they rarely listened to what you said afterwards. But during – that was another story.

'You are rather good at this, you know.'

It often enabled her to – well, to sort of catch up.

She also found that Edwin was eminently teachable, far more so than Nigel. Nigel was too full of himself; Edwin was grateful ...

At first, it had been simply someone to listen to him. Nobody else would. He had a tale of woe to tell – about a lonely young Saxon in a foreign country without his beloved dogs, and a cruel master who refused to take him to Brittany – and Adele was willing to listen. A sympathetic face became a sympathetic voice, then a sympathetic arm round the shoulder. From the chaste consolation of an arm round the shoulder to the warm comfort of a pair of thighs was for Adele the work of a mere two days – and a very enjoyable two days at that.

As they lay together, she caught sight of two empty beer mugs under a shelf. She frowned as if she could hear her father's voice.

Well, what else was she to do? No work, no company, no father, no comfort.

And she was no nun. Nor was she a milk-and-water priss like Arlette. Come to think of it, Arlette was no saint either. Purse-lips little hypocrite! She had been seen with her cosseted and much-protected Saxon hostage. The women who laundered down by the river missed very little ...

When it was over, she did not get up at once. She found herself content simply to lie. Edwin's arm did not fidget her.

On an impulse, she did what she had often done, with Nigel, and, truth to tell, with others. She kissed him lightly on the lips. But the kiss lingered.

Mystified, she drew back, and she saw Edwin watching her intently. Suddenly she found herself struck with an almost physical blow which momentarily caused her to fight for breath. Nothing in her previous life – no knowledge, no education, no experience, no vague hope, no dream – nothing had prepared her for what happened.

She fell in love.

* * * * * *

Chapter Seven

The Testing

Sir Walter Giffard looked sidelong at Sir Roger of Montgomery as they rode through the rain.

The Bastard had driven them hard. Another day, and they should be within striking distance of Conan. God's Face, what a ride! Aches and pains, camp cooking, awful weather, the Bastard in a foul mood. Never a word of complaint out of Roger.

There had been news about Mabel too. Roger had arranged for a courier to meet him at Falaise, to bring news from Bellême. Mabel, furious at being unable to meet Harold, had taken herself off to Paris. To do some social climbing, no doubt. What would worry Roger, of course, would be the money she would spend. It never showed on Roger's face, or in his speech.

Walter spat the rain off his lips. If he had half of Roger's patience. The secret seemed to lie in his friend's ability not to fret. Roger was content to leave deep thinking to Fitzosbern, to leave devilish scheming to Bishop Odo, morals to Lanfranc, subtle understanding of a man's mind to Geoffrey, and leadership to the Bastard. He was even prepared to leave the everyday running of Bellême to Mabel; whatever else he thought of her, he acknowledged that she was a good chatelaine. Nothing upset him.

No, that was not quite true. Honour. Honour moved him. It showed in his dealings with Fitzosbern. Two of his elder brothers had murdered Fitz's father. Many years ago now, and the brothers were long dead. Roger had redeemed himself by his loyal service to the bastard duke that Fitz's father had died protecting, but the memory remained. Too often Roger fancied that Fitz was wary of him. Probably not true, but Roger thought it was, and it worried him.

How odd life was – a fearless man is afraid of the very thing that all his peers can see he has no need to fear. Whatever you might impute to Roger – he was inclined to slowness, he was not especially inventive, he was frankly a bit dull – the one accusation you could never level at him was disloyalty or dishonour. And that was the only fear he had: that he might slip into the one or the other.

'God's Face, what a day!'

'Ah,' said Roger.

Sir Roger of Montgomery looked sidelong at Sir Walter Giffard. He had been poor company. It was not because of the weather; they had seen enough of that in their time.

Walter had not been happy about the whole Brittany idea. 'Half a campaign!

Worse than none at all. Conan will simply slip away into his mists and snap his fingers at us.' Roger smiled. What was really upsetting Walter was that a siege gave no scope for the deployment of knights. It was tedious, boring work fit only, in Walter's mind, for foot-soldiers and sappers. 'Earth-grubbers!' Walter almost spat his opinion. 'You do not win campaigns with the soles of your feet or the blisters on your knees; you win them from the seat of your arse – in the saddle.'

He had not been happy about Harold either. 'We are being too clever by half. We shall regret it – mark what I say.'

In fact, he had been in evil humour ever since the Bastard had summoned him to Rouen. Away from his precious Arabs. He longed for news from Longueville. And when it came, it was accompanied by a message from my lady – no doubt to Ermengarde's great satisfaction – that Judith had been put in the convent at St. Amand, together with her dowry. Walter had been purple in the face for an hour.

Roger sighed. Saints and angels, what a ride! What could he do to remove those deep lines about Walter's forehead and cheeks?

'A good thing this journey will soon be over. Another few days and Harold will have the entire column eating out of his hand.'

Walter snorted.

'I agree. The man is a miracle. All the more reason to kill him.'

* * * * * *

'Move over, Rollo, if you want a clean stall. Really, of all the ungrateful beasts ... '

Hubert raked out the last of the soiled straw, puckering his nose and making an explosive puffing sound with his lips.

'For sure, Rollo, they would never use you to perfume the bedchamber of the Sultan.'

He stood the rake against the wall, took out his knife, and cut away the binding from a fresh bale.

'Ah, well, the work is at the same time good for your body, and good for my soul. Perhaps I do wander too much; I should spend more time in the mother house. More time here, eh?'

The most he had been able to manage since his return from Rouen and Longueville had been a quick walk to the harbour at le Tréport, to exchange gossip with Aldred, ship's captain to Earl Harold. The work was proceeding well, and Aldred expected to have the ship ready by mid-July, or at worst by harvest-time ...

'We shall have the ship and the crew, but no Earl Harold. Gone adventuring at the other end of the duchy.'

Aldred hawked and spat. Hubert poured him another drink out of the cask from his waggon.

'He will return soon enough, my friend. It will suit neither the Bastard nor your earl to sit among the mists of Brittany for long. You could always watch for signs of movement from Guy of Ponthieu.'

Aldred drank, wiped his mouth, and grinned through his beard.

'You will not catch me like that, you tub. If you have come for gossip, you have come in vain. Guy of Ponthieu sits at Beaurain and gnashes his teeth, while Count Baldwin stands on his tail. You have poured your drink for nothing.' He held up the mug. 'It is good stuff, though.'

Hubert waved airily.

'Old soldier's distillation. Only for the favoured few.'

'Flattery will not get you anything either.'

'We shall see. We shall see. A drink and a willing ear are never wasted.'

Aldred sipped thoughtfully.

'I could take the ship there.'

'To Brittany?'

'Yes.'

Hubert shook his bald head.

'Out of the question, my friend. Out of the question. You could never sail it down the Channel against the westerly wind, and you have too few men to work it by the oar all the way. Besides, there are a hundred rivers between the Somme and the Couesnon; how would you know which is which?'

Aldred sighed. Hubert patted him on the shoulder.

'Patience, my old sea-hawk. Come and stay with us in the house when you have finished. I can tell you stories of every river-mouth from here to Mont St. Michel, the Wonder of the World. Now there is a tale for you – the founding of Mont St. Michel. Oh, yes, a real tale. It seems there was once a bishop of Avranches – long ago, you understand – called Aubert, and – a great wonder, this – he was visited in a dream by St. Michael the Archangel himself. Not boring you, am I. . ?'

Hubert paused as he spread the straw to speak directly into one of Rollo's long ears. He looked furtively to left and right first.

'But every day I spend here does put Father Abbot in a good mood. Every day builds up a small deposit of goodwill, which I can draw on when I have need of it. For there will soon be news from Brittany for the taking; I can feel it in the air. And Harold will return. That, my friend, is when Brother Hubert sets out on his travels again. Father Abbot will be unable to deny the privilege to such an obedient, hardworking brother.'

Hubert peeled an onion and held it in the palm of his hand to Rollo's mouth.

'And I tell you this, Rollo. They will have gone all the way to Brittany, and they will still not have caught him out.'

Rollo crunched it gratefully.

'Unless – unless – do you know what I think, Rollo? I think they will never catch him by being clever, by low cunning. But if they should – even by accident – happen to do something absolutely genuine, then ... Harold will not expect it, you see. He will be bowled over. He too may do something absolutely genuine. And that could be the undoing of him. Yes, the undoing. And I should wager that my lord Bishop Odo of Bayeux will be on hand to take advantage of such a misfortune.'

He stroked Rollo's nose, and whispered in his ear again.

'Still, we shall see, shall we?'

Rollo turned his head, and Hubert reeled from his breath.

'For sure, Rollo, you will die a bachelor like me.'

* * * * * *

'He will miss it then.'

'It looks like it.'

The admission was prised out of Ralph as if it were a rotten tooth.

It was the longest sentence he had uttered since dawn. For once it was Bruno who was the talkative one.

'They say the Bastard had the man almost flayed alive.'

'Who?'

'The cook, man. Mortain's cook. It was his dinner that laid everyone out.'

'Yes ... '

To be fair, Robert of Mortain had not been expecting so large a contingent in his brother's train, and there had been a tremendous rush to serve a meal of a suitable size and standard. There was always a rush where the Bastard was concerned. No doubt the poor cook had cut a few corners with suspect livestock and incomplete roasting.

Within hours there was a steady stream of men, clutching their stomachs and groaning like cows with over-full udders, on their way to the privies. Some never reached them, and added their putrid contribution to the straw that was already polluted by the waste of a dozen castle dogs. Some lay in corners in filth, unable to move.

By no mean an uncommon occurrence. The Bastard had been restive at the delay, but then he often was. What drove him to cold fury was that his son Robert was among those stricken. Earl Harold too, though not so badly. Trust the Earl to get off lightly. Men had already seen enough of him to shake their heads at his unfailing luck. But William felt the shame of a host whose guest is ill under his roof. Or rather his brother's, which was almost the same thing.

Ignoring Robert of Mortain's apologies and excuses, he had the wretched cook dragged into the main bailey and whipped before those of the garrison who could still stand. The man's screams sent the castle pigeons up in a cloud of winged applause.

The following morning, however, he was ready to set out for Pontorson.

'With half a force?' said Fitzosbern.

'Splendour of God!' roared the Bastard. 'We still have the surprise.'

Fitzosbern shrugged; there was no reasoning with him in this mood.

Ralph and Bruno, who had eaten in the stables with their horses, were still fit, and were sent ahead as usual. Giffard, Montgomery, and those knights who could sit on a horse followed an hour later. The captain of Flemings was among the casualties.

'Put Beaumont in charge.'

Fitzosbern opened his mouth to say something about Beaumont's inexperience, caught sight of the expression on William's face, and shrugged again. Beaumont was delighted. Here was something he could tell Judith when he returned. And his father.

Beds were dragged into the hall beside the fire, and were at once surrounded by a scuffle of eager servants. Harold waved them back.

'We are not at death's door.'

William came to say goodbye, and glanced at Robert's pale face.

'Do not fret,' said Harold. 'He is young. He will mend. I shall starve him for a day or two, and he will be in a saddle before you can fire an arrow. We shall follow soon enough, never fear.'

William looked doubtful. He left half the Rouen garrison as bodyguard. He began an explanation of the route. Harold waved it away.

'If Normandy is anything like England, there can not be many roads to Brittany. We shall find you.'

'One of our men was born in Avranches. He knows the country.'

So Gilbert found himself detailed to remain behind with Robert and the Earl Harold. Another was Nigel Fitzhenry.

Nigel, who, with his infernal luck, had escaped infection, looked forward to two days of indolent pursuit of the girls of Mortain, with a little teasing of Gilbert when time should hang heavy.

Gilbert was cast down at the thought of missing the excitement of a siege ...

Bruno looked at Ralph again, as they cantered along a ridge above the River Sée.

'There will be other chances, you know.'

'Yes ... '

The delight and eagerness that had flashed on to Gilbert's face when he had first heard the news.

'I am to go to Brittany? With you?'

He could scarcely believe it. He had been waiting so long. And now this ...

Bruno shook his head. Ralph was allowing himself to suffer with the boy, was dulling the edge of his judgment. Gilbert thought that glory was the only prize, that it was a quarry that stood behind every tree, waiting only be chased and caught by an eager hunter.

'Some people are simply not lucky.'

Ralph turned sharply, as if he had just woken up.

'What did you say?'

'Nothing.'

* * * * * *

'Holy Virgin – are you never satisfied, man?'

Geoffrey de Montbrai flung out his arms, and began pacing up and down.

Thierry and his friend Goscelin exchanged glances. At times like this, and, Heaven knew, there were plenty of them, it was best to remain quiet.

Geoffrey paused at the end of the hall, and shouted back at them.

'I find the timber for your scaffolding, and you say it is no good.'

Goscelin looked pained.

'It is unseas – '

Thierry nudged him in the ribs.

'I scour the whole of Lower Normandy for masons, and you tell me they are not sufficiently trained. What am I expected to do – steal them from his Grace of Avranches?'

Geoffrey came forward again, till he was right in front of Goscelin. He leaned forward in his agitation.

'Have you any idea of what this whole project is costing me? And what about the new wing to my palace? What about the court-room? As for repairing the aqueduct, I might as well pray for the moon.'

Thierry looked patiently at the rafters. When lord Geoffrey went on about the aqueduct, it was a sign that he was feeling particularly hard done by.

'I might also remind you that, in a short time, we shall be entertaining the whole of the Duke's train, as soon as he has captured Dol. Have you thought of that?'

Thierry and Goscelin shook their heads in humble contrition; no, they had not thought of that.

'If I go on spending money at this rate, I shall have to make yet another journey to see the Guiscard, and you know what that means.'

Thierry began to take notice. Yes, he did know what that meant. It meant months in the saddle, right through France, over the awful passes of the Alps, through the rains and mists of Lombardy, the snow of the Apennines, the blistering sun of Campania and Apulia – till they reached the headquarters of Robert Guiscard, the greatest adventurer in all Italy. Robert of Hauteville, and his brothers, came from a village of that name, and that village was in my lord's diocese of Coutances, and my lord had more than once gone on begging missions, to raise money for his new cathedral. The Hautevilles were usually generous, provided that appropriate memorials were to be raised to them in the new cathedral, and enough masses were to be said for their souls. Judging by the stories of their adventures that were told round firesides all over France and Italy, they were going to need all the masses they could get.

But it was a long and wearisome journey, and Thierry always dreaded it. You never knew where the next square meal was coming from.

Lord Geoffrey went on for a few more minutes, but it was clear that he was running down.

Goscelin knew well that his bishop was as devoted to the new cathedral as he was, and that it was worry rather than meanness that provoked most of the outbursts. Thierry knew too that lord Geoffrey was more than happy to entertain the Duke and his train, because it would mean that his great rival, Bishop Odo, would not. The Bastard would hold his council of vassals at Coutances, not at Bayeux. Satisfaction like that was worth some expenditure, begging trip or no begging trip.

Thierry suddenly woke up. Lord Geoffrey had stopped nagging, and was giving him some orders.

'My lord?'

'Time for you to earn your keep. Tomorrow you will go to Pontorson and Dol, and glean news about the campaign. Do not be afraid to ask his Grace himself, if you have to. He will know that you are only helping me to make a good welcome in good time.'

Thierry ducked his head.

'My lord.'

Geoffrey looked at him sourly, scratched a cheek with a fingernail, and turned away.

As Thierry was leaving the hall, Geoffrey called after him.

'Do not be lazy and take the short cut. Keep to the tracks near Pontorson. Do not cross the Couesnon too near the sea.'

'I know, my lord – the sands. I have been there before.'

As they crossed the courtyard, Thierry grunted.

'Goz, old friend, for once he has surprised me. I had expected him to send me for news to the lady Sybil at St. Amand. He must indeed have a lot on his mind.'

* * * * * *

'Who comes?'

'Sir Roger of Montgomery. Make way.'

'Sorry, sir. Sir William's orders. Foreign territory and all. Have to challenge everybody.'

Montgomery peered past the sentry.

'Where is Sir William?'

'Here,' said Fitzosbern, looming up from the shadows. 'Took you long enough.'

'I had no idea it was so urgent.'

Fitzosbern jerked a thumb behind him.

'If you had spent an hour like the one I have just had with him ... '

Montgomery grunted.

'That bad?'

'I can get no sense out of him or into him. I need numbers.'

'Ah. Who else have you called then?'

'Mortain. See if he will listen to his own brother.'

Robert of Mortain came up from the main camp.

'I have a joint on the spit. This had better be serious.'

'It is,' said Fitzosbern. 'I have failed. Three bishops have achieved nothing: Sées gave up after an hour; he swore at Lisieux, his own kinsman; Bayeux he refuses even to see.'

'Why ask me then?' said Robert of Mortain. 'If he refuses to see one brother, why should he see another?'

'Because you keep a castle,' said Fitzosbern. 'So does Roger here.'

'So do you – two.'

'Just so,' said Fitzosbern, unperturbed as usual. 'Together, therefore, we might carry some weight. We all know something about keeping people out of castles, so between us we should be able to offer some useful comment about getting into them – or not, as the case may be. Come with me.'

'Why should he be so put out?' said Mortain. 'The shock arrival has failed – that is all. It was a gamble in the first place. No man can get into a castle with knights and grooms. Conan has simply called our bluff. We shall get him in the end, when the Flemings and the sappers arrive.'

Fitzosbern shook his head.

'You do not fully understand the situation. He is torn by more devils than Conan's nerve.'

Montgomery frowned.

'No riddles, Fitz. Explain.'

Fitzosbern stopped before they came within earshot of the Duke's tent, but lowered his voice nevertheless.

'He has failed with the gamble – enough to eat the pride of a leader like William.' Fitzosbern was the only person outside the immediate family who referred to the Duke by his name. It was a measure of their intimacy and total reliance on each other, which all men respected. 'Worse, he has lost time, and you know how impatient he is.'

'What do you expect with a siege?' said Mortain. 'A volley of arrows on a spring afternoon and they surrender?'

'Come now, my lord,' said Montgomery, using the correct form of address to the kinsman of his Duke (he was neither familiar nor friendly with Mortain). 'We all know the dangers of a full siege. Patrols think that the castle is well provided. We have no clear idea of Conan's resources elsewhere. He may have a relieving army anywhere between here and Dinant or Rennes. Captured prisoners have suggested it. Look at our forces, here, at the moment. The longer we wait, the greater our chance of being caught between a hammer and an anvil.'

'In the open too,' added Fitzosbern. 'With our backs to the Couesnon and the sea.'

'We accepted that risk when we invaded,' said Mortain.'

'Not about the relieving force. That is a new factor.'

'The prisoners may be lying. Conan put them up to it.'

'Maybe. But that is a risk we can not afford to take. Even if the Flemings were here now, it would be too big a danger.'

Mortain grunted.

'There is something else,' said Fitzosbern. 'The other devil.'

'Of course,' said Mortain, snapping his fingers. 'Harold.'

'Harold is not here,' said Montgomery, puzzled.

'Exactly,' said Fitzosbern. 'He was looking forward to the chance of testing him.'

'Not the end of the world,' said Montgomery. 'There will be other chances. That is why we are watching and waiting all the time.'

'It is not only that, Roger. Think. Here was a chance of a brilliant stroke, in front of Harold. And it has not come to pass. It is not merely disappointment; it is loss of face. William feels it keenly.'

'Harold will understand. He is a soldier too. He is not small-minded.

Whatever else he is, he is generous.'

'Just so. But the troops. They are not generous; they will not understand. They will talk. Harold is already some kind of demi-god to them. He can do no wrong.'

'Ah!'

'So my brother,' said Mortain, 'is afraid that comparisons will be made.'

'Something like that.'

'Where do we come in?' said Montgomery.

'You back me up with a solution,' said Fitzosbern.

Mortain gaped.

'What do you expect us to do? Try again? Gallop up the motte into a cloud of arrows and leap over the wall from the saddle?'

Fitzosbern as usual refused to take offence.

'No. I expect you to tell him that his options are limited. He must forget Harold for the time being, forget his loss of face, forget the failure of his gamble. He must give up all idea of a protracted siege; we have neither the time nor the resources. I have been telling him that since Christmas.'

Mortain spread his hands.

'Then what *do* we have the resources for?'

'A short wait. In the hope that the Flemings and the sappers arrive. No more than four or five days. And plenty of patrols out in the meantime, all the way to Dinant, and Rennes if need be. We scour the country right down to Nantes.'

'For an army that may not exist.'

'Do you want to take that chance? Has it occurred to you that this could be the reason why Conan is sitting tight and defying us to do something?'

Mortain sighed.

'Very well.'

'And if the Flemings do not arrive within a few days,' said Montgomery, 'we go home. Is that it?'

Fitzosbern nodded.

'We swallow our pride and go. And to perdition with what Harold thinks.'

Mortain extended his hand towards his brother's tent.

'After you, then, Fitz. The sooner the better; my joint will be getting burnt.'

* * * * * *

Adele watched through a crack in the door as Edwin crossed the courtyard in the moonlight. Pulling the blanket tighter round her body, she went back to the bed and lay down.

How many hours was it to dawn? Dear God – how would she get through them?

She turned her head sideways and put out her hand to the hollow in the straw mattress where Edwin had been. It was still warm. She could smell him ...

It was the same every night. A few hours of separation seemed like a week; their hours together from dawn to dusk, or later, sped by like the flight of a swallow.

A thrill at first – a novelty. Adele gave herself up to the new sensation like a glutton revelling in an unfamiliar dish. Then there was the sense of challenge – of defying the whole castle. Their lovemaking was not forbidden, but it was secret; it added urgency. It was haste, almost violence; it was dampness in the small of the back; it was hair plastered across a glistening forehead; it was sweat running across a shiny red spot on the cheek; it was stifled moans and whimpers.

Before she could realise what was happening, it took over almost every conscious thought. She forgot her father's guilt and panic. She forgot Nigel's insolent hands. She forgot Beaumont's sneering rejection. She forgot Gilbert's cow eyes. She forgot everything in one blinding revelation after another that took her breath away as much with newness as with ecstasy. Absolutely nothing else mattered.

Within days she cast care who knew about it. The altar boys and scullions sniggered; the washing women nudged each other and grinned; Gerard let out his great booming laugh. The castle was half-empty, but if it had been full to the top of the towers, it would have been the same. The one shred of convention that clung to her was an inability to keep him with her right through the night; she insisted that he go back to his sheepskins by the kitchen fire.

'You must go.'

She never explained, and Edwin never questioned. He was still in a foreign country.

'In the morning then.'

'Oh, yes! And early – early!'

In the morning there were fresh joys. They went out, they sat by the river, they gossiped with Gerard, they ate and drank. Ordinary, so ordinary. But it was now, somehow, new. Adele noticed things she had never seen before. She took delight in quiet contemplations that she would have thought unutterably boring a week before. Their talk with Gerard was now empty of complaint and criticism and self-sympathy. There were times when Gerard fell into a mood approaching admiration.

'I should never have thought it possible. You two positively shine together.'

Adele was not sure that she understood his shake of the head, or the sad look on his face.

They devoured everything in the way of food that Gerard put in front of them. That did make him laugh.

'The food of love, eh?'

But Edwin was clearly putting on weight. He lost the grey patches under his cheekbones that had been there since his arrival.

After each excursion they could not stop their feet taking them back to Adele's bed in the tiny kitchen of Arnulf's house. They were being pulled by strings. Yet it was not a race to satiety, a contest of shuddering storms of the loins and gaspings for breath and flopping exhaustion afterwards.

Adele amazed herself. She was rushing to reach her bed not so that she could take further pleasure, but that she could give it. They offered the constant readiness of their bodies as a means of joy to each other.

'Use me! Go on – use me!'

They talked too. So many secret hopes and fears. They stared in wonder at the discovery of mutual worries and joys.

They laughed. Adele remembered that, almost from the first, he had made her laugh. Now they shared their laughter – at castle personalities, at accidents, at the rude words they taught each other in their native languages, at the funny noises their bodies made against each other.

Every encounter bound them closer and yet liberated their minds at the same time. Guilt had run away like rain off a steep roof. In the dazzling sunlight of their passion, they flaunted themselves to each other; they teased each other; they looked for new ways to prolong their own and the other's pleasure; they told each other what they liked best; they revelled in the sheer joy of playing with flesh ...

The mere thought of it all made her cheeks burn in the dark. Her chest pounded.

Adele lay in her blanket and put her arms across her breasts and hugged herself. God alive! How would she ever get to sleep?

* * * * * *

'I tell you, lads – this girl was so energetic, she was so frantic – talk about appetite – I almost fell off.'

Roars of laughter. More beer was passed round. Shakes of the head and wide grins. You had to hand it to Nigel; he was devilish good company.

Young Robert's face glowed. Nigel treated him as an equal; talked to him of men's matters.

'What then?'

Nigel glanced at him.

'What then, Master Robert?' He glanced round at his audience. 'Finished the course – naturally.'

More guffaws. Nigel was enjoying himself hugely.

'When once you have put your hand to something – '

'Your hand!'

Nigel shrugged.

'Well ... you know what I mean.'

He looked at young Robert again.

'If Master Robert feels sufficiently recovered, perhaps he might like to accompany me on one of my evening excursions, to sample the local – um – facilities.'

'For shame!' said Gilbert, who could contain himself no longer. 'His Grace has entrusted his eldest son to our care.'

Nigel spread his hands in a wide gesture of saintly innocence.

'And care is what he will have. I should never leave his side.'

'Might get a bit crowded – all under the same blanket,' said someone. More laughter.

Nigel leaned confidentially towards Robert, who was still in bed.

'The trouble with our friend Gilbert here – between you and me, Master Robert – is that he has a bit of trouble – how shall I put it – screwing himself up to the matter in hand.'

Robert heard the sniggers all round him, and nobly chuckled too.

'You see,' said Nigel, 'there is this girl, in the castle at Rouen. He worships her. Sadly, when the time comes, he finds he is not ... up to it. So she, understandably, feels – shall I say – let down. Not very flattering, after all.'

Gilbert put down his cup.

'Be warned, Fitzhenry.'

'Funny thing is, Master Robert – your father, his Grace the Duke, thinks he might be important. He comes from Avranches, you see. Knows the ground. So we have to take him along with us to deal with Conan. In case we get lost, I suppose.'

Gilbert slowly stood up.

Nigel looked up, but continued to talk to Robert without taking his eyes off Gilbert.

'Seems silly to me – all we have to do is cross the Couesnon. Why do we need the pathfinding skills of a ploughboy who gets lost on his way to the thighs of the castle whore at Rouen?'

The fight was over in a few minutes. Both were exhausted, both bleeding from nose and mouth.

As he turned over on to his stomach to sleep, Gilbert remembered something his father used to say.

'When you pay off an old score, son, always pay back in equal measure, and then add a little more.'

* * * * * *

Lanfranc read the official letter, the fair copy. His secretary had just left to put the draft into the archives.

'Lanfranc, Abbot of St. Stephen's of Caen, to His Holiness Pope Alexander II, servant of the servants of God, greetings ... '

His practised lawyer's eye skimmed quickly through the formal rhetoric ... 'unforeseen delays to the holy council which your Holiness had in his wisdom seen fit to summon at Rouen ... for the radical reform of the most sick and ailing body of Mother Church ... abuse of the holy sacrament of celibacy by ministers of Holy Church ... the joint wisdom of six prince bishops of Normandy – Sées, Evreux, Avranches, Coutances, Bayeux, Lisieux – and of the metropolitan archbishop Maurilius of Rouen, and of the lord abbots of ... the urgent desire of his Grace Duke William II of Normandy to attend to the heavy burden of responsibility placed upon his albeit willing shoulders ... the comparative paucity of decrees issuing from the above council in no way detracting from the zeal and reforming ardour of its ordained members ... lengthy deliberation would lead in the fullness of time to an even deeper understanding of His Holiness' wishes and desires and to an even more comprehensive fulfilment of those wishes and desires ... working together towards the performance of that most satisfying of all activities – the pursuance of God's Holy Will as transmitted to us lowly creatures on earth by the Bishop of Rome, just as the Blessed St. Peter had carried out the wishes and desires of our Lord Jesus Christ ... '

Lanfranc reached across his desk and picked up a pen.

'I trust this letter finds you in good health, and not prey to the many dank humours of the Eternal City. Such humours may not interfere with the longevity of the city, but they have been known to deprive many an unlucky servant of God of his hopes for a long life.

'Your cardinals, and no doubt Hildebrand in particular, will fulminate about the dilatoriness of our Duke over the matter of this council, but I should like to say on his behalf that there are particularly extenuating circumstances. Such circumstances may not carry much weight with Hildebrand or your more zealous, and – dare I say it? less imaginative – Vatican reformers. But William is a good son of the Church. Nevertheless, he will not be rushed. Nor will he be bludgeoned or frightened.

'Word has reached me that your archdeacon, whom you had nominated to represent you at Rouen, has had the misfortune to die of the flux on the journey. Is this God's way of telling us that the business of the council is not to be rushed? There are those who will interpret it thus. However, you and I both know that your determination to reform Holy Church will not be turned aside by a dozen such untimely deaths.

'All I would ask, as a friend and, I hope, trusted adviser, is that you take good advice when you appoint his successor. God, as we both know, does not abide sloth, but equally His cause is rarely served by blind impatience and rigid adherence to the letter of the law. Please, I beg you, do not send us another Hildebrand.

'I know this Duke of ours. He is hard, almost stark. But he means well. And he carries a great burden. Of responsibility and of ambition. If we are patient, this ambition could serve us well in the very long run. He covets a kingdom, no less. And a kingdom that, we both know, could do with a good deal of reforming. I should be just as pleased as you to see Stigand deposed from Canterbury.

'If we let our Duke do it in his own way, and if we give him good advice when he comes to appoint a new Archbishop of Canterbury, we could in a decade or two be able to add a glittering newly-reformed province to the rejuvenated body of Mother Church.

'Now I leave you. My thanks for your kind thoughts. I reciprocate similar wishes towards yourself. My thanks too for your compliments, the fulsomeness of which is no doubt enhanced by the mistiness of nostalgia. But I too treasure the memory of our joint quest for the truth while we studied together at Bec. You were ever a ready talker and listener – if a poor calligrapher!

'Your friend in God,

'Lanfranc.'

* * * * * *

Robert of Beaumont stood stiffly to attention.

'I have the honour to report, my lord – '

'Where is my son?'

'Your son, my lord?'

'Yes, you dolt. Where is my son?'

Beaumont blinked.

'On the road, my lord. Not two days behind, I am sure. If I might make my report – '

'You left him behind?'

'No, my lord. He is in the company of the escort you left with him. He has made a full recovery, and – '

'The Earl Harold?'

'A good recovery too. But then he was not taken as badly. If I might – '

'You are sure of that?'

Beaumont glanced uneasily at Fitzosbern and other senior vassals standing behind the Duke. They made faces to try and warn him.

'Upon my solemn word, my lord. The Earl Harold himself told me to make all haste. He assured me – '

'Yes, yes, yes.'

Giffard and Montgomery looked at each other. Harold taking the initiative again.

The Duke paced to and fro two or three times. Beaumont pleaded with his eyes to Fitzosbern, but received no guidance.

William at last stopped, turned, and stared at him.

'Well?'

'M – my lord?'

'You said you had a report.'

'Oh. Yes.' Beaumont scooped up his scattered wits. 'I – er – have the honour to report that I have brought the Flemish infantry. Not a man lost, my lord. If I may say so – '

'Is that all?'

'All, my lord?'

All? Forty miles in two and a half days. Without their captain – still heaving and retching on a soiled mattress in Mortain. Something of a minor triumph of improvised leadership, in Beaumont's private opinion. He had flogged the two chief troublemakers; bribed the senior sergeant; looted on the way to provide better camp rations. He had taken advantage of a distant kinsman's property to obtain good shelter for one of the nights on the march. And he had dismounted and walked with them for miles on foot. Though he said so himself, they had come to think of him as a good officer. It showed ...

'We thought you were a right pansy bastard, sir. No offence, sir.'

'None taken. Now – just you do what is needed at Dol, and I shall see you are all right afterwards.'

'Fair enough, sir. Man of honour, sir, I am sure ... '

Beaumont flushed.

'If I might make so bold as to point out, my lord – '

'Where are the sappers? Where are my brother's engineers? Where are the tools? The timber?'

'They are serfs, my lord.' He looked puzzled, as if the answers were obvious. 'You can not expect them to march like soldiers. Or knights,' he added, as he remembered his own exploits on foot.

William came right up to him. His eyes flashed pinpoints of light.

'You left them behind?'

Beaumont still felt baffled.

'I said, my lord. They are serfs. They will come in their own time. You can not make oxen gallop.'

William turned away to Fitzosbern.

'Take this idiot away before I break his neck.'

Giffard hustled him out of the tent and took him out of earshot.

Beaumont spluttered. 'What have I done?'

'Left your intelligence – if you have any – in Mortain. What do you think those serfs you are so sure about will be doing by now? Did you leave so much as a capable sergeant with them? No, I thought not. They will be halfway to their homes. What does any peasant do when he is not supervised night and day? Exactly.'

Beaumont turned pale. Giffard dusted his hands, as if Beaumont's jerkin had soiled them.

'The Bastard has a siege on his hands, and no means of pursuing it. Thanks to you. There may be a relieving army out there somewhere, and we have to do something in a few days. Though exactly what I have no idea. Perhaps your Royal Stupidness can think of an idea.'

'I brought his precious Flemings. And his smelly chaplain – bleating all the way. Had a donkey and cart too.'

Giffard spat.

'You did not bring assistance; you brought a feather to flaunt in your cap.'

Inside the tent, which William had left in a fury of impatience, Fitzosbern and Montgomery poured themselves a drink.

'Beaumont had better find a good use for his Flemings. That is all we have now.'

'I am sure Walter has enjoyed himself telling him that.'

'He would have enjoyed himself still more if he knew that Beaumont was paying court to his ward in St. Amand.'

* * * * * *

'God's Blood, Gerard – this place is like the grave.'

Matilda pushed away her plate, and plumped her elbows on the table.

Gerard noticed that the plate was clear. It took a lot to interfere with Matilda's appetite. It had been the same since she was five – none of the turned-up nose and 'Nasty!' from her. She wolfed food as if she had not seen a square meal for a week. A small army of nurses had despaired of teaching her table manners.

Gerard poured some wine.

'I suppose you have come here to cry on my shoulder. Get on with it then.'

Matilda glared as she licked her fingers.

'Well, if you must know ... '

Everything was wrong. Arlette for a start.

'She has lost nearly all control of the chicks. They tease her about Wulfnoth.'

'Hardly surprising. They are neither blind nor deaf.'

'You used to tease me about William.'

'Lady Matti, that is not a fair comparison, and you know it. Wulfnoth is not here for her to run to. Nor is she sure of him. Besides, she does not have a whiplash for a tongue, like some people I could name.'

Matilda glared again.

'William will let her be betrothed when he is good and ready. So mind your own business.'

'And Cecily?'

'What about her?'

'You said something about her being betrothed. Forgotten?'

'No, I have not. And it still might be a good idea. She behaved herself when Harold was here. Now she is impossible again. Jealous to madness about Robert.'

'He is a boy. What does she expect – to be given a horse and mail?'

Matilda leapt for once to her daughter's defence.

'I might have expected such a remark from a mere man. She is not asking for knightly attire; she is asking for fairness as she sees it.'

Gerard shrugged.

'Get her betrothed then. How about Beaumont? Well set-up young man. Good family. His father would be delighted.'

Matilda sniffed.

'Maybe. It is up to William.'

'Ah.'

'Gerard, you are a pox-ridden, interfering busybody.'

'Then why are you here? To tell me you have no troubles?'

Matilda bridled for a moment, then sighed in resignation.

'Arlette is partly right; the chicks are being difficult. Harold spoilt them – just like you – and has gone off to Brittany and left her to clear up the mess.'

'Easy. Send them to me. What else?'

Matilda threw up her hands.

'Ooohh – everything. No news. The place is dead. Nothing is happening. That dog boy of Harold's is in the clutches of Arnulf's whore of a daughter. I suppose you know.'

'No harm in that. It has taken away his loneliness. It has put some life into her.'

'That is just what I worry about,' said Matilda.

'Come now, lady Matti. Another castle bastard more or less. When have you troubled about that?'

'What about this council?' said Matilda, craftily shifting her ground.

Gerard frowned.

'What about it?'

'Maurilius shuts himself in his palace on the other side of the town. He sends me long letters which he knows I can not read. Avranches and Evreux do nothing but play chess. The council has done nothing but improve their game.'

She stood up and began pacing.

'I am so helpless, Gerard.'

For the first time Gerard felt some sympathy for her. She was used to presiding at councils of vassals when William was ill or absent at the other end of the duchy. Her authority was accepted, and she duly witnessed charters and writs. But a church council was different. No prince of the Church – not even a saintly scholar like Maurilius – would tolerate interference from a mere woman. She could hector about an agenda, and she could swear at bishops till she ran out of oaths. She would be met with nothing but polite manners and a wall of nothingness.

And patience was never Matilda's strong point.

'What do you expect, lady Matti? To turn the world upside-down? Not even the Holy Virgin told Jesus what to do. She knew her place.'

Matilda sat down again, and lifted her shoulders in a colossal sigh.

'So what I do, Gerard?'

'You cope.'

Gerard lifted his crutch.

'Like me.'

* * * * * *

'Please, my lord – one more chance. I beg you.'

The Duke, restless and red in the face, slapped his gloves against his knee. He turned about, walked away a few paces, and looked into the vivid Breton sunset.

The attack had been a failure. He had far too few archers to keep the garrison's heads down while the infantry went in. The steep hill of the motte proved too much for the discipline of the Flemish mercenaries, without their accustomed captain. It said a lot for the bravery and resource of young Beaumont that they actually reached the walls, never mind scaled them. At least the boy could lead. He held them on the withdrawal too – much more difficult. The real test of a good commander.

But Flemings were not sappers. They were useless with ladders. Swords and formation were their special skill. What was needed now was nimble hands and feet, quick wits, agility at jumping, speed at burning, dexterity with an iron bar to prise open the timbers of the walls. The most important thing was to get the main gate open, to let in the men who would do the real fighting. Swords and mail and tight ranks were little use half-way up a ladder. And by now over half their scaling ladders had been broken or burnt.

All Beaumont's fault, of course. If he had done his job properly and driven the sappers all the way, they would not be in this mess. How much time did they have left? Supposing there *was* a relieving army. Fitz had said barely two days. He was usually right, damn him. And he had rubbed the back of his neck, which meant that he regarded the situation as serious.

William turned back towards the group around Beaumont. For once he was not entirely decided.

'I suppose you realise the position we are in?'

Behind them Sir Walter Giffard grunted. Leave the job to boys and what did you expect?

Beaumont flushed at the sound, which he recognised perfectly well.

'We have a full day, my lord, maybe two. Sir William Fitzosbern has told me.'

'So?'

'All I ask, my lord, is the use of that day.'

He waved a gloved hand about them.

'The knights failed to get up there; we have seen that. We have not enough archers or sappers, I admit. But we do still have my Flemings.'

Montgomery smiled. So they were 'my' Flemings now, were they?

'Cover themselves with glory, will they?' said Giffard.

William silenced him with a curt gesture. He stood in front of Beaumont and fixed him with his eyes.

'You have my attention.'

Beaumont swallowed.

'My lord, all I ask is the chance to try once more. I – I think I have an idea.'

'Better than the last one, we hope.'

'Walter!'

'At least,' said Beaumont, 'it is an idea. I have not noticed any knight offering one.'

'What do you want to do?'

'One more assault, my lord. One more day. A free hand tomorrow. What can we lose? We shall be going home on Thursday whatever happens.'

There was a silence which weighed Beaumont down like a millstone. The Duke tightened his lips. Beaumont could see rejection coming like a black storm.

Suddenly Sir William Fitzosbern cleared his throat. William turned to look at him. Fitz lifted his shoulders in the smallest of shrugs.

William turned back.

'Very well. You have tomorrow. By the Splendour of God, it had better be a good idea.'

* * * * * *

'And do you know what they did then?'

'No, Gerard.'

Gerard took a swig from his flask, and stood it carefully on the side of the trough in the great outer bailey. He lifted his face to the spring sunshine and sighed with contentment. A blessed change from the smoke and smells of the kitchen.

Four children clustered round his feet. They had scooped up handfuls of loose straw to make cushions, and now sat cross-legged, their grubby hands dangling between their thighs.

'See that great gate?'

Gerard pointed with his crutch. Four heads turned.

'Well, the gates of the city in my story were bigger than that. Much bigger.'

Eyes widened. The two boys had another look at the gate to consider whether such a prodigy was possible.

'The Romans did not know what to do. Ten years they sat round the city trying to get in, and they could not think of a way.'

'Where did they sleep?' asked one of the girls.

'In their tents, stupid,' said Richard. 'Where else do armies sleep?'

Gerard cleared his throat before they fell into argument.

'Remember I told you last time that they tried to climb the walls, but their ladders were all broken and burnt. They could not dig tunnels because the walls were made of stone, and they were set on solid rock.'

A couple of horsemen clopped across the bailey towards the stables. Young William turned to look. Gerard leaned over and prodded him with the crutch.

'Pay attention.'

'Sorry, Gerard.'

'Now, where was I?'

'The Romans could not get into the city.'

'Ah, yes. Well, they had a meeting. It was decided that there was only one thing to do. They must send for the Guiscard.'

The boys clapped their hands.

'You remember who the Guiscard is.'

Richard and William fell over each other in their eagerness.

'Robert of Hauteville.'

'The son of Tancred.'

'Robert the Guiscard.'

'The giant.'

'The Crafty One.'

'The one who is never caught asleep.'

'The famous Norman adventurer,' said Constance, who liked long words.

'Exactly so,' said Gerard, beaming at one and all. He adjusted the position of his bad leg.

'Well, the Guiscard came, and they told him their troubles. "We can not get into the city," they said. "We have attacked many times and we have lost many men. They have burnt and broken our ladders. We can not dig mines because the ground is full of rocks, and we have not enough sappers and miners. We have been here for ten years, and we want to go home. But we can not go before we have captured the city, because it would be a great disgrace."

'The Guiscard listened carefully, with his head cocked on one side. He looked craftily out of the corner of one eye – like this.'

The girls laughed.

'The Guiscard had a plan,' said William.

'He did indeed,' said Gerard. 'He called all the leaders together and he said, "If you use my plan, you must do exactly as I say." They said they would. And he said, "We will use a trick." '

William fidgeted.

'The Guiscard always has a trick.'

Gerard stared at him.

'What did I say?'

'Sorry, Gerard.'

'The Guiscard said, "What is the one thing that the men in the city want us to do?" And they said, "Go away." And he said, "That is right. So we will go away."

'But the Romans said, "If we do that, we shall not take the city, and it will be a great disgrace." The Guiscard said, "That is the trick; we only pretend to sail away. We shall get into our boats and we shall leave Messina and we shall sail away, but we shall not sail all the way back to Italy.

' "But first," he said, "you must send some clever men up to the main gate of the city in the night, and they must measure how broad the gateway is." The Romans said, "Why?" and the Guiscard said, "You must do as I say; you promised."

'So they did as the Guiscard told them, and in the night they sent their cleverest scouts right up to the great gate, and they measured it. They came back and they said, "It is twenty paces across." '

Gerard stretched his hands wide. Gasps and open mouths.

'I did say it was a very big gate. Well, then, the Guiscard said to the leaders, "You must build a very big horse out of wood, and it must have a hollow belly, and you must put it on to a mighty trolley and the trolley must measure twenty-one paces across." '

'Why did they do that?' said Constance. 'Because you said – '

'Be patient, silly,' said William. 'Do you think Gerard has forgotten?"

'In the depths of their camp, the Romans built their great horse, where the people in Messina could not see. When the Romans had finished it, they said to the Guiscard, "What do we do with it now?"

'And the Guiscard said, "You push it right up to the walls of the city, and you all go back and pack up your camp and go into your ships and sail away, away from Messina – so that you can not be seen. But – " ' Gerard put up a warning finger ' " – you must leave one man alone beside the horse, and you must hide twenty brave warriors inside the belly of the horse." '

'Why did they leave one man outside?' said Constance. 'Surely the men of Messina would kill him if they saw him there all alone.'

Gerard nodded.

'They might, if they were ordinary men. But they were not. The men of Messina were very curious men. The Guiscard was cunning; he knew that they would want to know what this horse was, and how it got there, and what it was doing there. They would have to ask the man who had been left behind. Nevertheless, it was a dangerous thing to do, and there was no one who was willing to be left behind all alone like that. At last, the Guiscard said, "If there is any slave in the camp who will do this, we shall give him his freedom. And one man came forward and said he would do it.'

'What was his name?' said William.

'Joseph,' said Gerard without hesitation.

William sat back.

'The Guiscard said to – to Joseph, "When the men of Messina come out of their city and ask you, you will say that the Romans have tired of trying to get into the city and they have gone home. And they were in such a hurry that they could not repair one of their ships, and they had to leave behind one of their most precious possessions – the horse. Tell them it is – um – it is a statue of the horse of Saint George, the one he rode when he killed the dragon. It was a magic horse, and this is a magic statue, and it can do magic too. Tell them that. And if they ask why you are here, tell them that the Romans were cruel and left you behind as a sacrifice to the saint of horses."

'Did he do that?'

'He did indeed. The Romans, in the middle of the night, pushed their great horse right up to the walls of Messina, and they went back to the beach and went on board their ships and sailed away out of sight of land. When the men of Messina woke up, they saw the beach empty, and they said, "The Romans have gone away. The siege is over. We have won. Let us rejoice."

'And one of them looked over the other wall towards the plain and he saw the horse. And he said, "Look!" And they all saw it. They crowded on to the walls of their city and they leaned over and they pointed and they wondered among themselves.

'Then some of the braver ones opened the gates and came to have a closer look. They found Joseph leaning up against a wheel of the great trolley of the horse, and they said, "What is this?"

'Joseph said, "Ah, me, I am a most unfortunate man. The Romans have gone away, and they have left their most precious possession, and they have left me all alone because there was not room for me on their ships. It is not fair, because they will not come back, and I shall surely die."

'The men of Messina said, "You will not die, because we are a merciful people. Just tell us what this horse is, and we will feed you and care for you."

Joseph pointed to the great animal, and said, "It is, as you can see, a horse. But no ordinary horse. It is a magic horse. A horse of victory. It is a statue of the the horse of their Saint George, that he rode when he slew the dragon. A miracle horse."

'The men of Messina were wonderstruck. They touched the great hooves and stroked the wood and whispered among themselves, and they leaned back to gaze up to its noble head, and their mouths opened.'

Four tiny sets of teeth gaped before him. Gerard managed a furtive mouthful of wine.

'The men of Messina said, "Can this horse do magic for us?" Joseph said, "It can do magic for anybody, provided that they give it a home."

' "You mean," said the Messenians, "that we must take it into the city?" Joseph said, "That is so. Otherwise the magic will not work." '

Richard smiled to himself at the subtlety of Joseph's cunning.

'So,' said Gerard, 'they began to drag the trolley towards their city. But when they came near to the gates – '

'It would not go through,' said Constance, glancing in triumph at her brothers.

'And do you know what they did then?'

Four heads shook.

'They were so anxious to possess this magic horse that they took down their gates and they took some stones out of their city wall, so that they could make a passage wide enough for the horse to pass.

'They dragged it into their main square, and they left it there for the night, while they went off to drink and make merry, because their enemies had gone away, and they had captured the most precious possession of their enemies. It was a great victory.

'All through the night they feasted and drank, and they fell into a deep sleep.

At the very darkest hour of the night, Joseph came into the square and he climbed up under the belly of the horse, and he opened the secret door, and he let out the warriors who had been hiding there.'

'Was the Guiscard there?' asked William.

'To be sure,' said Gerard without blinking. 'It was his plan. It was only fitting that he should be there to see that it was properly carried out. If there was to be danger and difficulty, you would always find the Guiscard there.'

'Ah.'

'So,' said Gerard, 'they climbed down out of the horse, and one man slipped and broke his neck – '

All four laughed loudly.

' – but the rest ran about the city and started great fires. There were no sentries because everybody was asleep after the drinking, and they thought the Romans had gone away. But the Romans were waiting, and when they saw the light of the flames against the dark sky, they came swiftly back to the beaches. They ran up to the city and poured in through the great open gate, and they captured the king's palace, and they took all the weapons of the soldiers because they were still sleeping. It was a great victory. And it was all because of the clever plan of Robert the Guiscard.'

Richard and William leapt to their feet.

'We shall do that. We shall play sieges.'

'I shall be the Guiscard,' said Richard. 'I am the eldest.'

'And I shall be Joseph,' said William.

'I want to play too,' said Constance and young Matilda.

'You can be the men of Messina,' said Richard.

* * * * * *

The Duke glanced up at the bright morning sun. A coastal breeze blew gently towards the castle of Dol.

'It seems that God is on your side. Get on with it then.'

It was the third day of warm weather. The ground had dried out after the rains that had drenched everyone during the approach march. Beaumont had been wondering how he could use this. He had also noticed the morning breeze off the sea. When they intercepted two waggons piled high with skins, destined for Conan's walls, the parts of a plan began to come together.

'They are short of water,' Beaumont told his sergeants. 'And now they have no means of keeping their walls from drying out. I want ten good men, who are prepared to take risks for an extra week's pay.'

To the Duke he said, 'Remember, my lord, plenty of noise.'

'You shall have it.'

On the Duke's order, the trumpeter blared his signal.

A hundred paces from the walls of Conan's castle, Beaumont's Flemings dragged forward scores of hay bales and set light to them. As soon as they began to blaze, buckets of water were thrown on them. Beaumont watched in satisfaction as the smoke drifted on the breeze towards the castle. He looked at the Duke.

'Now, my lord.'

The trumpet blared again. The boy, excited at being so important, blew lustily.

The Duke's knights, in full battle gear, trotted to and fro in the crackling straw, sometimes emerging for a moment, then retreating, but always coming forward with the drifting smoke.

'*Diex aie*!'

The Norman war-cry was carried towards the walls of the castle, where the defenders crouched and squinted. Before long, flights of arrows were being fired towards the smoke.

'Back,' said Beaumont.

William nodded to his red-faced trumpeter, who blew again.

The defenders gradually ceased firing, as their targets disappeared.

'Half an hour, my lord, and we do it again.'

Resting behind the smouldering bales, Sir Walter Giffard blinked and wiped smuts out of eyes.

'God's Face, what a way for a knight to make war!'

Montgomery coughed beside him.

'If either of us had had any better ideas, Walter, I am sure the Bastard would have listened to them.'

Giffard grunted.

'We have no way of knowing if this is going to work.'

'They are exhausting their arrows. And they have no way to retrieve them. That at least can not be bad.'

More fires were lit, and the same manoeuvre was performed. More arrows flew harmlessly into the murk. Hardly a man was struck, and nobody was seriously injured.

'Satisfied?' said the Duke.

'One more time, my lord, if you please.'

Giffard swore, but they did it again. This time far fewer arrows were fired.

Beaumont nodded to himself. Either they were running short of arrows, or they were seeing through the ruse. Perhaps both. Good.

He gathered his ten volunteers.

'When the smoke starts again, take your straw right up to the foot of the walls. No, no – use these bales.' He indicated a pile of them set aside. 'They are special. No water this time. I want fire – fire. Understand?'

'Very good, Sir Robert.'

It was a change from the days when they had sworn at him across their gaming boards.

When the next false attack went in, the defenders shouted taunts and insults from the walls. Some even disdained to remain at their posts. Scarcely an arrow was loosed.

Beaumont's men ran forward, flung down the bales, and set them alight. They were surprised by the speed with which they burst into roaring flames, and needed no trumpet to get them to fall back.

'Again!' roared Beaumont.

More bales and more fires. One man, as he was about to retire, saw something shining among the crackling stalks. Suddenly overwhelmed by curiosity, he bent, gasped, and drew out a silver penny. A shout above his head sent him dashing back from the wall.

At a safe distance, Beaumont turned to the Duke.

'Have they gathered the arrows?'

In the excitement, he forgot the niceties of formal address.

'Yes.'

Beaumont turned to the platoon of Flemings who fumbled unfamiliarly at bowstrings.

'There is no need to hit anybody. Just get the arrows over the walls. Now!'

As random shafts began to whine in the vague direction of the outer bailey of Conan's castle, Beaumont turned to the rest of the Flemings, drawn up in two ranks. Their swords were sheathed. In their hands each man carried an axe or an iron bar – the fruit of two days' scavenging in surrounding manors. Villeins had fought so hard to save their hay crop from theft that they had had no time to notice the other looting.

'Right, lads – up to the wall. A bushel of silver awaits you in the ashes.'

They blinked in bafflement. The curious soldier shouted.

'He speaks the truth, boys. That straw is something special.'

'We can see that; he soaked it in oil.'

'He sowed it with silver, too. Look. Plenty more where that came from.'

'And your pay,' bellowed Beaumont. 'And your loot afterwards. What are you waiting for?'

'Are you coming with us – sir?'

The irony creeping back again.

Beaumont seized a sword.

'Try and catch me.'

He raced towards the walls. With a great shout, the Flemings followed him. Some were so excited that they ran through the remaining flames and hurled themselves bodily against the charred timbers. The lighter ones bounced off, but their heavier comrades crashed through. The remainder got to work with irons and axes.

In the smoke and shouting, they heard the Bastard's trumpet blare yet again. The boy, his cheeks grimed with dirt and dried tears from the smoke, forgot his split notes, and blew like the Angel Gabriel.

The Duke turned to his vassals, standing awkwardly apart from their horses.

'You want some fighting, Giffard?' He flung out his arm. 'Do you fancy following Beaumont?'

Red in the face, from the smoke, the effort, and now the insult, Giffard wrenched out his sword, tore off his spurs, and began to run towards the walls, without waiting to see if Montgomery or the others were following.

'Diex aie!'

Timbers split and burst; splinters impaled the unwary; fountains of sparks flew into the air. Curses and groans arose like a thousand rooks screaming: sergeants in the garrison bellowed desperate orders; grindings and wrenchings and crashings marked the destruction of the outer bailey wall. Breton archers, after hours of smoke-filled eyes and false alarms, were appalled at the sight of real knights in front of them – on foot. It was against nature. Unbalanced and unnerved, they soon broke and ran. Over the back wall, into the shelter of bailey storehouses, into stables, in the desperate hope of stealing a horse. Some ran to hammer on the doors of the tower, only to find them barred against the enemy. Turning at bay, they fell on their knees and flung away their bows, covering their heads with their arms. Some ran through the gaps in the walls towards the Normans, their faces streaked with sweat and dust, their hands opened in token of surrender, their voices crazed with panic.

Within minutes, the outer bailey was in Norman control. The Duke appeared, also on foot, and came to stand in front of the tower. He looked up at the great door from the foot of the mound.

His knights gathered round him. The Flemings, rather pleased with themselves, and many counting silver coins and comparing successes, stood about in groups. Beaumont, flushed and panting, came to the Duke.

'Do you want me to go on, my lord? Secure the rear gate?'

William shook his head. He was watching the walls of the tower. Clusters of heads were visible on the tops.

William raised his voice. Its raucous tone was known from one end of

Normandy to the other, so there was no mistaking it.

'Open the gate now, and you will go home. Resist, and we give you the fire again. Make it hard for us, and … '

He gestured to some of the Flemings to bring forward a cluster of cringing prisoners.

'It will be Alençon all over again.'

The prisoners shrieked with terror.

'Jesus and Mary – no! No, my lord!'

One of the Flemings turned to his friend.

'Alençon?'

'Yes. Oh, I was forgetting – you are new. Some years ago, the Bastard was trying to capture Alençon. They resisted. Worse still, they hung skins over the walls and shouted, "Work here for the son of the tanner's daughter." He brought a batch of prisoners in sight of the walls, and cut off their noses, their ears, their lips, their hands, and their feet, and had them thrown over the walls. Some say he had their eyes put out as well.'

'God Almighty!'

'Did the trick though.' He gestured towards the top of the wall, where a strip of white rag was flying. 'Works here too.'

In one corner of the bailey, Ralph and Bruno were seeing to their horses, knowing that they would soon be sent on scouting duty, to watch the retreat.

Bruno pointed.

'Look at that.'

The great gate was now open; the fearful garrison was straggling out, and stumbling down the motte. All eyes were on the front of the tower.

At the rear, someone had climbed over the wall, and was letting himself down by a rope. On the ground, he sprang at once through the back gate; the victors had left it open for the defeated garrison to pass through after they had been searched and looted of everything of value.

Ralph gasped.

'Conan!'

'How do you know?' said Bruno.

'I should know that red hair anywhere.'

Bruno prepared to mount. Ralph stayed on the ground.

'Well?' said Bruno.

Ralph shook his head.

'Let him go. Revenge achieves nothing.'

'It may not for you; you have told me. But this is the Bastard's business.'

'I am concerned with the Bastard's business. Ten years ago, when Fulk had

Enguerrand killed, it was against the Bastard's clear orders. What happened? Enguerrand's brother, Guy, becomes Count of Ponthieu, and sworn to pay off a bitter score. If the Bastard had not acted quickly, what might he not have done to Harold? And what might he not be cooking up right now while we are at the other end of the duchy?

'And if we kill Conan, what will his brothers and cousins do? Come and ask the Bastard to be their friend and overlord? No. They will wait to cook up mischief at this end of the duchy when we return to Rouen. I say let him go. He will have to live with the disgrace – far worse than martyrdom.'

Bruno relaxed.

'So long as it is you who tells the Bastard.'

Ralph shrugged.

'Why does he have to know? What the eye does not see ... As far as he is concerned, Conan could not be found. That can only mean that he deserted his own men before the end. So he becomes not only a loser and a fugitive; he is a coward.'

Bruno lifted his eyebrows. Scouts like them learned to be judges of economy of effort, learned when to be quiet, learned when to stay at a distance. Now, it seemed, they were about to do the Bastard a favour, and all by doing nothing at all. Not a bad day's work.

* * * * * *

'Why? Why us?'

There came a time when Adele had to wonder. The pause brought bafflement; it made her uncomfortable at her ignorance.

The same pause also made Edwin ask questions.

'Did you lie like this with Nigel? Did you miss him when he went to Brittany?'

The pause brought guilt too. At times she felt almost wretched. Not guilty that she had made love before, but that she had been so good at it. When she caused Edwin to cry out with pleasure, it was joy for her that she loved him so much, and that he rose to her lovemaking. But it was guilt too that part at least of his joy was a result of the many tricks she had learnt. For the first time in their passion she felt shame.

She was a wanton. She could not escape the truth that she now saw so clearly. Her guilt became agony one evening, when he lay beside her, stroking her thigh.

'I never knew it was possible to feel such love for anybody except the Holy Virgin. You are perfect.'

Adele burst into tears, wrenched up the blanket, and turned away.

'You must not say that. It is not true.'

He put his arms round her, and she clasped his hands across her breasts. As her cheeks dried and her breathing became steadier, she looked blankly at the wall.

She had recoiled at Edwin's words, but, in her heart, she understood what he was trying to say. She felt the same. This – this – thing that they both shared in such drunken measure was so big, so strong, so – so complete that there was no escaping it; it was in them, around them, everywhere. She felt her heart thump – like God! *It was God!*

She knew now something of what it must be like to feel possessed as a saint was. She understood why pilgrims toiled on such long journeys solely in order to stand on the very spot where a saint had stood, to touch a tree made holy by his magic, to drink from a spring called from the living rock by his prayers, to pluck a bloom from the earth where drops of his blessed blood had fallen.

How many times had she caressed the back of a chair where Edwin had so lately sat? If she washed a shirt of his, she often pressed it to her face – before she put it in the water.

Some mystery – some magic – had put a sort of light inside her eyes which shone on everything. Or rather which changed everything she looked at. She had once known a nun when she was a girl; this woman had looked at the whole world just like that. Adele had thought her a fool. That stupid smile! Now she had that same smile so often on her own face, and she knew it.

She sighed and pulled Edwin's arms tighter round her.

'God is here somewhere,' she muttered.

Edwin nuzzled her ear.

'What did you say?'

'Nothing.'

* * * * * *

'Where is that fat priest?'

William paced up and down inside Conan's hall at Dol. He gestured in disgust at the debris around the main hearth.

'Sweep that offal out of here. Get some clean straw, if Beaumont has not burnt it all. Find me Wulfnoth.'

As the messenger bolted through the door, William bawled after him.

'And bring me Beaumont too.'

He sat down at a bench, and slid off his mail coif.

'Some morning, eh, Fitz? Ha!'

Fitzosbern, and Giffard and Montgomery and the other senior vassals, flopped down as well, exhausted after unfamiliar work. Bishop Yves of Sées undid the laces on a boot, and eased it off a sprained ankle. Bishop Hugh of Lisieux watched a servant bind a cut on his forearm.

Bishop Odo of Bayeux appeared dragging Arnulf by the scruff of the neck.

'Hiding in the stables,' he said, flinging the chaplain down at William's feet. 'I swear he did not even know it was all over. Sickening.'

Arnulf got to his knees, and wiped his jowls.

'My lord, I – I was only putting the altars in a safe place. The relics, you see. It must be my first concern – '

'Yes, yes,' said William. 'Set up the altars here, in this hall, tomorrow morning. I shall hear Mass at dawn.'

He put his hand up to the neck of his hauberk, and felt under the mail the small holy relics that he always wore in action. It was only right to give thanks.

'Of course, my lord. But why not the chapel, my lord?'

'A shambles,' said Odo. 'If you had put your sweaty nose anywhere near the action, you would have seen. Why do you think his Grace wants the travelling altars? Idiot! See that everything is ready in time.'

He kicked Arnulf out of the door.

'Why you tolerate that wretch, brother ... '

'Mind your own business,' snapped William. 'You will be here at dawn, and you will say Mass. Sées and Lisieux here will assist. Arnulf will serve. See that the altars are properly ... charged.'

Odo coloured slightly, but bowed correctly, and withdrew. Altars ... relics ...

Wulfnoth passed him in the doorway, and was nearly knocked aside.

'My lord?'

William gestured to the mess around them.

'I have sent for a fatigue party to clear this away. Get a meal organised. And some fresh bedding.'

Wulfnoth flushed.

'My lord, I have just been in action, like these knights here. May I suggest – '

'You are my under-chamberlain, not them. Do as I say. You have the authority. You can use the prisoners too.'

'If that is all you think I am fit for, my lord. '

'Take him away, Fitz. Make him see.'

Fitzosbern took Wulfnoth's elbow and propelled him towards the door.

'See, you foolish boy. Observe. William trusts you . And do not drape yourself in the cloak of rank. So far, this morning, Sir Robert of Beaumont has lit fires like any sapper, and the Flemings have served as archers and miners. To say nothing of knights of honour attacking on foot. The least you can do is to forget your dainty dignity and provide us with bed and board.'

'And what about the prisoners? Stupid Bretons.'

'After the fate they thought they were going to suffer, they are grateful to be alive and in one piece. They will do anything. Now see to it.'

Wulfnoth flounced out in a huff. It was Beaumont's turn to be nearly knocked over.

He marched up to the Duke, and stood stiffly to attention, awaiting the words of praise, even perhaps a reward. He flashed a smirk of triumph in the direction of Sir Walter Giffard. The Duke barely glanced up.

'You can turn the Flemings loose. They can waste as far as they can reach. Teach Conan a lesson.'

Montgomery and Giffard exchanged glances. They had guessed as much. It would cow the locals, and make them think twice about providing for Conan's troops again. If the Flemings found enough loot, they would probably start to drift home and so would be less of a nuisance about their pay. If they got greedy and ranged too far, and there really was a relieving force, it would catch them, and the Bastard would be saved from an awkward problem. If there was no relieving force, and the Flemings came back to Dol, they could be kept occupied as a temporary garrison until a proper one was collected.

Giffard inclined his head in appreciation.

'Neat.'

Beaumont remained at attention before the Duke. William frowned.

'Well?'

Beaumont coughed.

'The small matter of the silver, my lord.'

'Silver?'

'The silver I sowed into the hay. There was – I mean, I did use rather a lot. When can I expect that you will – um – and then there were the bribes.'

William's eyes sharpened.

'Are you asking me for compensation?'

Beaumont swallowed.

'Yes, my lord.'

'Out!'

Beaumont stared.

'My lord?'

'It was your mistake in the first place. I do not pay for you to put it right. Fitz?'

Fitzosbern now steered the aggrieved Beaumont towards the door.

'But my lord.'

What made it worse was Giffard's laugh.

Fitzosbern took him outside. He gestured at the mound below them, where ashes and charred timbers were already being cleared. A group of prisoners, with spades over their shoulders, was being marched through the bailey gate to dig graves.

'Do not fret. All this. He has noticed, and he will not forget. And he has Robert on his mind.'

'Robert? That is me.'

'I mean Robert his son. Left behind with Harold, remember? He is anxious about the boy. And about Harold.'

Beaumont growled.

'He should be more grateful.'

Fitzosbern pushed him towards the steps.

'Some day, you will command men – perhaps. Then we shall see if you have time always to be grateful. Have you praised your Flemings?'

'I came to get some money for them just now. On account, as you might say.'

'Just so. Only it will have to be your money, not William's. Burden of command, as you might say.'

Giffard and Montgomery came to the door and watched Beaumont stumping down the motte, kicking rubbish to one side or another.

'Arrogant puppy!'

'He got us in, Walter.'

'Yes – on foot. Almost as dishonourable as surrendering.'

'It was an interesting idea. Would you have thought of it?'

'Certainly not! Too clever by half.'

Montgomery wisely changed the subject.

'Why is Odo looking so pleased with himself. Did you see the look on his face when he left?'

'Yes.'

'What is he up to?'

Giffard shrugged, then grinned. 'When we go to Coutances, we shall ask Geoffrey. He is the expert on Odo's mind. He will find some devious motive to impute to him.'

* * * * * *

Thierry helped himself to three ladlesful of soup from the great pot in Gaimar's kitchen.

'To be sure, he paced up and down, and he asked me where the money was coming from. But he is pleased – really. The honour, you see.'

Gaimar cut some bread.

'He must have known already, surely.'

Thierry nodded, already midway through his first spoonful.

'Yes. The Bastard warned him. But he did not know when. Now that Dol is taken, they will be here earlier. Just so soon as they have picked up Robert and Harold. But that is not all.'

Thierry looked up and waited for Gaimar's full attention. He knew how to make the most of fresh news.

'There is to be a full council. They are summoning vassals from all over – not just those at the siege. From the Bessin, the Auge, the Ouche, the Roumois, as far as Perche and the Vexin – everywhere. Odo's idea, I gather.' Not 'my lord Odo'; just 'Odo'.

'Why?'

Thierry lifted his shoulders.

'With Odo you can never be sure.'

Gaimar looked about his kitchen.

'Where is all the meat coming from? I never expected this.'

Thierry ran his tongue across his teeth.

'Just what my lord Geoffrey said. Only he said it rather more loudly than you did.'

Gaimar still looked worried.

'Never fear,' said Thierry. 'Lord Geoffrey will find whatever is required. Just think, Gaimar – a full council, here, at Coutances.'

* * * * * *

'How far now?'

'Not long, my lord.'

Gilbert looked back at the column behind them. The captain of mercenaries was still riding with discomfort. The few knights and men-at-arms exchanged swearwords about the journey, the campaign, bad food, the accursed awfulness of life in general. Their stomachs were quiet at last, but they were empty and they were painful. Nigel was entertaining young Robert with his usual ribald stories.

Harold looked back too.

'The boy has recovered faster than anyone. Ah – youth!'

He saw concern on Gilbert's face.

'Have no fear; we shall reach Pontorson tonight in good time. And if we are delayed, blame it all on me. It was I who wanted the detour.'

'Very good, my lord. But the Duke did make me the guide.'

Harold leaned towards him.

'I said it was my fault. How can his Grace expect you to overrule a Saxon earl? He will understand; it is not every day that a man can see one of the great wonders of the world.'

'If you say so,' muttered Gilbert.

'Believe me,' said Harold. 'His campaign is successful. Dol is captured. Conan has gone to ground with his tail between his legs. You heard the scout – what was his name?'

'Ralph.'

'Ralph. What with that, and the joy of seeing Robert again, and in good health, he will forgive everything. Or he will by the time I have finished talking to him.'

Gilbert could think of no man who was so confident of a meeting with the Bastard going well. But then Harold was a very unusual man. The last few days in his company had shown him that. It was impossible to dislike him. It was impossible not to respond to him.

'What is this river?' asked Harold.

'The Sélune, my lord.'

'You were born near here, I understand.'

'Yes, my lord. I am Gilbert of Avranches.'

'Ah.'

Harold had heard Nigel baiting Gilbert throughout the whole journey. Every man in the column now knew that Gilbert was born on some tiny manor well away from Avranches, and had probably visited Avranches no more than two or three times in his life. Gilbert still clung to the name. Harold saw no point in adding to the boy's diffidence. He liked him. He had an open face, an innocence that was engaging. He obviously wanted so much to perform well, to be esteemed. With his lack of deviousness and sophistication, he was easy meat for the likes of Nigel Fitzhenry.

Harold had seen scores of Nigel Fitzhenries in every army in which he had served. They were as common in England as they were in Normandy. They would get their just reward sooner or later.

'Close, did you say?'

'Yes, my lord. Just round this next bend in the river.'

'There is a story about this place, no doubt,' said Harold as they jogged along.

'Indeed there is, my lord.'

Why was it so easy to talk to this English earl?

'Long, long ago, long before Duke William or his ancestors, long before Count Rollo, there was a mighty forest here. Out of the forest God had raised up a great rock – a rock of granite, you understand. The bishop of Avranches in those days was St. Aubert. He took himself to the rock to live a life of solitary prayer. One night he was commanded in a vision by the Blessed St. Michael the Archangel to build a chapel on the summit of this great rock. But St. Aubert was afraid that this vision was a trick of the Devil. As you well know, my lord, we are told that the Devil can come to a man in many guises. So St. Aubert took no heed of it. A second time the Blessed St. Michael came to him, and again he paid it no attention.

'A third time, the Blessed Archangel came to St. Aubert, and this time he pressed his hand so firmly on the saint's head that he left an indentation there. A clear mark of his holy finger.'

Harold smiled. Gilbert noticed it.

'I assure you it is so, my lord. As I shall make clear to you in due course.'

Harold composed his features.

'I have no doubt.'

'When the saint and his flock began the work of clearing the ground, they found a great stone in the way, which the workmen could not move. St. Aubert prayed to the Blessed St. Michael, who told him to go into the forest and look for a small child. This the saint did, and brought the child to the rock. He touched the stone with his foot, and at once, by the spell of this innocent child, the stone rolled to the foot of the rock. St. Aubert then struck the stone with his crozier, and a spring of the purest water gushed out from it.

'When the chapel was complete, the saint sent some monks to the mighty church of St. Michael the Archangel at Monte Gargano in Italy, to ask them to send some relics of the Blessed Archangel to place under their new altar.

'It was while the monks were away that God wrought the greatest of his miracles: he caused the sea to rush in and swallow up the forest. Nothing was left above the water. Silent – like a great wet tomb. But the miracle – God had left the great mount untouched. The water ran right round it, but it stood above, and so did its chapel. Pilgrims came to see this miracle.

'They came also to see the skull of St. Aubert, which itself became a holy relic. For there, in the head, is an indentation – the very mark left by the finger of the Blessed St. Michael.'

'Ah.'

'A village grew up round the foot of the rock. His Grace's ancestor Duke Richard the Fearless endowed it with lands. More monks were placed there. His Grace's grandfather, Duke Richard the Good, began to build a mighty abbey, a mighty abbey which would be the wonder of – and there it is, my lord! See!'

The tolerant smile vanished from Harold's face like breath off a blade. Just behind them Nigel Fitzhenry stopped in mid-sentence. Robert went pale with the shock.

Before them stretched the estuary of the Sélune, miles of grey sand as far as the horizon. An afternoon sun tinged the countless grains with silver and pearl.

But that was not what took away the smile from Harold's mouth, the joke from Nigel's lips, the colour from Robert's cheeks.

Three or four miles from the coast, rose a vision in lilac and amethyst, yet caressed too with afternoon gold, which managed to be both ethereal and immovable at one and the same time.

'Great God Almighty!'

One of the gaping men-at-arms tried to put into feeble words the wonder of what they were gazing at.

Gilbert, who had seen it many times, nevertheless felt bound to make a great announcement.

'The Abbey of Mont St. Michel, St. Michel au Péril de la Mer.'

The entire party sat motionless in the saddle. The horses ceased tossing their heads. A coastal breeze ruffled Harold's moustache.

'Like a granite ghost.'

If Gilbert had not reminded them of the lateness of the hour, there was no knowing how long they would have remained there.

Harold nodded to him, and turned away his horse's head.

'Very well. Lead on.'

They followed the coastline towards the west and the River Couesnon, the boundary between Brittany and Normandy. Leaving horses to pick their way, every man kept his eyes fixed on the vision to his right.

Harold shook his head.

'If I had not seen with my own eyes ... truly a thing apart.'

Gilbert drew alongside, and, reassured by the effect it had had on all of them, took it upon himself to elaborate further.

'The tide goes out further here than anywhere else in all France,' he said. 'And when it comes in, it is swift, swifter than a galloping horse – or so men say. And higher than five tall men.'

'And the sands,' said Harold. 'They are remarkable too.'

'Deadly,' said Gilbert. 'They dry quickly in the sun, and beckon to the unwary with their pearl-clear innocence.'

'But the water runs in underneath,' said Harold.

Gilbert turned towards him, amazed.

'Yes. How did you know?'

'I have lived near a great river mouth in England – the River Severn. I too have seen mighty tidal waves and quicksands.'

'A trap for the stupid or the unwary,' said Gilbert. 'It is said – '

He broke off suddenly, and gazed away. Harold looked at him to see why. Gilbert turned in the saddle and glanced back at Nigel. As he settled himself again to the trail ahead, he had forgotten what he was saying, and to whom he had been saying it.

Gilbert's face and his movements were so open that Harold had little difficulty in following his train of thought.

'Nigel does not know the sands, does he?'

Gilbert's face now registered alarm. Harold smiled.

'Have no fear. I have seen Nigel with you. A lesson would not hurt him. Provided it is no more than a lesson.'

'You would not betray me?' said Gilbert.

'Silent as the grave,' said Harold. 'It should be fun. You are sure you know your way on the sands.'

'It is all a matter of light,' said Gilbert. 'And sheen. You – '

'Yes, yes. I see you understand.' Harold dug his heels into his horse's flanks. 'Let us be about our little plot then. To the Couesnon. I could do with a little mortal entertainment after our brush with the Almighty out there.'

* * * * * *

The Duke flung himself from the saddle, rushed across the small square at Pontorson, and swept Robert into his arms.

'I am well, father. Well.'

Despite the shadows of sunset, he looked pale and shaken.

Harold leaned down from the saddle.

'A piece of foolishness and bad luck, William. No more. Soon mended.'

William indicated Ralph behind him.

'I have heard the story. The full story. Where is the man who saved him?'

Harold beckoned Gilbert forward. Gilbert handed his reins to another horseman, and came to stand in front of the Duke.

'My lord?'

'You saved my son.'

'My lord.' Gilbert could think of nothing else to say.

William looked him up and down. Gilbert's jerkin was still streaked with grey mud.

'You are one of my men-at-arms?'

'Yes, my lord, in a manner of – '

'Why have you no hauberk?'

'I can not afford one, my lord.'

William turned to Ralph.

'Get him one. We took plenty at Dol. See to it.'

Ralph inclined his head.

'My lord. On the morrow.'

'At dawn. Mind you do.'

Gilbert spluttered his thanks. William waved them away. He looked round for Beaumont.

'Go with Ralph here to Dol. Count Conan's horses – they are yours.'

Beaumont's face lit up.

'My lord! I can hardly tha – '

'Then save your breath.'

Fitzosbern whispered to Beaumont.

'I told you he would remember.'

William patted Robert on the shoulder, and began walking round the square, as if looking for something. He had begun his tuneless humming – always a good sign. Fitzosbern and Harold exchanged glances.

William stopped.

'Is there no church here?'

'I think not, my lord,' said Fitzosbern.

'A middling heathen race, my lord – the Bretons,' said Sir Walter Giffard.

'Then we build one,' declared William. 'For thanks. Fitz, make the arrangements.'

'My lord.'

William came up to Harold.

'I am in your debt.'

Harold shook his head.

'It was nothing, William. The credit belongs to Gilbert here. Gilbert of Avranches.'

'Nevertheless ... ' William turned away. At the edge of the square, Bishop Odo of Bayeux frowned; a train of thought had begun.

'It was Gilbert who tried to stop him,' said Harold. 'I merely assisted.'

William suddenly stopped humming.

'Bring out the idiot.'

Nigel Fitzhenry was pushed before him. He was sweating.

'M – my lord?'

Without warning, William struck him across the face. Nigel stood still and silent, the blood running from the corner of his mouth.

'Tie him to the well-head over there,' said the Duke. 'Fitz? Fifty lashes. Make sure the sergeant lays it on.'

He turned back to Nigel.

'By the Splendour of God, man – think yourself lucky.'

* * * * * *

The white skin of Nigel's back was streaked with red and blue. The toes of his riding boots made furrows on the earth as two burly men-at-arms dragged him to a trough and dumped him in it.

Ralph looked at Gilbert.

'Satisfied?'

'Yes.'

Ralph spat.

'Revenge. Is that what you enjoy? A man out of action for days because of a stupid prank that went wrong? So that you can drool over blood?'

'He was a fool. All I did was prove it.'

Ralph gestured towards the trough, where one or two women were trying to lift Nigel to a sitting position. He was barely conscious.

'Was it worth it?'

Gilbert whirled on him, his lips drawn back.

'Yes! And get me that hauberk! You heard the Duke's orders.'

As he strode away, Ralph swore to himself. Bruno came and stood beside him.

'You should be pleased; that is the first time he has stood up to you.'

* * * * * *

The evening shadows stretched right across the square at Pontorson. Dark shapes of wooden buildings were graven against a blood-red sky.

Gilbert sat on the edge of the trough.

For the tenth time he went cold at the thought of what might have happened.

At first it had been all too easy ...

A wager.

'The first man across the Couesnon.'

'Done!' said Nigel, spurring his horse.

At the bank Gilbert reined in.

'I – I think not. Not this time. The sand.'

Nigel reared his horse beside him, glowing with strength and arrogance.

'Dry as a bone. See for yourself.'

Gilbert turned away, and kept his head down.

'The horse is not willing.'

'You mean you are not. So be it, dog boy! When I reach the other side, you owe me. Remember that.'

Harold came up beside Gilbert and watched.

'Well done. A neat job. How long, do you think?'

'Fifty – a hundred paces. No more.'

Suddenly Robert spurred past them.

Horrified, Gilbert shouted.

'No, Master Robert. You must not.'

Robert stopped and turned.

'I am no coward even if you are. I heard the wager.'

Harold joined in.

'Gilbert is right, Robert. It is not a good idea.'

Robert stood in the stirrups.

'No common soldier tells me, the son of a duke, what to do. And no Saxon either.'

Gilbert made ready to dash after them. Harold put a hand on his arm.

'Why not teach both of them a lesson?'

Harold put out a hand to stop any more soldiers following.

'It is a wager. Leave them be.'

Suddenly Nigel's horse seemed to stumble. Nigel was thrown over its neck, and landed on his back. The horse, terrified at the unfamiliar ground, thrashed with its hooves, throwing sand in Nigel's eyes. It began to sink. Nigel's wrist was caught up with the reins.

Nigel tried to reach the shield tied behind his saddle, but the horse's flying hooves prevented him. Nigel's legs sank below the surface. He shouted to Robert, but Robert too had fallen.

On the shore, men gazed in helpless terror.

'Christ and Mary – what do we do?'

Two men were for going in.

'Do you want to face the Bastard if he goes down?'

Harold put out his hand again.

'Wait here. We know the sands. You do not. Give me your shields.'

He collected four or five of them, and took two lengths of rope from a saddle horn. He turned to Gilbert.

'Ready?'

Gilbert nodded.

'The sheen, my lord, remember?'

'You lead. I shall follow. It is your river.'

Picking his way, Gilbert began. Nigel was bellowing for help. Robert was now in the sand up to his waist. He was screaming.

'Does it swallow them completely?' said Harold.

'Not normally. To the chest. Maybe to the neck. It is not the sand that kills them; it is the tide. Higher than five tall men, and – '

' – and swifter than a galloping horse. You said.'

'Jesus and Mary – help me!'

Nigel was making it worse by his wild and purposeless thrashing of arms.

They reached Robert first. The boy was nearly mad with panic.

'I shall take him,' said Harold. 'You go on for Nigel. Enjoy your moment. Here. Take this rope.'

Harold dragged out Robert, who was in a state of collapse, and paid the rope from his saddle to try and save the horse. He laid out two or three shields, and tried to encourage the crazed animal to put hooves on them. It was a mess of neighing, and mud, and flailing legs, and straining rope, and much flaring of nostrils and swearing, but the animal at last struggled to firm ground, and stood, steaming and shaking all over.

Gilbert dismounted in front of Nigel.

'Get me out, damn you.'

'All in good time,' said Gilbert. 'First – you are a fool. Yes?'

'Curse you to Hell!'

'Very well.'

Gilbert turned about and made for his horse.

'No! Wait! For the sake of Christ!'

'You are a fool.'

'I am a fool.'

'And you are sorry for your filthy tongue.'

'I am sorry.'

' – for your filthy tongue.'

' – for my filthy tongue.'

'And you will not do it again.'

'I will not do it again – get me out, you son of a sow.'

'On the soul of the Virgin?'

'Yes, yes, yes – on the soul of the Virgin.'

'And I win the wager?'

'Yes. Anything you like. Only hurry.'

Nigel cut his hands on the edges of the shields, but took no notice. He clutched at Gilbert like a blind man feeling for the lock on the door of a burning room.

It took the combined efforts of both Harold and Gilbert to get out Nigel's horse.

Harold wiped some mud off his hands, took a deep breath, and blew.

'Some rescue, eh? Now – you take the horses, because they need more care. Leave the stupid humans to me.'

Robert could not stand, and Nigel was still prostrate. So Harold lifted the boy on to his shoulder, grasped Nigel by the scruff of the neck, and started after Gilbert towards the shallow bank.

As they landed, the other soldiers gave a great cheer.

'I can face the Bastard now,' said one. 'I was just beginning to think of going off to serve the King of the Moors ... '

'Not celebrating?'

Gilbert jumped. He had not seen Harold approach.

'Thinking, my lord. I was thinking.'

Harold sat down beside him.

'Bad practice – thinking.'

'Suppose the Duke finds out.'

'Who is going to tell him? Nigel? Will he own up to a stupid wager?'

'Robert then.'

'Is he going to admit to his father that he was a foolish, arrogant puppy?'

'The others.'

'Will they confess to his Grace that they stood by while Robert went into the river?'

Gilbert sighed. Harold patted him on the shoulder.

'The world thinks you are a hero. What is wrong with that?'

'But the Duke is so grateful. For what?'

'For saving his son's life. When honesty gets in the way of gratitude, Gilbert, honesty gives way.'

'But I started it all.'

Harold shook his head.

'Waste of words, son. If the world thinks you are brave, you are brave. Why spoil it with a little too much truth?'

'The world is wrong.'

'That is the world's worry, not yours. It is not what is true that so often matters, but what men think to be true.'

And if the Normans think I am up to something, then I am up to something.

* * * * * *

Chapter Eight

The Plotting

'How do I look? Good fit too, eh?'

Harold span himself round. Wulfnoth tossed his head in annoyance and frustration.

'Do you realise what you have just done?'

'I should hope so. I was there.'

Harold patted his belt and walked across to a trestle where servants had finished laying out food and drink. Wulfnoth came after him.

'Can you be so blind? So stupid?'

'It all depends on your point of view. You can see nothing but foolishness in what I do. I, on the other hand, see sense.'

Wulfnoth leaned forward to say something else, but caught sight of eager looks on the faces of the servants, who hovered as close as they dared. He motioned a Breton prisoner towards him.

'Tell them they are dismissed – for the time being. Wait for my orders in the kitchen.'

Harold watched.

'You have learnt no Breton then?'

'I have been here only twice in twelve years – and stick to the subject. I say again, do you see what you have done?'

'And I say to you, do you see what I have not done? Do you see what has not happened to me?'

Wulfnoth frowned.

'What do you mean?'

Harold poured himself another drink.

'In your never-ending litany of impending doom, you have missed what has actually happened. I was shipwrecked. Did I lose a single man? I was seized by Guy of Ponthieu. Did he keep me in chains? When he escorted me to Duke William – with full honours, I may add – did a ransom change hands? Did the Duke cast me into prison? Has he treated me with anything other than correct respect and full attention? Has one of his vassals uttered a word out of place? Has anyone put my life in danger on this campaign – except myself, when I went into the Couesnon?'

'You make it sound as if you have been on nothing more than a summer social progress. Is that why you came here?'

'The reason I came here is – what anybody cares to think.'

'But look at what the Duke has just done.'

'He has shown his gratitude to me for saving his son's life. I should have done the same if I thought he had saved a son of mine. Purely personal, I assure you.'

'Will the world see it like that?'

'It is none of the world's business. It was between William and me. It showed he was human. I like him for that.'

'Was that your object then?'

'What do you mean?'

Wulfnoth sneered.

'Building a wonderful friendship?'

Harold remained infuriatingly calm.

'William has been concerned to behave as a correct host, and I have been concerned to behave as a correct guest.'

'You have done everything the Duke wanted you to do.'

'A good guest goes along with his host's arrangements, generally. I have found them quite acceptable.'

'Did you have any choice?'

'There you go again. Doom and tragedy. That is not truth, Wulf; it is only a point of view. You see it as choice, or the lack of it; I see it as opportunity.'

Wulfnoth began to look baffled. Harold smiled, and put a hand on his shoulder.

'Wulf, you and I both know that one day – one day – your Duke and I may become rivals for a very great prize. I am sure you would want me to win that prize. One of the best ways to win it is to study your rival. Now – look at the last few weeks. What better chance could I have had for such study? I could never have arranged it this way if I had schemed and plotted for a year. Opportunity, you see. You must seize it.'

Wulfnoth remembered Gerard's words ... 'to seize life, all you have to do is put out your hand' ... It unsettled him. He shook off his brother's touch.

'And how do you plan to get home? Have you found an opportunity for that yet?'

'I shall, never fear. The chance will present itself, as surely as the night follows the day.'

'How will you know?'

'Because I shall see it before me. The man with doom in his eyes will not.'

* * * * * *

Hubert took a deep breath and sucked in the sweet soft breeze of a lovely summer morning.

'Rollo? If the Almighty were a man of mood – which God forbid! – He would truly be in a good one today. What beautiful air! And so much in it.'

He caressed Rollo's haunches with his hazel stick.

'Do you want to know what is in it? Well, Brittany is in it for one. I said it would be. It is good news, or I am no Christian man. What sort of good news, you say? Ah, there you take me into deep waters.'

He made an awkward gesture with his injured arm to try and embrace the whole surrounding countryside.

'But what else is there? Every vassal of substance in Bray, Caux, and the Roumois, that is what. All going in the same direction – west. And all unwilling. Their grooms told me so. And I would wager my best arm that they are riding from the Hiesmois and the Avranchin too – coming east. Now where are they bound, Rollo? That is the question. And why now? Because of our Saxon earl, that is why. What has he done? Has he made a mistake at last? Was it as I suspected? Has he done something on impulse, on genuine impulse? Or are they trying to get him to make a mistake?'

Hubert laid his stick in his lap, and groped behind himself for his flask.

'Perhaps we shall find some answers in Rouen, eh, Rollo? And see my young Englishman too? I wonder if he took my advice about that buxom priest's daughter. While away the long summer evenings ... '

'Father Abbot, it is time that I journeyed to Longueville, to relieve Brother Stephen. May I have your permission?'

Father Abbot allowed himself the ghost of a smile.

'On one condition, Brother Hubert.'

'Name it, Father Abbot.'

'I expect an answer to my letter from my lord Lanfranc. Bring it. And, while you are about it – ' he raised innocent eyebrows ' – you can also bring back to me the news that you intend to gather at Rouen. Especially about Earl Harold in Brittany.'

Hubert stared. Father Abbot let his smile spread wider.

'Abbots get things out of the air just as often as ex-soldiers, my son. And they can be prey to just as much curiosity. You, however, have the advantage of being able to satisfy that curiosity.'

'Only with your permission, Father Abbot.'

'If I deny you that liberty, you will of a certainty take it, and then endanger your immortal soul by prevaricating when you return. In your own interests, it seems, I must give in to your worldly interests.'

'Argued like a Vatican archdeacon, my lord, if I may say so. How fortunate I am to have a spiritual father such as yourself to watch over me ... '

And what if the search for news should lie beyond Rouen?

'Ah, well, Rollo, we shall cross that bridge when we come to it. If random threads of the story should pull us further west, I am sure the Father Abbot would be just as interested as I if they could be gathered up and woven into a full tapestry.'

* * * * * *

The courtyard was deserted. Sir Roger of Montgomery dismounted.

'Funny.'

Sir Walter Giffard looked all round.

'Middle of the morning.'

'Ho there!'

Giffard dismounted, drew his sword, and banged with the hilt on several doors.

At last a frightened stable boy shot out of an archway like a rabbit chased by a ferret. He almost ran into Giffard, recoiled, and cringed.

'Where is everyone?'

He cowered back so much that Giffard thought it wise to catch him by the shoulder in case he scuttled back inside again.

'Where is his Grace?'

The boy struggled with the question.

'Grace?'

Well, at least he could talk. Giffard shook him.

'Your lord. His Grace. Where is he?'

'His Grace the bishop,' added Montgomery.

The boy, now thoroughly baffled, looked round the courtyard.

'Not 'ere, surr.'

Giffard shook him again.

'I can see that, idiot.' He thrust his florid face near the boy's nose, and spaced the words. 'Where – is – he?'

The boy frowned.

'S – surr?'

Montgomery stepped forward, before Giffard hit him.

'Just a minute, Walter.'

He took care to keep his voice calm and level.

'We are in Coutances. This is Coutances – yes?'

'Surr.'

The boy was watching Montgomery's lips intently, as if anxious not to miss a single step in the argument. Montgomery glanced at Giffard before continuing.

'We are in the episcopal palace – ' he corrected himself ' – we are in the house of my lord Geoffrey de Montbrai, Bishop of Coutances. Yes?'

'Surr.'

'My lord Geoffrey is expecting us – he knows we are coming. I am Sir Roger of Montgomery. This is Sir Walter Giffard.'

The boy's eyes opened wide.

'Oh, surr!'

'Where is he?' said Montgomery, pouncing.

'S – surr?'

The wretched boy looked baffled again.

'Where is he?' bellowed Montgomery.

The boy flung out an arm.

'There, surr.'

Montgomery turned round, and back again.

'Where?'

'He be standing beside you, surr.'

Montgomery stared.

'That is Sir Walter Giffard, you blockhead.'

The boy brightened.

'I know, surr. You told me.'

The famous Montgomery patience gave out. He flung the boy away and walked off with his hands on his hips.

A hinge creaked. A door opened in a chapel adjacent to the hall. Geoffrey himself appeared, in full episcopal robes, and carrying his crozier.

'I thought I heard your voice, Roger. Hallo, Walter.'

Behind him the congregation trickled out of the chapel, blinking at the light. They began to gather in twos and threes, caught sight of Geoffrey still there, and trudged off to their household duties.

Geoffrey stopped directly in front of Montgomery and Giffard, and extended his hand bearing the episcopal ring. They knelt and kissed it.

'In the name of the Father, the Son, and the Holy Ghost, I welcome you. Well, how are you?'

'Stiff as a board,' said Giffard. 'Your roads are diabolical.'

'At least we have some,' said Geoffrey. 'More than you can say for Brittany.'

He turned to the poor boy, who hovered, still baffled, at a respectful distance.

'Now, Lambert – go tell the cook to prepare three fresh meals. Off with you.'

Lambert's face cleared, but remained watchful. He ducked his head and sidled away, never taking his eyes off Sir Walter. More boys appeared and took the horses.

Giffard gestured towards Lambert's disappearing heels.

'Is he the best you can do?'

'Everyone was at Mass.'

'Why not him?'

'He has fits if he gets too tired kneeling.'

'Oaf!'

'Do you have no Lamberts at Longueville?'

Giffard merely growled.

Montgomery interposed.

'I must admit the roads began to improve as we approached Coutances,' he admitted. 'There is always something new to see whenever we come here.'

'I see you renewed your scaffolding,' remarked Giffard.

'I had a bit of luck,' said Geoffrey. 'A Swedish ship put into Granville with pine trunks for masts. Seasoned. We bought the lot.'

And Geoffrey always said he was a pauper. Giffard and Montgomery exchanged glances.

'Come and see what we have been doing,' said Geoffrey. His new arrivals sighed. Any visitor to Coutances was forced to make a tour of the rising cathedral before anything else could be done. It was a duty which everyone had long since learned to accept, like dipping one's hand into holy water in the entrance to a church.

It was indeed impressive. Montgomery and Giffard tramped obediently across the town square, ducked below boards and poles, and kept an eye open for falling trowels. They both got a crick in their necks gazing up at the soaring tower. Buckets and pulleys rattled everywhere.

'I see you let your workmen cut Mass, then,' remarked Montgomery.

'No. They go. At dawn. I say another for the household. The palace chapel is not big enough. But, when this is finished ... ' He waved a hand around the nave. The roof was nearly complete. Tilers' boys slid down ropes like acrobats.

'Saints and angels, Geoffrey – you will get half Normandy in here.'

'It is bigger than Odo's at Bayeux,' said Geoffrey, smiling smugly.

He saw his two visitors exchange glances again, but made no comment.

'Come and see the very latest addition.'

Behind the site of the altar, he stopped beside some tall objects covered in cloth which itself lay under a crust of stone grains as fine as flour. Taking one of the corners, he tugged. A cloud of dust enveloped them. When it had cleared, there before them was a freshly-carved statue.

'Who is it?' said Giffard, still coughing.

'Sir Tancred of Hauteville,' said Geoffrey. 'Recognise him?'

'The father of the twelve?' said Montgomery.

Geoffrey nodded.

'This is their contribution. Or rather my payment for their contribution.'

Giffard and Montgomery both knew that Geoffrey had journeyed more than once to southern Italy, where the many rogue sons of Sir Tancred were carving fortunes, and estates, for themselves. Hauteville was in his diocese, and Geoffrey was not above a little blackmail in his dealings with them to raise funds for his treasured cathedral. In return for his prayers for their souls (souls which, in the general opinion, were more in need of prayer than most), they would contribute money and treasure to help build this monument to the glory of God. The most wily of the brothers, Robert the Guiscard, drove the hardest bargain. He wanted in addition a row of statues, of his father and mother, and of himself and his eleven brothers.

Geoffrey pulled off another cover. Giffard gasped.

'The Guiscard – to the life!'

'Good, eh?' Geoffrey was very pleased with himself.

'Where did you get the mason who could do that?'

'Bought him. From Bayeux.'

'From Odo?'

Geoffrey grinned from ear to ear.

'Money talks. Odo has not found out yet.'

Giffard and Montgomery turned towards each other once again. Geoffrey at last reacted.

'Why do you two keep looking at each other whenever I mention Odo?'

Montgomery cleared his throat.

'Do you think we could have something to eat, Geoffrey? We have been riding for several hours.'

As they walked back towards the hall of the palace, Geoffrey, for all his curiosity, could not help keeping up a flow of commentary.

'Small wonder young Lambert reacts like a frightened fawn. This place was the end of the world, you know, when I first came here. Fear and superstition stalked like feral cats. No town, no church, no palace, no court, no market, nothing.'

Montgomery found it impossible to resist, or to hide, a further glance at his friend. Geoffrey saw it.

'Well, you must be proud too of what you have built at Bellême?'

Inside the hall, tables groaned under the weight of great piles of blankets, napkins, and towels. Towers of dishes and platters swayed as their footsteps made the nearby floorboards give beneath their weight. Trestles and benches were stacked everywhere. Huge piles of logs almost obscured the hearth. New torch brackets gleamed on the walls. The rushes smelt fresh and sweet.

Three meals had been set out at a clear table. Geoffrey waved them towards a bench, and himself poured them a drink.

'Well, when are they coming? Today? Tomorrow?'

Montgomery hesitated with his cup halfway to his lips. Geoffrey leaned forward.

'And if you look at Walter once more, I shall knock that cup out of your hand.'

'Conan is finished,' said Montgomery.

'Thierry told me that. Answer my question. When are the Bastard and Harold coming? When does the council meet?'

'It does not,' said Giffard.

Geoffrey blinked.

'You mean it has been cancelled?'

'No. It has been moved.'

Geoffrey's face darkened.

'Where?'

Montgomery coughed. Giffard came to his rescue.

'To Bayeux.'

'What!'

'Just – just soften your spurs, Geoffrey,' said Montgomery. 'There has been a change of plan.'

Geoffrey began pacing.

'And the poor devil who has to pay for it is the last to find out.'

'Be fair, Geoffrey. Walter and I have ridden as fast as we could. And we did come in person. The Bastard could have sent a courier like your man Thierry.'

'Odo is behind this. Odo. Admit it.'

Montgomery began to carve himself some meat.

'Do you wish to hear the real reason, or do you wish to carry on complaining about the expense and about Bishop Odo? We have heard you on this subject before, you know.'

Geoffrey sat down.

'Very well. What is it?'

'Location, chiefly. The Bastard has decided that Coutances is not central enough. He had thought at first that by having the council here, so near to Brittany, that it would overawe Conan and help to bring him to heel. But his rout has been so complete – young Beaumont did very well, by the way – that he feels safe in changing the place to somewhere further east.'

Geoffrey sneered.

'And Odo just happened to mention Bayeux.'

'It is central, you must admit.'

'And Maurilius has agreed to come from Rouen,' said Giffard. 'I doubt you would get him as far as Coutances. Getting him out of his palace is as hard as getting you out of yours.'

'Evreux and Avranches are coming too,' said Montgomery. 'Sées and Lisieux are already with the Bastard. You and Odo make the tally complete.'

Geoffrey raised his eyebrows.

'Almost as if he were having two councils – lay and spiritual. Why?'

'No idea,' said Giffard.

'Odo,' said Geoffrey.

'He could be up to something,' admitted Montgomery. 'He has been closeted with the Bastard several times. But just what it is ... ' He shrugged.

'If it is directed at Harold,' said Giffard, 'it will have to be something very special to place us ahead of him. I have seldom seen a man whom it is so difficult to put in a false position.'

'Even sickness – when half the force was prostrate at Mortain. He stayed with young Robert. Missed the action. And never lost any face.'

'The Bastard trusted him,' said Giffard. 'Trusted him to look after his son. Good thing he did.'

'You can not outface him,' said Montgomery. 'You can not embarrass him. And you certainly can not frighten him. The man is impossible.'

Giffard forgot his meal and leaned forward.

'He could have played the distinguished visitor. But he joined in everything. All the way from Rouen to Mortain. No march is interesting. He made it almost a triumphal progress. He even shared sickness with them. Their faces light up when they see him. God's Face, he even risked his life in the Couesnon.'

'I suppose you know he saved Robert.'

Geoffrey nodded.

'I heard. Thierry's appetite for news, fortunately, is almost as good as his appetite for food.'

'I must say,' said Montgomery, 'that his grasp of war is remarkable. His comments are always worth listening to. I never thought I should hear myself say it, but I am forced to admit – the man is a brilliant soldier and a born leader.'

Geoffrey grunted.

'Roger, *I* never thought I should hear you say it either. What are you two about? We are supposed to be plotting the man's downfall, or at the very least his discomfiture. And he has charmed the pair of you into becoming dewy-eyed boys at the feet of a fireside minstrel. Pull yourselves together.'

'That is unfair, Geoffrey, and you know it.'

'To listen to you, anyone would think it was Harold who led this expedition, not the Bastard.'

'He did not – and you know that full well too.'

They fell into silence. Giffard turned his attention at last to the food. Montgomery cut himself some cheese and tore off a hunk of bread. Geoffrey, who had fasted since dawn because of his two masses, also ate vigorously.

Each followed his own thoughts.

At last, Geoffrey brushed some crumbs from his knees.

'What would you do, Roger?'

'I know what I would do,' said Giffard with his mouth full.

'We all know what you would do, Walter,' said Geoffrey. 'You have told us enough times. I asked Roger.'

'You mean if I were the Bastard?'

'Yes.'

Montgomery picked his teeth.

'I am not a deep thinker like Fitz. But I am beginning to agree with him. Remember what you said at the outset? Try and trap him into a mistake? Well, we have failed. The man's armour is impregnable. It is impossible to discomfit him. The troops admire him out of all proportion. Leave him here much longer and they will not want to fight him when the time comes. Worse, we may be in danger of making fools of ourselves. We all say it would be bad politics to – er – remove him.'

'Not me,' said Giffard.

'All of us – except Walter – say we can not remove him. So I might be inclined to cut our losses and let him go. Remember what Fitz said: let him deal with the other claimants for us. I should think he will eat young Edgar.'

'And Norway?'

'I should back him against Norway. Saints, he has *our* troops practically eating out of his hand. His own will be invincible faced with a threat like Hardrada.'

Silence fell again.

Geoffrey looked round at the evidence of his vast preparations. Ah well! At least he would save on food. Might even hire another mason or two.

'Was there anything else?'

Montgomery frowned.

'Anything else?'

'Any other news.'

Giffard poured another drink.

'There was one other thing – after the rescue. You remember he saved young Robert ... ? '

* * * * * *

'How long?'

'A week.'

'A week!'

'You know what armourers are. You can never rush them.'

'There were plenty in better condition than that one.'

'Yes – all sewn on to cheap leather. Bretons for you. Only one with the welded links. You saw.'

'But the hole in it.'

'You should have seen the stomach of the man from whom it was cut.'

Bruno grunted.

'You are paying, I suppose.'

'It is I who wants the repair.'

'Spoiling him.'

'Oh?'

Bruno undid his saddle girths.

'How old were you before you had a hauberk like that? I had to work up to mine.'

'What I do with my money is my business.'

'He will not be any the better for it.'

'He will be better protected. Deny that.'

'He will need it.'

Ralph flung down his gloves beside the fire.

'Why do you have such a down on the boy?'

Bruno arranged the saddle beside the fire so that it formed a support for his back, and sat down.

'It is not I who drives down; it is you who raises up.'

'You are nothing but a misery.'

Bruno began to fix a small carcass on a spit.

'Where is he now?'

'On leave. He lives near here. You know that.'

Bruno tilted his head a fraction.

'Ah, yes – Gilbert "of Avranches". '

'And why not? You are Bruno of Aix. I am Ralph of Gisors.'

'You do not need me to tell you the difference. Did he invite you to go with him to his home? Well, did he? I would have invited you to mine.'

'He wanted to tell his family about his exploits. Is that so wrong?'

The bird began to sizzle.

'Ah, yes – saving the Bastard's son from the deadly sands. Sands he was born near. I will wager he knows them better than he does his vaunted "Avranches".'

Ralph forgot his horse for a moment.

'Nothing he does is right, is it? Nothing I do is right either. When I avoid going on leave, I am wrong. When he goes, *he* is wrong.'

Bruno, his head down, paid careful attention to the fire. Ralph leaned down towards him.

'You belittle everything. A misery, that is what you are. What about your home? We never hear anything about that. I suppose you do have one.'

'I do. Like you. And I had a brother. Like you. And my brother died. Like yours. But it is not I who is the misery. It is you.'

'How do you work that out?'

Ralph regretted the words as soon as they were out, and steeled himself for the reply. Bruno looked up.

'Your brother is dead. So is mine. Dead. Gone. You are trying to bring yours back. And you will be miserable until you stop.'

* * * * * *

'He gave Conan's horses to Beaumont. He founded a church at Pontorson – on the spot. He turned the Flemings loose – wasting. Mind you, that was killing two birds with one stone. He gave a hauberk to the boy who went in after him – ordered a scout back to Dol to get a good one. He has sent for Matilda. I tell you, Geoffrey – I have never seen him in such a mood.'

'He has never had his son snatched from such danger before.'

Giffard leaned over the table and helped himself to strawberries.

'These look good.'

Geoffrey snorted.

'You can live on them for a week – now. Is that all you have to say?'

'One more thing,' said Giffard, reaching for a spoon. 'He has given him arms.'

'Who has given them to whom?'

Giffard scooped out some honey from an earthenware pot.

'I never expected to see it, but I suppose, on reflection ... '

'Walter!'

'What?' He paused with his spoon in mid-air.

'Make yourself clear.'

'Clear? Ah. Yes. Well ... '

He took another huge spoonful. Geoffrey raised his eyes Heavenwards.

'The Bastard has given arms to Harold. Decorated him. Grateful, you see.'

Geoffrey leaned forward intently.

'And he accepted?'

' Of course he did. I will say this for Harold – '

'You have done nothing but say things for Harold.'

'I say this for Harold,' repeated Giffard. 'He knows how to behave like a true knight. Knows the correct form.'

'He did it very well,' commented Montgomery.

Geoffrey whirled on him.

'Not you too – please.'

'Why are you so annoyed?' said Giffard. 'It was just a friendly gesture – from one father to another – and accepted in the spirit in which it was given.'

Geoffrey drove his fist into his other hand, stood up, and began pacing.

'Praise be to God!'

Montgomery and Giffard looked blankly at each other. Geoffrey stopped in front of them.

'But see what this *means.*'

'I do,' said Giffard. 'It means that, after all these weeks, they have acknowledged publicly what we have all been seeing anyway – that they have developed a healthy regard for each other. Perhaps they even like each other a bit.'

Geoffrey tossed his head in despair.

'Dear God! Walter, think! Look, look. The Bastard gave Harold arms. Yes?'

'I told you.'

'Did he carry out the investiture personally?'

'Yes. It was his son that was saved.'

'Was this in front of witnesses?'

'I should say so. The surviving garrison of Dol, most of the Bastard's task force, half a dozen senior vassals, three bishops, Fitz, and us.'

'Ah!' said Montgomery, the light beginning to dawn. Giffard still spooned strawberries and looked blank.

Geoffrey took the bowl from his hands and laid it on the table.

'Walter, concentrate. Harold gave thanks for this – yes?'

'I told you! Harold knows how to – '

'He rendered homage.'

'Yes, I told – aaahh!'

Geoffrey sat back in relief.

'So,' said Giffard, eyes now alight, 'if Harold has gone on his knees and given thanks and rendered homage – '

' – he is now the Duke's man, his vassal,' said Montgomery, eager to show his new comprehension.

'By all law and custom, recognised throughout Christendom,' said Geoffrey, 'he is the Duke's feudal subordinate.'

'So if Harold makes any move against the Bastard – '

' – he will be guilty of violation of the oath of homage. He knows the Bastard claims the crown. If he now makes a bid for it himself, he will be challenging his feudal overlord, violating his knightly oath of allegiance.'

Giffard came out of his trance of excitement.

'Do you think that will stop him?'

'No.'

'Well then.'

'But it will stop him being in the right any more. We have at last – *at last* – put the man in a false position.'

Giffard picked up his bowl again and took a second helping.

'We are still going to let him go, he will still snatch the crown, and we shall still have to fight him. We have gained nothing.'

'We have gained a moral advantage,' said Geoffrey.

Giffard pointed with his spoon.

'Wait until he is coming at you with a battle-axe, and see how much good to you is your "moral advantage". '

'We shall see,' said Geoffrey, unimpressed. 'The Bastard is thinking beyond the battle, remember. He wants the crown of England as its rightful king, not as thieving brigand. He has to be in the right if he wants the support of the Pope. Putting Harold in the wrong will help him to get it. It is Harold who will be the usurper now, whatever happens.'

'Look at the overall picture, Walter,' said Montgomery. 'Everything is now moving our way. You must admit that our boundaries have never been so secure as they are now – especially after we have cut Conan's claws. A boy on the throne in Paris, Anjou divided, Maine conquered, Ponthieu chastened, Flanders an ally, and its count the Regent.'

Giffard wiped his mouth, folded his arms, and waited for Montgomery to finish.

'May I mention one small detail you seem to have overlooked? King Edward is not dead yet, never mind Harold.'

Nobody replied at once, so he took advantage.

'You are all plotting and planning and being clever. If you had taken my advice in the first place and done away with him, we should be one clear step forward, and no if's or but's. Now where are we? Congratulating ourselves on a "moral advantage". Midden muck! We may see it like that, but not Harold ... Outfaced? Outwitted? Rubbish! He will ignore it. And it is his view of it that counts.'

'No, Walter, that is just where you are wrong. It is the world's view that counts.'

Giffard laid down his empty bowl.

'I may have thought so, just now, when you carried me away. But no. The world's view is the common sense view. To Harold, to the world, and to any normal man, this whole thing is nothing but a public compliment from a grateful father.'

'You are forgetting one of the witnesses,' said Montgomery. 'Bishop Odo.'

'Oh?'

'We thought he might be planning something – remember? My guess he can use this as well. For once I fancy Geoffrey will not begrudge to Odo his devious mind. Am I right, Geoffrey?'

Geoffrey sighed.

'Yes – I think you may be. Something is going to happen at Bayeux. So I suppose the sooner we make our way there, the sooner we shall find out.'

Geoffrey poured three drinks and handed them round.

'To Bayeux.'

'Bayeux,' said Montgomery, and nudged Giffard.

'The council at Bayeux,' said Giffard. 'And much good may it do us.'

* * * * * *

Adele gazed up into the dark above their bed, where she knew mice ran along splinter-strewn, smoke-blackened joists. It did not matter. A draught came under the door; that did not matter either. She drew the blanket up over Edwin's shoulders, and returned her hands to cradling his sleeping head.

She was not worthy of this. She was a wanton, a trollop – yes, a whore if you like. The men despised her – deep down. She despised herself. Nigel? Ha! The only thing he valued was what he carried between his legs.

So why this? What had she done to deserve it? She felt as if she were the survivor of a disaster in which hundreds of worthy people had perished. She stroked Edwin's hair.

She had been given this – this great prize without having done anything to compete. To whom, or to what, should she offer thanks? Life up to now had been a procession of sins and penances, of guilt and fear of punishment, of wagging fingers and shaking heads. Pleasure was something you squeezed in between the fading security of the last penance and the certain guilt that would follow the commitment of the next sin. The demands of her body shrieked against the shackles of the spirit. Sometimes her mind tried to break through; sometimes she wondered if there was anything beyond the darkness, beyond the nooks and holes and shadows that took up so much space around her. There was always so much to fear: death of course; disease, and the awful dying that could follow; that was always there, at the end, for everybody. But on the way too: demons in cellars, evil spirits in woodland depths, the Devil himself everywhere, waiting to pounce on the unwary. The ghosts, the goblins, the trolls, the dwarves, the giants, the freaks, the fairies; the spells, the incantations, the necessary prayers.

Adele had never before thought about them all together. Now, since this miracle – she caressed Edwin's head again – she did not fear them. Not that they were not dangerous; everyone knew that they were. She was still able to realise that life grew a forest of traps round the careless and the careful alike. But she felt, now, free from fear.

She opened her eyes wide as further revelations came to her. Was this why hermits never feared the forest and the wilderness? Was this why monks often built their houses in remote places? Not because they believed the Devil was not there (of course he was), but because they did not fear to go and fight with him on his own ground. Was it because they too had this – this thing? This way of looking at the world? Did this explain why they were always on their knees, giving thanks?

To whom? To God?

She frowned. It seemed stupid, but was she, in a way, now looking at the world as God would look at it? With mercy? With love? Had God given her His eyes?

She recalled sermons by Father Lanfranc – a frightening man. But he was not frightening when he talked about the love of God. She had not understood him, but she remembered his saying something about God being love. A riddle. She was surprised that it had stuck in her mind. She had heard her father say the words too, but she knew he was mouthing things he had only half learned. He did not know the truth. Father Lanfranc did. So did Archbishop Maurilius.

So had they solved the riddle? Had she? Was God love? Was this why she felt no fear, here, in Edwin's arms? Was this why holy men feared only separation from God? For the first time, excommunication meant more to her than the flames of Hellfire. Was this why she feared, not losing Edwin, but losing the love that they shared?

She gazed up once again into the shadows. Why did the mind run on in the dark? Was it a kind of sleeping? Was she merely dreaming with her eyes open? Was this whole thing a dream? Would she wake up one day soon?

No, surely not. This dream, if dream it was, was so much more powerful, so much more real, than ordinary life. Yet her mind told her too that ordinary life had been around her since she had been born. So – which was reality? The darkness and fear of life as it was lived, or the blinding light and beating of the heart as she now felt it?

She recalled something else that holy men went on about. Something about this world being not the real world, about its being merely a preparation. Heaven was the reality. And she was not good enough for Heaven.

Edwin stirred. Adele lifted his head off her breast and kissed him.

'It is late. You must go.'

'Yes.'

* * * * * *

'It is a measure of William's regard for you that he deems the occasion incomplete without you.'

'It is a measure of the Duke's regard for you that he sends you as the only person he thinks capable of persuading me. I have said it before, Sir William – you are a loss to the legal profession.'

Fitzosbern bowed to the compliment.

'I thank you, my lord abbot, but I hesitate to accept the accolade until I know whether my advocacy has been successful.'

Lanfranc scratched an ear.

'Why does this man always want me to be somewhere else?'

'Bayeux is not very far, to be sure. And it is central.'

'So is Caen – here.'

Fitzosbern allowed a twitch of irony to appear about his mouth.

'Odo does not have a cathedral at Caen.'

Lanfranc nodded.

'I thought I detected his hand in this. I must say I am not entirely surprised.'

'Especially as you dropped some hints to him in the first place.'

'Which he quickly gathered up, it seems. May I say that you are exceedingly well informed.'

'Odo is generous with information that he thinks will be helpful to his purpose.'

Lanfranc smiled.

'So I am to be gathered in by the stray threads of the net I myself began to weave in Rouen? You and I both know that my purpose was to hasten the business of the Church council.'

Fitzosbern lifted his eyebrows innocently.

'Well?'

Lanfranc thought for a moment with lowered head. At last he lifted it.

'I take it that I am absolutely indispensable to this meeting?'

'William thinks so. That is why I am here.'

'But you told me that every vassal of note and every bishop in Normandy will be there.'

'Maurilius too.'

'Maurilius! Who was sent to persuade him – John the Baptist?'

Fitzosbern emptied his cup.

'Enough of this, Father. You profess indifference to politics, but allow me to set out once and for all the situation, of which I have no doubt you are already aware. You know what is on William's mind; has been on his mind for thirteen years. The crown. Since the Confessor promised it to him. Every move he has made has been with this in view. Now look at his position. Especially after Brittany. Conan has had his claws cut. A delegation is on its way now to Rennes to claim his homage. We have garrisons at Dol and Dinant. He can not move without William's permission. Anjou is riven by civil war. Maine is ours. William's father-in-law is the King's guardian. The Vexin is quiet, and Guy skulks in his kennel in Ponthieu.

'Now this Harold is among us. The second man in England. Imagine – if William can obtain a pronouncement from him about the future – a public pronouncement – then we have not only Normandy prepared, but England too.'

'But why me?' persisted Lanfranc.

Fitzosbern shook his head.

'Your modesty does you credit, Father. But it does not mask your intelligence. You are the most illustrious scholar in Normandy, in France, possibly in Christendom.'

'Ridiculous.'

'No! True. The Pope himself is an ex-scholar of yours, and freely acknowledges his debt to you. Having you at Bayeux will be almost as good as having the Pope himself. Better, in William's eyes.'

Lanfranc inclined his head by way of acceptance.

'Is this entirely Odo's work?'

'The public statement part, yes. It is my idea to add the part about a possible betrothal.'

'Harold has a woman. Several children too.'

'But no wife. What better way to bind him to William than to join him to the ducal family? Think of it! The allegiance of the most able, experienced, popular, and powerful man in England. Better still – if William offers to continue with him as the second man in the kingdom. What finer offer could Harold have?'

Lanfranc gazed steadily at Fitzosbern.

'Perhaps you had better ask Harold that.'

'I understand he is prepared to make this statement. Is that enough for you?'

'Not quite. You may recall that the reason why all six bishops, and Maurilius, were gathered together in Rouen was for a Church council. Now, it seems, all seven will be gathered again at Bayeux. If I were to attend, that would provide a perfect occasion for this Church council to be put in session. Do I make myself clear?'

Fitzosbern nodded.

'I had expected as much. William will guarantee you the Council as soon as this matter is completed.'

'At once?'

'At once.'

'At Bayeux?'

'At Bayeux.'

'With William?'

'You have his word.'

Fitzosbern made to get up. Lanfranc put up a hand.

'You may recall, Sir William, that one of the causes for the summoning of this Council was the matter of non-celibate priests.'

Fitzosbern hesitated in mid-air.

'Well?'

'This priest of William's – Arnulf – has a daughter.'

Fitzosbern sat down again. Lanfranc drove a harder bargain than he had expected.

'It would be surely fitting, Sir William, if the president of this Council were to set an example by dismissing his worldly chaplain. I should be only too pleased to nominate a more – suitable candidate.'

Fitzosbern inclined his head.

'My lord abbot is too kind.'

Lanfranc rose.

'I shall come with you to the gate.'

Nigel Fitzhenry stood waiting with the horses and two other soldiers of the escort. He positively shrivelled in front of Lanfranc.

'God's Blessing on you, my children, and a safe journey.'

'My lord.'

'My lord.'

Nigel could get no words out at all. He clambered painfully on to his horse.

Fitzosbern grunted.

'Good to see you show respect for at least one of your betters.'

Nigel shivered.

'That man! He is better than anybody. Has eyes that come straight from God.'

* * * * * *

It would have been such a good story too – the frustration, the failure of the first attacks, his own brilliant idea to use the wind and the dryness, his clever plan to induce the Flemings to push home the assault, the noise and the fire and the smoke, the breakthrough, the hand-to-hand fighting, the final victory, the Flemings all round him, cheering. Above all, the Duke's reward. In front of Fitzosbern, of Earl Harold, of that puffing old fool Giffard, in front of everybody.

Judith would have listened with parted lips, would have clapped those swift white hands of hers, would have skipped round in a circle to show her delight.

Robert of Beaumont dug his spurs savagely. Tears of mortification pricked his eyes …

'No offence, Sir Robert. Orders, sir. Captain's back.'

'But I led you. I gave you all that silver.'

'I know, sir. Generous. But will you get us home, sir? Can you pay us what is our due? That is what we ask ourselves, sir.'

'You went looting for miles. You are loaded down with stuff.'

'We must provide for the future, sir. And then there is the contract, Sir Robert. Bastard's business, not yours. No disrespect, sir.'

'So what I did for you means nothing. What we did together.'

Lothar, a dark-jowled ex-weaver from Brabant with a split ear, shrugged.

'Fortunes of war, you might say, sir. Things come and go. We had to look after ourselves. How could we know when you were coming back, sir? Very sorry, sir … '

They were not, of course. Even through his tears, Beaumont could see that.

What could he say now? What could he tell Judith? That the men he had led into battle, the men who had said that they respected him, who had cheered him amid the smoke of victory – that these very men had stolen his horses, sold them – to the Bretons – and put the money into their own pockets, to 'provide for the future'.

'No disrespect, sir.'

* * * * * *

Arnulf laid on the whip as hard as his flabby muscles would permit. The donkey took no notice. The cart shook as the solid wheels bounced over another stone. Rain whipped the puddles into rebellion.

How many hours to Bayeux?

Arnulf blinked the water out of his eyes. His bones ached, his joints complained, his stomach rumbled. As if that were not enough, God had opened the heavens for pure spite.

He swung the whip savagely, and cried out as a twinge cut through his shoulder.

He glanced behind him. The rain roared on to the canvas canopy. The boxes at least were secure and dry …

But was he?

Fitzosbern had left Pontorson in haste, and had gone to see Abbot Lanfranc. Sentry gossip soon spread the word.

'The Bastard wants him to the council. They say he is going to excommunicate Harold for him.'

The council. Was it to be only a feudal council, or were they going to re-open the Church council as well? Was there going to be a declaration after all about incontinent priests? Dear God – what was he to do?

'Do? On your life and survival, get there!'

Bishop Odo's spotty face glowed with intensity. He seemed to know everything.

'Take your altars, the covers, the furniture, everything.' He paused to lay particular stress. 'Everything. Do you follow?'

Arnulf swallowed and nodded, without entirely understanding. Odo grasped his collar.

'And not a word to a soul. Not a soul. If you do, you will be on your own. But – if you go direct to my palace when you arrive, and make yourself known to my constable, and stay there, and await my instructions – I shall make provision for you. I am thinking of raising the number of canons in my cathedral. Coutances now has twelve. So I must have fifteen.' He laughed unkindly. 'You never know – I might even provide for your whore of a daughter. She can ply her trade as well in Bayeux as in Rouen.'

Arnulf wiped his wet hands on the sides of his habit.

'My thanks to your Grace ... '

He swung the whip again, and winced.

And while he was torturing his aching body, on vile roads, all over Normandy, always trying to provide for the future, what was Adele doing in Rouen? Was she providing for the future? Or was she still throwing herself at anything in leggings?

Arnulf wiped his streaming face.

Hussy!

* * * * * *

'See? I have made this one slightly shorter, especially for you.'

Gerard pointed with a huge hairy forefinger.

Young William seized the wooden sword and swung it, making battle noises.

'Mine is better,' said Richard, and began fencing with him.

Matilda cuffed them.

'Say thank you to Gerard.'

'Thank you, Gerard.'

'Thank you, Gerard.'

'And you two – say goodbye.'

Constance and young Matilda piped up.

'Goodbye, Gerard.'

'Goodbye, Gerard.'

'Take them away, and dress them for the road,' said Matilda to Arlette. 'And come back here.'

'My lady.'

Gerard noticed Arlette's tight lips, and gestured a silent comment to Matilda.

'Oh, her?' said Matilda, not caring that Arlette was still in earshot. 'It might stop her mooning. She is a worse drag than a ten-month womb.'

Arlette sniffed loudly on her way out.

'She finds it difficult with the boys,' said Gerard. 'I could take them, you know.'

Matilda stuck her finger into a bowl.

'Yes. And spoil them rotten.'

'They would learn more here than they would bouncing on the road to Bayeux, with a dozen wailing women like Arlette.'

Matilda pulled out her finger and licked it.

'William wants them all.'

Gerard shrugged.

'Even Cecily?'

'Especially Cecily.'

'Oh?'

Gerard kept his eyebrows raised for a moment. Matilda wiped her finger on the side of her dress.

'Mind your own business.'

'Does she want to go?'

'What do you think?'

In chorus they mimicked her whine: 'Do I have to?'

'She will change her song when we get there,' said Matilda.

Gerard decided to probe from a different direction.

'It may be the last time you see Harold then?'

Matilda narrowed her eyes.

'What is that supposed to mean?'

Gerard made an innocent face.

'Love one's enemies.'

Matilda sat down on a bench and cut herself a piece of cheese.

'He is not an enemy. And – yes – I do happen to like him. If I met the Sultan I might like him too. It changes nothing.'

Gerard grinned.

'You would probably like his woman. Edith.'

'Yes, I probably would. He told me a lot about her.'

'In confidence, of course.'

Matilda broke in with her mouth full.

'Whatever the reason, it will get me away from this graveyard of a castle.

Travel! Action! No more listening to the nonsense of cripples and potboys in smelly kitchens.'

'I see,' said Gerard. 'Get away from the truth and wallow in the mush of fluttering women and trembling valets. A great step forward.'

'I am taking Arlette.'

'Exactly.'

'She will have Wulfnoth to look forward to. Might put a smile on her face.'

'I am sure she will be wonderful company.'

Matilda stood up and smoothed out a dress that was decidedly grubby.

'If you think you are going to persuade me to take you.'

Gerard threw up his hands in mock horror.

'By the Nails! A fate worse than death.'

Matilda grunted some swearword. Gerard pointed with his crutch.

'Sit down a minute.'

The tone in his voice was completely different. Matilda obeyed. Gerard leaned forward intently.

'Are you with child again?'

Matilda looked wary.

'What if I am?'

'I thought so. Something about your face, your eyes.'

'Well?'

'Does the Duke know?'

'No.'

'And you are still going to Bayeux?'

Matilda stood up again.

'If that is all you have to say.'

'In this weather? In a waggon?'

Matilda stopped at the door.

'Mary went to Bethlehem – in winter – on a donkey.'

She nearly collided with Arlette on her way out.

'Follow me.'

'At once, my lady.'

But Arlette, after an anxious glance at her, came on into the kitchen.

'Gerard, is it true you said something to Wulf about seizing life?'

Gerard shrugged.

'I may have done.'

Arlette clasped her hands excitedly.

'Well. I shall.'

'Explain yourself, girl.'

Arlette unclasped her hands, and adopted the stance of a martyr at the stake.

'Wulfnoth would not ask the Duke. So I shall.'

* * * * * *

'Is it worth it?'

'Nothing will happen here, for sure.'

Bishop John of Avranches shrugged.

'It is half-way home for me.'

'I hate travel, as you know,' said Maurilius. 'But – if it is the only way to pursue this council – so be it.'

'You know it is Odo's idea – Bayeux.'

'Yes.'

'Do you trust him?'

'No. But I trust Lanfranc. He will extract a price for this. He was a lawyer before he was a monk.'

'Will Odo keep his side of the bargain?'

'By that time it will be out of Odo's hands. The Duke will preside.'

Avranches hesitated, but said it at last.

'Do you trust the Bastard?'

Maurilius swept a beetle off the table.

'No. He has broken his word to bishops before, but he will not break his word to Lanfranc. If there is to be deceit, it will come from Odo, not from his brother. And I do not see how it can hurt us.'

'Will Evreux go too? He is visiting his sister at Longueville.'

'Oh?'

'Said it made a change from eternal chess. I was beginning to beat him.'

'I have sent to him. I have suggested that he takes Ermengarde with him. My guess is that half the wives in Normandy will move Heaven and earth to get to Bayeux. Their last chance to get a look at him. And the Bastard wants as many notables as possible. How can he refuse them?'

* * * * * *

'It is good news.'

'From Brittany?'

'Yes.'

'For the Duke, you mean?'

'For Harold too.'

'Yes. Yes. I suppose so.'

Adele giggled.

'Everyone knew except us. Gerard said we were too busy to notice.'

Edwin smiled.

'Yes.'

Adele leaned back against his knees. They gazed into the river.

Neither spoke for a long time.

At last Edwin said, 'The lady Matilda has gone then.'

'Yes. Taken all the children. And Arlette.'

At any other time Adele would have added some abuse about her. Instead she sighed ...

'A council, girl. At Bayeux. Huge one. Everone will be there.'

Gerard was a fount of information as usual.

'What will happen?'

'Not sure. But something. It will resolve this whole business. By the Nails it will ... !'

Edwin was a foreigner. No land. No rank. No lord – not in Normandy anyway. What could she do? She could not go against the world so far as to keep him with her all through the night – in a friendly castle where everybody knew everything, and understood. How could she go against the world – the harsh, open world of strangers – in all other things? Her father would disown her, and be grateful for the Heaven-sent opportunity. And be justified.

Edwin stirred. Adele looked up at him.

'I saw you talking to that fat monk with the donkey.'

'He rescued me – remember? Brought me here. Well, almost. He said he trusted an Englishman to travel only the last few miles by himself.'

They laughed. Edwin put his arms tight round her. They fell into silence again ...

'Rollo wanted to go on his travels once more. I could not deny him.'

'Hubert, you are impossible.'

'So my lord abbot says, often. But am I not rewarded for my hardships on the road? To see you so happy? Much happier than when I left you. Adele is her name, is it not?'

'Mind your own business.'

'Oh, I do, my boy, I do. But that does not stop me being interested in other people's. Was that not our Lord's mission?'

'Stop being clever, Hubert.'

'Very well. I shall tell you something you wish to hear.'

'What is that?'

'News, my boy. News to make you move. Captain Aldred tells me that my lord Harold's ship is ready for sea. At le Tréport. It awaits only his orders ... '

His mother's face came up as clear as a reflection in a summer pond. His dogs. Home. He felt Earl Harold clapping him on the shoulder. 'Nothing to a ride in a boat, son. It has to be better this time. Enjoy it.'

For a moment he almost relished the prospect. There was no resisting that man's superb confidence and relish of life.

'What are you thinking about?'

'Oh – nothing. What were you thinking about?'

'Nothing.'

Without another word they stood up, held hands, and began to walk back to the tiny lodging, to the familiar shelves and shadows, the dark sheen of the furniture. To the familiar noises – the scuffing of a loose door plank on the floor, the fall of the latch, the rustle of clothing, the creak of the bed timbers, the smacks of damp flesh.

The ghosts of the future faded as they took refuge in another world. For a few more moments of agonising preciousness, they reached out to touch eternity.

* * * * * *

Chapter Nine

The Swearing

'Try this on.'

Gilbert took it in his arms as if it were a new-born baby.

'Is this – ?'

'Yes. Yours.'

Gilbert kept his head down; he dared not trust his voice. Every link shone. It nestled as blithely as a fresh blanket. When he moved his hand to caress it, it gave out a soft jingle like a miser stirring a million very tiny silver coins. He could find no trace of any damage, or of any repair, and he knew it had been cut from the body of a dead Breton. It must have taken countless hours of an expensive armourer's time. This was a garment to live in, with pride – to die in.

'Somebody say something,' said Bruno. 'You two sound like me.'

Gilbert forced himself to raise his eyes, and smiled through tears.

'It is beautiful.'

Ralph looked at his young face – shining, pale, alight – just like Michael's. He cleared his throat.

'Well – there you are. The Duke said you were to have one.'

Gilbert took a huge breath.

'When I said those things – after the Couesnon – I was in rage. I – '

'He understands,' said Bruno.

'I mean, I should not want you to – '

'He understands,' repeated Bruno. 'That is why you have it in your hands now.'

Gilbert nodded. Ralph nodded. Bruno looked at the pair of them, and raised his eyes Heavenwards.

'When I went home,' said Gilbert, 'I wanted to boast. And I did ... '

He never stopped for several days. His family were a devoted audience. But he noticed that with each telling, his elder brother Robert became more and more sparing in his praise. Robert was the one who had stayed at home. He had no stories to tell, except the daily round. Nobody wanted to hear about the spring rains or the plague of rabbits several times over.

Little by little he found excuses to reject Gilbert's offers of help about the holding. There was a toolwright coming to see to the scythe and sickles; they were going to pull down the old pig-sty anyway; weeding was not necessary in the plot by the meadow – he was thinking of leaving it fallow for a year or two.

His sister Mahaut's local gossip now included references to people he did not know. Repetition did not enhance the acquaintanceship. His mother constantly mothered him. It was embarrassing, especially when she did it in front of neighbours.

When at last he stopped telling the story, his father Hugh took it up, and repeated it endlessly at every opportunity. Gilbert writhed at every fresh inaccuracy and embellishment. By the time Hugh had finished, his brave soldier son had almost pulled the Duke himself out of the Couesnon ...

'But nothing could be better than this.'

Ralph gave him a soft punch in the chest.

'Well – take care of it.'

Gilbert looked hesitant.

'Do you think I can wear it for the council?'

Ralph seized the opportunity to laugh and so break the tension.

'That is the general idea. And keep your eyes and ears open. Everybody will be here. You will learn a lot.'

As they watched him go, Ralph spoke without looking at Bruno.

'Right now, I do not feel miserable. But if you speak, I shall.'

* * * * * *

Walter Giffard slowed his horse to a walk.

'Be glad to get back.'

Roger of Montgomery took off his gauntlets, transferred the reins to one hand, and eased the fingers of the other.

'Good day though.'

They were content to let the main party draw ahead. Giffard grunted.

'There is something else the man does well.'

'What?'

'Arrow or spear – it is all the same to him. He is a natural. Damn the fellow.'

'Scared of no obstacle either,'said Montgomery. 'He took two fallen trunks in his stride that I would have gone round. Strange horse too.'

'I suppose you heard the beaters joking with him. Charm the birds off the trees.'

'If Geoffrey hears you say that ... '

'But you have to hand it to him.'

'Or that. Still, Odo's little council should find a weak chink in the mail somewhere. Not long now.'

Giffard allowed himself a mirthless laugh.

'At least what we have taken today should feed everybody.'

'They are still pouring in,' said Montgomery. 'Wives and all.'

'Yes. Did you know Mabel was coming?'

Montgomery hesitated.

'Let us say that it did not surprise me.'

'Ah.'

Montgomery looked sideways at his friend, who kept his eyes straight ahead …

'Did you see those wives from the Cotentin? How old were those clothes they dug out? Even I noticed … How their husbands allow them out like that defeats me.'

'Well, it must have caught them; they have to be there … '

Mabel put more pins in her hair.

'Oh, Roger, you surely did not expect me to stay at home at a time like this. You are not ashamed of me, are you?'

'Is everything well at home?'

'Yes, it is. And the children, to save you asking. And do not change the subject. Did you see Ermengarde? I swear she is still wearing the dress she was married in. And her hair!'

'Ermengarde is a good friend.'

'Of course she is, and I would not say a word against her. I am very fond of Ermengarde. But really!'

'Have you paid your respects to Matilda yet?'

'Yes. I suppose you realise she is with child again.'

'Oh? Nobody has said anything.'

'You men would not notice. You are never interested in the consequences of your actions. But the signs are there. You see – there will be some announcement. That is, if the Bastard himself knows yet. Men!'

'He is somewhat preoccupied at the moment.'

'Not too preoccupied, obviously. They really ought to – well, take more care. Six children in a dozen years, and pregnant again. And she travels, you know, bulging like a sow – I have seen her a dozen times. Disgusting.'

'You said six just now.'

'I have *seen* her a dozen times. She cares nothing. No sense of dignity or discretion.'

'I see.'

Mabel stood up and patted down the folds of her new dress.

'And it is no good your looking like that, Roger of Montgomery. If I have nothing else, I do have a sense of dignity and a sense of discretion … '

'Did you know Ermengarde was coming?'

Giffard coughed.

'She had news about the Arabs … '

'And fancy letting Judith out with that young stag Beaumont. Anything could have happened. He is totally unreliable.'

'I hear he did rather well in Brittany,' said Ermengarde.

'Nearly ruined the whole enterprise by letting the sappers desert.'

'But he rescued the situation.'

'Been gossiping already, have we?'

'Stop wriggling, Walter. You are annoyed not because of Beaumont, but because of Judith's dowry going to St. Amand. At least you can not get your hands on it. If you had gone on the way you were going, we should have had nothing left.'

'You are only paying me back for borrowing the other.'

'Hah! Borrowing!'

'You should have consulted me, Ermi. It does not look right.'

'I suppose I should have consulted you when one of the Arabs was taken sick. Waited weeks while messengers dashed all over Normandy looking for you. Done him a lot of good, that would.'

'That is different.'

'I see. I am good enough to take decisions about horses, but not about human beings. And you are far more concerned about the Arabs than you are about anything else – including me. And in any case, I do not see what you have against young Beaumont. He strikes me as a very nice young man.'

'Exactly. He is a young man. Spoilt too. Do you know what he is doing right now? Going round every important man he can find, to complain about losing his precious horses that the Bastard gave him.'

'Was it his fault the Flemings stole them?'

'Maybe not. But look at him: running to the Bastard, or Fitz, or his father. I shall say this for Roger of Beaumont – he thinks the sun shines out his boy's backside, but he sent him off with a flea in his ear over this.'

'Well?'

'Well? Young Beaumont needs a lesson. We have a great council any day now, and all he can think of is horses, horses, horses. Nothing else matters but his precious horses,'

'Well?

'Well, what?'

Ermengarde flung her arms in the air.

'I give up ... '

Walter Giffard sniffed.

'Do you know what, Roger?'

'No.'

'Politics and women do not mix.'

* * * * * *

'Are you with child?'

'How did you know?'

Harold laughed.

'Edith has presented me with five children. And we lost two more.'

'The Lord giveth ... '

'Has He taken from you?'

Matilda crossed herself.

'No. A great blessing. All the chicks have survived.'

'Does William know yet?'

'No.'

Matilda laughed.

'I imagine he is the only one who does not. Gerard asked me before I left Rouen. And I saw the Montgomery woman staring at me. If she suspects, it will be all over Bayeux, with her tongue.'

'Why not tell him?'

Matilda shook her head.

'Did Edith tell you if she thought you had things on your mind?'

Harold raised his eyebrows.

'Does William have things on his mind?'

'God's Blood, Harold. Do not play games with me. Give me more credit.'

They both laughed.

'I apologise,' said Harold. 'Now – how is that serving-girl of yours – Arlette?'

Matilda grunted in disgust.

'About as miserable as usual. No – perhaps not quite so much. She thinks she is going to secure a private audience with William to – you will scarcely credit this – ask him to allow the betrothal.'

'With Wulfnoth?'

'Yes. So she is going to be even more miserable pretty soon. Have you noticed that the young have no sense of timing?'

Harold grinned.

'True,' said Matilda. 'She hopes to flutter her eyelashes and win William's complete attention at a time like this, for a mere betrothal. I am still trying to tell him he is going to become a father.'

'If she did ask him, Wulfnoth would be furious.'

'Who would blame him? Fancy – a girl asking for a boy's hand. Unheard of. But she and Wulfnoth are the centre of the world, you see.'

Harold inclined his head by way of half-agreeing.

'I will give him credit for worrying about me. He thinks I am about to make a mistake.'

Matilda looked sharply at him.

'Are you?'

'If I were to think that, would I be doing it?'

'William thinks he is making a sound move too.'

'I have no doubt. We shall have to see.'

Matilda smiled.

'Harold – as Roger of Montgomery says – you are impossible.'

'But not intolerable, I hope.'

'Not that. When will you go?'

'As soon as the ceremony is over. There will be no further reason to stay.'

'We shall look after Wulfnoth for you.'

'I am sure you will. And have some mercy for Arlette. She is only a little miserable.'

'Like Wulfnoth.'

Harold grinned.

'They will make a good pair then. Suit each other down to the ground. When will you tell William? About ... '

Harold indicated Matilda's girdle.

'When you have gone.'

Harold rose, took Matilda's hand, and kissed it.

'In case I do not have the opportunity again.'

Matilda bowed her head in acknowledgment of the compliment.

'Thank you for saving Robert.'

Harold shrugged.

'It was nothing. William would have done the same for one of my boys.'

'Nevertheless – you were there. I shall always be in your debt.'

Harold gave her a slight bow.

'William is a lucky man.'

'Edith is a lucky woman.'

* * * * * *

Geoffrey looked round the hall, where Arnulf fussed over last details. Well, at least it was now costing Odo a fortune too.

The decorations were not in the best of taste, but then Odo had not been to Italy. His loss. Too many objects were simply too big and, somehow, too loud. Odo trying to prove something again.

What was it he had said the previous day, when he could not resist showing Geoffrey round the cathedral. . ?

'I have not finished with the hall yet, you understand. This council is merely an interruption to my long-term arrangements.'

Poseur!

'Yes – I have it in mind to hang a mighty tapestry that will stretch right round the hall – every wall.'

A tapestry! Was that the best Odo could manage? Geoffrey thought of the mighty statues of the Hautevilles that were to grace the nave of his own cathedral. And Odo wanted a strip of embroidered linen to gather the smoke round his hall where his vassals got drunk. Pathetic!

'Of course I am taking great care before deciding upon a suitable subject. Something on epic lines, do you not think, my lord? More fitting, perhaps, than commemorating the dubious exploits of a family of bandits in a cathedral nave.'

Geoffrey could have hit him …

'I trust you approve, my lord. We know how high your standards are.'

Odo's voice – no mistaking it.

Geoffrey whirled round. The reply that leapt to his lips died there, because he saw the Duke close behind.

William halted just inside the main door, his restless eyes taking in the whole picture.

'You have done well, brother.'

Odo bowed, glancing in triumph at Geoffrey.

'We try our best, my lord.'

Arnulf hovered in the background, wiping his hands down his habit.

Odo indicated the dais.

'If, when your Grace sits here, he were to carry a naked sword, I fancy it will add to the atmosphere. I have taken care to ascertain that Harold intends to be unarmed.'

'Naturally,' said Geoffrey. 'As a guest, he would not insult his host by wearing weapons.'

Odo flashed a scalding look in his direction before turning back to the Duke.

'Nevertheless, my lord, as it is a formal occasion, the wearing of the insignia of rank will not come amiss.'

'Wearing,' said Geoffrey, 'but not open display.'

The more Geoffrey saw of these arrangements, the less he liked them. They smelt of trickery, they reeked of Odo's devious mind. One of Walter's favourite dismissive verdicts came back to him: 'too clever by half'.

'Enough,' said the Duke. 'Leave that decision to me. It is my council, not yours, Coutances.'

Geoffrey bowed.

'My lord.'

William pointed.

'You, brother, will stand at the foot of the dais – here. And you, Coutances, will stand there, opposite.'

'My lord.'

'And the reading?'

'We shall read clauses alternately,' said Odo. 'First myself, as the presiding bishop.' Another flash of the eyes at Geoffrey. 'Then my lord of Coutances, as the assisting bishop.'

William nodded.

'He is clear about it?'

'The text has been read to him, several times. He fully comprehends it.'

'Where will he stand?'

Odo pointed.

'There, between those two tables. A copy of the text will be laid out on each table. Harold will stretch a hand over each one while he recites.'

Odo picked up one of the parchments.

'If my lord would care to cast his eye ... '

William waved away the offer.

'And the witnessing?'

Odo carefully replaced it, went to another small table, and picked up a much longer document.

'Listed, in order, awaiting only the marks. The seals are over there, with your chaplain. He has been fully rehearsed.'

Arnulf tried to look pleased.

'And while we are away?'

'Your chaplain will be here, my lord, from this moment until the council begins to assemble. Nothing amiss will happen without his knowing. He knows well that a great deal hangs upon his success in – in this matter.'

Odo looked directly at Arnulf while he was speaking. Arnulf produced another sickly simper, and wiped his forehead.

'Sentries – trusted men – will be posted at once at all the doors and all around the walls – inside as well as out.'

Geoffrey could not resist an interruption.

'In a matter requiring such subtlety as this, my lord, you may rely upon my lord of Bayeux to attend to every detail with his customary thoroughness.'

'I expect your full compliance, Coutances.'

Geoffrey bowed.

'You shall have it, my lord duke.'

William looked round once more. He began his tuneless humming as he turned and left.

Geoffrey hitched up his sword belt.

'Then we had best dress ourselves, my lord, as befits such a – a solemn occasion.'

He would not put it past Odo to show off a new gold-stitched cope.

When he had gone, Odo snapped his fingers to Arnulf, who hurried to come close.

Odo recoiled slightly at the nearness of his glistening cheeks.

'As you value your reward, make doubly sure. Of everything.'

Arnulf bowed.

'It shall be done, my lord. And may I take this opportunity, my lord, to thank you for your hospitality and your generosity in this matter. It is a rare nobleman who – '

'Yes, yes, yes ... '

* * * * * *

'Shall we just put our heads in?'

'Harold!'

Harold had not stopped for a reply, so Wulfnoth was forced to follow.

Harold whistled.

'Odo has certainly spared no cost.'

Wulfnoth looked too.

'It was his idea. And you feel no concern?'

'No.'

Harold entered the great hall and gazed about him. Again Wulfnoth followed.

'Harold, they are preparing your downfall.'

'If that is what they think – yes.'

He tried the Duke's chair for size, leaned back, and patted the wooden arms, grimacing in appreciation.

Wulfnoth came and stood before him.

'You are about to throw away your life's ambition.'

Harold nodded readily.

'It might well seem like that. To the careless observer.'

'Dear God!'

Harold took pity on him, stood up, and came close.

'Wulf. I said it might *seem* like that.'

Wulfnoth's face lit up. He looked about to make sure there were no servants. The Duke's chaplain was at the other end of the hall.

'You mean you will change your mind. You will refuse – at the last minute.'

'Wulf.'

'You *do* have a plan. I have been so – for a moment I thought – '

'Wulf.'

'You have it prepared, worked out, I know.' He turned away. 'Home. England.' He hugged himself. 'England.' A sudden thought struck him. 'And Arlette. I may take Arlette?'

Harold grasped his arm.

'Wulf, listen to me. Listen!'

He motioned him to sit down, and stood over him.

'First, I love you. You are my brother. You are the youngest and dearest son of our beloved mother. You are also an Englishman. I ask you now to think of England. To think of England with the Confessor dead. Do you want the Viking barbarian from Norway on the throne? Or the baby Saxon prince? Or Duke William, for all that you admire him so much?'

Wulfnoth remained silent, so Harold answered his own question.

'You want me there, I am sure. I want to be there. I am in all honesty the best man for it. To get there, I must follow my own counsel, do what is best for that end.'

Wulfnoth's face set into stone.

'You are going to leave me here. Admit it.'

Harold hesitated only a moment.

'Very well. Yes. I am.'

'So the crown means more than your brother.'

'Stop talking like a child.'

'I should have known better. I too nearly fell for it – the famous Harold charm.'

'You are not returning now,' said Harold. 'I did not say never.'

'No matter. Whenever you ask, the Duke will say no.'

'Who said anything about asking?'

Wulfnoth sneered.

'You must be as stupid as you are selfish. He has the whip hand. He has always had the whip hand.'

Harold adopted his careless air again.

'I have no wish to push William any further than I have to – at this stage.'

'*You* push the *Duke*? *At this stage*? Harold, open your eyes. Look. Look. Why are you doing this – ' Wulfnoth waved an arm around the glittering hall ' – this thing? Because you feel like it?'

'Because I think it is a sound idea at this time. You speak as if I shall be swearing some kind of sacred oath. I shall simply make a pronouncement. A very carefully-worded pronouncement.'

He bent and aligned three bowls on a table. Wulfnoth followed him.

'Yes. In full view of every bishop and abbot in Normandy. Every vassal from the furthest borders. The lady Matilda!'

'Oh? That will be nice. We get on very well, you know.'

'God in Heaven, Harold! Will you take this seriously.'

'I am as serious as you, I assure you.'

'They will twist it – this statement.'

Harold shrugged.

'If it can be twisted one way, I can twist it another. It is William's word against mine.'

'But the record, the record. It will be recorded.'

'I should hope so. I have taken enough trouble with the wording.'

Wulfnoth flung away.

'You are impossible.'

'No. Just careful.'

Wulfnoth turned back again and spread his hands.

'And what happens to me?'

'Nothing. Have you seen these knives? German, I swear. For once, I admire Odo's taste.'

'I stay here and rot.'

'You can if you wish to. But I imagine, when I am King, you will prefer to come and join me in England.'

'If you become King, what reason will the Duke have for keeping me alive?'

Harold replaced the knife, and carefully adjusted its position.

'What reason would he have for killing you? Once I have the throne, your death will not help him to get it. William will never kill you out of temper or blood lust. I have seen enough of him to know that.'

'So?'

'So – you are much safer here than in England. When I get the throne, William will invade. If you were with me, you could easily die in battle fighting against him. Is that what you want?'

Wulfnoth sighed.

'Now you are tying me in knots.'

The main door opened, and men-at-arms began trooping in to take up sentry positions.

Harold patted him on the shoulder, and lowered his voice.

'Well, be guided by me, and remain a good subject of Duke William for just a little longer. If I get the throne, you will live. If he defeats me, you will still be alive – either way in England, I have no doubt.'

'I have little choice, do I?'

'Not choice, remember – opportunity.'

* * * * * *

Gilbert looked at the crowded benches and marvelled. Vassals from every corner of Normandy were crammed and jostling on them. A small forest of bishops' croziers and abbots' staffs waved near the front. Their clerks, priors, and chaplains formed a dense blotch of black at the back, on the right. On the left, a shrill buzz betrayed the presence of a large number of vassals' wives, their newly-made head-dresses swaying like ears of corn in an early gale.

He turned to Nigel Fitzhenry beside him, who, unlike the other guards about the hall, was not leaning against a post.

'Not wearing mail then,' said Gilbert innocently. 'Still smarting, are we?'

Nigel sneered at Gilbert's new hauberk.

'My, my. Shining like a virgin's wedding ring.'

'Jealous? I am afraid the Bastard gives rewards only for pulling sons out of the river, not for pulling them in. Unfair, if you ask me. Would you like me to put in a word for you?'

'Go to Hell.'

Gilbert looked across to the other side, where Ralph and Bruno stood together. Ralph winked at him, and made a motion to polish the hauberk.

Between them, Sir Walter Giffard edged up to allow Sir Roger of Montgomery to sit down.

'Will he do it?'

'He will do it.'

Giffard shook his head and smiled.

'Not so long ago, you were all saying that it might be better to let him go and have done with him, because he was outfacing us all. We had plotted our heads off, and we were going to give him best. Now – without any further effort on our part – he says he is ready to make a public renunciation of all his claims – something we would never have hoped for in our wildest dreams.'

'How do we know it will be a renunciation?' said Montgomery. 'Fitz is not saying.'

'Why else are we all here?' said Giffard. 'To wave him goodbye?'

'It is almost as if he were playing with us,' said Montgomery. 'He always goes along with what we want, yet somehow we never get out of it what we plan for, and he carries on as if there were nothing wrong at all. The man is impossible.'

Giffard cursed as someone trod on his toe.

'Surely we have had the initiative all the time. God's Face, he was the one who was shipwrecked in a foreign country.'

'Does it occur to you, Walter, that this apparently obvious implication seems to have escaped Harold? Does it also occur to you that the obvious implication of everything else has escaped him? His shipwreck, which put him at the mercy of Guy of Ponthieu. His rescue, which put him under obligation to the Bastard. His service in Brittany, and his acceptance of arms, which places him in feudal subjection – at any rate formally. Why does he not see what we see?'

'How does he keep up his morale?' said Giffard. 'Not a thegn, not a groom, not a single English servant with him. All he has is that miserable brother of his – enough to depress anybody.'

Montgomery waved a hand round the hall.

'And now this. The entire vassalage and episcopacy of Normandy – everyone that counts anyway – to witness what? We have no idea. The Bastard may have summoned them, but they are here to see what Harold will do. Curiosity. Why are all those wives here – ours included? Who is making the bear dance – we, or Harold? I tell you, Walter, he is either very dense, or very, very clever.'

'All the more reason for killing him when we had the chance,' growled Giffard.

There was a buzz as Harold entered, with Wulfnoth at his elbow. There was no announcement. Harold looked as casual as if he were attending a Christmas feast. He paused here and there to exchange greetings with acquaintances.

Wulfnoth pulled him away to a corner.

'Harold, there is still time.'

'Time for what?'

'To refuse.'

Harold pretended to be shocked.

'To go back on my word? I told William I was willing to make this statement. Would you have me deny it?'

'You are going to deny the statment when you get back to England. What is the difference?'

'Oh? Do you know what I am going to say?'

'Who cares about the wording? You are going to perjure yourself afterwards.'

'*I* care about the wording, Wulf. I have taken great trouble with it. And I have no intention of perjuring myself, I promise you.'

Wulfnoth stared in bafflement.

'You are surely not going to let William have the crown.'

Harold placed both hands on his brother's shoulders. He looked about the hall, but the noise was high enough for his remarks to be inaudible to anybody else.

'Wulf. This is your brother talking to you. This cup before me is for me only to drink. The responsibility is mine alone. It would be unfair for me to share it with anybody, even with you. For that reason I will not share my thinking, because it would place a burden upon you that would also be unfair.'

Wulfnoth pulled himself away.

'What you mean is that you do not trust me.'

'That is not so. You are my brother. How can I not trust you?'

'Because I am half Norman. It is true; I do understand Normans. It is because I understand them that I beg you to think again. They are devious; they are subtle. Have you played their game chess?'

'I have seen it many times.'

'They have a passion for it.'

'William does not, I notice. Wulf, I deal in politics and power, not games. So does William. You know about Normans, I grant you. But little about politics and power. Not from the inside. People on the outside think they do, but they do not.'

'Then take me in. Show me, share with me. I am your brother. I am Saxon. I have a right to know. Harold, please – I have been on the outside for so long.'

Harold took hold of his arm.

'Then, as you love me, I ask you to be patient and remain on the outside just a short while longer. It is not easy to be in ignorance, I know, but the burden of ignorance is light compared to the burden of knowledge and responsibility.'

Wulfnoth looked down at Harold's hand.

'Then you will not be advised by me.'

Harold's face shone with affection, but he shook his head.

'I must keep my own counsel. The decisions are mine, and the consequences will be of my own doing.'

Wulfnoth wrenched away his arm.

'Then make your accursed decisions. Put forth your hands. Swear it all away. Make a fool and a coward of yourself. I am ashamed of you as my brother.'

Harold restrained him.

'Wulf, before you leave me, do I have your hand?'

He held out his own.

'Go to the Devil!'

A herald banged a badly-tuned gong.

'My lord Duke William II, by the Grace of God Duke of Normandy, Count of Maine, overlord of Brittany, Perche, and the Vexin, heir to the throne of England.'

The assembly rumbled to its feet.

First came a detachment of men-at-arms, followed by the Bishops of Bayeux and Coutances, in full episcopal robes, attended by a flurry of yet more chaplains and clerks. My lady Matilda came next, and was shown to a seat on a front bench.

'She will never see a thing if she sits anywhere else,' whispered Mabel of Montgomery to the wife beside her.

Finally came the Duke himself, with Fitzosbern at his elbow. He strode briskly to the dais, and took his seat, with his sword drawn and resting against his right shoulder.

'They will never teach the Bastard to walk like a bishop,' muttered Giffard to his friend.

Odo and Geoffrey led the formal prayers. Odo had scarcely lowered his hand after the final blessing before William opened the proceedings.

'Is everything prepared?'

Odo bowed.

'It is, my lord duke.'

William nodded towards the herald, who cleared his throat.

'The Earl Harold of Wessex, lord of Hereford, guardian of the lands over against Wales.' He had a little trouble with the unfamiliar names.

Harold stepped forward, and stood before the two tables, on each of which rested a freshly-written parchment.

Odo of Bayeux turned towards him.

'Earl Harold of Wessex, you have declared your intention of making a solemn statement here before our lord Duke William, before his bishops and abbots, and before his pledged vassals, and in the sight of God. Do you stand by your declared intent?'

'I do.'

Wulfnoth put his face in his hands.

Odo stepped forward.

'Place your hands as I shall direct – here – and here.'

'Like that?'

'Thus.'

Harold was now standing midway between the two tables, so that with his arms outstretched he could lay a hand comfortably on each.

Odo stood back.

'I must ask you to remain so while I and his Grace the Bishop of Coutances read in public the words of the declaration which you have agreed in private. Do you so consent?'

'I do consent.'

Odo picked up his own copy, and handed his crozier to a chaplain. He stretched his neck – a nervous trick he had. His small head, set above the elaborate, broad episcopal vestments, looked even smaller. He was visibly sweating.

'This is the text of the statement privately agreed between my lord Duke

William of Normandy and my lord Earl Harold of Wessex, and now to be publicly declared. Earl Harold, you will repeat after me … '

When the recitation was complete, Harold bowed to the Duke, who inclined his head by way of returning the compliment. Amid a frenzied hubbub of conversation, Harold resumed his seat beside his brother.

'Well?'

Wulfnoth looked haggard with chagrin and disbelief.

'You can talk freely,' said Harold. 'Nobody is going to hear you.'

'How could you? How could you?'

'Necessary, I am afraid, Wulf. You are a prince of a noble house. You know about these things.'

'But not to have told me. Me!'

'It was a confidential matter, until this public statement. Only the Duke and Fitzosbern and me; that was the agreement.'

'But it is my fate.'

'Well, you know now. You make it sound like a death sentence.'

'And what about Arlette? What do I tell Arlette?'

'She will accommodate herself to it in time. Women are used to this kind of arrangement.'

'And what about me?'

'What about you?'

'Arlette and I have been – '

'Betrothed?'

'Well, no.'

'No harm done, then.'

'But there has always been an understanding.'

'Do you love her?'

For a fraction, Wulfnoth hesitated.

'I – it has always been understood.'

'Do you love her?'

Again the hesitation. Harold brushed some invisible specks from the front of his cloak.

'She will be no great loss then.'

'And if I do?'

'If you do – if you do really love her, then you need never lose her. I have never lost my Edith. It matters not who is my formal wife.'

Wulfnoth wiped a hand across his brow.

'But this – Cecily. She is a child.'

'Twelve.'

'There you are.'

'So there is no difficulty, is there? It is only a betrothal, not a marriage. Between now and then, anything can happen.'

'What do I do in the meantime?'

'Nothing. I hope.'

'Trust you to make a joke at a time like this.'

'Do you want me to have a long face, like yours? Wulf, this is a political arrangement. Surely you understand that?'

Wulfnoth sneered.

'And the rest of your wonderful "pronouncement". Is that a mere political arrangement too? Just listen to Bishop Odo.'

Odo had taken another document in his hand, and began to read.

'I call upon all here assembled to bear witness ... '

'That,' hissed Wulfnoth, 'is a list of every name of every person here. They are all going to make their mark as having witnessed what you have just said ... '

'Maurilius, lord Archbishop of Rouen, Yves, Bishop of Sées; William, Bishop of Evreux; John, Bishop of Avranches; Odo, Bishop of Bayeux; Geoffrey, Bishop of Coutances; Hugh, Bishop of Lisieux; Lanfranc of Pavia, Abbot of St. Stephen's of Caen ... '

'You might as well have the Pope here,' said Wulfnoth.

'I rather wish he had been,' said Harold. 'It would lend more force to it.'

Wulfnoth stared.

'And when the clergy have finished, every vassal will do the same.'

'Good. That is the general idea.'

Wulfnoth flung out an arm.

'They are not rushing to make their mark about Cecily and me; they are rushing to witness what you have said about yourself and the Duke.'

'Of course.'

'You have just told the world that you renounce the throne.'

'I have told the world nothing of the sort. Clearly you were not paying proper attention.'

'I have eyes and ears.'

'And heart. But no head – at the moment.'

'I see. Still the baby brother. Too young to be let in on the men's secrets.'

Harold sighed wearily.

'Wulf, you must be patient.'

'I have been patient – for twelve years. And now, after twelve years of waiting, here is my first chance of freedom.'

'That is not true.'

'Of going home. And you have just thrown it away. For ever. And why? Because you lost your nerve and abandoned your judgment. And you are not man enough to admit it.'

Harold began to look grim.

'We shall see.'

' "We shall see." The fool's forecast. The coward's clairvoyance.'

'Be silent.'

'You are no longer my brother.'

'Then you are no longer my conscience. Be silent!'

Odo was coming to the end of his list ...

'Wadard of Pontaudemer ... William of Briouze ... William of Warenne.'

Odo handed the list back to a clerk.

'My lord Duke, all the aforementioned lords spiritual and temporal have given their word of witness, and thereto will make their mark, to note the solemn statement of the Earl Harold.'

William nodded.

'So be it.'

He looked at Harold, who also nodded.

'So be it.'

Odo took up his crozier again, and stretched his neck. His face was shining. He pulled at a red spot on the side of his jaw. Taking a deep breath, he raised his voice a trifle higher.

'Now that the Earl Harold has made his solemn statement in the sight of man, we must now give proof that the Earl Harold has made his solemn statement in the sight of God.'

He made a sign behind him, and Arnulf hurried forward to stand between the two tables. He grasped each embroidered coverlet by a corner.

A tense silence had fallen. Odo gave the slightest of nods. Arnulf twitched the coverlets away. There was a slight intake of breath, and a sigh, almost of disappointment. It was as if they had expected two puppets to spring upwards.

Odo nodded again. Arnulf took hold of a small handle in the middle of each table, lifted them, and raised a small panel. He looked towards Odo. Every eye in the hall followed his.

Odo swallowed.

'Earl Harold, you have given your pledge not only to the lords spiritual and temporal assembled here, but to the saints whose holy relics lie within the altars whereon you placed your hands.'

The hall shuddered.

Odo raised his voice still higher.

'The following holy relics will bear witness to your solemn oath! Saint Rasyphus, the head. St. Rhadagaisus, the shinbone. Saint Wandrille, the hands. Saint Sebastian, part of the first arrow to pierce his side on the occasion of his blessed martyrdom. Saint Veronica, three drops from the phial of sweat off the Holy Brow of Christ on his way to Calvary ... '

Each name brought a gasp.

Wulfnoth hissed in Harold's ear.

'Do you believe me now?'

'Be silent.'

'Listen to those saints. Do you deny them?'

Harold stood grim and expressionless.

Wulfnoth pressed him.

'They are not vassals, nor yet bishops. They are God's anointed. You have spoken to God Himself.'

'Be silent,' said Harold again. 'Or, by our mother's life, I shall strike you.'

Odo completed his list, and turned to the Duke.

'My lord, all the aforementioned holy saints and their miraculous relics here bear witness to the oath of the Earl Harold.'

Bishop Geoffrey kept his face a mask.

He had guessed that Odo was up to something, but nothing like this.

The Duke rose, and sheathed his sword.

'So be it.'

He opened his mouth to speak again, when he was interrupted by a commotion in the front rows below him.

Abbot Lanfranc stood up, white with suppressed anger, and edged his way to the end of the bench. Without turning once in the Duke's direction, he stalked towards the door. Long before he reached it, such was his demeanour, two frightened sentries had it wide open. He swept out without a sound.

It was impossible to translate the murmur that followed.

Odo tried pathetically to rescue the situation.

'If there is anyone else with a call of nature, he will have to wait only another minute or two.'

The Duke snapped his fingers. Silence fell.

'My lords, you will remember – all of you – what you have seen this day. There will come a time when I shall recall it to your memory.' He turned towards Harold. 'My lord of Wessex, you have long been a guest here in Normandy. It is fitting now that you should return to your native land. You will be provided with all your needs, and with an escort appropriate to your rank and estate, for the journey to the harbour of le Tréport, where your ship now lies renewed and ready. We shall pray for your safe return.'

Harold bowed slightly.

'I thank my lord Duke of Normandy. It is indeed time that I returned, loth though I am to depart this pleasant land of yours. But I remind myself that I am second man in the kingdom of England, and there is much that demands my attention. I shall take with me – good memories of the many – interesting things I have seen and heard during my stay among you. I am in your debt.'

William bowed in return.

'Finely spoken. And as I reminded my court of the words they have witnessed, may I remind you. As I shall some day recall them to the memory of my vassals, so I shall some day have occasion to recall them to you.'

'That is your privilege,' said Harold. 'I shall be at your disposal – in England – whenever you choose so to remind me. As I have enjoyed many things of great interest while I have been your guest, so I can promise you, should you come to England in the future – near or distant – a reception and an entertainment just as interesting – and eventful.'

'Then we understand each other,' said the Duke.

'We do.'

'So – I bid you farewell – until we meet again.'

'I look forward to the day.'

* * * * * *

'How could you? How could you?'

'It was not of my doing.'

'But you are his brother. If you can not speak to him, who can?'

'Arlette, I tell you I had no idea. I am just as surprised as you are.'

'Surprised! You make it sound like a birthday present.'

'Talking of surprises, what are you doing here? I thought my lady was going to leave you in Rouen.'

'I – er – she changed her mind at the last moment. Not that it matters now.'

Arlette turned away and wiped her eyes.

'How could he? How could he?'

Wulfnoth frowned.

'What does that mean?'

Arlette wrenched her face into composure.

'Nothing. Nothing.'

'I saw you talking to the Duke.'

Arlette went white.

'When?'

'Yesterday.'

'Did you hear?'

'No. That is why I am asking. What is going on?'

'Nothing. Nothing. A family matter. About the other girls. It is nothing.'

* * * * * *

'May I take this opportunity to bring to your Grace's recall the small matter of the canons at your cathedral? Your Grace was so generous as to assure me that, after my assistance in the administering of the oath, he would be kind enough to include me in the fresh appointments to the chapter.'

' "Consider". Not "assure".'

'I beg your Grace's pardon. But your Grace is a kind lord, and a man of honour. A man of great affairs too, with many things on his mind. I have merely taken the liberty of reminding – '

'Yes, yes, yes ... '

* * * * * *

'Still not speaking to me?'

'Not to a fool, no.'

'Still not prepared to listen?'

'Not only a fool. A dupe.'

'You still think I am William's dupe?'

'From start to finish.'

Harold spread his hands.

'Do I look baffled?'

'No – you are too foolish to realise that you have been duped.'

'Shall I tell you where the bafflement has been?'

Wulfnoth sighed.

'I can not escape.'

Harold ignored the long face.

'It began with Guy of Ponthieu. He had no idea what to do with me. Within a week I had clothes, horses, falcons, weapons – all on credit. Is that the work of a dupe?'

'Guy of Ponthieu is a stupid brigand.'

'I see – even more stupid than I am. Well, look at Fitzosbern. Look at Giffard, Montgomery, the rest of those stolid vassals. When have they looked as if they were in charge of the situation? When has the Duke smiled in satisfaction?'

Wulfnoth said nothing. Harold answered his own questions.

'Never. And shall I tell you why? Because I have fallen in with every one of their suggestions – the one thing they did not expect me to do. And they are baffled. Now – tell me – who has had the initiative?'

Wulfnoth pointed towards Bishop Odo's hall.

'Did you have the initiative in there?'

'I was as content with the arrangement as they were.'

'The crown as the price of your passage.'

'Nothing of the sort. You were not listening, obviously.'

'They think it is.'

'Oh? Have you asked them?'

'No need to. They are not looking baffled now.'

'Lanfranc is; he is furious. Coutances is none too pleased either.'

'And Bishop Odo?'

'Ah! The trick with the relics, I admit, was a surprise.'

'There you are then.'

'A trick, Wulf. A false oath – an oath by deceit – is no oath. Ask any cleric, any lawyer.'

'All right, all right. You said you were content with it all. Tell me what you have got out of this – this arrangement, as you call it.'

'Everything I want. A full recognition of my status. A public ceremony of the whole Norman establishment at which I was the central figure. An assured, and immediate, passage to England. A set of rivals who think they have outwitted me. And the retention of the initiative.'

'Exactly. They have outwitted you. What good is the initiative at a time like this?'

'I said they *think* they have. It has been my experience that a very good place to have a rival is in a state of over-confidence. That is precisely where I have put the Normans, and it is precisely where I want them. Not a bad day's work, I should have thought. Oh – and I have provided for your future too.'

'Thank you very much."

'I do not mean Arlette. I mean a guarantee from William about your safety.'

'I meant Arlette.'

'I said before – you have not lost her. If you love each other, you can still enjoy her as much as you like. You will both be here, in exactly the same circumstances. I take it you have already enjoyed her.'

Wulfnoth ignored the dig.

'And Cecily? She is a pain in the neck.'

'Oh, come, brother. You are a prince. You understand that much politics. Matilda had a shocking reputation before William began his courting, but a match between Normandy and Flanders made good political sense. Brother Tostig is not exactly besotted with Judith, but an alliance with Flanders made sense to us too. King Edward was persuaded to marry our sister because our father wanted greater power.'

'So I just breed with her.'

'Twelve, Wulf. She is twelve. A lot can happen.'

'Like what?'

Harold dropped his voice.

'Like a coronation.'

'Then what is the point of the betrothal if you are so sure?'

'A foot in a dynastic door is never a bad idea. It makes William and me related. An adventurer may think twice about invading the land of a kinsman.'

'Ha! It did not prevent him executing rebels from his own family. The last Archbishop of Rouen was a kinsman; he deposed him.'

'Nevertheless ... '

'Then why not take her yourself? You said it would not interfere with your – arrangement with Edith.'

'I could then suggest taking her with me to England. William would look askance at that. I did not want to drive him too far at this stage.'

'*You* drive *William*?'

'Yes. I wanted a solution that he felt happy with.'

'So I was convenient?'

'Yes – as a matter of fact, you were. As my brother, I thought you would understand. It seems I overestimated your maturity.'

* * * * * *

'Splendour of God! How dare you walk out of one of my councils.'

'How dare you abuse holy relics.'

'It was Odo's idea.'

Lanfranc remained still.

'My lord duke, do not take refuge behind your brother's devious mind or behind the expediency of cheap advantage. One word from you and the whole shabby farce would never have taken place.'

'You have no understanding of politics.'

'Thank God! That is exactly why I walked out. I should do so again.'

William glared.

'I created you abbot, remember.'

'If you are not satisfied, depose me. Send me back to Bec.'

William went red in the face. Lanfranc could run rings round him like this for ever if necessary. Worse, he had no pride, no lust for honour. He was untouchable.

While William fumed, Lanfranc stood before him, waiting for his moment.

'My lord duke, what you presided over was a cheap piece of market-square chicanery – no more. A tawdry trick which would not impose on a ploughboy.

If by so doing you expect to gain some political advantage which is relevant to your worldly ambitions, that is your business. Do not expect me to be a part of it. I came here in good faith to witness a solemn occasion, and because you asked me. And because you made promises contingent upon it.'

William sat down. Lanfranc still stood over him.

'I kept my side of the bargain. Maurilius and the bishops have kept theirs. I now expect you to keep yours. You may flush and threaten, but I tell you, Duke William of Normandy, that the Church council will begin its sessions, and it will begin its sessions within the week. Or the Pope himself will hear from me direct of the way that one of his bishops, aided and abetted by a bastard ruler who cares more for his personal profit than he does for the dignity of Holy Church, prostituted the miraculous nature of holy relics in a parody of politics that turned a dignified occasion into a posturing pantomime.'

'Very well. Very well! You shall have your precious council. Satisfied?'

'Within the week.'

'Within the week!'

'With yourself presiding.'

'I must see to Harold's departure. From le Tréport.'

'See him off from here. Send Robert with him instead.'

'Very well. I preside. Now are you satisfied?'

'Not quite. There remains the small matter of your worldly chaplain. He must go.'

'Saints, man. He married us.'

'In defiance of Holy Church. And you had Maurilius marry you again. So much for your regard for Arnulf's dignity as a priest.'

William hesitated.

'What will become of him?'

'You need not concern yourself. I shall see that he is provided for. And I shall introduce a new chaplain.'

William sneered.

'Some milk-and-water saint, I suppose.'

'A properly-ordained priest, with no whore of a daughter clinging to his skirts – or he clinging to hers, from what I hear.'

William narrowed his eyes.

'Have you been talking to Gerard – that cripple in Rouen?'

Lanfranc ignored him.

'Do I have your word?'

'Yes, yes, yes, damn you. Now are you satisfied?'

Lanfranc bowed.

'Totally, my lord duke.'

'Good.'

'For the time being.'

* * * * * *

'You might have told me.'

'I did.'

'Not about Wulfnoth. Cecily thought she was going to get Harold himself.'

'Teach her not to jump to conclusions.'

'She will have a long face.'

'I know.'

They looked at each other, and began together in chorus.

' "Do I have to?" '

Matilda folded her hands in her lap.

'All the same, you did drag me here specially. I think you might have told me.'

William flung out an arm.

'With all those wives? What sort of secret would that have been?'

'They would not have heard from me.'

'That Montgomery woman would have found out. She already knows you are with child. So will everybody else by now.'

Matilda stared. William raised his eyebrows and looked smug.

'I am not blind. Or deaf.'

For once Matilda could think of nothing to say. William turned his face away. Another favour that Harold had done for him.

* * * * * *

Hubert patted the leather wallet that he always carried.

'Consider it already delivered, my lord abbot. Already delivered.'

Lanfranc allowed a slight tremor to disturb the corners of his mouth.

'I have no fears about its delivery, my son. It is the directness of its delivery that concerns me.'

Hubert's face was a great wide circle of purity.

'As fast as my Rollo will carry me, my lord abbot. You may rest assured.'

'See that it is so. The letter is overdue. I do not wish your father abbot to be kept waiting.'

'Rollo's feet will be like the winged sandals of Hermes himself, I do assure you, my lord abbot.'

'Hmmm. No casting of shoes in Caen.'

'None.'

'Or sudden fits of the flux at Rouen.'

'We can but hope, my lord abbot. It is in the hands of God.'

'Or pauses to gossip with Brother Stephen at Longueville.'

'Perish the thought, my lord abbot.'

The tufty eyebrows were raised in an arch of injured innocence.

Lanfranc pursed his lips.

'And just to make doubly sure – a sort of guarantee, as you might say – call it my lawyer's passion for closing loopholes – should you find some unfortunate and unforeseen occurrence that could delay you unduly upon the road, I might – I only say "might" – find occasion to inform your father abbot that you so far breached his instructions as to go beyond Rouen – as far as Bayeux, no less – in your passionate and ceaseless search for unofficial information. Most reprehensible!'

Hubert swallowed. Lanfranc examined the back of his hand.

'I am sure you would agree that such a dereliction of duty would deserve a suitable punishment involving a curtailment of future freedom.'

'Oh, indeed, my lord abbot. Richly deserved. Indeed, richly deserved.'

'Good. Then we understand each other.'

'Man to man, my lord abbot. Oh, yes.'

'Good.'

Why were great men always so well informed? Was that what made them great?

'Then I had best be on my way, my lord.'

'One other thing. One final commission.'

'Name it, my lord abbot. I am at your disposal.'

* * * * * *

'Gerard says within two or three days.'

'Everyone?'

'Robert will escort Harold. The Duke is staying in Bayeux for the council.'

'Another council?'

'A Church council.'

'Will your father remain there?'

'Gerard did not say about that.'

'Did he say anything else?'

'No. He just looked sad. Straight at me.'

Adele slid her hand out of Edwin's and folded her arms about herself.

Edwin bowed his head.

Within minutes they were having their first quarrel.

* * * * * *

Chapter Ten

The Parting

'So you are leaving?'

'I see no point in further delay.'

'Needed in England, are we?'

'If that is what you choose to think.'

'The Duke has given his permission then.'

Harold continued to supervise the grooms.

'We both agree that it is time I left. I do not wish to overstay my welcome.'

'You still regard yourself as his guest. You fool!'

'When have I been treated otherwise? Tell me that.'

'You were shipwrecked, captured, imprisoned – '

'Not by William.'

'Held here throughout the summer.'

'On the contrary, I have enjoyed it. When have you seen my movements restricted? When has he treated me other than as an equal? When has he shown a flicker of distrust?'

'And Brittany?'

'Would he have consented to that if he feared my escape or my treachery?'

'He gave you arms – made you his man.'

'Wulf, I saved his son's life. What he did was a gift, a reward, an expression of gratitude from one father to another. And from one equal to another. I am an Earl; he is a Duke. Only kings are greater than either of us.'

'The oath then. You have signed everything away.'

'I have put my mark to nothing.'

'The text of the statement was agreed between you and him.'

'Yes. So at least half of it must be mine.' Harold patted a saddlebag. 'And I have a copy.'

'This promise to act as William's representative at King Edward's court. Was that your half or his?'

'I can act as anyone's representative anywhere without impinging upon my own interests. That is no burden.'

'You also said that you would do all in your power to secure the peaceful accession to the throne – '

' – of the rightful king of England. It remains to be seen who shall be proclaimed the rightful king.'

Wulfnoth began to struggle.

'But the other clauses.'

'They were all – did you take sufficient notice – tied to the same proviso: "insofar as it shall not prejudice the interests of the English people". I consider it one of the most important phrases of the entire statement.'

Wulfnoth struggled to find a reply.

'If you have provided yourself with so many loopholes, why did the Duke agree to it? He is not a fool.'

Harold glanced up at the sky to decide whether he needed his travelling cloak.

'He was making the best of a bad job.'

Wulfnoth stared.

'*He* was!'

'Yes. He has been waiting for weeks for me to make a mistake. In vain. He knows I can not stay for ever. He will look foolish. But how can he agree to my going without appearing to have gained some advantage? So I suggested making a public statement.'

'*You* suggested?'

'Yes. It allowed him to save some face. Never push a man's back to the wall unless you wish to destroy him. I happen to like him. And I think he has some regard for me.'

Harold nodded to a servant to unfold the cloak. Wulfnoth spluttered.

'But – but the statement. In front of the world.'

'My dear boy, the more public it is, the better. William has now put himself in the position of appearing to wring public promises out of me. By doing that he is admitting that mine is the better claim, or why would he go to such lengths to secure my word?'

Wulfnoth rescued some composure by remembering something.

'And the relics? Was that your idea too?'

'No. I told you, that was a surprise.'

'Well then.'

Harold leaned forward intently.

'Wulf, a false oath is no oath.'

'But he will say that you broke it when you take the crown.'

Harold shook his head.

'I shall take nothing. I shall be *offered* the crown, brother. William is the one who will have to take it, if he still wants it by then.'

'You will still appear to be in the wrong. A perjurer.'

'No. Nobody swears on relics in ignorance and is then held to account for it. The fact that he – or brother Odo – has descended to trickery is further proof of the weakness of his position.'

'Supposing he says otherwise. That you knew about the relics.'

Harold swung the cloak round his shoulders.

'It will be my word against his. Yours too, presumably. I take it you are still on my side.'

'Of course, but – '

'I was beginning to wonder.'

'I shall stay loyal to you – even if you do not stay loyal to me.'

'What is that supposed to mean?'

'You are going back to England, to see to your crown. You do not care about your brother that you are leaving here.'

'I care a great deal.'

Wulfnoth pounced.

'Then take me with you.'

'It would not be politic at this stage.'

'You mean the Duke would not let you.'

'I mean,' said Harold, fastening the clasp, 'that I wish at this stage to give William no avoidable offence. If I drove a harder bargain by demanding you – '

'*Demanding* me!'

' – by demanding you, I should be pushing William too far too early. It would appear too obvious that I was clearing my ground.'

'So you are gambling my life for the crown.'

'Not in the least. Your life is in no danger with William. I have seen him and I know. He is a man of practicality, who would never kill anyone if he thought it would get him nowhere. Besides, he likes you.'

'And the crown?'

'The crown is no gamble either. Believe me, brother – I shall be offered the crown by due process of law and custom. Getting it will be no gamble. Keeping it – that may be a different matter, I grant you.'

'The Duke will challenge you.'

'Of course he will. Everyone knows that. I shall have to fight. When that happens, I shall gamble not only your life but my own, and those of our brothers, even possibly our mother's. When I put my army in the field – to meet the invasion of a usurper – I shall gamble the life of every able-bodied man in England. A mighty issue. Now – tell me – what is the guarantee of your safety put against the peace and security of England?'

Wulfnoth sighed.

'Now you have mixed me up again. You always do.'

Harold turned round before him.

'How do I look?'

Wulfnoth shrugged sadly.

A servant offered the reins. Harold put out a hand to delay him.

'Now stop feeling sorry for yourself. Show yourself a man, a Saxon, and a true son of Godwin our father. What I ask is not easy; I should not ask it of any other man but a brother. Because I know you can do it. Now – wish me goodbye.'

Harold flung his arms round him. Responding to the pressure, Wulfnoth suddenly returned the embrace, fiercely.

'Dear Wulf.'

There was a catch in Harold's voice.

'Have no fear. I could never desert you. Believe me, we shall fish again in the Severn, and you will be the brother of a king.'

He took the reins, mounted, and looked down.

Tears pricked the back of Wulfnoth's eyes, and he kept his head lowered. Harold waited for him to raise it. When he did not, he dared not wait longer, in case Wulfnoth should see the twitch in his own face.

When he heard the hooves, Wulfnoth at last looked up.

'Goodbye.'

Harold did not hear him. Wulfnoth raised his voice slightly.

'Give my love to mother ... to Gyrth ... to Leofwine ... to England.'

Harold, now further away, did not hear that either.

Wulfnoth gazed after him till he rounded a bend in the road towards Caen. The tears now streamed down his cheeks.

'I shall never see any of you again.'

* * * * * *

'What will you do now?'

'My business.'

Matilda sniffed.

'Very well, what do *I* do now?'

'You go to Caen to have the child.'

'That is months away.'

'No chances, remember? How else have we kept the others? It is not all God's work. We have to help too.'

'I shall be bored to madness.'

William turned away to pour some water.

'Then see to your abbey. I have finished mine.'

Matilda made a face at him behind his back.

'Why? Are you so anxious to put a smile on Lanfranc's face?'

William turned back again.

'It was our promise. An abbey each – for the marriage.'

Matilda sniffed again. William was good at putting himself in a strong position. Like all men.

'I still say you want to put a smile on Lanfranc's face.'

'More important to put a smile on God's Face. We promised.'

An even stronger position. Matilda shifted her attack.

'What about Cecily?'

'Take her with you.'

'She will not want to.'

'She did not want to come here in the first place. She never wants to do anything, so what does it matter?'

'And Arlette?'

'What about her?'

'In case you have forgotten, you took away her husband. She is heartbroken.'

William shrugged.

'She will mend. The boys will keep her busy.'

Matilda sighed. Men again. William put down his cup.

'I shall find a husband for her soon enough.'

'Who?'

'Who knows? Someone – eligible. Someone like – um – Beaumont. Someone like that.'

Matilda knew better than to press further, so she shifted again.

'So you want me to go to Caen? In this weather?'

William let out a hoarse chuckle.

'Is that the best you can do? The weather has never troubled you yet.'

Matilda fell silent. William touched her arm.

'I shall come to Caen – in time. Maybe earlier if Brittany remains quiet and Conan gives homage.'

Matilda punched him gently in the chest. He had missed only one confinement.

Matilda poured herself a drink, and looked at him over the rim.

'I might catch up with Harold.'

'Ha! He will be too quick for you.'

'I have never seen you give so many gifts to anybody.'

'Maybe.'

'Maybe nothing. What I say is true.'

'My business. I notice you gave him one yourself.'

Matilda made a casual gesture of dismissal.

'Something for his woman. Nothing else.'

It struck William as a little too casual.

There was a silence, broken at last by Matilda.

'Very well – so we both liked him.'

* * * * * *

'Cecily says I must call her "my lady" now. Little bitch!'

'Ah!'

'Much joy you will have there.'

'Mm.'

Arlette stamped her foot.

'Is that the best you can do?'

'Arlette, what *can* I do? How could I know what was going to happen?'

'Wulf, why is that things always seem to happen to you? You never make them happen, do you?'

Wulfnoth ran a hand through his blond hair.

'Arlette, I am a hostage. I have no status, no rights, nothing.'

'Harold was a castaway, a prisoner, a forced guest. He managed well enough.'

'If I were Earl of Wessex, I should too.'

Arlette put her head on one side.

'I wonder.'

'Do you think I want this – arrangement?'

'I wonder about that too.'

'If you must know, I asked the Duke to give me a fief – land – a house – something.'

'For what?'

'For us of course.'

'Bit late.'

'Arlette, I did my best.'

'Did he give it?'

'No.'

Arlette nodded.

'He refused me too.'

She gasped with horror at her mistake. Wulfnoth stared.

'He refused you what?'

Arlette blushed.

'Nothing. It was nothing.'

Wulfnoth grasped her arm.

'What?'

'Wulf, you are hurting.'

'What did you ask?'

Arlette wriggled.

'Well, if you must know, I asked him if he would consent to the betrothal.'

Wulfnoth could scarcely believe his ears.

'You asked him!'

'It was before the oath. I had no idea what he was going to do.'

'You asked him – for my hand in marriage!'

'It was not like that – honestly, Wulf.'

Wulfnoth turned about and stepped away, flinging his hands wide.

'Is nothing left to me? I can not go to serve my brother. I can not go home to my country. I can not serve my master here as a landed knight. And now I have women going behind my back to claim me in marriage.'

'Wulf, what else could I do? I was desperate. For all I knew Harold might have been planning to take you home with him. I did not want to be left here.'

Wulfnoth whirled back towards her.

'Well, you now have nothing. No marriage, no betrothal, and no man. He is being reserved for the Duke's household. A tame son-in-law, when the right time comes. Meantime, he will make do as an under-chamberlain – a master of ceremonies, a guest-master. See that the bishops are well fed and watered.' His voice nearly broke. 'A puppet to dance to whatever tune the piper plays.'

Arlette shouted back at him.

'At least I tried to make our relationship a proper one. Would you have me remain your paramour? Like that blowsy little whore in Rouen?'

Wulfnoth stared at her as if she were loathsome.

'How could you?'

'Well, it is no matter now, is it? All you have to do is wait for Cecily to grow up. And that is arranged for you too. Something else which has simply happened to you.'

'It has happened to you too. And serve you right.'

They stood face to face, each weeping tears of mortification.

* * * * * *

'Will there be anything more, my lord?'

Geoffrey looked up.

'Are you still eating?'

Thierry swallowed.

'A morsel, my lord. A mere morsel.'

Thierry looked round, then leaned forward.

'May I speak freely, my lord?'

Geoffrey nodded.

'If I may say so, my lord, his Grace of Bayeux keeps a mean kitchen.'

'You mean the cook will not feed you ten times a day.'

Thierry shook his head.

'I have seen what goes on the table in the great hall, my lord. I have seen your face when you have eaten it.'

Geoffrey let it go. It was difficult to tell Thierry anything that he did not already know. But then, his business was to gather news. That was why Geoffrey was sending him off now.

Two weeks into this misbegotten Church council, and there was no knowing what was going on at Coutances. It was not as if it had been time well spent. Archbishop Maurilius had made pious speeches about the scandal of the buying and selling of church benefices. Well-meaning clerics had been making pious speeches about that for thirty years or more. Geoffrey himself had had his own bishopric bought for him by his brother Mauger. He had tried to get out of it, in vain. Now he was stuck with it.

Bishop John of Avranches had droned on incessantly about his particular obsession – clerical celibacy. Sent everyone to sleep. Even Bishop Odo – who had at least one bastard.

One abbot had put in suggestions about forbidding clerics to bear arms – when, sitting beside them, were Bishop Yves of Sées and Bishop Hugh of Lisieux, who had taken recent part in the assault of Conan's castle at Dol.

Others had aired issues like fasting before the marriage ceremony, the scandal of clerics engaging in usury, armed attacks on priests, and so on. Fringe stuff. Nobody raised, in clear terms, the business of canonical election as against lay appointment. Who – to put it simply – was to appoint bishops? The cathedral chapter, on Papal suggestions, or the lay ruler, on considerations of politics? Nobody met that one head-on. Hardly surprising.

The Duke, as he had promised Lanfranc, presided for most of the sessions, though Geoffrey doubted if he understood some of the finer points of canon law. Still, he was there. His very presence sent a message to the outside world.

Geoffrey sighed. Not much would be decided, but the very fact that the entire senior clergy of Normandy was met in one place to discuss reform was a sign of the times. And more Church councils were held in Normandy than in most other provinces of France. This was the way the world was moving. Something definite would come out of it sooner or later.

'Time and patience, patience and time,' Lanfranc had said to him.

'My patience is not limitless, and neither is that of the Duke.'

'No, but God's is,' said Lanfranc.

There was never any arguing with Lanfranc.

Geoffrey fidgeted.

Even so ... Thierry was right. Bayeux was a mean place. Odd how an establishment took its nature from its master. Odo was a mean man, in every sense of the word.

Look at his ridiculous idea of a tapestry. What person, other than one supremely vain, would think up such a scheme? Half a furlong long it would be – or so he boasted. Mania. Mania of grandeur. He was so taken with the cleverness of his idea that he had overlooked the obvious fact that this wonderful monument to his power and conceit would not last six months – fire, beer stains, the rats. How stupid could you be! It would cost him a small fortune too. Ha!

Geoffrey took a mouthful of beer, and frowned in thought.

But his face cleared when he remembered something else about Odo. Lanfranc, with the backing of the Duke, had taken several of Odo's best monks from his house at St. Vigor to increase the numbers at the new house at le Tréport.

'I had a letter from the abbot,' he told Geoffrey. 'They are desperately short of good men. I can send them back with that tubby little ex-soldier with the donkey. He knows all the roads.'

Geoffrey smiled at the recollection.

Lanfranc had also taken one of Odo's prize canons to become the Duke's new chaplain. That brought down the total to only nine. Against Geoffrey's twelve at Coutances.

Coutances! How long would it be before he could get back? Was the new scaffolding coming up to expectations? Goscelin would almost certainly not approve. Had he put up all the statues in the nave? Had the new blocks from the Montjoie quarries been delivered in good order? Were the new masons behaving themselves? Were they skilled enough to carve the heads on the west front?

Holy Virgin – so much to see to. And that was only the cathedral. What about the school? When would that see the light of day? There had been no time even to discuss it with Lanfranc, though Lanfranc had promised to recruit some teachers for him from his old school at Bec. And as for the aqueduct – fifteen years as Bishop of Coutances, and it it still awaited the merest preliminary survey. It was still a Roman ruin. He had always planned an endowment too, for Sybil's convent at St. Amand.

Geoffrey lifted his shoulders in a huge sigh. A polite cough brought him back to earth.

'Before I go to Coutances, does my lord wish me to take any message to – er – to my lady Sybil at St. Amand?'

Thierry, as usual, had read his mind.

But, as for managing to see her ... the whole summer gone, with this business over Harold. Now, the Church council. And Coutances as soon as possible, or there was no knowing what might happen. Then winter. The town courts, the taxes, the market, the housing problem – it was never-ending.

So it would be spring at least before ... Sybil's broad, open face came up before his mind's eye.

She was right.

* * * * * *

Adele sat on the edge of the bed, her back rounded, her head bowed, her hands limp between her knees, her hair a curtain of lank tails before her blotched face.

Behind her, the pillow no longer carried the warm indentation of his head. The familiar smell of his flesh had gone.

Drying tears were cold, and smelt of nothing ...

'I shall come back. By the Heart's Blood of the Virgin, I shall come back.'

'I know ... '

How often had they sat by the river and gazed at the water, at the whirls and eddies, at the many things carried along by it.

Two small fallen branches twined together by a rushing stream, only to be torn apart in an instant by a jutting rock. Bonded in ecstasy and severed in pain by a stony God whose Mind they could not read.

It was the emptiness, the awfulness beyond words. Adele was totally unprepared. Just as she had been stunned breathless by the joy of its discovery, so now she was reeling in disbelief at the misery of its loss.

There was no hope. Edwin meant what he said, but what could he do? What could *she* do?

Yet she must do something. Her father was not returning. The news from Bayeux was clear about that. Dismissed from the chaplaincy. Fine time to choose. After all these years. Hypocrites! Did the high-and-mighty lord abbot Lanfranc know what pain he was causing by his precious rules?

So – no father. Soon, probably, no house. Who to confide in? Nobody. Not even Gerard. Not now ...

It was over. Heaven was past. The 'ever' of love had come to an end. There was no God – not in the way she had come to learn. There was no company. No parent. No-one to listen. Nothing.

For the first time in her life, she was alone.

She sat up, stretched her back, and pressed her hands against her stomach. Well, perhaps not completely alone.

* * * * * *

A novice stood at a discreet distance, leaning slightly forward in hope of my lord abbot's approval.

Lanfranc skimmed through the official letter he had just dictated, checking that the main points had been well made ... the sessions of the Council, the attendance record … the Duke's chairmanship … the issues discussed … progress and agreement … views of individual bishops and abbots … the dismissal of the Duke's incontinent chaplain … recruitment of brothers to enhance the strength of the new house at le Tréport … the state of other Norman houses … his own establishment at St. Stephen's of Caen … the building of the Abbaye aux Dames by the lady Matilda … looking ahead to the next council.

After what seemed an eternity to the dry-mouthed novice, Lanfranc looked up.

'Yes. You have done well.'

A huge weight was lifted from the young man's shoulders.

Lanfranc held out the parchment.

'Get this copied. Ask Brother Amaury.'

The novice's face fell. Lanfranc tapped the document.

'This has to go to the Vatican – to His Holiness himself. How long have you been training – is it seven, eight months?'

'Nine and a half, my lord.'

'Ah. Nine and a half. Brother Amaury has been in vows for twenty-three years. Now, would you have His Holiness think ill of this house, that we do not use our best scribe for correspondence to him?'

'No, my lord.'

Lanfranc looked at the expression on his face – trapped, glum, cast down. He reached out for a pen.

'Of course, there is always the matter of a copy for the files.'

The novice brightened.

'I will do my very best, my lord.'

Lanfranc examined the point of the quill.

'And I should like a copy for myself. Could you handle both?'

The boy beamed.

'Most certainly, my lord.'

'How soon?'

He swallowed in his excitement.

'By the morning, my lord. If I have to stay up all night.'

Lanfranc smiled.

'Not, I hope, to the neglect of Divine Office.'

The boy left in a flurry of smiles and skirts. Lanfranc pulled out a fresh parchment, dipped his pen, thought for a moment, and began a postscript.

'To Anselm, greetings.

'I have stolen three days to catch up on business here at St. Stephen's. Ah – the blessed peace!

'The council, as you will have seen from the official letter, proceeds. I can offer no great hopes of sweeping reforms to come out of it, but you are as much a realist as I. The great benefit is that the council has been held. Every synod, every council – every assembly which brings together the clergy of this dukedom under the Duke's chairmanship – is a step forward. Every time we induce a warrior bishop to sit at a conference table – chain mail or no chain mail – we move ahead. Every record of reform aspirations, however empty-sounding, to which these worldly vassals put their mark is an advance.

'I would liken the reform of Mother Church to a great mountain of sand, which it is our God-given task, and precious duty, to build. Unfortunately, it can be built only grain by grain. Each time we add a grain, we do not see the mountain grow any bigger. But we know that, by God's Grace, it is. One day that mountain will move, and, when it does, the world will not be able to stop it. Alas, we shall not be here to see it, but it is enough that we are doing God's Work in helping to bring it about.

'And let us not be too dismissive of these rough men in Normandy. Since I set up my first school in Avranches all those years ago, I have seen a score of new houses established and endowed, by men of war. And they are sincere, according to their ways. Some, like my old friend, Herluin, will probably finish their days in a monastery – if only to escape from their awful wives!

'The hardest of the soldier bishops at least appreciate efficiency. Odo of Bayeux is aware of the value of scholarship. My friend Geoffrey of Coutances also wants to establish a school. He would be the last to admit that he takes his episcopal duties seriously, but believe me he does.

'The Duke himself – ah, there is a puzzle for you. Harsh, restless, ambitious. A man of mail if ever there was one. But look at his start in life – bastard birth, attempts on his life from the age of eight, constant civil war until he was twenty. No wonder he is proud of what he has achieved. Capable of inspiring great loyalty too. Continent – look at his marriage. Planned in disobedience, but pursued in virtue. Not a breath of scandal. Most important for us, he wants to do well by the Church. He treads with nailed boots, but he treads far and he treads bravely. He does try.

'As for his recent little episode with the Earl of Wessex, you will have heard about the statement and the oath. We need not concern ourselves with such a charade. But it is part of the exercise of our talents to be practical. If what William has done helps in any small way towards the English crown, that is a circumstance to which Mother Church should incline some thought. If ever there is a field which is ripe for re-planting, it is England. A false archbishop, out-of-date liturgy, neglect and abuses rife – I do not need to go on. My point is that William, for all his faults, may well repay the support of your Holiness in his work.

'I have at least prised William's incontinent priest from his court. Poor man, it is not his fault. I shall see that he does not suffer. I thank you for sending to our deliberations an archdeacon of moderate views. At least we are not in constant danger of excommunication from a scowling saint!

'I go on too long. Forgive me. But it is not often that I can avail myself of the opportunity to talk easily and frankly with an old friend. Teachers and abbots can not be gregarious creatures, though I know that my loneliness is as nothing to the chasm that now surrounds you on the Papal chair.

'I thank you for the many and undeserved compliments that you heap upon me – to the danger of my immortal soul. I happily return them – to the danger of yours!

'Until it pleases Almighty God to let us meet again, or until He gives you leisure to write, I remain

Your friend in God

Lanfranc'

* * * * * *

'You are not concentrating.'

'What?'

Gerard pointed.

'I said you are in check.'

'Ah.'

Wulfnoth glanced at the board.

'Do we have to continue?'

'You sound like Cecily.'

'Cecily!'

Wulfnoth rose with a curse, and began pacing the kitchen. Peter the scullion looked up from the spit. Gerard caught his eye and dismissed him with a sharp jerk of his head.

When he had gone, Wulfnoth came and sat down opposite Gerard again.

'What am I going to do, Gerard?'

'Nothing. There is nothing to do.'

'But Cecily!'

Gerard poured two drinks.

'Which would you rather – the daughter of a duke, or the daughter of a dead vassal?'

'What does it matter? Either way it would be arranged for me. Either my brother asks the Duke or Arlette does.'

'Then *you* ask him.'

'I did. For a fief. He refused.'

'If you were the Duke, and the brother of your chief rival asked for land and promised homage, would you trust him by giving it to him?'

Wulfnoth said nothing.

'But,' said Gerard, 'if you were to become his son-in-law, that would be a different matter.'

'So Arlette is to be cast aside?'

'Not long ago you wanted to wring her neck for shaming you.'

'That was then, in Bayeux. Now ... '

'And if she were to arrive here in Rouen?'

'She will not. She is to stay with the lady Matilda in Caen, until – '

Gerard waved a hand.

'Yes, yes. I know all about that. Do you think I enjoy staying here, while ... '

Wulfnoth forgot his troubles for an instant.

'You can not be nursemaid for ever, Gerard. And you most certainly can not be midwife.'

Gerard grunted.

'No. I suppose not. Well – if we are unable serve, we are able at least to drink.'

He proceeded to do so. Wulfnoth twiddled the stem of his cup. Gerard wiped his lips.

'Accept, boy. Accept. Either you either love the girl or not. If you do, then you prepare yourself for a life of love on the side, like your brother. If not, then you wait for the next girl. They are like sheep; there is always one coming along behind.'

Wulfnoth sighed.

'It is not only that. It is ... '

Gerard topped up his cup, in the hope that he might be tempted. Wulfnoth ignored it.

'Have you any idea, Gerard, what it is like to be a hostage? Away from your own country? For twelve years?'

Gerard tapped his leg.

'Have you any idea what it is like to be a cripple? A Fleming in Normandy?'

'But that is life, Gerard. That was Fate. I am the victim of other men's decisions. The Duke refuses let me serve him. He refuses to let me marry Arlette. Harold refuses to take me with him. And, one of these days – '

'One of these days,' said Gerard, 'they will come up against each other. There will be danger.'

'Yes. And where will I be?'

'You will be here – safe.'

'Ha!'

'By the Nails, boy. Observe. And think. Think! It is *because* they care. It is *because* they both love you that they have left you out. If Harold wins, you will be the brother of the King of England, and you can marry whomsoever you wish. Arlette, if you still want her. If William wins, you will be the son-in-law of the Duke of Normandy and probably of the King of England too. What a prospect!'

Wulfnoth rapped himself on the chest in his agitation.

'But I shall have done nothing. Nothing!'

Gerard put down his cup and eased his bad leg.

'The hardest thing to do, when there is nothing to be done, is nothing.'

Wulfnoth almost sneered.

'Like you – the frustrated nursemaid.'

Gerard's beard bristled.

'If you wish, yes. But I was thinking of your brother. Look at what he achieved this summer. And all by doing nothing. There is a man for you.'

Wulfnoth stood up again and made to go.

'There it is again. The great Harold. Harold the charmer.'

He slammed the door.

Gerard fixed his crutch under his arm and heaved himself to his feet.

'And there goes Wulfnoth the loser. A great pity!'

* * * * * *

'Pleased to see me?'

'No.'

'Give me five minutes and you will be.'

Nigel stood behind Adele and put his hands round her waist.

Adele shook herself free and started to knead dough. Nigel pursued her.

'Oh, come on, Adele. I understand. It is all over the castle. If you want to make do with a Saxon dog-boy while the men are away, nobody would blame you.'

Adele continued kneading.

'As you made do with the red-faced Breton girls.'

Nigel laughed.

'Yes, if you like.'

'When you were not drowning in the sands of the Couesnon.' She turned round. 'No time to poke the fire then, eh? Especially with a sore back.'

Nigel flushed.

'What do you mean?'

Adele leaned forward.

'That is all over the castle too. If I want a "man", as you put it, why go for a fool who falls in the Couesnon? Surely better to go for the one who fished him out.'

'Gilbert! The ploughboy!'

'Do you ask a man's trade before he saves your life?'

Nigel waved a hand airily.

'I was getting myself out before he arrived. And did you know he shied away from a wager when he thought it was dangerous? Like a rabbit from a shadow. If Earl Harold had not dragged him on to the sands, he would never have had the guts to come himself.'

He sidled up to Adele again.

'Anyway, I came here to talk about you, not about cow-eyed ploughboys from the Avranchin.' He put his hands round her waist again. 'I came here to talk about something much more interesting.'

Adele made no attempt to remove his hands. She went on with her work as if she were complexly alone.

'Do go away, Nigel. Take your dog-heat somewhere else. You will find plenty of bitches in the town willing to cool it for you.'

Nigel looked down at the top of her head. She was treating him as if he were a groping young scullion trying to get a hand up his first skirt.

'You are different.'

'Eyes in your head as well as your privates. My my – growing up at last.'

* * * * * *

'I expect he will be home by now.'

Sir Walter Giffard leaned on the new bridge across the River Orne at Caen, and tossed a twig into the water.

Ahead lay the road to Rouen – and Longueville. And his Arabs. At last! Ermengarde had gone home ahead of him ...

'I see I am to be trusted with the horses then ... '

It would probably be better not to mention Judith when he got back.

He sighed. One way and another, not a particularly fruitful summer. And that damned Saxon charmer had gone off with a smile on his face.

'I expect he will be home by now.'

'Precisely where we want him,' said Fitzosbern.

They were waiting for Montgomery to get a lost shoe replaced before they went their separate ways.

Giffard tossed another twig.

'Like a triumphal procession.'

'What?'

‘The whole business.’ He stood up gestured expansively. ‘Look at it. From the moment we picked him up at Eu on the frontier. Eu – Rouen – Brittany – Bayeux – and now Eu again, and le Tréport for his ship. Full circle. A triumphal procession. With us scrambling around him trying to be clever. And we still have no idea why he came in the first place.’

‘For his brother, I suggested.’

Giffard shook his head.

‘No proof. And he has gone home without him. So if it was his purpose, he has not fulfilled it. Does he look one whit put out? He made the whole business at Bayeux look like his idea. What have we got out of it?’

‘Not much,’ admitted Fitzosbern. ‘On the face of it.’

‘There you are then. We should have killed him when we had the chance.’

‘No. No. And no again. It does not matter whether he made fools of us or we made a fool of him. We wanted him back in England in one piece to deal with the other two claimants, and now he is.’

Giffard growled, and continued tossing twigs into the water. Sir Roger of Montgomery joined them.

‘Not long now. We found the smith and sobered him up.’

He caught sight of the look on Giffard’s face and turned to Fitzosbern.

‘What is wrong with Walter? Anyone would think one of his precious Arabs had gone lame.’

Fitzosbern grinned.

‘He thinks we have been wasting the whole summer. But not you, Roger. Is this right about Mabel?’

It was Montgomery’s turn to grin – very broadly.

‘Yes. Our fourth. She is furious. No Christmas feast in Paris.’

Fitzosbern clapped him on the shoulder.

‘Are congratulations in order?’

Montgomery nodded, but looked a little rueful.

‘I expect I shall pay for it one way or another. But that is a long way ahead.’

Giffard suddenly turned round from his wall.

‘Here! If our only concern was getting Harold back to England, why not pack him straight on to the first boat? Why all the plotting and planning? And why all that rigmarole of the oath?’

‘The oath was necessary,’ said Fitzosbern.

‘Why? He will break it.’

‘Of course he will. Then he will be in the wrong. How many times have we told you, Walter: an enemy’s place is in the wrong.’

‘It was a pretty feeble oath, Fitz,’ said Montgomery. ‘The clauses had more loopholes in them than a castle keep. Even I could see that.'

'Exactly,' said Giffard. 'And when has a sacred oath been binding when the swearer had no idea what relics were there? Harold had no idea there were any relics there at all. What is the point of half an oath?'

'You are forgetting the man whose idea it was,' said Fitzobern.

'Odo?'

'Yes. When Odo has completed the records about that whole ceremony, you will hardly recognise it.'

'Why bother? Harold is still in England, and we still look foolish.'

'Walter, you are not looking far enough ahead. You are still gnashing your teeth because you think Harold has been allowed to escape. But we want him in England – to deal with young Edgar, and especially with Hardrada.'

'Why is the oath so vital to that?'

'Because Harold, by that time, will have been crowned King. We shall be the invader; William will be the challenger. But if Harold can be proved a perjurer and a usurper, we shall have the right on our side.'

'I should have thought an army would be rather more useful.'

'Have sense, Walter. William sets great store by world opinion.'

'What about our opinion? We know the oath was a farce.'

'Our opinion counts for nothing. It is what Odo tells the world. It is military support William wants from us. From the world, he wants moral support. He wants the holy banner of the Pope, to provide the blessing of God. He wants the approval of a rightful invasion to depose a usurper, to remove an unlawful archbishop. We must have the law on our side.'

'How will you do that?'

'Odo will tell the world what he wants it to hear. To you, at the moment, Harold is a visiting prince, a charmer, a gallant soldier, and a consummate politician whom it is near impossible to outface. When Odo has finished with Harold, you will scarcely recognise him. He will be presented as a helpless castaway, a dupe, a feudal subordinate, and a deliberate, pre-meditated perjurer.'

'And what about Harold's version?'

'You are forgetting something else, Walter,' said Montgomery. 'Records are written by the winners. How will Harold's version survive after his death? And if we lose, which of us will be here to worry over Odo's version?'

Giffard looked from one to the other.

'Well, if that is politics ... '

A groom came up with Montgomery's horse.

'Ah. Pepin. How is it, boy? Fine, eh? Fine?'

Montgomery patted a foreleg, lifted it, and examined the handiwork before tossing the man a coin.

He mounted.

'Until the spring, then, my friends.'

Giffard put his foot in the stirrup.

'Well, I have said it before, and I say it again: we have all been too clever by half. All I know is, we had him, and now we have lost him. The next time we see him, he will not be a dupe or a perjurer; he will be the leader of a line of mailed housecarles.'

Fitzosbern gestured to the men-at-arms to follow, and heaved himself into the big wooden saddle.

'Never mind, Walter. If he gets shipwrecked again, we can do it your way next time.'

* * * * * *

'You kept us waiting long enough, sir.'

' "Frontier to frontier", it said in the contract. I had it checked by three separate clerks.'

'We delivered him to le Tréport two days ago.'

'Formalities,' said Beaumont. 'You know how tricky these things can be.'

Lothar took another swig of beer. Flemish beer this time. He smacked his lips.

'Why have we been paid so short?'

Beaumont looked innocent as he picked up his cup.

'You must ask your captain that. He was paid the lawful amount. I just carry the money. Messenger boy, remember?'

'He says no.'

'Then he is lying. You were paid the correct amount according to the contract – in full – '

Lothar paused, his cup in mid-air, waiting.

'Yes?'

' – apart from stoppages.'

'Stoppages? You penalise us for looting?'

Beaumont spread his hands.

'Now would we do that? Of course not. We recognise fortunes of war.'

'Well?'

'But we do penalise theft from our own side.'

'Theft?'

'Six war destriers, belonging formerly to Count Conan.' Beaumont refilled his cup. 'Costed according to the full going rate. I checked it with Sir Walter Giffard. There has been no malfeasance.'

Lothar looked him stonily in the face. Beaumont raised his eyebrows.

'No disrespect, Lothar. Eh?'

Lothar scratched his split ear, stood his cup on the table, and stood up.

'What you might call fortunes of war, sir.'

'Exactly. I could not have put it better myself.'

Lothar hitched up his belt, and swung his short cloak over his shoulder.

'What I say is: war teaches you something new every time. It has taught you too, sir. When we started this little caper, I thought you were a right pansy bastard. Now – you're a real bastard. Well done, sir.'

* * * * * *

'That feels better.'

Ralph rubbed a freshly-shaven chin.

'How is the head?'

'Better too. I feel human again.'

'About time,' said Bruno. 'If you will drink with Flemings.'

'Yes, I know. Asking for trouble. With their beer.' He grinned. 'Did you hear them say which way they are going home? I should like to see the look on Guy's face when he finds out.'

Ralph began to pack his saddlebag.

'What were you drinking – milk?'

'I was drinking to enjoy myself, not to try and forget something.'

For once Ralph did not take offence.

'I shall go.'

'To Gisors?'

'Yes. Mother and Father will not live for ever.'

'Can the ploughboy spare you?'

Again Ralph did not take offence.

'He is too busy playing with his new hauberk, and being the hero. Saviour of the Bastard's boy. Ha! He does not need me for a while.'

Bruno began cleaning a buckle.

'And there is always the priest's daughter to make eyes at. He has no need for you there either.'

'Priest no longer. I wonder what will become of her.'

'When will you go?'

'Now, I suppose.'

Bruno reached out for some more polish.

'I shall be here when you get back.'

'Going home yourself?'

'I shall be here when you get back.'

Ralph had long since learned not to press him.

He completed his packing, picked up his gear, and made to go. He paused at the door.

'With Michael. I do try, you know.'

'I know. So do I with mine. Come back soon.'

* * * * * *

Rain dripped from gaps in the thatch. Logs spat in the hearth. A dog jumped and ran under the table. The main door opened, and a draught sent loose straws from the floor wheeling round the food on the table.

Guy of Ponthieu swore, and turned towards his constable.

'What do you want?'

'A messenger from Count Baldwin of Flanders, my lord.'

'Well?'

'The Count says he has no knowledge of a regiment of mercenaries such as you describe, certainly not Flemings.'

Guy swore again. The constable stood his ground.

'There is one other matter, my lord.'

'Yes?'

'The tradesmen, my lord. They are still here. Want their money.'

Guy picked up a plate and flung it.

'I never said *ask* them to go. I told you to throw them out. Set the dogs on them. Think of something! Or by the saints you will lose it from your own money.'

'My lord.'

When he had gone, Guy poured himself a fresh measure of drink. Before he could drink it, he had to pull out scraps of chaff with his fingers.

What an end to the summer, and it had promised so well.

No ransom. No thanks. No credit with either of his powerful neighbours. All the tradesmen and huntsmen who had swarmed round Harold were clamouring for their money. Well, they were going to get nothing from him. And Harold had long since forgotten them.

Worse, the Flemings hired by the Bastard had decided, from sheer perverseness, to go home through Ponthieu, and had gone out of their way to cause trouble all along the way. Now Count Baldwin was saying mercenaries? Mercenaries? What mercenaries? When he knew perfectly well.

The dog whined under the table. Guy kicked it.

A raindrop fell down the back of his neck.

* * * * * *

Gilbert rubbed and polished for the hundredth time. He paused, reached out for a drink of beer, and looked round the empty guardroom. Most of the regular garrison had been sent on leave, as harvest time approached.

He had stayed. The few days near Avranches after the Brittany campaign had been enough. Nor did the emptiness of the guardroom bother him. He bent over his hauberk. Ralph approved of him – that was enough. He held the evidence of Ralph's approval in his hands. True, the Duke had ordered him to get it. But the time and money spent on restoring it – that was all Ralph's.

Bruno had said nothing. Which was compliment in itself. All too often Bruno could make a whiplash out of two words.

Gilbert rearranged the rag over his two fingers and dipped it into the grease. He lifted his shoulders and dropped them again, totally absorbed ...

'I like the hauberk.'

'Thank you, my lord.'

Harold winked at him.

'Our secret, eh?'

'I did not deserve it, sir.'

'If the world thinks you are a hero, you are a hero. Sit back and enjoy it.'

'It nearly went terribly wrong.'

'But you saved the situation.'

'*We* did.'

'All right – *we* did.'

'So I did not deserve it.'

Harold grinned.

'Want to give it back then?'

'No.'

'Good. Then, if you did not deserve it, work to deserve it in the future. Nobody need know.'

'You do.'

'Am I going to tell the world from Winchester? No – it is your secret now. A little piece of advice, son: we all too often think, because we know something, that everyone else does. They do not ... '

Gilbert held up the hauberk and examined it. Two or three blemishes offended his eye. He laid it in his lap again and picked up the rag.

Nigel Fitzhenry had learned a lesson or two. He probably continued to scoff behind Gilbert's back, but at least he was civil to his face. Another surprise – he was not hanging round Adele any more. In fact, Gilbert no longer saw any young men there when he went to visit – wearing his hauberk.

Best of all, Adele was pleased to see him.

'I like you. No, I really do ... '

* * * * * *

'Quite a millpond, eh?'

'Yes, sir.'

Harold leaned his elbows beside Edwin's.

'Bit of a change from last time.'

'Yes, sir.'

'Turn the other way, and you will see England soon.'

'Yes, sir.'

Harold cleared his throat.

'We can get more dogs, you know.'

'Yes, sir.'

Harold gazed towards Normandy through a long silence.

'Nice, was she?'

He saw Edwin's face pucker in pain.

'Hard, sir – leaving.'

Harold put an arm round his shoulders.

'Me too, son. We both left something.'

He ruffled Edwin's hair, and moved forward, to talk with the captain.

'Should be a good crossing, my lord,' said Aldred.

'Yes.'

'Home, eh?'

'Yes.'

'And not a man lost. A fine achievement, sir, if I may say so.'

'Yes. Thank you.'

'Funny.'

'What?'

'Well, I nearly lost my ship, and there was danger. Foreign country and all that. But you know, sir, all things considered, I would not have missed it.'

'Neither would I.'

'I mean, you learn things. Stuck in that one-eyed little seaport, God knows it was boring at times. But with fellow-professionals, language is not such a barrier. Like I said, you learn things.'

'Yes.'

'You keep your eyes and ears open. Surprising what you pick up.'

'Yes.'

'You never know when it might come in handy.'

'Very true.'

Aldred squinted up at the sleepy sail, revealing the cavernous gaps in his teeth.

'Excuse me, my lord. Must chivvy those oarsmen along a bit. In this calm. Getting lazy.'

Harold pulled his cloak round him, and leaned on the side.

Dear Wulf! If only he would stop seeing every event as a mishap, every situation as a trap. If only he would see them as opportunities, not disasters. Open his eyes.

Ah, well – perhaps one could not put old heads on young shoulders.

He heaved a colossal sigh. It was good to relax. After so long. Not a man lost – not one. Not bad going, though he said so himself. He was pleased Aldred thought so too.

He smiled. If nothing else, he had given the Normans plenty to think about. Yes, he agreed with Aldred – all things considered, he would not have missed it.

* * * * * *

'As soon as I saw you, Father Arnulf, I knew we should get on. Oh, yes, we should get on. Well, I mean, of a certain age. Men of the world, as you might say. These monks from St. Vigor – rather too keen on their own dignity. Nose in the air, to coin a phrase. No company on the road. Keep to themselves. Hard to get a civil word out of them. Between you and me, my friend, a bit of a pain in the arse, if you will overlook the vernacular.

'Hup, there, Rollo. Much more cosy on this cart, eh, Father? Just the two of us. As soon as Father Lanfranc said to me, "Hubert," he said, "I want you to conduct Father Arnulf to your house at le Tréport," I knew I was in for a treat. Both of us know what it is to fall on hard times. Look misfortune in the face, as you might say. And I was right; I have enjoyed the last few days enormously.

'You will like le Tréport, for sure. New house, of course, and understaffed. You will be welcomed. We need men of energy and vision – oh, yes – energy and vision. I am sure you will make a fine assistant sacristan. Indeed, a fine one. You see, Brother Martin is – well, rather old, and, between you and me, not very efficient. Now, I am sure you will be the new broom sweeping clean.

'And you have no more worries about your daughter. Fine girl, that. Fine girl. Mind you, you were right to be concerned, as any good father would. But young Gilbert is a well-set-up young man, and very fond of her by all accounts. Oh yes, very fond. They make a fine couple. Great relief to you, I am sure.

'Interesting how the Lord always provides. Now look at me. Piece of wreckage, I was. Cast up from the wars. Crippled arm – look. Been everywhere too. But had enough. Wanted to go home. And what did I find when I got there? I say, what did I find?

'I shall tell you what I found. Nothing. That is what I found. Father dead. No house. No land – stolen. Family split up. Well, I tell you, I went to pieces. Quite to pieces. Sank to the depths. Oh, yes, the depths. Like an animal. Dirt, lust, drink, crime – it was terrible. Terrible. But, like I said, the good Lord provided. I met a saint.

'I was pulled out of a ditch near Brionne. Near the great house of Bec? You have heard of it? Well, as I say, I met this saint – not boring you, am I?'

* * * * * *

THE END

Acknowledgements

As with many of my previous publications, I owe the appearance of this book to the interest, help, advice, and combined talents of Mark Webb of Paragon Publishing, Stephen Goodwin of sgssdesign.co.uk, Yvonne Reed, proof reader of Error Terror.co.uk, and my son Stephen.

Also by Berwick Coates:

978-1-78222-791-5

978-1-78222-893-6

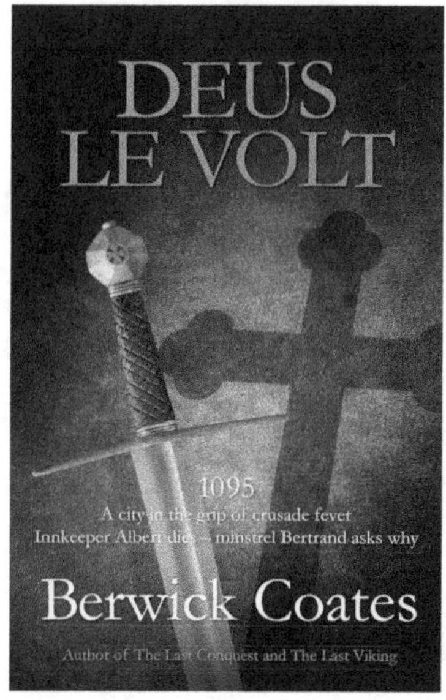

www.ingramcontent.com/pod-product-compliance
Lightning Source LLC
LaVergne TN
LVHW010541100826
845148LV00001B/256

* 9 7 8 1 7 8 7 9 2 0 3 1 6 *